A TRAG

THAT DESTINED THEIR LIVES

JORDAN

His passion for Yukiko was as intense and as suddenly ended as a summer storm. When he returned to her and his son, he was years too late... with fateful consequences for them all.

YUKIKO

Soft and gentle as a fragile flower, she lived for the day her handsome G.I. would return ...having given up her life to spare the child of their love.

JOE

Outcast because of his American blood, made to suffer for his mother's sin, he knew only hatred for the man his mother would always love.

WANDA

Jordan's wife, who despaired of giving him what he wanted most in the world, was helpless to stop him from pursuing a delusion that would destroy him.

Brocade

Jan Merlin

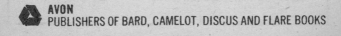

AVON
PUBLISHERS OF BARD, CAMELOT, DISCUS AND FLARE BOOKS

BROCADE is an original publication of Avon Books. This
work has never before appeared in book form.

AVON BOOKS
A division of
The Hearst Corporation
959 Eighth Avenue
New York, New York 10019

First Avon Printing, June, 1982

AVON TRADEMARK REG. U. S. PAT. OFF. AND IN
OTHER COUNTRIES, MARCA REGISTRADA, HECHO EN
U. S. A.

Printed in the U. S. A.

WFH 10 9 8 7 6 5 4 3 2 1

FOR MY SON,
Peter William Merlin

When a man makes a name for himself in the world, it is said he clothes his village in brocade.

JAPANESE PROVERB

Nansei Shoto
AUGUST, 1945

The fuselage of the Zero shuddered. Power surged, the propeller whirled furiously, then reduced speed to whine to a sluggish halt. The frustrated pilot's carefully balanced tranquillity wavered. Clenching his fists, he slumped upon the cockpit seat. His palms were sticky and he wiped them across the faded cloth of his uniform. It was shabby, stained with grease and oil and coral dust. Nothing was first-class material anymore, even the skin of his plane had been patched with flattened food tins...his task seemed an impossibility without help. The sweet odor of petrol was nauseous after inhaling it so long. During past weeks, he smelled it everywhere. Last night it haunted him at the far end of the beach where he hunted crabs and gathered sea urchins. No matter. There was no one else to be disturbed by it. The flaw in the engine must be cured before enemy reconnaissance spotted him. They had flown by to buzz the treetops; miraculously, they hadn't seen through camouflage covering the Zero nor the brush scattered over his makeshift runway. They didn't suspect his existence....It was like being invisible...or a ghost....*Life duplicates a fragile flower, blossoming, then drifting apart; the fragrance of it cannot be expected to last forever....But you of the Dai Nanko Unit, you are the divine winds, immortals*...a noble message for Admiral Ohnishi to have sent the Special Attack Corps volunteers...but a short course of instruction regarding emergency engine repair would have been more practical.

Grazing the pilot's stubbled cheek, a mosquito rose into the dome of the steaming canopy and dove at him again. The slight wind of its thin transparent wings calmed him. His own target was chosen recently from among a formation threading the islands and bypassing this one whenever the maze of its circuits brought it near—a powerful blue ship with two low stacks, twin-barreled naval cannon bristling fore and aft, and many, many anti-aircraft guns. The exact center to aim for on its hull was below the cartoon of a minotaur painted in bright primary colors upon the full length of the second stack—such fools to provide so perfect a guide!—but the Zero's engine failed him at takeoff. The ship could not be his unless he became airborne. He wanted it badly because of its conceited symbol—*hai*, even at the cost of searching and using too much fuel...

And on the fantail of the U.S.S. *Bulman*, sailors listened to a drawling shipmate wail over the pick of a guitar; the rebel was playing a lilting, deck-stomping tune scored out of the war's theft of his green years and mournful to the ear. Stragglers of the ship's company filed numbly to evening chow while those fed earlier wandered or loitered throughout the decks as though lost. The veteran destroyer was one of a vast armada cabled against the tides in a wide bay, well protected from swells of the East China Sea. The battered task force was resting, exhausted from kamikaze raids hurled nightly upon the Ryukyu chain. Battle seemed endless; though many were brought down and some taken aboard into ghastly fiery embraces, suicidal attackers continued to drone toward the Allied fleet occupying Okinawa. In their scores and pairs they came. Or they arrived singly.

Seeking. Aiming themselves. Diving.

Diving...

Diving into the eruption of their encounter with radar picket ships at the outer perimeter of the invaded islands... and again diving when they appeared over this vulnerable anchorage, Nakagriskaku, now renamed Buckner Bay.

"Jordie?"

Jordan Asche made room on the steel bitt for his friend Dave, and they sat facing the sea to talk quietly, vaguely conscious of a sharp tang radiated from tar line laced to the taffrail before them. They were not quite twenty... and older than years could make them.

"Got a cigarette, Dave?"

"Yeah... here..."

"Thanks."

A Zippo clicked; then flared. Smoke drifted to the mel-

2

ancholy singer. They waited for darkness, savoring peace before the expected call to General Quarters. Every dawn and twilight had been sweated out or fought into the relief of full day when Hellcats and Corsairs could be launched aloft for protection. It was better to be at sea than at anchor...Flank Speed into the cooling wind! Elevators on the escorted carriers loaded flight decks rapidly; wings unfolded, each bird darting forward to drop sickeningly over a bow before rising into the clearing sky; I spy a bogey, tally ho! they cried, and chased the bandits from the scene or shot them down...but not at night. At night, they roosted below decks impotently.

"Weather's nice..."

"Yeah...but we'll have fucking stars...three-quarter moon, too, maybe..."

It wasn't possible to admire the beauty of constellations during this fickle typhoon season without looking for bogeys within them. A star sprang into being muted by vivid sundowns, then gleamed brighter to settle into a quivering constancy with so great an assembly of companions that nights were made terrifying; the silvery illumination revealed ships at sea...or those chained to harbors...

"What do you think is going on over there, Jordie?"

A carrier flagship blazed with electricity in the dusk; a surround of motor whaleboats and gigs stood off from its massive bulk. Jordan puffed at his cigarette nervously. The smoking lamp should have been proclaimed out for men on deck; blackout conditions were strictly enforced west of the International Dateline and it was getting darker rapidly. "Search me," he answered with apprehension. "Everybody sent a boat over. I guess we'll be hauling ass to sea again..."

"Wonder why the word hasn't been passed to darken ship?"

"Will be soon as the Admiral sticks his head out a porthole."

"Hell, he ain't gonna risk getting a sore asshole."

The joking remark wasn't worth a grunt, and the Admiral was a mean son-of-a-bitch anyway. Orders in his command were carried out at the double and woe to a tardy ship. If anyone was going to get reamed, look to the lower ranks.

"You'd think we were in the States."

"Yeah...if you were crazy..."

They first met when the *Bulman* was being prepared for commissioning; twenty-seven hundred tons of destructive warship needed three hundred seamen. Upon edging out of a torpedo tube, blond crewcut spiked with grime and cleaning solvent, he saw Dave Bell, freshly arrived from Colby, Kansas, via boot camp at Great Lakes...a typical farm boy the color of a sorrel horse with stiff hair sprouting above jughandle ears. Jordan had to laugh, not that he was himself God's gift to mirrors, not with an ordinary face and plain nose bent a little from scrapping in city streets. Raised on the Lower East Side of Manhattan, he had the wiry frame of a survivor and was leaner than Dave. Both were apprentice seamen then, the lowliest members of the torpedo gang. Strikers, they were called; they wanted to be ratéd men. In those uncertain days, strangers became buddies, more than confessors and less than lovers, though some relationships reaped the scorn of crews from whom nothing can be hidden, for sailors sleep in bunks toe to opposite face, defecate side by thigh on a many-holed plank, sit hip to elbow at mess tables, shoulder to jowl at crowded battle stations. Where could a secret exist? Yet close friendships evolved. And this was one.

Activity livened the carrier gangway. Small craft dashed in to take on passengers and sped to their own ships. Jordan stood abruptly, heart quickening its beat.

"Hey, take it easy, Jordie."

"Jesus, doesn't anything bother you, Dave?"

"Everything but clap and sea duty...because you can't get them both at the same time."

One familiar boat raced steadily to their ship. It stopped alongside and the Captain and Exec sprang purposefully up the accommodation ladder. As they vanished into officers' country, the boat was winched aboard into its davits. A stillness thickened into a sinister hush; after other gigs and whaleboats delivered officers to their destinations, Buckner Bay was silent. Jordan finished his cigarette irritably. Flipping the stub over the railing into black water, he heard a short hiss as it hit and then heard the loud snap of the ship's communication system activated.

"Now hear this..."

4

Not the tobacco-juiced expectoration of the Master At Arms.

"**Attention all hands: This is your captain speaking...**"

A pause crackled and fizzed loudly from the bridge. Identical words echoed from other ships nearby.

"**Eight days ago an atomic bomb destroyed the city of Hiroshima, and five days ago, the same action was taken against the city of Nagasaki...**"

Shit, everyone knew it. He'd passed that word each time with a tremor but now his voice was measured and strong.

"**Today...our...President...President Truman... announced to the world...that Japan has accepted our terms...for an unconditional surrender....**" A murmur began, swelled into loud cheers and shrill whistles. "**...repeat...unconditional...**"Jubilation roared from every ship. A destroyer exulted with the crazed whooping of its siren. Rescue flares rocketed skyward and a few manned guns fired tracers at the stars. In a night which had fallen without an alert, the sight became glorious. The Captain's concluding words were smothered by general pandemonium as he intoned, "**...and we thank Almighty God and may He bless...**" Nobody heard more.

On every side, portholes and hatches burst open to spill their light. Navigation and masthead lamps flicked on; signal flag bags emptied and their bunting ran up the halyards; rows of yellow bulbs beaded the fighting ships into a fleet of luxury liners. Foghorns joined sirens; large searchlights raked the receptive firmament with a crisscrossing fan of dazzling beams which faded into nothingness at their farthest reach. Dave seized Jordan, hugging him, "You're crying, you crud, you're crying!" and Jordan clung to him, answering, "So are you! So are you..." And they were, the tears streaming unhindered over their laughter. A wild and incoherent uproar resounded throughout the ship. Wiping wet cheeks with a rough swipe of a palm, Jordan said earnestly, "We've got to celebrate...we'll drink all the torpedoes dry!"

"Hell, I can do better than that for us!" Dave yelled happily. He dragged Jordan to the crew compartment where they bunked. The noise in the confined space was deafening; a path had to be forced through a wrestle of

5

boisterous sailors stripping fire-retardant covers from bedding and hammering upon the bulkheads with excitement. Kneeling beside a footlocker, Dave lifted the lid to rummage among his possessions. Neatly rolled uniforms and linen were tumbled aside hastily. He produced a sampler of brandy he'd picked up in Honolulu as a souvenir. There wasn't more than a taste but it was genuine liquor. Unscrewing the cap, he raised a toast too enormous to be spoken aloud and drank half, then passed the rest to Jordan. "I was saving it for something special..."

"We made it," Jordan breathed reverently. There was much to add but the words balked. There would be no more nights of dread; no more praying during piston jabbers of ship's gunfire and salvoes of exploding five-inch shells. No more bloodied decks or whirlpool epitaphs closing over oily seas. No more bloated corpses ebbing from blasted beachheads. No more evasive letters to be written; no more yearning ones to be read. No more. Tomorrow was reinstated. And tomorrow after tomorrow, thank you God who was only remembered in the valley of the shadow amen. He drained the bottle, then tossed it at Dave with an ecstatic shout, "We're going to live forever!"

They charged up the ladder to exit the open hatch, joining exuberant shipmates on the main deck. It was hours before anyone slept—and that was done reluctantly, as if afraid the next waking would show all to have been an unkind dream.

But it was true.

Everywhere, men heard the news and rejoiced. Everywhere. Except in the stunned country of Japan, which faced the disgrace of occupation. And everywhere...except where contact was broken. In jungles. In caves. Upon embargoed islands. And upon an isolated atoll where Lieutenant Akiro Ishimoto, lacking a mechanic's knowledge and skill, patiently attempted to repair a balky Zero engine through trial and error.

And while he worked, he was given the precious gift of time. The *Bulman* received orders to sail north to Japan.

6

Suspicious as hounds, the destroyer squadron nosed into
Kii Strait, coursing at angles across the mouth of the sea
with mine-sweeping devices arrowing from their jaws.
They flushed one deadly ball after another to open a channel for the ships steaming grandly from the south. Sharp-
shooters sent the harvested bobbing menaces the impulse
which detonated inadvertent salutes to the invaders, hair-
triggered veterans, conquerors of the fallen island empire.
Nothing else was in sight upon these waters, no craft of
any kind, no sign of life upon the shores. The incredible
beauty of the twisting seaway was still hidden, blocked by
mountainous landfalls and cloud-crested Awaji Shima,
that great castle of land which must be skirted before
entering Osaka Bay. With his mates, Jordan kept grim
watch, sweeping the land with hard eyes. His search was
long; he shifted binoculars only after noting that nothing
moved. Where were they? Where, the enemy that was and
may still be? White shrouds over pine-studded peaks kept
the answer secret.

Geysers rose half the day, bellowing beneath the water-
cushioned steel plates of the ships until it was evident
their spread paravanes would bring nothing further to the
surface. Still the destroyers cast back and forth across the
strait, cleansing it thoroughly to ensure a haven for themselves and larger vessels. This was not an arrogant conquest but a civilized entry by victors, though they came
finely honed and prepared to resume battle. First the sea
lords, smarting from outrageous losses sustained over
Okinawan deeps, then would follow the rest in their di-
visions and brigades to spread across the humbled country.
When the squadron hove to in the gloom of nightfall, its
crews harkened to clarion klaxon calls to General Quarters
and spent the punishing hours at battle stations. Hollow-
resounding pings tallied clockwise electronic surveys but
nothing glowed on the screens to warn of intruders. From
his watch on the torpedo deck, Jordan tensed whenever

a dim light flitted a short cakewalk on the sinister shore. His squadron patrolled in its own circular wakes; unwilling to anchor, ready for war. Who said it was over? The Bay and her four seas lay ahead of them...Harima, Hiuchi, Iyo, and Suo...like a great winding, wild salt canal separating the big island Honshu from her smaller sisters, Shikoku and Kyusho...

At dawn, the destroyers were unleashed to enter Seto Nakai, trailed by a lumbering supply tender and two tankers bearing their fuel. Instead of opposition, they encountered a fantasy clad in gossamer disintegrating fog. Seto Nakai was the unbelievable rendered real, revealing a strange cultured beauty upon every side unlike the barricaded fortress everyone imagined. Jordan saw sharp volcanic outcroppings crowned with twisted pines and spumes of low-hanging clouds; crude rope bridges stretched languidly between sets of pinnacles, and close to scant beaches were camphorwood torii wading steadfast in sky-dyed waters as stately portals to Shinto shrines. From the land wafted an indecisive scent—an incense of musk and human waste. He didn't know this was a holy place, the spawning reservoir where the gods Izanagi and Izanami gave birth to the islands of Nippon.

His ship voyaged deeper into the westward-coiling passageway. Constricting its great expanse, the Harima Sea narrowed into veins, threading jagged rocks on currents of foam. Then the s⁓ ⁓dron eased past hundreds of islands, large and small, some bearing forests of dark pines and the occasional orange flash of tiled rooftops to mark fishing communities. Rising from stained perches to greet the newcomers, sea birds keened above the radar webs revolving atop each ship's mast. On the shores could be spied that living scroll from the era of the first Emperor, his people etched in attitudes of arrested toil to see the *hakujin* arrive. Patiently waiting to be prodded on their way, bullocks stood with lowered horns, laden carts held sulkily over huge wooden wheels. Beside them, conical straw hats shaded the peasants, the *hitotachi,* and when the foreign ships slowed at a predesignated minor port and began to drop anchor, astonishment and dismay reigned. The people thrashed their bullocks into a run and melted from view, rush capes bristling with the haste of their departure.

The port was of considerable importance, which was

unknown to its inhabitants. The Americans were making their initial landing in this port, one with a name ending in the inevitable "ma" sound and like any other. Its reactions would predict those of the nation. Jordan and Dave were chosen for duty along with other sailors from their watch when every vessel assigned a Shore Patrol. They were all volunteers, for this was an unknown risk and highly critical for the Occupation forces to come—unlike the scene in the North, where a solemn signing was being witnessed in Tokyo Harbor under the watchful might of admirals and generals. This unsupported excursion had to be totally dependent upon itself; should resistance arise, the men going ashore were lost.

Speeding whaleboats from each ship bounced roughly as they converged to form a column heading for the port, which was smudged against the hazy jade of mountains; boats moored at wooden piers were untended; slight activity had been observed in the town. It was an uneasy journey. As the whaleboat vanguard drew nearer, a few male citizens watching the armed men arrive froze into position on the streets.

Emptying one by one, the boats disgorged helmeted, wary boys with tense hands closed over the butts of loaded .45s holstered at their sides. Sweaty palms swung truncheons as the Shore Patrol gathered into a tight protective band. Officers assigned pairings, Jordan making sure to remain with Dave, and short, bandy-legged men stared at them from the safety of doorways and building corners. The quiet of the street was broken only by subdued, rumbling American voices. An LCV had delivered several jeeps from the tender and these growled restlessly under the fists of their drivers. At length, it was time to separate; the cluster of warriors edged from the waterfront, stamping hard upon their heels to reassure themselves. Their watchers inhaled deeply, shrinking smaller as the larger men passed by smelling of gun oil and tobacco and Lifebuoy soap.

The town was deathly still. Peeking and hiding at once, those indoors remained there. Jordan and Dave didn't talk; they had to absorb the strangeness and a scent of fear emanating from the surroundings. Mistrusting alleys, slowing whenever they saw several civilians together, they kept to the center of the roads. Impaled upon anal

9

knots of alertness, both urged unwilling feet into the sorry district. They felt the eerie pressure of being the focus of innumerable apprehensive eyes. Jordan wasn't thinking of them as belonging to a timid humanity; they were The Enemy's eyes; there were fangs and muzzles pointed toward him, following him, hungering to rip him down. He didn't feel brave...had he ever? It was more frightening to wait than to go after them, he decided, but this had every element of what should have been over. His respect for Marines and dogfaces doubled. This was his turn to walk the thousands of vulnerable yards to establish a beachhead, forcing through the rising tide of body heat with perspiration slicking armpits and crotch. To break the tension he muttered, "When are we going to stop crapping in our pants?"

"Listen, they didn't put us ashore to get murdered."

"Balls. It's the old charge-follow-you bullshit. How much gold braid do you see around?"

"They're too busy setting up an Officers' Club to be on the streets with us, Jordie."

It made him grin. Dave and his funnies. Anytime, anywhere. There was a recruiting poster which Dave stole from a subway train long ago pasted inside the flash shield of the aft torpedo tubes: JOIN THE NAVY AND SEE THE WORLD. It mocked the duty watch over tracking dials and firing mechanisms...and a thin slit through which to sight targets manually. SEE THE WORLD. Yeah, they'd been to Dago and Pearl, to Wake—his baptism of fire—and to the bottom of the ladder that led here: gentle Funafuti in the Ellice Islands, and clawing through the bloody Gilberts and Marshalls to the Carolines and Marianas; Truk, then Guam. Then Saipan and Iwo Jima; and the Philippines led to the Ryukyus, where he knew nothing could ever be so bad again for the rest of his life, if he lived through it: 17 ships sunk, 198 damaged. SEE THE WORLD. Till now it was mostly ocean and islands with blasted tree stumps...well, not all of it. San Diego had seemed foreign, with its pink and green and yellow cottages pinned to lawns by bougainvillea and avocado trees. There was Honolulu, too; Paradise lost with but a single dirge repeating itself in Hawaiian melodies. Yet those weren't big changes. This was a big change. Japan had been artificial during the voyage, just out of reach except

10

for zephyrs of turned earth to give it substance—which meant the ship was within shore-battery range and kept the squadron's intimidating gun turrets swinging. They were aimed at the port now, manned by crack gunners. Jesus, it didn't make him feel better; *he* was part of the target.

"Notice anything strange, Jordie?"

"Yeah, there's no mob waving flags to watch us go by."

"No, look. We've seen only men here. Where the hell are the rest of the gooks? The women?" Dave gawked at windows nearby, hopefully. "They must have locked them up the second we dropped the hook."

"I'll bet it was sooner, Dave. I'll bet it was the day they heard you enlisted." Dave threw a punch at his arm and they felt better. But it was odd. They had looked forward to seeing the women. Each turning they reached was another funnel of compressed housing. Corrugated shutters covered store fronts; windows were blanked out with oiled paper or blackout material. The streets had become empty of anyone but themselves. A man in khaki leggings dashed across an intersection, startling them. He wore a white cotton mask, surgeon style, intended to protect him from airborne germs. They halted, hands ready upon their weapons. Then they laughed nervously. Jordan elbowed Dave to get him moving again. "Just one of the local bandits, Dave. We don't have to worry about him."

"Bandit, hell. He can't stand the stink around here, either."

The pervasive reek of excrement was strong in the town, vented from drainage ditches serving the dwellings and shepherded by clouds of flies. It was loathsome but they accepted it as indigenous and tried to ignore the odor. They approached the intersection with care. Streets angled from it and they had to make a choice. Each was equally forbidding; not a soul in sight. They felt dangerously separated from their mates. Deciding, they turned a corner and Jordan pulled Dave to a stop. Pointing, he whispered, "A kid...first one we've seen."

Busily peeing into the street, a child, head down, gravely studied the trickle of urine as it snaked along cracks in the pavement. When he looked up at the sailors, his expression was so assured they knew at once he wouldn't flee. He was beautiful; a doll cunningly animated

11

and set out to ensnare the gentlehearted. His face glowed unnaturally with deep color, a betrayal of the tubercular devil afflicting him. Neglected and forgotten, his thin stream stopped. He was small; almost seven. He grinned.

"*Ohayo gozaimasu!*"

Jordan exchanged a baffled glance with Dave.

"Ohio? What the hell does he know about Ohio?"

"Maybe he thinks we came from there."

Jordan searched his pockets. "Hey, Dave, got any gum to give the kid?" Squeezing fingers past cigarette packages tucked into their breast pockets, they both checked to see what they could offer.

"Yeah. Hell, it's all bent up but he won't give a shit." Smoothing wrinkled paper as best he could, Dave held out a mangled stick of gum. The boy eyed it curiously, with hands folded behind his back and shriveled penis suspended like a loose button inside his open fly. "Here, kid...Spearmint-oh..." Dave made believe he ate the gum, chewing like crazy and aping exaggerated enjoyment. The boy crowed with joy at the performance. Dave cocked his head at Jordan. "Maybe the kid doesn't want it."

"Give it to me." Taking the gum, he walked slowly to the child to avoid frightening him. Crouching on his haunches, he offered the gum with a low, friendly voice. "Here, kid." They were being watched by someone in a building across the street. A woman, probably. If it was the kid's mother, she'd be in a panic. He held the gum encouragingly, without moving closer. The little boy snatched at it suddenly and danced out of reach. Sniffing at the gum as an animal might with something new, he grinned once again and tore off the wrapping. The gum vanished into his scarlet mouth and was gone after a brief chew. "You dumbbell, you're not supposed to swallow the damned stuff," Jordan lectured cheerfully. The boy shared his amusement, then spurted to the house. The door opened swiftly to admit him and was shut as quickly again. They were alone on the street. Only a gum wrapping and a wet trail proved they had seen a child.

It took three days for children of the town to appear in force. And five for the women. After that, throughout Japan, the serious Occupation was transformed into a grand

12

tourist mob being set upon by merchants of every degree. The Bays and Seas were cleared instantly of harmful ingredients and barriers, except for the bomb-gutted battleship *Haruna*, sunk at her moorings like a fat dowager in her bath. A brisk barter was established with the Americans, there being no use for invasion currency, which was issued to all hands in advance. Within two weeks Jordan was exchanging real dollars for paper yen and featherlight aluminum coins. Invasion troops and fleet heaved a collective sigh of relief; these feared people, so compulsively dedicated to death during the war, had become gracious hosts and subtly reversed the capitulation.

Moving on, his destroyer squadron followed Hiuchi Sea over its millrace to a bay above the sea named Iyo, where they rested again. Kure, the famed naval base, lay strick here... and that infamous crater of ashes and fission-dried riverbeds that was once Hiroshima. The captains dared the ultimate test; was it of their own men or those upon the land? Sending crews in watch sections to shore, they put them aboard commandeered trucks to be driven over the shards of the poisoned plain.

Jordan rode silently with his matew, swaying erratically on the jouncing vehicle to view the incredible devastation caused by a single bomb. It was another sea, a flooding of burned particles destroyed beyond recognition or salvage. Not a living thing grew anywhere; naked tree trunks slivered the ruins. Once a teeming metropolis, every building was down, leaving handfuls of vacant cement and steel-caged shells looming with skeletal supplication over the evenly distributed debris. And there were citizens, too. They beheld the sailors with mute, calm faces, thus rebuking them beyond what any shaking fist might have done. Everywhere were hospital signs posted over temporary canvas structures for tending casualties. The walking wounded waited stoically outside; soon to die, dying, they wrapped their final struggle in bandages to hide the unspeakable from the living. As those bundles seared themselves upon him, Jordan was ashamed to be whole; he felt unclean, like the stoker of some vast oven stirring the remains of his labor, sifting it to study whatever had not been consumed. Swirls of ashes thrown up by the wheels of the truck clogged his nostrils; there was some-

13

thing ghoulish about their flow, as if directed toward him purposefully. Bile burned in his throat.

His truck stopped at what used to be an intersection to permit a man and a woman to pass. Though the man walked at a distance from her, they could only be husband and wife, having taken on that resemblance of each other which comes from close living side by side. The woman was hunched, shuffling at a slow pace and carrying a light burden heavier than mothers should bear. Refusing to cross, they paused and looked cinder-eyed at Jordan. Unable to meet their gaze, he avoided it and saw the pitiful char filling her arms, so cauterized it could not bleed past the scabs disguising it. But it lived. Whimpers spewed from it without stop. His stomach heaved and he thought it easier to look into the woman's face. He saw her then differently. She became human; tragedy rendered her features into a universal sameness which was not Asian or Japanese or unknown to him. He knew her... and the man beside her. They were everyone. Parents to the child; parents to the dead; parents to himself...

The truck jerked into motion and drove around the couple. They turned slowly, holding their eyes upon him and remained in place to see him depart. He wrenched his face away, digging fingernails into his rib cage to keep from vomiting. How could he have compared them to his own father and mother? So far from home. So far... so far... and suddenly here. He wanted to cry. Not once during that hideous ride did any sailor speak. They didn't glance at each other when they returned to the wharf... It became a rout aimed at the whaleboats. Take us to Kure, to anywhere but here! Yet later, seconds later, a man said, "Fuck 'em. It stopped the war, didn't it?"

Jordan couldn't sleep. As he twisted under the sheet for a better position, the light near the ladder pried at his eyelids. Red. Red lights in corridors and at passageway hatches throughout the ship kept men from stumbling in

14

the dark. The crew moved within arterial atmospheres everywhere inside the ship. And when they did not, when they settled to sleep with men on duty stations watching over them, the *Bulman's* restive noises intensified. Not the vibration of screw shafts and great turbines—those were the heartbeat of being under way—it was the fugue beneath which remained after securing from sea. When the anchor ran before its chain and held, the snipes, they of the engine room, shut down to minor power. The ship swung to the moon's pull and became quiescent; steel thumped and creaked; plumbing chattered and gurgled or sang a steady stream; the metallic tread of the Officer Of The Deck prowling midwatch rounds of compartments echoed for a long time; barnacles fastened below the waterline emerged from razor shells to sieve the calmness, and even their avaricious silence had volume. Jordan tossed restlessly, turning against the hook of his thoughts.

The man and woman rose from the past day to stare at him—*Jesus, why haunt me? I didn't do it*—yet they wouldn't leave and he tasted again their loneliness and their loss. He'd seen that loss before, hadn't he? And dismissed it then. He had seen them, just so, with a space between themselves as if the comfort of a touch would enlarge the pain, and they knowingly compounded it by not clinging to each other. In the red glow he understood it was the ache he saw when leaving his parents' care. No, not their care, he hadn't left that...not their loving loving...not their loving care. They had stood before the building containing the recruiting office, one of many families milling before its soot-streaked granite waiting for the bus to take their son from them. To the train station, "*Jordan, don't go.*" To the training camp, "*Jordan, stay.*" To the ship, "*Jordan, pray.*" To the separating oceans, "*Jordan, we pray for you.*" To the grave they feared was opening—and they censured him wordlessly for leaving them behind to live in dread. They must have seen his young body already lifeless to have that same look he'd seen ashore. He twisted again on the bunk. A man coughed; another began to snore. But it's okay now, he protested to the red glow. I'm alive, I made it. I'm not going to die like that baby...not like those...

What? Ah, that was it. The people ashore weren't

15

Japs anymore. Indoctrinated to think of them as The Enemy, he now couldn't believe them savage animals to be distrusted, nor the unthinking wyverns attempting to kill him without thought to their own cost. They had become what he saw ashore, though he wished he had not been there. Why was the tour conducted? Was he to take the image home as a glory? This is how the war was stopped; that's what somebody said on the ride back to the ship. That's right, he whispered to the stark redness, it stopped the war, we stopped the war twice to make damned sure. Is that what I'm to tell everybody? This is how it's done. No one will have to tell the baby in the woman's arms....

"What's the matter, Jordie?"

He opened his eyes and the red mist faded, was a light bulb near the ladder. From the next bunk, Dave studied him with concern.

"Nothing. I can't sleep..."

"Why not?"

"I don't know. I was thinking about home..."

"If we were draftees, we'd be counting the days."

"There's not long, anyway."

"You crud. Your hitch is up before mine."

"I was smart. I signed for the baby cruise, not six years."

"Don't rub it in."

"Change your mind about staying in the service when your hitch is over, Dave?"

"Depends on how horseshit peacetime Navy is..."

"I wouldn't sign up again..."

"You homesick?"

"I don't know." *How do you go home after ending the war? How if you can't cheer?*

"You know, I was homesick as a hound in a pound my second week of boot camp." Dave would have reached to touch Jordan in sympathy but refrained. Touching was done in mock battles, affection masked beneath pushes and shoves and punches. On these bunks, separated by the width of a man's breath, there could be no touch. "I thought I got over it. Till the surrender, I thought I got over it...and then it started again."

"I guess that's how it is with me..."

16

Falling silent, they thought mournfully about home and family, turned their backs upon one another absently and fell asleep. Being young, resiliency was to fend off the fright of what they'd seen. And concurrently, the memory would burrow inside, pretend to be lost or set aside or accepted. Cain's brand is deep and never obliterated. For Jordan, there were further sins to be consummated.

Roving onward through the Inland Sea, Jordan's squadron dropped anchor at various ports for reasons known only to the Supreme Commander for the Allied powers. The quality of their reception ashore and a total absence of belligerence made the new guests soften; it became possible to slough away past anguished years. The sailors were enchanted by exquisite diminutive women determined to treat them like noblemen, using impeccable mannered customs which led them to believe it was deserved. Whenever free of the ships, the crews became involved in that fleeting honeymoon of chivalrous confrontation which existed for a time...so very brief a time before the impact of the main body of the Occupation forces hardened the life and brutalized what it touched. Although the season was late in the year, it had a tender air of beginnings...

Once the malignancy of Hiroshima was left behind, restricted to itself and far beyond to the other side of Kyushu where Nagasaki had been, Jordan longed to be on the land which always lay tantalizingly close. Each visit exposed more of the delights of the western island straits. Being so small a military group, the crews of his destroyer squadron could be absorbed into communities without overwhelming them. He thought they must be awesome enough, dwarfing the people. He felt highly visible, even when stooping to examine lacquerware or trinkets spread out upon the ground by enterprising salesmen. Why didn't piles of explicit erotic silk paintings seem out of place amid carved trays and strings of lumpy pearls and dolls? The ports he liked best were the lesser ones, hardly worthy of

17

the name, innocent of anything but what was heard over a radio or by word of mouth. There was one in particular.

The village lay at the cusp of the sea, resembling a small nest which had fallen and submerged part of its body in the waters. Frail wooden houses, tiled gray or blue on sloping roofs, huddled about a sand-colored cement ramp. This was a substitute beach constructed by the community because the island had none. The quay was perhaps the size of a football field, immaculately clean, a berth for a line of fishing boats drawn up side by side with blunt prows raised in perfect symmetry, like chorus girls in a show. A breakwater of stone calmed a lagoon before them. Houses topped the ramp and extended to stone wharves at both sides, so streets beyond were difficult to see. Rising in irregular steps at the rear, simple dwellings snugged closely to one another emitted an odor of burning charcoal and wood smoke. On the mountain above, past cultivated parcels of land, stood forests and shrubbery made damp by mists from the upper airs. It was a village similar to others along Seto Nakai, and it was also pleased to welcome the foreigners.

Children watching the liberty party arrive from the somber warships scampered merrily over the ramp, kicking up water and printing the shapes of their feet everywhere. The whaleboats made for the wharves, their personnel not knowing they were a buffer for the port from devouring seas in time of storm and had no mooring cleats. The children had to be entreated to catch thrown lines to hold the boats fast while sailors sprang ashore; the children seized the lines in tumbling groups, giggling as they competed to see who held on most securely. They seized Jordan's heart, too. Spared bombings or strafings, they were untouched by war; children hear an elder's fears but continue to play unless something visible confirms the words. Dressed in summer whites, Jordan leaped briskly from a packed boat to join the throng and help his mates disembark. It became an established routine. Every day he went ashore he looked forward to helping them with their task and then swaggered inland with Dave as the whaleboats returned to the ships, distributing candy like confetti upon his milling escorts before entering the village in a disintegrating band of sailors and imps taking different paths and alleys to explore.

18

As for older members of the village, they knew little of the *hakujin*, the white people, save what they had read or been told. These foreign ships, it was reported, would remain in their harbor to use it as a permanent base of operations. Permanent. It was a thing to discuss in whispers. But the crews were certainly not the monsters spoken of in days gone by; if anything, they were undisciplined youngsters, overgrown and most peculiarly friendly. There were black men among them, too; not many in number, nevertheless they were also considered *hakujin* and objects of interest. It wasn't easy to comprehend the ways of any of these sailors, yet not without profit to deal with them, for they were wildly generous and one was sore put to find appropriate gifts to repay them. The solution was simple: They turned the exchange to commerce.

Stalls promptly constituted a pedestrian hazard in the village. Every craftsman and enterprising householder had something for sale, be it the work of hands or commonplace articles thought to appeal to the sailors. If they would not buy brooms or clay bowls, what of lacquered trays and fine boxes? Flags of cotton and silk were popular, and pornographic art in any form. Sewing machines were treadled night and day when it was learned the sailors would buy kimonos for their women at home. The commercial revolution in the village was a microcosm of what happened enthusiastically in the cities on the main island of Hoinshu. The act of surrendering had been transferred and grown men found themselves at the mercy of small boys with wads of yen in their hands and propositions upon their lips. They could supply anything. Their eagerness endeared the children further to the customers, who struck what they thought sharp bargains in exchange for cigarettes and candy without paying mind to hundreds of yen they poured into the small cupped hands as payment for fancy contraceptives of intricate and humorous design or bottles of suspect alcoholic beverages. Little girls were not so bold, leaving it to older sisters to bewitch the men. To satisfy passion, a crib of whores was available, discreetly enlarged by the addition of women from another district. Not geishas, these. Untrained peasant stock with stamina for the constant trade.

The trouble was, the village had only itself to present. Nothing about it had historical significance; there were no museums and no old castles to see. The sailors soon exhausted the few entertainments and contained their restless wandering. They patronized the whores and sellers of spirits and it grew rarer to see them on side streets as they had charted every one and marked them as doldrums. And so it was remarkable that Jordan and Dave came upon something they had overlooked.

"That's got to be a theater—it can't be anything else," Dave called to Jordan. He had been attracted to a gateway before a low structure because of bright banners hung above its ample court.

"Why didn't we notice it before?"

"We did. But they didn't have these decorations up."

They examined the premises eagerly, for it was a new place to them now. A stake fence enclosed the area, surrounding a clean yard pebbled with smooth oval stones. At one side, a row of potted plants eased the austerity; a full branched tree shaded half the court. There were wooden stands displaying hand-tinted photographs and large paper posters depicting fiercely visaged warriors in ancient costumes. The sailors rested their forearms atop the fence to look inside.

"What's it doing in a dinky burg like this?"

"We have *two* theaters in Colby," Dave bragged.

"Yeah, but that's movies," Jordan retorted scornfully. "Everybody's got movies."

"You don't think they show movies here?"

"No." Jordan indicated the wooden stands. "Those look like stage pictures. See where the edge of a stage shows on the bottoms? You can make out the top of somebody's head in the audience. I saw the same kinds of pictures on Broadway."

They studied everything from a distance, reluctant to enter the court. A sallow man in a plain gray yukata appeared. Shuffling between the potted plants on straw zories, smiling and speaking in low tones, he beckoned at them. They smiled in return and advanced shyly.

Whatever was said, they had to deduce by what was shown. He led them into the building, which proved to be a theater as they suspected. Extending an ell through the audience space, a long wooden stage occupied one end of the large room. Its polished boards gleamed beneath a simple scenic setting of a house exterior. The talkative

20

guide lifted a trapdoor on the platform, repeated the word
seridashi several times and pantomimed it was used by
actors for exits and entrances. He would not permit them
to step upon the stage but took them past it to the side of
the building and outside into a family living quarter.
There, seated upon his heels, an elderly man held a male
child firmly before himself and manipulated its arms and
legs as he sang a whining, startling chant. Jordan and
Dave, seeing the art of the old one transmitted to another
generation, nodded understanding at words of explanation. From the cottage beyond, they were scrutinized by
others of the household, women and older children who
had been entertaining a visitor and now were hushed as
they saw the foreigners in their midst.

The old man stopped his training session. The child ran
to the safety of the cottage, pausing in the doorway with
crossed legs. He watched as the old man dipped his head
solemnly at the sailors. Dave offered a cigarette. Accepting, the old man allowed him to light it and sat regarding
these round-eyed striplings through the satisfying smoke.
They enjoyed a moment of stillness, feeling friendly and
wondering what to do. The little boy panicked and fled
into the cottage. Dave offered a cigarette to the guide.
Bowing deeply, the man took it, also accepting a light from
Dave's Zippo. They all grinned at one another.

The peace was broken by a spill of feminine voices from
the small house; the visitor must make her departure and
she took leave of her hostess with a flurry of polite phrases.
Emerging from the cottage timidly, she took a moment to
gaze at the men. She was minute; a lark surprised to be
earthbound. A white smock covered her ordinary black
dress and she clasped a cedar picnic box, such as that
which every member of an audience brings to the theater
when watching a performance. Her eyes widened slightly
as she beheld the sailors. They were alarming so close.

Jordan smiled broadly at her and said, "Hi."

She blushed with confusion. Covering her mouth with
a hand, she spoke softly to the woman behind her, asking
why this *hakujin* said yes to her when she had requested
nothing of him, and her companion tittered in answer. It
would be necessary to pass the military strangers in order
to leave. How vexing! Although her elder sister's husband
invariably had company, it was unbelievable to find

21

American seamen at his door. Her new box could have been shown another day. How odd the foreign warriors were taking an interest in people of the arts...and how blue were the eyes of the one who spoke...

How black her eyes are, thought Jordan, enraptured. She seemed to hover in front of him, so fragile and tense he felt clumsy in her presence. Her face wasn't what he was accustomed to think of as beautiful, yet he was captivated; her slender figure was well proportioned and did not bottom out in the manner many of the girls of the country displayed. He was making her uncomfortable and regretted it. If only he could speak her language! She bowed at him then, a low ceremonial procedure, and without raising her head slipped past to hurry beyond the plants dividing the court. He didn't want her to go but there was no way to prevent it. Unsettled, he looked back at the others and tried to retain his smile. Those in the doorway of the cottage resisted being pushed entirely into the yard by inquisitive souls behind; though everyone wished to get near the *hakujin,* they were yet fearsome things. Jordan backed a step, then cleared his throat nervously to say, "I guess we better haul ass, too, Dave." He tugged at his friend's sleeve and they retreated from the court. The assembly bobbed many short bows, and the Americans imitated them awkwardly. At last they were on the street again. Jordan looked around anxiously.

"You after a date, Jordie?"

"I'd like to get to know her," he said evasively. "She was...well, you saw her."

"Scuttlebutt says they brought in a new bunch of beauties up the mountainside. They took over a shrine or something."

He shook his head. "I'm not talking about that."

"Don't you even want to find out if it's true?"

"I want to see if I can meet that girl again."

"You want to search for her now?"

"Yeah...I was thinking of it."

"You've gone Asiatic, Jordie. I'm going after the sure thing."

The girl was nowhere in sight. He turned to Dave. "You know I don't screw around with whores, Dave."

"I know you still got your cherry." Dave started off

22

was not for him. Such altitude required an oxygen mask. He didn't like anything covering his face.

There was another drawback. The final dive was too critical. If the wrong angle was begun at that height, it couldn't be corrected; a pilot lost control of his plane as gravity took charge. He preferred the low-altitude approach, sneaking under the enemy's radar at sea level and climbing sharply at the final moment to dive at the target. It took full control for the maneuver, more so with a plane salvaged from remnants. Had the Zero been assembled from original parts, it would be running smoothly by now. Well, then. He was doing better with it. Having learned how one function affected another during the process of stripping the machine, the fault was being remedied. His supply of water was another problem; this task was taking longer than expected. When the remainder of the unit was transferred here from Oroku on Okinawa, they brought supplies for four men to exist for a while. Even alone, the water was dwindling fast.

Alone.

They had been ground crew for each other. Their mechanic was in charge of maintenance; having none to order but himself, he had done his job superbly—nobody drives a man better than himself—but the eel in his bowels had emptied him of life. How the pilots dreaded dysentery! Did Dai Nanko suffer it during his final battle centuries ago? Like him, the Unit was outnumbered by the enemy, and its petals dropped from the bloom of glory in turn—and he was alone finally. To have been chosen by his brothers in arms for the honor of being last was painful. Now there was no one to encourage him as he had them.

Flap...flap...flap...flap...flap...

A broken sound. Like the engine. Ishimoto began to run through the trees to the plane so that he could work again.

Whenever Jordan went ashore, he searched for the girl of the courtyard. Dave ragged him, saying he'd do better at the busy brothel on the mountainside. The men of the fleet were making such a habit of going there in fraternal bands that from a distance the slim path seemed thronged with pilgrims. On a day when Dave decided not to pay his respects to the converted monastery, he was asked to help search through the streets of the village. They checked the theater compound but did not stay, not caring to smile and nod with folk who could not tell them what Jordan wanted to know.

They came to an enclosure serving as a market and walked slowly past stalls filled with farm produce and gleanings from the sea. The farmer in Dave was critical of what he saw for sale, unaware that he and his shipmate were also undergoing an inspection. There was a crone nearby with an eye for foreign warriors. Among her wares, she had stacks of dried seaweed which had been toasted and, to her thinking, ideal to give seafarers. When they passed, she clutched at Jordan's elbow with a gnarled hand, thrust a tidbit into his palm and bared her gums in what she believed an appealing smile. He looked at the object in his hand with doubt.

Dave murmured, "If it kills you, I'll sic the Shore Patrol on her."

The old woman moved Jordan's hand to his mouth to goad him into tasting the goodness, but he resisted.

"Anohito wa nippon shoku wo tabetakunai to omoimasu."

He turned to see the girl he sought, her head slanted with humor as she told the tradeswoman the sailors wouldn't like Japanese food. Jordan nibbled at the crisp seaweed and found it palatable. Grinning, he patted his stomach affectionately. The women broke into laughter, inclining their bodies toward each other so their shoulders touched. The girl carried string bags into which she placed

26

her purchases; radishes, greens and taro roots poked foliage through networks of beige twine.

"Very good," Jordan said. "I like it." He smacked his lips and rubbed his stomach again.

"Hai," the girl answered sweetly, looking from him to Dave and back again. She wore Western shoes with high heels on her bare feet, and her legs were straight and sleek as those of a young cat.

"Hi," he returned. She repeated her word and Jordan realized it meant yes and exclaimed at the discovery, "Oh...yeah! *Hai, hai, hai!"* And both beamed over the exchange.

"Scratch one bogie," grinned Dave.

Excusing herself, the girl devoted her attention to the old woman's stall to choose vegetables and a clutch of eggs. Their transaction was a courtly drama, filled with elegant haggling and mutual satisfaction. The girl's absorption concealed her agitation. The color of his eyes had made her so bold—she wanted very much to study them closely—and who could not notice that he seemed equally fascinated? It was far more exciting than being singled out by boys she knew, but there were none her age in the village; they had gone to the war. She didn't know what to make of this new feeling inside. It was time to pay her money. She counted yen into the tradeswoman's hand and started to leave. Jordan blocked her path impudently.

"We'll walk you home, okay?" He pointed from the bags to himself and Dave.

She guessed they wanted to play servant and refused, saying *"Iie, arigato,"* but the crone cackled and urged her to allow the giants to unburden her. She eyed them with uncertainty.

"Okay," Jordan said. "Maybe you don't monkey around with strangers. This fella is Dave Bell. My name's Jordan Asche." He tried to be personable as he thumbed his chest and repeated his name. "Jor-dan...Aaashhh..."

"Ah," she replied, "Joe-dan...Ashhh."

Pleased to have made a beginning, they paused. He pointed to her, raising his eyebrows in question.

"Hai," she stuttered, *"hai..."* Drowning in the dark blue of his eyes, she whispered, "Yukiko...Yukiko Shimada..." The market crone nudged her with an insistent finger to start them toward the street. Outside,

27

people passing were careful not to turn heads till after they had gone by, diverted by the sight of two tall sailors carrying groceries and shortening their strides to match the steps of the girl.

Her family lived among crowded houses upon a ledge of rock overhanging the sea. There was Oka-san and Oto-san, her mother and father, and a stern mummy of a woman introduced as Ooba-san. It was apparent this aged grandmother had ruled the household for many years with an iron fist. She alone regarded the sailors frigidly, refusing to put them at their ease. Watching with contempt as they learned to remove their shoes before entering her domain, she was a bleak stone gargoyle seated beside an open pit which exuded heat from an ashen skin of hot coals in one corner of the room. The sunken firebox was set into the floorboards; an iron kettle steamed from a hook above. Bundled into a quilted jacket and capped with a head scarf, Ooba-san could keep herself comfortable in whatever weather while she ran the family's affairs. Her daughter-in-law served everyone like an indentured servant, but this was customary and not resented. Wriggling leathery bare toes in the cinders, Ooba-san observed how her son and his wife welcomed the foreigners. The size of the *hakujin* shrank her abode; her family diminished further in the depths of their numerous obsequious bows.

Neither Jordan nor Dave understood the conversation as Ooba-san grunted belligerently, "What awkward fools you make of yourselves for these long noses from Beikoku which your second daughter dares to bring into our house!"

Oto-san declared respectfully, "But Revered Mother, now that they are here, they are our guests."

"I have not forgotten taking the ashes of my youngest son to be laid to rest in the cemetery on the side of the mountain."

"It may be these men did not fight against my heroic brother in the battle of Luzon."

"If it was not they who took his life, then it was done by others of their kind." Ooba-san spat into the coals at her feet. *"Hai,"* she continued with indignation, "your second daughter has lost responsibility. My stomach rises at having this impudence forced upon me." She ignored the others in the room thereafter.

The *hakujin* were brought bowls of broth from the ket-

28

tle. Everyone but the dragon at the hearth felt inadequate for lack of knowing how to behave correctly. Having given food, which is never wrong, Oka-san wished for invisibility and did her utmost to escape attention. It was extraordinary for her daughter to bring the men here but she would not have done so without good reason. They arrived carrying her bundles as though she were their mistress and could command them! Oka-san hoped her good husband would see they didn't disgrace themselves before the baffling strangers. The Beikoku-jin had been discussed with alarm in weeks past and the family was instructed by their hamlet leaders to obey the edict of the government and to be compliant and serene. It was amazing that none of the fierce tales about the enemy heard during the war seemed to suit them . . .

Oto-san, being at a loss, did nothing. If he did nothing wrong, then it followed that the *hakujin* would think all he did was right. If only his magnificent mother would stop rattling her armor! She might incite them and all would pay dearly! They might bind him and rape each of the women, perhaps call in more companions from the streets and then set the house afire. They appeared to be calm, though. They seemed to like his poor wife's broth. The instruction to be placid in the presence of the Beikoku-jin accomplished its purpose; they were not plundering the countryside, and the village was at peace. It was so in the rest of Nippon, he had heard. How much time must he spare from his labor in the rice paddy to play host? Ah, banish the thought lest it make him ungracious. Oto-san darted an optimistic glance at his stupid daughter, for she knew much of these newcomers and how to treat them, having the ability to read the new simplified newsprint and having books and schooling. She would prevent the family from disgracing itself.

Yukiko thought the sailors were enjoying themselves. It wasn't possible to think of the blue-eyed one as *hakujin*, a bad name having to do with vomiting and given to the Western people long ago. He smiled much and looked admiringly at everything in the room. Had he noticed her arrangement of leaves and twigs in the tokonoma? Her grandmother hadn't upset him and his friend, which would have been an embarrassment for everyone. There must be something more to do to be hospitable. Oto-san and Oka-san knew what was proper. Oto-san defended them to his mother to silence her, and Oka-san fed them immediately. It was only miso with grated dried fish floating around but there was little else. Should they have had rice? She sat quietly, leaving the matter to her wise parents. They knew how to keep the family from disgrace.

Jordan swallowed manfully despite his aversion to the heavily salted flavor. A revolving disk of an eye had been hard to take. It wouldn't do to offend the family by putting the bowl down without emptying it. Dave was avoiding looking at him. What did he find in his soup? The family was relaxed, not running around excitedly as they might. The old lady wasn't as talkative as she'd been, but that was natural since he and Dave didn't speak Japanese, and the family must have heard everything she ever had to say. What to do next? If the party broke up too soon, the family might feel hurt. Approving sounds regarding stuff in the room perked everybody up; well, there wasn't much in sight. These poor people didn't have anything. Sitting on his legs as the family did was a mistake; the pain had been awful till his feet fell asleep. Jesus, he was going to have a bitch of a time getting up. So would Dave. Jordan wanted to laugh out loud. He was happy. This was a nice place and he was having a good time...and he was happy.

When all had been thoroughly subjected to growing discomfort and distressing boredom, and when there was nothing further to do, the *hakujin* lurched to their feet like bumbling oxen to depart. They brayed in their strange tongue and bowed and behaved idiotically and were gone. A man could return to work. Oto-san hurried to get his hoe from the veranda. His mother refused to speak to anyone; his relieved wife was almost faint with gratitude for having survived the peculiar event, and his stupid daughter had gone down the road to watch the men march away. Though winds blow, he must stand like the mountain. As he took hoe in hand, Yukiko ran to him, breathless with excitement.

"Still a child and running?" he reproved her sternly.

"Do you think they liked us, Oto-san?"

"What made you bring them to my house?" he demanded. "I should beat you for it." And he raised the hoe menacingly. She shrank from him without alarm. It was right to be scolded but she had entered a new era daringly and allowed impulse to guide her and was too exhilarated to be afraid. Oto-san was gruff. "You are out of favor. Go inside to make amends." He left abruptly, stared at by his neighbors, who had come to their doors to see what other outrageous thing his family would do. Yukiko composed herself. Her outward appearance was demure...but she entered the house on wings.

Before Jordan and Dave could call upon the Japanese family again, storm warnings routed the fleet from the Inland Sea. The ships were to lay off on the ocean expanse, where they would fare better against a threatening typhoon. A number of lesser vessels were left behind, since it was thought they would be sheltered in the coves. Those departing sailed under lowering skies, showered with torrential rains preceding the fury from the south. Jordan's ship steamed out in tandem with the destroyer squadron, followed by the supply ship and the wallowing tankers. At a distance beyond Shikoku and Kyushu judged safe for maneuvering against the weather, the naval group waited for the assault.

It arrived with enormous energy, transmitting giant waves and throwing the ships into winds which howled after them as they sank into bottomless troughs. The *Bulman* yawed, dipped beneath maelstroms of foam, rolled and plunged under washes determined to drag it down forever. Maintaining sporadic contact with other ships, trying to hold position and course, its bridge and radar room were as frantically alert as they ever had been during the war.

It was impossible to stand, sit, or do anything without clinging for dear life to whatever seemed secure. Battened down tightly, passageways and compartments became foul with fetid air; men with battered bodies sucked in their breath at sounds of thunderous blows hammering at the hull. Where a seam showed signs of strain or buckling, men worked furiously to shore it up, bolstering it with lumber, mattresses, anything to prevent an ominous

31

trickle from becoming a Niagara. Two days and nights were fought before the eye of the storm was upon them, bringing slight respite and a promise of agony to come. One of the tankers was gone. No one knew if it had sunk or been blown off course.

During that brief lull, the sailors sat in Neptune's jaws so wearied none believed in survival. The Chief Torpedoman entered the mess compartment where many of the crew, wearing foul-weather gear and life jackets, tried to gulp hot coffee from unsteady cups. Seeing Jordan, he said, "Get your ass topside and check the charges. Make sure they're not working loose." Jordan set his cup down, too tired to pursue it when it fell to the heaving deck. "And pick up Bell on the way. Tell him to check the tubes fore and aft." Jordan staggered to the hatch to go into the next compartment, where he located Dave in his bunk.

"Dave, we got the duty."

Dave buried his face under a damp pillow. "I just got in the sack," he whined.

"You won't be able to sleep, anyway. Chief wants us to have a look-see at the tubes and depth charges."

Groaning, Dave abandoned his bunk to pull on oilskins and a Mae West. He trailed Jordan out of the compartment, up a steep ladder, and along a corridor to a heavy hatch. They undogged it and stepped out onto the main deck.

Above, a slate sky loomed over colossal swells crested with spittle. Trembling wildly each time her propellers lifted free of water, the *Bulman* rode the sea helplessly. Everywhere, liquid mountains rose and fell in torment. Dave climbed laboriously up a slick steel ladder to the torpedo deck while Jordan clung to handrails at the side of the slippery main deck to work his way past hedgehogs and depth-charge racks. A sea roared along the deck, broke against the racks and threatened to tear him from his hold. He gripped the greasy railing tightly, blinking hard into blinding salt spray. When the ship righted herself, he continued to the stern. All secure. Rounding the port side, he found nothing amiss and looked to the aft torpedo deck for Dave. The minotaur on the stack gleamed brightly under its sheen; its frozen charge towered over Dave as he skidded below it, slid toward a ladder when the wind blew him off his feet, then missed grabbing a stanchion to fall heavily to the main deck. Jordan had to scramble to catch his arm as he went by. Seawater carried Dave's legs and waist under tattered tar line webbing, pulling him downward as it poured in a ferment over the side. They suffered another sucking heave of the ship, then forced themselves from the brink of the chasm at the gunwhale.

Hearts pounding, they snatched at the railing. A life raft, torn from its cradle, careened past to catch momentarily at a 20mm gun mount before flying overboard. It floated upon the marbled side of a wall of sea and remained a long time, matching the struggling destroyer in speed until another convulsion bore it into billowing curtains of rain.

"Come on, let's get below..."

"My leg's broke."

Jordan wiped streaming drops from his face and reprimanded Dave angrily. "What the hell did you have to fall for? Jesus!"

Dave managed to grin past his wince. "Tough titty, Mac. You'll have to give me a hand..."

Dragging themselves painfully beside the railing, they struggled along the deck. A torrent pinned them down badly once, almost tearing them apart. Jordan locked his arms around Dave as the water flooded over them. It pulled, seethed around them and away. Sputtering mouthfuls of brine, they were able to crawl to safety. When they got to the hatch, he twisted the dogs open and hauled Dave inside. Securing the steel door, Jordan panted, "You be okay here?"

"Oh, yeah. I wasn't going to do any dancing."

It was stifling. The dark resounded with deep thunders from below. Their labored breathing slowed; strength seeped back into strained muscles. After a moment, Jordan braced himself against the bulkhead and got to his feet. "I'll scare up a corpsman to help take you to sick bay."

"Oh...hey, Jordie..."

He looked at his friend. Dave was tucked uncomfortably against the closed hatch and was serious as hell in water pooling on the metal deck under him.

"Yeah?"

"You know, Jordie...if I can ever do anything for you..."

33

"Ah, fuck off, will you?" Jordan snarled sourly. "Now I've got nobody to go ashore with for a while." He walked unsteadily down the corridor under the red battle lights to sick bay.

Dave leaned wearily against the steel. Some moron had scratched the mindless graffiti signature left wherever American troops went, a goon head peering over the base seam: KILROY WAS HERE...

The letter could not be mailed but Ishimoto continued to write. It would be left in the bunker when he made his sortie; if someone found it in the future, he hoped it was taken to Nippon. The storm was abating. Rain leaked from between the earth-covered logs of the roof. A candle guttered on the crate he used as a desk. When the candle burned to its end there was no other. He would be in the dark at night hereafter...

"...and just this moment, I thought of lanterns we bought in Gifu when we were on vacation. I know they are hanging in the same place in your house and shining with beautiful light as I write these words. I can see them clearly, yellow and blue silks glued over bamboo strips in graceful pagoda shapes. I'm happy to know I shared them with you, my dear parents and family, and that you can be reminded of me when you look at them. My favorite has white peonies painted on it. But you will wonder why I haven't carried out my mission. The engine of my Zero is repaired! Inclement weather delays me now but I shall meet you at Yasukuni Shrine very soon. As the sun rises, so shall I. I don't mean tomorrow but when everything is ready. The runway must be cleared and then I will wrap my *hachimaki* around my helmet with its red sun centered upon my forehead and I will put on my white muffler and read once more the words you wrote on the flag you gave me. I keep it inside my jacket close to my heart. The inscription inspires me: *Hio wa itidai, na wa matudai!* A man is the length of his lifetime, his name is longer...."

34

The flame of the candle went out and the heavy smell of the wick assailed him. They would be proud reading his letter. They would pass it among themselves, from father to mother and among his younger brothers and sisters, and it would be shown to the neighbors. How easily he wrote "your house" as if he had not lived there, had not been born there. A man is the length of his lifetime...He would be twenty-three years old in a few months...*iie*, he would not be...not *be*.

Ishimoto groped to the opening of the bunker. He squatted under folds of burlap covering it, pulling the material aside to feel the rain. A gasoline drum outside was filling to the brim. Dancing splashes. Plenty of water now. Was he permitted regrets?

When the squadron returned to its anchorage, everything was as before, scoured cleaner and once more the tranquil coastline and islands of a myth. The scene was marred by an overturned landing barge and some larger craft driven onto rocks. Their castaway crews waited like cavern-eyed *haniwa* to be absorbed back into service. Busy figures swarmed over the wrecks to plumb sunken compartments and to pick them bare; later the hulls would be rusting ogres guarding the shores. And this time, the villagers greeted the Americans like relatives, for the survivors of any mutual calamity always undergo an unsolicited union...and the aftermath of the typhoon was as the unfolding of a flower.

Jordan's next liberty began with a sense of loss; his friend couldn't leave the ship. As he dressed, Dave lounged on the footlockers, scratching irritably at a heavy plaster cast on his leg. The itch inside wasn't eased. "I wish I were going with you, Jordie."

"So do I."

Dave examined Jordan's locker. Canned food, cigarettes and candy bars were jammed among the clothes. "You taking this loot with you?"

"Not all of it. I can't smuggle everything off the ship at once." A directive had been issued against taking material from the ship which might end in black-market hands. Everybody ignored it.

"What do you expect to get for it?"

"Nothing. I'm giving it away."

"Sure you are."

"No. I want to give it to that Japanese family we met."

"Oh. You need an excuse to see the girl again."

"She's got nothing to do with it."

"Don't shit me, Jordie. You were grinning like a tomcat with a hard-on the whole time we were with her."

Jordan wriggled into his jumper and combed his hair carefully. "Listen, I'm not a sex fiend like you. They were nice. I thought we could take them a few things they didn't have."

"You mean *you* could do it."

"Oh, you'll be sprung loose when you can get around without falling down."

"You might wind up becoming their welfare department, Jordie."

"That's okay with me."

"Even if you get your ass in a sling for it?"

"I'm only taking a few things ashore, not enough to notice."

"And the girl's got nothing to do with it." Dave leaned against the bunk springs. The lowest bunk had been raised to allow access to the lockers and provided a cushion for his back. "The Japs were killing us a month ago."

"That was a month ago."

"They're still gooks, Jordie."

Jordan concentrated on polishing the shine of his shoes. "You know what, Dave? With a droopy moustache, the girl's father could be a match for mine. Remember the way he treated his wife? Respectful and calm. That's my Pop with my Mom. Same thing. Old Country-style people. And the granny sitting by the fireplace. Okay, it was a hole in the floor but I've got somebody like her in Poland. I've never seen her but I bet she doesn't say a word to strangers, either." He put his shoe brush aside and put on his tie. A carton of cigarettes and several cans were slipped into a ditty bag.

"I wish I was going with you, Jordie."

36

"Me, too, I won't know what to do with myself."

"You won't have any problems."

Clapping a freshly laundered white cap to the back of his head, Jordan hoisted the bag under his arm and left. Dave started to shut the locker's lid, saw the candy bars and called after him, but Jordan was already out of the hatch. He forgot the candy bars. Whatever he would admit about the girl, Jordie sure as hell didn't have little kids on his mind if he could forget to take those along.

Getting the contraband ashore was simple for Jordan; pushing past importunate beggars on the wharf was not. Seeing him, the children clamored at his elbows, tugged to see what was in his bag, and were astonished to be given nothing. "Choco-rat-oh! Choco-rat-oh! Hey, Joe, choco-rat-oh!" He promised to make up for it next trip. They pursued him halfway through the village before they believed he had no candy with him.

Yukiko met him on the path below her house, chattering about how terrible the storm had been and how near a thing it was that her family's home had not tumbled into the sea. He didn't know what she was saying, though he tried to grasp the meaning and nodded agreeably in her pauses. She told him how she worried about him during the dreadful week, how her thoughts flew seaward even as the house of her neighbors sank in a rumble of stone and earth at the height of the squalls. The doomed cottage broke apart immediately upon entering the cauldron at the foot of the cliff and its splintering timbers soon ground up the trapped inhabitants. With earnest sadness, she guided him to the raw site of the disaster and mourned that there was no one left of the unfortunate family to claim the salvage. He saw steps her father carved into the barren portion of the hill, making it possible to climb to the upper road without having to follow the original path. It was a useful monument.

Her parents were not home when they got there, having gone to work in the *dandan batake*, the agricultural plots, above the village. Ooba-san was perched dourly in her accustomed place beside the fire pit. She frowned as her granddaughter brought Jordan inside.

"Ooba-san, he brings gifts of luxuries from his ship!"

The old woman gnawed the insides of her cheeks; she measured the bulk of his bag. "So," she said, "a pony is to

37

come out of a gourd. Why should he be generous to us, this long-nose?"

Hoping Ooba-san would relent and accept the presents with good grace, the girl made no reply. Jordan unloaded his collection one at a time, arranging each at Ooba-san's side in a row like a toy train. The carton of cigarettes attracted her attention and she grunted as if in thanks. She looked questioningly at an unlabeled can and he pried it open to show her the contents.

"Sugar...sug-ar-oh...you know, sweet stuff." He didn't know how to explain it better.

Dipping a finger into it, Ooba-san tasted the grains tentatively. "Ah...*sato*," she said. It was a grumpy comment; Jordan was almost tempted to sample the contents himself to see if he had mistakenly filled the can with salt, which they surely didn't need. Then he produced his cans of Spam. Pictures on the labels clearly showed what was inside. "Ah...*nango*," she purred reluctantly, acknowledging these were certainly treasures to receive. Perhaps she would remove her helmet for a time to see what more would transpire.

Pleased her grandmother was softening, Yukiko knelt quickly to open the cigarette carton. She extracted a package of Lucky Strikes and handed it respectfully to Ooba-san, who exclaimed with surprise as she saw it.

"It is marked with the flag of Nippon!"

"Hai, Ooba-san." Yukiko had no idea the logo was changed because of war needs in the States; the red circle on the package was on a white field instead of green.

"This foreigner takes care to please us." Ooba-san examined the slick compactness of the package and anticipated the pleasure to come. She undid the top carefully and tapped out a cigarette. When she put it to her lips, Jordan was at her side to offer the flame of his lighter. Ignoring him, she bent to the ashes at her feet and picked up a coal. Holding the ember between two fingertips, she lit the cigarette slowly, then pitched the hot coal back into the pit. He was astounded.

"What's she made of...asbestos?" He had the impression she was invincible. She wouldn't look at him directly, nor did she move when he spoke other than to take long, gratifying drags. The cigarette smoke wreathed her as it combined with haze from the fire pit.

38

"Joe-dan-ash..."

Yukiko beckoned, indicating they leave the dragon in peace. Jordan nodded, muttered "See you" at Ooba-san and followed the girl out of the house. They slipped into their shoes and she took him along the winding street to orderly tiers of rice fields which edged the forested upper region of the mountain. Her parents were in one of the flooded pans; an earthen dam enclosed a low pond reflecting straight rows of full-grown rice. In the next paddy, a man worked a black ox over a drained field to turn the mud in preparation for seedlings. The many paddies were a charming causeway of terraces stepping down to the village, each ledge either green or yellow and contrasting sharply with the intense blues of the sea below. Oto-san saw Yukiko and the sailor and waved. She bowed in reply, then led Jordan higher.

Farther up the mountainside they passed plots of vegetables, also terraced and planted in long even rows, and then they entered the cool shadows of the forest. They walked upon a mat of dank pine needles and thick moss, shielded from the sky by tall irregular trees. The serenity was disturbed only by sudden bird calls and a tripping run of slender streams which carved caverns beneath ferns before reappearing in dashing channels lower on the slopes. She brought him to a shredded cobweb of a waterfall, difficult to see from the trail. He thought it must be a favorite haunt since she was so completely at ease there. Inviting him to sit, she shared a bank of soft moss and they listened to the sounds for a while. He said, "Pretty," looking around with pleasure at the glen and then, looking at her, he said, "Pretty" again. She became brave and touched the side of his face, saying the word after him.

"Pretty."

Jordan flinched. The muscles of his groin contracted; he felt the high, delicious electricity of another touch when Everybody's Girl from Second Avenue tried to teach him how to waltz on a tenement rooftop... and inched exploring fingers inside his belt. She had scared him. He wanted to do anything but didn't know how to begin without making her laugh. He missed his chance because she scared him, as this girl did. But Yukiko had touched him innocently and was smiling into his eyes, admiring them intently to her heart's content.

39

"Pretty...*kawaii,*" she said. Her r's were clouded as milk.

He denied her praise, saying, "I'll never sign autographs."

"Nani?"

"Where I live...back home...kids like to think they look like somebody famous. Me, I just look like me." She was shaking her puzzled head at him; his words meant nothing. "Look, if we're going to get anywhere, you have to learn English...or me, Japanese. Yes? *Hai?* I teach you, you teach me. Okay?" She shook her head again but waited to hear more. The language lessons began with the naming of things.

"Hair. Hair?"

"Kami-no-ke."

"Say hair."

"Hair." She didn't get her sound quite right, which enchanted him the more.

"Okay, that's fine. See up there? Cloud...cloud. What's that?"

"Naku!" she exclaimed and hugged her knees.

He pointed to her nose. "What's nose? Nose?"

"Hana...nose."

"See how easy?" He wiggled a foot. "What's this?"

"Ashi." And she giggled, adding mischievously, "Joe-dan-*ashi!"* and pulled his shoe to make fun of his long legs. He felt better, released from the awareness of being alone with her. They were playing a game. He told her of stickball, skates and hockey pucks, and of crowded, sooty streets, tall buildings, pushcart markets on Avenue C, and he told her things he seldom said aboard ship. Missing his parents. The unhappiness of war. And he stopped, then continued happily because the war was over and the unhappiness ended with it. There was just anticipation to suffer now; everyone aboard ship wanted to go home. Yukiko listened.

Listened.

Said *hai-hai* whenever she got a cue from his intonations. And was captive to the blue of his eyes. She was falling in love with him.

40

Ooba-san snuffled at her food. The family sat closely around the fire pit, eating soba from plain dishware with the chipped rims of long usage. To the mix of buckwheat noodles in sea bream broth flavored with soy, they had added generous amounts of sugar the sailor brought each week. Forgetting its scarcity, they were using sugar lavishly; packages were delivered to the daughter in the theater compound for the pleasure of her family as well. Relishing the sweet taste, Ooba-san ruminated over the recurring presence of the long-nose. Her son and his wife permitted much they should not between a child budding into womanhood and the foreigner who was already a man. All for the sake of a bountiful flow of luxuries they could not resist. Without fail, he arrived every other day to exchange what he had with him for the company of the girl. If the parents would not pay heed to the danger, perhaps the offspring would. Because Ooba-san believed indirection served best, she presented her case by starting with an observation.

"The soldiers of Beikoku are in every city now. Soon the seamen in our harbor will be sent away."

Yukiko paled slightly. "Ah, no, Ooba-san. Why should that happen?"

"Is it not so, my son?"

Oto-san glanced at Yukiko over his bowl. "That is the way of seamen. They travel the world like lice at the command of their admirals. And it is not they directing the army of the Occupation. And the army is an army. So the ships are not needed as they once were."

"Why would they go?" she asked. "There's nothing else for them to do."

Ooba-san's unwavering obsidian pupils shone at her across the coals. "It is rumored in the village that the ships of the Beikoku-jin will escort our own soldiers home...those who survived." Yukiko looked to her father for confirmation.

"The rumor is true," he agreed. "They are gathering them from all the battlegrounds."

"To be brought home, ships are needed," said Ooba-san. "Like those in the harbor."

Yukiko protested plaintively. "The ships of Joe-dan-ash are not big enough to carry troops."

"What fleets pass on our sea have smaller ones to escort them. I say the ships in our harbor will be sent to fetch the soldiers."

"Then that means Joe-dan-ash will return."

Slyly, the old woman sabotaged her hope. "When a ship leaves port, no one can truly know its destination. There are changes of orders, there are storms." Pleased with herself, Ooba-san smacked her lips and hunted among dishes at her side. "Is there no *tsukemono?*" she demanded with the rising inflection of annoyance.

Oka-san hastened to the brine barrel to bring a bowl of pickled relish. Begging pardon for her lapse, she served it meekly to the older woman. There were households in which a mother-in-law observed the custom of *shakushi watashi*, the handing over of the spoon to the new mistress, but Ooba-san refused to do it. When Oka-san crossed the threshold as a bride, the new husband was content to permit his mother to keep her power. It was thought she waited for the male child who was to appear after a female birth. That was the established formula: first the girl, who is born easily, then the boy. Alas, it was not so; and Ooba-san did not budge from her throne. Lately she was getting crankier and created tensions in the house.

Everyone ate the supper silently, reflecting upon the discussion. Ooba-san stabbed food with her wooden *hashi* and delivered the warning to her granddaughter at last as if an afterthought. "It occurs to me, Yukiko, that you might become *aki no ogi* the fan in autumn which is discarded when the heat of summer is gone..." Yukiko bent her head lower over her bowl. Her mother and father regarded her inquiringly but were unable to catch her eye. Above the roof tiles, wild geese fluted discordantly in the dusk, trailing the call behind the arrowhead of their flight.

"I was speaking with Mr. Nakatsuru this morning..."

Oto-san had their attention. Mr. Nakatsuru was the

42

moneylender of the village and a venerable leader of the community. He spoke through intermediaries if at all.

"He was waiting for me at the rice paddy," Oto-san said with awe. "Can you imagine? I was very humble."

"What had he to say?" his wife asked.

"He wanted to show me he had most of his teeth."

It wasn't necessary to explain the meeting. Mr. Nakatsuru was following up on spadework done by his go-between. It was vexing to have a widower suing for Yukiko's hand. She was not to hope for a marriage of love, yet it was hoped she could wed someone closer to her own age. Old men seed weak sons. Without malice, Oto-san observed, "Mr. Nakatsuru is not very intellectual."

Ooba-san quoted caustically, "Money improves wit."

"I mention his lack of interest in books, other than his accounts, because of hers."

"Mr. Nakatsuru wouldn't care for her books, in any case," Ooba-san sniffed. "She's studying the *hakujin* language."

"So? Then he would not. He's of the old school." He addressed his daughter. "Can you speak Ei-go well now, Yukiko?"

"*Iie*, it's too soon, my father, but I progress." During days Jordan had the duty, she studied diligently, having borrowed helpful grammars from the schoolmaster, who had them from a missionary few people remembered. Her English was improving considerably; she was striving for perfection.

"Did you see the sailor today?" There was hostility in the question. She spent too many hours with the foreigner. Was she chaste?

"We watched the potter at work. Joe-dan-ash will be back to honor *meigetsu* with us." Though the crews enjoyed a ten-o'clock curfew, they frequently returned to their ships for evening meals.

Oto-san could not oppose her plan. The people of the hamlet were to celebrate a seasonal event. Many had composed fine verses in praise of *meigetsu,* the harvest moon. It was overdue this year; they had not done it earlier, during the autumnal equinox as was usual, for the confusion of having the Occupation descend upon the nation disrupted the practice. Everyone, family and neighbors, were looking forward to sitting upon their verandas or

43

journeying to favorite viewing sites to gaze at the moon. Well, then. He couldn't turn the man away. He had brought so much from his ship they were in his debt. And the ceremony took place among crowds...

Jordan couldn't comprehend what it was at first, that one chose a seat on the veranda or stood in a specified place merely to look at the moon, which was the same as it always was no matter its phase. It seemed to compare with stoop gatherings his parents attended at home; on humid nights, they sat idly with friends on the steps of the tenement to fan themselves, drank cold beer, and watched games on the wet street, wet because smaller kids had a hydrant opened to give them a chance to prance under sprays of water until firemen turned it off. He couldn't explain that to the Japanese family, who had never seen a hydrant, manned by a master, spewing fountains to the sky.

Oto-san and Oka-san elected to remain with the old dragon and wouldn't go with Yukiko and himself. He waited with them upon the veranda while the girl completed a ritual of placing a handful of rice flour dumplings and a few wild flowers on a shelf. They were an offering to the moon, she said. Taking leave of her family, they went to her viewing place, picnic box in hand, to join others of the community.

"I don't know if I can eat anything. You could have saved yourself the trouble." He could tell by the weight of it, the cedar box was packed full.

"Not only for us. For everyone."

She brought him to a spur of ground beyond the stone wharf. A dozen or so neighbors welcomed them politely, illuminated like phantoms of her ancestors by the white disk above them. Its double shimmered toward them in a wide strip across the water of the lagoon; islands in the distance were edged with silver. The picnic box was opened to be left with similar ones, each filled with autumn cakes of chestnuts, clover and rice. There were taros boiled with the skin left on, and green soy beans, and bunches of grapes; it looked like a banquet to him. She paused to exchange pleasantries with a young friend, a girl she introduced as Natsu, but he barely saw her. His eyes followed Yukiko's every movement. More than anything, he wanted

44

to hold her against himself and take the tender kiss of his imaginings which now plagued his hours. He shifted to ease the pressure rising at his crotch. His predicament worsened when she put her arm through his and coaxed him to admire the moon.

"Yeah, it's a beauty. Looks bigger than at sea."

Her joy faltered. Should she ask if he had heard news of leaving? But, if so, it would spoil the evening to be told.

"What's your girlfriend saying over there? Everybody's so quiet around her."

"She's telling the poem she made for *meigetsu.*"

"Oh."

"Everyone has a poem."

"You too?"

"Hai."

"What is it?"

"Oh...it is too poor a thing to hear."

"Not for me." He wanted everything from her. Everything.

"You wouldn't understand."

"Is it in Japanese?"

"Iie, it was, but the schoolmaster helped me to put it into English."

"Then it's okay. You can tell me."

"It is only a haiku."

He didn't know what that was. He was hoping to distract his thoughts so he wouldn't have to turn his back to her. "Come on," he cajoled, "let me hear it."

"Well, then..." She removed her arm to hold her hands at her sides like a child in class and turned her face up to the moon. He felt worse; the warmth of her touch burned harder in its absence. Her face was beautiful in the pale light...and knowing it, and wishing she had the courage to say the haiku was about themselves, she recited the required seventeen syllables in a subdued tone:

> "Sedate the moon
> Where flamed summer's sun.
> Together, a dance of lions..."

She didn't repeat the poem to him. It was a spell; she was certain of its efficacy and was patient in her impatience for the desired result.

45

Pacing naked under moonlight, Ishimoto scuffed the cool sand, exposing pockets of heat left by the sun. He was debilitated from the effects of dysentery; that was his reason for not wearing clothes. He didn't want to soil the uniform. The letter to his family had many postscripts now: apologies for the delay; rational explanations for living. He was convinced they were true. Surely he had not lost his dedication by being alone. Surely not. His bravery revealed itself not two days earlier when a torpedo boat swept close to the shore, searching the shadows behind coconut boles for signs of life. He had been prepared to make a stand, loading his store of rifles and waiting with one leveled from behind the burlap of his bunker. They couldn't see him . . . or the plane. Everything was kept well camouflaged above and around. *Iie,* they couldn't see any of it. They couldn't see him aiming . . . aiming. . . .

The Enemy was stupid. The torpedo boat coasted leisurely out of range, and a loudspeaker blatted above the surf roar rolling to the shore: **Come out! Come out, the war is ended! Come out at the command of the Emperor! Come out and be taken home to your loved ones! Come out, the war is over!** *Hai,* stupid. As if he could be enticed into surrendering by a lie. They knew nothing of Bushido. As he was already dead to the nation, life would discredit him. They had called to him for a long time, slowly circling offshore. He heard the bark of the speaker on the wind when they moved farther down the beach; they sailed completely around the atoll, the fools. It made him doubly cautious for the rest of the day—they might have landed men out of his view.

But they hadn't. His inspection found the entire length of sand lying smooth and untouched from tree line to water's edge. His bowels were running again. He sprinted to squat in the lees of the surf to relieve himself. It was agonizing; nothing but fecal trickles lost in the wash of the warm ocean current as it lapped over his knees. The sea pushed him off balance and he struggled to remain in place. A flutter against the moon drew his eyes and he saw a thin line of geese bannering across it. Was it so late in the year? The calendar of his days wasn't kept anymore to make waiting for the ship less difficult. Two brief sorties into the air after the engine was repaired had been unsuccessful and he fled back to the atoll to conserve fuel. There were spare drums of gasoline buried, enough to guarantee a few more searches. Fighters hadn't pursued him, though his flights must have been reported. Perhaps that was what brought the torpedo boat. They were testing to see if this was his base. It worried him to think they knew he was there, after all. If he were strafed, a lucky hit could explode the Zero's bomb; 250 kilograms makes a big hole, and it was destined for the minotaur, not this island. Ah, the sea...rocking him, bathing him...if it would only wash his sickness from him. It was water that caused it. Rain gathered in the discarded gasoline drum had swirled with rainbows. He had known it was tainted, had filtered it through rags before drinking, but the brackish liquid made him nauseous within an hour of his thirsty taste. He should have restricted himself to the small green coconuts in the trees, but they loosened him, too.

Ishimoto bobbed in the water, steadying himself to break the swell of the surf breaking over him. **Come out and be taken home to your loved ones!** He attended his own funeral in Japan. He could not return. Would anyone?

Covering the ramp and strung along the wharfside, the villagers waited for a soldier's return, straining to see the barge that was bringing him from the mainland. Jordan and Yukiko stood on a street above the crowd, looking down easily over the row of fishing boats and assembly of people.

The barge was one Americans used for ordinary tasks along the Inland Sea. It chugged out of the mist, bucking

47

a choppy current and drove into the quiet inlet to ram itself gently onto the ramp. The soldier clambered over its side to drop into the shallow water. He was an emaciated, haggard man worn rancid and pale from the rigor of living in caves. In one hand he clutched a bundle containing the scraps of his possessions carried not for value but for sentiment. Without waiting, the barge backed away to transport its threadbare cargo to other ports of call. The villagers were mute, staring at this prodigal upon their shore. Ankle deep in water, hugging his bundle with both hands, he looked back at them. His mother and father, tearless, stood directly before him amid the spread netting of their own fishing craft. No one spoke. What is this man who did not die for the chrysanthemum? It was a question of welcome, foreseen and decided and become a question once more. He bowed gravely, shorn head ducking to his knees. The *hitotachi,* every one, returned the bow with equal formality. Splashing slowly out of the water, he trudged up the ramp toward the village and the people followed after, his parents leading the throng. As the procession passed, his eyes flicked at Jordan and Yukiko. He knew the girl; she had grown fair and become a woman. And the foreigner saw him. Not with the blind seeing of other Americans. He saw him as one man sees another. The soldier continued, entered the village, and the silent people filed with him up the mountainside to the Shinto shrine beside the cemetery. Sailors having to do with the brothel watched curiously, while discomfited monks who shared their monastery with the whores went out to meet the returnee. Japanese soldiers were to arrive home like this for decades...there were many who would choose not to.

There was too much melancholy in the incident for such a promising day. The weather was brightening rapidly and was uncommonly warm. Jordan had donned dress blues to his regret. Since they planned to spend their time at sea and fish for their lunch, they rented a cockleshell with an ancient engine from a fisherman. He lent them sturdy twine and several hooks and clams they could use for bait. Helpfully, he offered the use of his heavy net but they declined, thanking him solemnly, and set out into the lagoon without further delay. They were going to chug around the nearby islands until they found an appealing one, and there they would stop to cook their meal.

The sea rippled sunlit sparks from shore to shore. Of many foam-edged islets floating in the vicinity, few had acceptable landings. Too many stood sharply stark before the hazy mainland, toothing the sky with broken crags. There were other boats in the channel, some anchored near buoys where strings of cultivated seaweed were fetched up upon long-pronged poles. Jordan couldn't resist steering the boat past the *Bulman* to show his ship to Yukiko... and at the same instant to exhibit her proudly for those on deck to notice. Unnerving ribald remarks flew across the water at them and he was glad distance made them too faint to understand. Phallic-fingered fists shot up to salute his luck; blushing, he distracted the girl's attention. She was awed by the giant minotaur on the stack; a painted tally of shot-down planes on the ship's bridge was meaningless to her. Answering envious jeers with farewell waves, they motored into the channel.

The island they chose was larger than most; a few houses hugged one side and activity was confined to them. Jordan and Yukiko deliberately went to the opposite side for privacy. At a dwarf beach, they dragged the boat onto the sand, leaving the stern waterbound, and tied the bowline securely to a pinnacle of rock to make all fast. Seated in the stern, they cast baited lines into the clear salt water and watched small sea bream flirt with their hooks. The fish were gold in color, with dark bands. Yukiko hauled one in after another, thrilled with the struggling catch and pleased to be so lucky while Jordan fished badly. He jerked his line so hard the bait fell off or was torn from the mouths of the fish. He didn't care. He was not fishing at all. It kept him from throwing himself at the girl—and he didn't know how she would respond.

They amused themselves until they had a sufficient catch for a meal, then cleaned the fish and skewered strips of flesh to slivers of bamboo. A driftwood fire cooked the meat into a succulent glory. Eating, they dabbled toes in the water from the rear of the boat. The fish left their mouths dry, which led them to discover they had forgotten to bring anything to drink. She suggested looking for a stream on the higher reaches of the island and, if unsuccessful, they could beg water from the community on the other side. Barefoot, they climbed from the boat and began to ascend the rocks toward the weathered trees of a forest.

49

It was a dappled world of sea smell, snug thickets and picturesque glens. There were places they could see the mainland across the water, and once they managed to catch a glimpse of the boat far below. Birds ceased pecking for seed and insects to perch saucily upon branches to scold the invasion of their sanctuary. Cedar, birch and beech trees intermingled with pines, flashing fall colors and adding a musky mulch of leaves to the floor of scented needles; stands of larch and cypress surrounded stately oaks leaning awry under the training of winds; wild flowers were bright exclamation points among moss and brush, quivering from the departure of unseen creatures as they escaped the intruders...and it was all embroidered upon the rich azured air overhead...

They came to a shallow basin, a catch for waters from above. Combed by polished stones, a rill fed it, and the sun filtered to a stoop of grass enclosing the pond. Everywhere, only the tapestry of the forest was to be seen. Yukiko kneeled at the pond to cup her hands for a drink of the sweet water. The sun's rays had not taken the cold from it. She smiled at Jordan; he was tall as a god to her, his white hat tipped over his brow at a jaunty angle. The climb had beaded his skin with perspiration...his tan was darkened to burnished copper...whisps of corn-silk hair glinted with light...and there were his dark blue eyes...

"*Suwaru*," she said, patting the turf at her side. He knelt beside her and drank as she had done, dipping a cupped hand into the pool. Though they weren't touching, she felt embraced and wanted to hold him closer. As if he heard her thought, he darted a glance at her, face furrowed with doubt. In English, she declared, "good" as she leaned forward to gather water into her palm and let it fall through her fingers. He grinned at her. She tugged at her neckline, saying, "*Atsui-ne?*"

"Yeah...it is hot. I should have dressed for summer after all."

Was he then as warm as she? She lowered her feet into the pond; tiny fish surrounded her toes to inspect them. An outraged frog flipped to the reeds to chirp steadily. The sun moved straight overhead...she felt the heat of it, and shifted uncomfortably. Joe-dan-ash was sweating. She was sweating...in a private place...

"Hey, you know what? I'm going to take this jumper

off. You mind?" He pantomimed his intention and she nodded, thinking it sensible. Writhing out of the heavy, constricting cloth, he folded it carefully inside out to retain its press. His neckerchief fell across it like a pirate flag cut from the mast, showing sharp creases and the wrinkle from its knot. Then he removed his damp white T-shirt. She admired him sidelong...sweating...

And the sun bore down.

"You know, if we wanted to, we could take a dip. Nobody would see us, and we'd get cooled off..."

She hesitated. It wasn't the same as sharing a bath somehow, and yet that was precisely all it was. Rising, she slipped from her outer clothing—a plain black skirt and white blouse from her schooldays. She wore no brassiere, only brief cotton underpants which were drawn tight by a string. Almost a child, her fullness had not yet ripened into womanhood; her breasts were firm, smaller than the hollows of his hands. He tore his stare from her and turned his back. Taking off his trousers, he took pains to fold them properly; it gave him additional seconds to control himself. Then he sat quietly in his skivvy shorts. Neither dared to look at the other. Did custom differ? They had only imagination and hearsay for guide. Eyes shining with a delirious anticipation, they agonized about how permission was to be asked...and how granted. They studied the water, alive with the baring of nerves.

She murmured gently, "*Itizyu no kage, itiga no nagare....*"

Turning to her questioningly, he could see her nipples—pointed, wine red on the small bosom.

"The shade of a tree, the water of a river," she explained. "It is said when two strangers meet by chance."

"What does it mean?"

"Because it was fated to be, the strangers share the water of the stream...and they lie in the shade of the tree to rest."

Afraid to touch her, he leaned forward as if to kiss her mouth. Trembling with insecurity, he stammered, "I...I was named for a river."

"*Hai?*" Her breath beat against his, drawing him in.

"From the Bible. Where John baptized Jesus..." She was a well and he was in danger of falling. The blood flamed in his cheeks. Christ. He'd never done it before. IT.

51

He struggled to catch the Sunday subject so it could save them. "The River Jordan...where he was baptized."

"What is baptized?"

The spell was broken. She was listening now. He expelled his breath with a short laugh. "Oh...one person sprinkles water over another."

Giggling merrily, she moved from him. "Come," she chirped, indicating the pond. "We baptize. Let us enter this cold *furo*..."

And they stood and became naked, each shedding garments carelessly to conceal the anxiety of desire, she releasing the drawstring at her waist swiftly while he removed his shorts with a clumsy caution, mortified that his penis was indecently erect. They scrambled into the water. Because the level was not above their knees, they splashed at themselves and sat gingerly to get wet. The frigidity of it calmed them but they warmed their blood by raising a grand turmoil, churning the water between them with hands and feet. They touched. Accidentally. Both then touched with calculated deliberation. To quell his excitement he tried to swim, learned he couldn't, and settled to the dangerous seat opposite her. As she surmised, it was only a bath. They could play like children without guilt in the center of this island forest. It was as near as she came to thinking of her parents or their strictures...

And when they left the pristine bath, young bodies sequined and without shame, they lay down together upon the lush grass to let the sun dry them. Bearing the dazed face of love, she went into his arms pliantly, granting all without being asked. In the reeds, the frog sang. Its complacent croak was muffled by the whirring wings of a spying bird's flight...and both were witness to the wisteria and the pine entwined in the dance of creation as it was ordained from the beginning...

"What the hell are you so glum about?"

Dave clumped behind Jordan on the chow line at the port side of the ship. Dave's leg was still encased in the plaster cast, which had acquired a gray patina of dirt. In the cold dawn, everyone bunched up eagerly to get below.

"Our watch has the duty."

"No shit. Happens every other day."

They shuffled another foot closer to the ladder leading down to the mess compartment. Sailors crowded to continue the line behind them. "I want to be ashore every day."

"I'd like to get ashore any day."

"When does the cast come off?"

"Another week, they said. The last couple of months has been a pain in the butt."

"I'm glad I didn't break my leg."

"No shit." They moved another few feet. An undefinable odor of food wafted from the hatch. A couple of men scuffled at the ladder, ending an argument with harmless threats. Life in the Navy was abrasive these days; men counted what time was left to serve out regular hitches; draftees speculated upon how long they had to wait to be discharged; length in service was calculated like ration points. Most wanted to go home. "You never say anything about what you've been doing with Yukiko anymore."

"Oh, mostly we've been teaching each other our own languages."

"You learning?"

"Some."

"I bet she has." He fended off the expected punch, then sang teasingly, "Poor Jordie... still doesn't know how to get any. Or maybe you have been and don't want me to know."

"Is that all you can think about, Dave?"

"I'm tired of Old Lady Fivefingers and that's all I can think about."

53

"Good thing you were laid up or the path to the whore-house would have a groove ten feet deep."

"First thing I do when this fucking cast is off is run like a skunk to the shrine."

"Serve you right if you wind up with a monk."

They descended the ladder to the mess compartment, opening their heavy jackets. Taking aluminum trays from a pile, cutlery and plates, they passed along the serving counter. Large portions of creamed chipped beef were ladled into their plates over pieces of toast, the derisively named shit-on-a-shingle which was routinely offered in spite of unpopularity. They accepted mugs of freshly boiled coffee; good GI coffee brewed in kettledrum vats and tasting of scrubbed steel and chicory and strong dark beans, the common comforting communion of every meal and every watch and an excuse for respite in any situation...the American version of British tea. It was also suspected of containing saltpeter. Dave and Jordan sat on a temporary bench at a temporary table, those scourges of mess attendants on every ship which were assembled and taken down three times daily. The friends ate without zest in the din and cigarette smoke of the confined area; working days began with numb tolerance.

What had he been doing with Yukiko? Jordan was disturbed about his relationship with her. It was locked into dreamtime, so separated from reality he had not considered her role in his future. From that merging in the forest, they were infatuated with each other, taking every opportunity when he was ashore to escape others and to make love. Even as the season changed to winter, they accomplished it many times, behaving guiltily in the presence of her family...their trying for innocence gave them away. Her father was remote with him now; the grandmother more antagonistic. They knew, he thought. Or did not but had lost their trust of him. Oto-san attempted to ask about his commitment to anyone at home, but gave up when they got mired in misunderstandings. But he knew what the man was getting at. He was saying the fuck's off; that's what fathers do, isn't it? Unless there's to be a marriage. Hell, there was no chance of that...marriage between Americans and Japanese was strictly prohibited by Occupation decree. He didn't know what she thought along those lines. When they talked, it was of anything else. Jesus, Christmas Day she had to know all about Santa Claus and why she found chocolates in her sock. Those were the kinds of things that concerned her. And when they were intimate, she didn't speak but for whispered endearments. They lived for the moment with no future to trouble them. Yukiko. His depression dove. He'd leave her eventually. But she knew that. Just didn't talk about it. She had to know everybody would go home someday.

Home to your loved ones! The enemy hadn't returned since that exceptional visit. When was it? Ishimoto knew many weeks had slipped by: Geese no longer flew southward high above the atoll; another typhoon caromed from it to follow the route of the birds beyond the Tropic of Cancer to blow itself out in equatorial climes. During calmer days and nights, he saw ships on the horizon and didn't hurry to clear the runway. Hai, he could run again; his dysentery was gone. He was near death for a while, but Bushido pulled him through. A useless death is not for one prepared to die. He waited for the minotaur...did he, indeed?

It was winter at home; hard to believe it here. Hai, the corpse was privileged to distinguish changes of temperature. He had taken to sleeping in his flight jacket now that the nights were cooler. It wasn't as clean as it should be. Nothing was. His own fault. The letter he once kept safely stored on a ledge in the bunker was destroyed and buried deeply under the sand of the floor. Weeping one night, he had torn it to shreds; it was composed of so many lies he could not bear to dishonor his family with it. The mortifying fact was that he feared a final sortie and viewed the fatal plunge with terror. Why is it when a man chooses his own death it must be painful to him? Seppuku needs the assistance of a beheading to bring the ceremony of self-inflicted disembowelment to conclusion...but he would have gone through with it anyway upon realizing he was making excuses for himself had not the Way of the Warrior cautioned him it would be wasteful. There was no place to run from himself, nowhere to hide. He was fixed in a dilemma which was none since he was nothing but the name his family remembered and there was no choice open to him. They were thinking of him today, his natal day, and he wished he were back in the womb, wished he could substitute his nonbeing for that of a babe quickening now into a destiny unlike his own.

The wish was a futile one. Its destiny was much the same.

In her room, Yukiko lay curled within her cozy *futon*. She had slept late and wondered why no one awakened her. She would have risen at once upon opening her eyes but recalled that Joe-dan-ash did not have liberty, and she remained abed to think about him and relive the feeling of his hands upon her body...and his weight...she touched herself in imitation of his caresses. Her thighs closed over her fingers, squeezed to contain the ecstasy. Ah, if she could hold him there forever! There must be a way; it was inconceivable such happiness should end. Her ingrained reticence had prevented her from discussing it with him, though she knew he must feel as she did...and her hands moved to her waist, stroked back and forth from belly to mound of desire. She was filled with content. Sleepily, she rubbed the silken flesh as he would have done and noticed a minutely perceptible thickening. She was getting plumper...it must be due to her happiness...

And she sat bolt upright, her hands arrested upon the telltale sign. An ungovernable panic and chilling shame slew her initial joy.

But about another thing, she was wrong. None of the crews had liberty that fateful morning. She soon knew why she wasn't called from her bed. The villagers had left their homes to watch the squadron lift anchors and sail majestically into the icy fogs of the channel. Her parents wouldn't awaken her; they were glad to see the ships go. And Ooba-san occupied the corner of her firebox smugly. Her prediction was fulfilled and it wasn't needful to crow *aki no ogi* with unseemly haste. When the girl entered from her room, wan and disconcerted as though having heard the news, Ooba-san puffed a cigarette and told what a neighbor had said not an hour ago, eyes alight with prim satisfaction. Yukiko's alliance with the American was an irritant to everyone; hadn't Mr. Nakatsuru withdrawn his suit because of it?

"The *hakujin* are gone."

"Gone?"

"Not long after daybreak. You've only just missed seeing them leave."

Yukiko rushed to the window to look at the harbor. Empty. Not a warship anywhere.

"Natsu's mother told us. Your parents went with her to watch the sight. What, tears? Why are you crying?"

She didn't answer. He couldn't leave her now.

"They are going to Okinawa."

"They'll come back!"

"Not here. They are to escort steamers carrying our soldiers to Yokohama."

"To Yokohama..."

"It is where most of our men are repatriated."

"The ships will come back..."

"Look at me, child. *Ite?* Then let your stubborn shoulders heed. It was decided not to permit you to see the foreigner again."

"I will see him."

Ooba-san dropped her cigarette in astonishment. "Defiance? Be sure not to have it when your father returns."

"This is their base, Ooba-san! Joe-dan-ash must come back to us from Yokohama." In a panic, Yukiko ran to her tiny cubicle and slid the door shut. Ooba-san heard her stifling her misery in the bedding. She reached to retrieve her cigarette and smoked thoughtfully. It seemed that the fan in autumn, having mixed with vermilion, was stained with red.

Okinawa was more than three hundred miles to the south, basking in the Kuroshio Current. The destroyers sailed at high speed and sent crews to General Quarters to keep them alert. There was grumbling about the drill; the war was over, wasn't it? The weather improved and the ocean flattened to a calm lake which flying fish skimmed to cross the bows of the racing ships. Achieving flank speeds, rooster tails of water flared in white-lathered emerald curves twelve to fifteen feet high above burrowing sterns; the destroyers took on the stirring magic of living beings, true sirens of the sea ensnaring the sailors forever.

In the beginning, the sailor thinks it is the port to which he looks forward, but that is not true. A landsman makes journeys with final destinations in mind; the seaman, never. He is in constant motion, an elemental. And when the ships are done with him, and if the sea does not choose to keep his body, porpoises are assigned to guide it to shore, aided by the ever-giving tides... or fathom-gowned crustaceans will render him to pearls. The voyage from anywhere to everywhere is far too short...

As short as life, which Ishimoto thought too long. Denied death by his lack of courage, he entombed himself in the bunker in a fit of rage. It was at most a passive suicide attempt. Lacking conviction, he fought the smothering earth, kicked his way to air, and survived. Feeling contempt for his foolishness, he was grubbing in the ruins for the flight bag when a ship crawled over the horizon. Radar antenna, foremast, gun-control director, bridge, forward five-inch mount, then the slicing bow... and another speck grew behind it. And another. And another. And as the last appeared, they maneuvered toward the atoll unnoticed until the cadence of their turbines and pumps telegraphed to shore. He threw up his head, shaggy now, with hair falling to his shoulders. Something. Something disturbing the atmosphere. Springing from his knees, he stumbled to the edge of the trees. He thought they were an invasion force, then saw them swerve. They were identifiable as destroyers without assault craft following. They changed course again and charged the atoll, then heeled smartly in review, sending swells to fatten rollers moving toward the beach. The surf rumbled louder. Ishimoto saw the minotaur on a stack. He dropped to the sand, shocked. Well, then. The target was here. The ships were undoubtedly heading for the bay in Okinawa. His head buzzed and did not cease, though they were gone into the maze of Nansei Shoto and the waves subsided on shore.

The squadron roared into Buckner Bay like mustangs, whooping blasts from each ship to announce themselves. A crusty admiral admired the arrival from the bridge of his carrier flagship and though amused by the performance, he gave them hell for it. Goddamned tin cans always did look disrespectful and rowdy at sea; no cause to let them practice the image.

Several days passed; they took on stores and refueled. Bum boats pestered the ships and made off with garbage, even seining the waterlines to collect effluence from each ship's heads for use as rich fertilizer for fields ashore. Each nightfall, the crews of the destroyers gathered for movies projected upon jury-rigged screens, films they traded back and forth to view again. On the *Bulman,* the prized show was *Shadow of a Doubt* and not swapped with any ship Teresa Wright played the heroine so sweetly, the sailors had fallen in love with her to a man, cheering for Charlie, namesake niece of a murderer, when Joseph Cotten was foiled at the end. Watching for perhaps the tenth time, Jordan didn't see Charlie as his ideal girl anymore; he saw Yukiko instead.

To supply recreation while waiting for the convoy to be formed, beer parties were organized. Off-duty watch sections carried cases of three-point to a secluded beach, away from the critical eyes of Okinawans, and the men were given free reign. It was countless cans of beer, swimming, ball games, and countless cans of beer. They stripped down to the buff and cavorted in the sand; it was too much trouble to peel clothing for a swim, dress again for a short turn at bat, and then swim again. Those less energetic guarded the beer dump and did not swim at all. Dave was among them. Though rid of his plaster cast, he was taking

59

it easy. Shaded by a cluster of palm trees, he played mother hen to Jordan, cautioning him about toying with rusting dud grenades kicked up from the sand.

"Get rid of the fucking things."

Laughing, Jordan tossed one from hand to hand playfully. "Catch," he taunted.

Dave scrambled to his feet, limping awkwardly. "You crazy?" he demanded, terror-struck. "Throw it away! What if it goes off?"

"Catch."

He ducked as Jordan faked a toss. Jordan howled with glee and spun to hurl the grenade into the calm bay, where it sank swiftly before its sensitivity raised a thunderclap and blew spray over him. Men paused everywhere to look, then resumed their play.

"Idiot!" Dave shouted furiously. "You fucking idiot!"

"I wasn't really going to throw it at you, Dave."

"You could have killed yourself with the fucking thing!"

Jordan chortled, mimicked him by hopping on one leg and said, "No chance. War's over, we're going to live forever!" He helped himself to a can of beer from a carton under the trees and threw another can to Dave. They knifed holes into the cans and put their mouths quickly over warm foam as it jetted out under pressure. Taking his denims from a pile of clothing nearby, Jordan dressed, allowing the cloth to absorb drops of seawater remaining on him from the explosion of the grenade.

The reconciled friends drank, studying the baseball game's thirty-first inning. It was a ludicrous sight, every man adangle and marked with the uniform of the day, suntanned arms and faces sharply delineated from white bodies and legs pinking under the blazing sun.

"I wish we'd leave soon," Jordan said.

"We gotta collect all the suckers we're taking north first." Dave smiled. "You're more anxious to get back to Japan than they are."

"For now. But I wish I was going home, too."

Cocking his head skeptically, Dave asked, "What about your welfare family?"

"Oh . . ." Jordan turned the beer can reflectively in his hands. "They'll make out. They know we have to take off someday." The image of Yukiko's body stirred him. He sat beside Dave, drawing up his knees to hide his discomfort.

"I wouldn't mind trying to smuggle Yukiko to the States in my seabag as a souvenir." He lay down and rolled to his stomach and began a Crosby song. Dave joined at the chorus, which brought another sailor, the rebel and his guitar, and soon there was a yearning of them gathered under the palm trees; and the singing and the beer and the comradeship knit all of their homesickness together.

Perched on the aft torpedo tubes with a comic book on his lap, Jordan glanced often at the ragtag vessels which had been converted into transports. Each ungainly ship had a sullen complement of dun-colored, gaunt Japanese soldiers bunched into close herds like dumb beasts led to a charnel house rather than from it. Many of them had been pried laboriously from sandbagged dens and makeshift ramparts in the thousand strategies it took to convince them the war was truly over.

Almost reluctantly, the convoy was sailing north to Yokohama. To atone for earlier behavior, the destroyers held point perfectly around the fat ships under their charge. The day was cloudless. Sailors stole hours from duty to smarten up their clothes; that same sea into which the defeated spat disconsolately churned clothing lashed to lines dragged behind the ships by lazy mariners disinclined to scrub.

A solitary divertissement slowed the convoy when a mine was sighted. Round and ominously spiked, drifting with lonely menace. Sunlight picked delicately at algae scabbing the ball. On the nearest destroyer's main deck, a sharpshooter trained his rifle at the object. He fired and the mine bobbed playfully. On the ship's bridge, officers and men regarded the mine with disgust. It revolved merrily, an entertainment for the squadron. A pattern of purpling barnacles displayed white tips on the rusting metallic hide to tease the sharpshooter some more. He braced himself against the roll of the ship and took aim again. The mine floated gracefully a moment before vanishing

61

within a tremendous upsurge of water and splintered sunbeams and crimson flame. A cheer rose from the ships and normal sailing speed was resumed.

Otherwise, it promised to be a dull journey for all hands. None of the islands being passed were admired; they were reminders of sleepless nights and fatigued days on picket station when the Divine Wind sank and damaged a deplorable number of ships. Scraps of atolls were dismissed as flotsam ejected from lost worlds; it was easy for Jordan to imagine a pterodactyl rising from one to threaten him. His head was bent over the adventure strip again when the attack came.

No one saw the Zero. No one reported a bogey in the sky. Lieutenant Akiro Ishimoto flew low over the water, scraping waves with the tips of his wheels. It was the classic low-level approach, and he was in sure control. Upon sighting the convoy, he released the bomb safety as he learned to do long ago in practice periods at Oroku Field. Everything this morning was done according to the book. His freshly laundered uniform was donned after he bathed in the surf; the damaged boot was repaired with a stitch of wire, and both boots were polished and rubbed with a rag till they gleamed. He wound the *hachimaki* around his head, centering the red circle carefully, then folded the long white scarf about his neck under his jacket. He meditated over his flag for a short span of time; the drop of saki saved for this final sortie was tasteless in his mouth. He drank it ceremoniously, standing before the Zero at the head of the cleared runway and sensing his departed comrades at his side. Climbing into the cockpit, he relished the cleanliness of it. It was scrubbed as spotless as a coffin at home would have been. Rapidly closing on the convoy, he adjusted course to head for the *Bulman,* not surprised to find the destroyer there. Had it not been, he would have streaked past the ships to search in Okinawa's bay for his target. The minotaur mesmerized him and he miscalculated the precise instant to climb sharply for his attack.

"Bakayaro!" The worst expletive cursing himself and the minotaur.

Unnerved, urinating uncontrollably as he gunned the engine, he savaged the controls to skim above the upper deck. Accidentally, he jettisoned the bomb and soared wildly into the sky. The bomb dropped like a discarded feather. To Jordan's upturned, startled face, it was forever in falling; he threw the comic book at it, as if to deflect its direction.

Broooomphhh!!

General Quarters! General Quarters! Klaxon clanging frantically as men raced to battle stations.

Load! Load! Load!

The Zero straining into the vanishing blue, screwing into a turn at the top of its arc.

Commence firing! Pom-pom-pom-pom-pom-pom-pom-pom-pom-pompompom . . .

Ishimoto diving. Aiming. Aiming.

Pom-pom-pom-pom-pom-pom-pom!

Tenno heika banzai!

Pom-pom-pom!

Diving.

Pom-pom-pom-pom-pom-pom-pom-pom-pom-pom-pom-pom-pom-pom-pom-pom. The Zero was hit at the median of its dive, Ishimoto screaming with remorse and disappointment until he crashed to his death. *Tenno heika banzai!*

The bomb damaged part of the main deck; the ship's store was a tangle of shredded steel and merchandise. The head and its sinks and showers were riddled. Above them, on the torpedo deck, the tubes had received a minimum of shrapnel, sacrificing just one fish to the blast. Compressed air whistled from the ruptured tank, condensing into a thin, dissipating vapor. The minotaur was unblemished, slanted against the sky as the ship curled upon its wake to run over the wreckage of the plane. Injured by several hot fragments, Jordan had been blown off the tubes by the concussion of the explosion. He struck his head during the fall and was mercifully sinking into unconsciousness and his world dissolved into the vague interior of the sick bay; white on white on pain.

Yukiko wore an old heavy coat belonging to her father, buttoned and pinned against the wind. She walked quickly along the narrow street, shivering with cold. To gain a moment's respite from the raw weather, she stepped into a shop doorway bristling with straw brooms and gourds and baskets. Inside, her friend and former schoolmate sat beside bins of vegetables, plucking feathers from a newly killed hen. Natsu beamed with pleasure to see Yukiko there.

"I was going to call upon you when I finished this, Yukko!"

Yukiko forced a smile and entered the store. "Oh? You look happy, Natsu."

"I've been told I will marry!" she squeaked delightedly.

"How wonderful."

Natsu peeked toward the shoddy interior. Her widowed mother was busy in the living quarter and taking no notice of them. Natsu turned back with a glowing face, so excited her plump body quivered. "I beg it can be done soon."

"Have you met your future husband?"

Lifting a palm to prevent mirth from breaking into more than a rapturous smile, Natsu nodded. Eyes dancing, she said, "We saw each other briefly at the *omiai* yesterday evening."

"Who is he?" asked Yukiko.

Her friend recalled the formal engagement meeting and her voice faltered. "Masao Masuda. He's shown an interest in me." Her eyes were anxious as she said defensively, "We need a man in our family. I think I shall like him."

Masuda was the solitary soldier brought back from the war. His acceptance by the community was guarded; the marriage was not an advantageous one. Yukiko pitied her. "May you learn to love him."

"Perhaps you will also find a husband among the returning troops." Yukiko looked at her blankly and the girl added apologetically, "Everyone knows Mr. Nakatsuru

64

won't marry you...and a ship arrived in the harbor just now...the America-jin have brought more of our countrymen home." Before she could say another syllable, Yukiko had spun away and out of the shop to dash down the street.

She plunged headlong through alleys and lanes. Laughter began bubbling out to interfere with her breathing. *Joe-dan-ash! Joe-dan-ash!* Not till she reached the upper edge of the ramp did she slow to gaze at the harbor. A steamer was anchored among the destroyers. She saw the minotaur among their stacks, underlined with a splash of new paint on the hull beneath it. And more, she saw whaleboats filling with sailors at the sides of every ship in the squadron. Above them, gulls spiraled from mastheads to sea in a frenzied search for food. The sailors hurried down laddered gangways to press into the tight confines of their liberty boats; coxswains pushed off to head for shore; the gulls shrilled and beat into the sky with knife-edged wings. The distant buzz of engines gained power as they approached until they rivaled the hammering of her heart. She hugged herself to contain it. Surely it would leap from her breast! Children ran past in a gay swirl. Caught up in their charge, Yukiko went with them and did not stop till she reached the end of the wharf.

One by one, the boats arrived. They emptied and sailors waded among the welcoming committee. The boat she looked for threw lines and was snugged to the wharf. Men poured out in a confusing jumble. Dave had limped past Yukiko but she ran after him to ask about Jordan.

"Oh....Yukiko. I didn't see you." She had a premonition then and stared at him. "Well...let's not just stand here. I think we ought to go someplace you can sit down. Okay?"

"Hai." Her voice was small. It was a forbidding beginning.

"Where do you want to go?" He wondered if he was being too gentle; she was reacting in a distressing way and he hadn't lowered the boom yet.

She pondered. It would not be possible to speak to him in her house. The length of the stone wharf was deserted but for them; the last of the whaleboats was retracing its journey to the ships, and the liberty parties had gone into the village. "Stay here, *hai?* We stay." They sat at the end of the wharf, dangling their legs above the restless water of the lagoon. The whaleboat shrank in the distance, got lost among the warships. It was bitter cold. Moisture-laden clouds were sickening the weather. Attempting to be light, she exclaimed, "I'm so happy! You've come back!"

"We sure as hell have."

"I looked for your ship every day."

He stuffed his hands into the pockets of the pea jacket and tucked his chin in against the chill. His leg was aching. "Well...Jordie said you could talk real good in English now." She was waiting to hear something else. "Well...we had to stay in Yokohama for a while."

"Hai...so long. But you've come back!"

"Yeah...this is our permanent base."

"Hai," she said with relief, then added brightly, "You saw Fuji!"

"Yeah. Real nice...just like the postcards." Water slap-slapped below them, sending up an odor of kelp and traces of frost. She was shivering. He wanted to put an arm around her but thought better of it.

She leaned forward, straining to see the *Bulman.* "Joe-dan-ash. Where is he?"

Hating to tell her and forcing casualness, he said, "Oh...he's not with me, Yukiko."

"Hai." She looked at him with dismay. "He said you would come ashore together next time...as before."

"That was because my cast was going to be taken off. But we left too soon."

"Hai...too soon."

"We always got liberty together because we had the same duty watch."

"No more?"

"No." Damn, Jordie had done a fine job of teaching her. Yukiko was trying to read his eyes.

"You don't work with Joe-dan-ash as before?" she asked.

"No."

She appeared to relax as she glanced to the harbor. He gritted his teeth and went on doggedly.

"We had a bad break coming back from Okinawa. We got hit by one of your kamikaze jerks who wanted to keep the war going." When she blanched, he quickly added, "No, no, Yukiko...nothing like that! We took a bomb on the main deck and had to lay in for repairs at the Navy Yard in Yokohama. That's what kept us so long."

66

It was as though the sun came out. Smiling at him, she asked, "Ah, then Joe-dan-ash will be ashore later? He has the duty today?"

Dave shook his head. "No, he hasn't got the duty." There was nothing left but to be blunt. "He's gone home. Back to the States. When the plane bombed us, Jordie got mangled some, too, and they've patched him up and taken him home."

She was aghast. "Joe-dan-ash was hurt? Badly?"

"Don't get me wrong. He was wounded but he's okay. Not much more than a couple of gashes. He'll be good as new."

"But they sent him home."

"Well, in a way. You see, the hospital ship was due back in Honolulu and Jordie wasn't in any shape to be returned to duty. So they took him along. You see?"

Her expression froze into one of appeal and he got desperate.

"Yukiko, there was no way he could have come back to our ship...no possible way."

"Hai. I understand. It was orders. He had to obey."

"Yeah, that's right. I packed his gear and took it to him. They'll take better care of his wounds on that hospital ship." He wanted to leave her; the damp stone was making his rump itch. "You want him to be okay, don't you? They'll make him all right again."

"Will Joe-dan-ash return to your ship?"

"It's not likely, Yukiko. They usually give you another berth in a case like his."

"What does that mean?"

"Jordie will finish his hitch on another ship."

"Hitch..."

"Jordie has less than a year to go before he gets his discharge from the Navy."

Frightened, she grasped at straws. "Will his next ship bring Joe-dan-ash to Japan?"

"I don't know. Maybe. I'd hate to give you a bum steer. Jordie asked me to tell you good-bye for him."

She was crying soundlessly. "Does Joe-dan-ash have someone in America?"

"Oh, sure. Didn't he tell you? He must have. Regular Oka-san and Oto-san like you've got. They'll be happy as hell to see him."

She shook her head. It wasn't what she meant. "I wanted to tell him something...something to tell..."

"You want to tell me? I'll drop him a line. Or you can write to him. That's a good idea, Yukiko, I'll give you his address."

Continuing to shake her head negatively, she said fiercely, *"Iie*...I wanted to tell..."

He didn't understand. There was no handkerchief in his pockets to stem tears running down her cheeks. She looked ugly, her mouth parting in that smile of grief which later is a quivering frown. And still she made no sound.

"Well..." He struggled to his feet, cursing softly at the tenderness of his leg. He wanted to help her up but dropped his hand when she refused it. "Well, I don't know...I guess that's all I have to say. Maybe he'll write to you...." She sat so forlornly he had to get away immediately. "Well...I got a date...I told Jordie I'd see you first crack and then...yeah. Well, see you around." It was cruel to leave her but he could talk to her again sometime. The ships were scheduled for a long stay.

As he limped to the village, she kept her gaze upon him. The sob welling from her throat snagged at tightly held lips; then, covering her face with her arms, she bent over her knees. She cried a long time. When Dave returned hours later to catch the whaleboat back to the ship, he was sure he sensed her presence on the windswept stones. As if she left her moans there.

The *Mercy* was positioned beyond the hurrah of drydocks and piers which served warships in the West Loch. The berth was considered to be secluded, but nothing was in that port. The reverberations of December 7 had not ceased; no one would drowse in Pearl Harbor again. Jordan felt sore along one side; the last of his bandages were removed that morning. His scars were livid welts running below a shoulder blade. How the hell did he get hit there? His seabag was packed. They were transferring him today.

If he didn't ache, he would have danced a jig. It would be fun to grab some shore time and spoil himself with a special meal in Honolulu. Steak and eggs and pancakes, smothered with thick sweet syrup and washed down with a strawberry shake. It wasn't a peculiar menu, just what sailors couldn't wait to devour when they unlimbered after long months at sea.

A hospital corpsman looked in at the entrance to the compartment, caroling, "Asche, Jordan, torpedoman second class, get your ash down to Personnel to pick up your orders!" Jordan was tired of the pansy's lousy pun and glad to be getting away from him. His gentle disposition made a good nurse of him, but the questioning, limpid eyes did not. Jordan refused to be friendly; guilt by association was common aboard ships, more so on this one, where favors could be traded for additional drugs to kill pain. The corpsman smiled at Jordan, a nice face with wounds embedded in wide brown irises, and he asked, "Want me to carry your seabag to the quarterdeck for you?"

"No thanks, I can do it."

"We hate to lose you, Asche."

"Yeah? I thought you were in business to get me back to my ship."

Limpid agreed with a small moue. He knew why this sailor was touchy with him. Most were. But he wasn't what they thought. He wanted desperately for everyone to know he wasn't and yearned to discuss it with each recoiling person... only to be rebuffed further. Patients could cry out and tell about their hurts in agonizing detail; his seemed superficial by comparison and he tended them and kept prospecting for the one manly listener who'd be sympathetic. There's somebody for everybody. He hadn't found his body yet. "You were a good patient," he said. "That's all I meant."

Jordan swung the seabag to his shoulder. There was a twinge of pain, not enough to bother. He left the compartment without another word.

Orders had been cut for him to be transferred to the base at Pearl. When he protested, it was pointed out he had few months left of his hitch; they weren't sending him to his ship in Japan only to bring him back immediately. He went through the boring process of reporting in and being assigned a temporary billet. A sailor between ships is a drifter upsetting the balance; he was given menial jobs. Jordan hated shore duty. It was boot camp without the rigorous training and double the horseshit inspections. An officer's white cotton glove was wiped behind unreachable pipes to find dirt, and a seabag's contents had to be displayed just so. The peacetime Navy was being resurrected. He felt sorry for Dave Bell, who had two more years to go.

Yukiko was fading fast from memory. Spring in Hawaii is redundant; there was an imitation of romance there which heightened the sexual inclination of servicemen. He saw her in the black-haired golden wahinis, but they were coarsened by having the Occidental attitude of their American mainland sisters. He couldn't get next to one, anyway, unless he paid a fee. And he did that, too. Went through the line at the Canary Cottages, suffered the indignity of being rushed, and loathed the pro station afterward. Fuck 'em. But the stay in Hawaii broke Yukiko's hold; she had lost him.

She lost respect in the village as well. Her secret was known; people looked to see change in her. How was it they knew? Her family would not have revealed so shameful a thing; they had forbidden her to stray away from the house. She was restricted to her own small room and to the plots of ground they farmed. Oto-san had beaten her when she confessed she was with child. Did the neighbors learn of it from her howls? Her mother was too timid to soothe her...it was Ooba-san, stealing into the dark like a wraith to feel her body, ascertain the hurt and smooth an unguent over the bruises. Her old palms had rasped on the tender skin. There was no sympathy from her; Ooba-san accepted life as it was.

"It's too late to abort the child, Yukiko."

"*Hai*, Ooba-san."

"Why didn't you tell us sooner?"

"I was frightened."

"You waited till long after he was gone. The foreigner was in no danger from us."

"I was frightened."

"The child could have been aborted."

A twitch; had it moved in response? Ooba-san asked her to turn to the other side.

"You were willful. You didn't listen to my warnings."

"I did nothing willfully."

"You weren't forced."

"Iie, I wasn't forced."

"If the man had been one of ours..."

"I would have been beaten."

"You would have been beaten."

"I love him, Ooba-san."

"You loved what was done. When a woman is not forced, the first is always the best and you'll get over it."

"I did not feel I was doing wrong, Ooba-san...not when it happened the first time. Only later. But I didn't want to stop."

"I know."

"Why couldn't I stop, Ooba-san?" She felt her grandmother stiffen.

"Ask of the honeybee..."

The rough but kindly treatment ended and she was left to herself. Obedience. There would be no questions to answer if she had observed the rules of her upbringing. Hereafter, she would do whatever she was told.

As Jordan did, without question, five thousand miles distant when he was transferred from Pearl Harbor to San Diego on the mainland of the United States.

LA JOLLA.
BARBECUE.
SEVENTH-DAY ADVENTIST FAMILY.
NONDRINKERS WELCOME.

The notice was tacked to one of the bulletin boards beside the Naval Station's phone booths where Jordan waited his turn to make a call. Everyone killed time by checking messages on the boards. BRING SWIM TRUNKS. Surrounding the item were ads offering secondhand tailor-made uniforms for sale or share rides to various cities. He read them out of boredom, having noticed them before.

71

When he got to the phone, he put through a long-distance call to New York, then grinned through the tearful broken English of mother and father as they said how they looked forward to seeing their baby soon. He hung up, somehow at a loss, and started to go back to the barracks. The words on the board got a second look. LA JOLLA. BARBEQUE. He'd never been to one. The religious and prohibition aspects weren't appealing but it would be something different to do. He had run out of entertainment in San Diego.

The base lacked discipline; its major function was processing men into civilian life. It was a strange transition for most. Leaving the military regime wasn't the problem. They had led carnival lives when loosed in a town; men generally got what they looked for. Sailors and Marines migrated from shooting gallery to movie house to saloon to burlesque show for lack of better to do. USO's were where the fairies met or mature ladies served doughnuts and slices of pie. Having been accustomed to such recreation from induction to separation, it was jarring to renew the inhibitions uniforms removed. Jordan had seen what the city had to offer and didn't care for it. Nothing was fun without a buddy. Except for the zoo. He'd enjoyed each visit, watching animals at first and then went to see the children. They were like those of the Inland Sea—lovable, adventuresome, eager to please. And they were not the same, since they weren't scheming businessmen conning passersby. Couples coping with their sprats made him envious. He wanted their security; it reflected the peace of his earliest years and the promise in those to come. More than anything, he wanted to begin his civilian life.

The notice listed a time for pickup at the Main Gate. There was one for Sunday, which was the next day. He debated the dullness implied and decided it couldn't be worse than wandering alone for hours. Importantly, it wouldn't cost a dime.

In the morning, always the same in Southern California, two doubters waited at the gate with him—a Marine and a Cook, Third Class, looking starved. They introduced themselves suspiciously. What the hell kind of guys go on this kind of outing? Then they were friendlier and joked about what was in store, but they were unanimous in wanting to do *something*. A large station wagon arrived promptly at 0900. Augustus Fleming, cherubically foolish

72

in a ten gallon hat, Bermuda shorts and a luau shirt, hailed them in an unmistakable Texas accent.

"You hands for the bar-bee-kew? My name's Gus. Hop in!"

They got into the vehicle, the sailors sitting behind him and the Marine. Gus drove into traffic at a fast clip, attention fastened upon the cars ahead.

"By jingo, we won't have to pester folks to send over any of their girls today!"

The servicemen were unresponsive. He gave them a resumé of his history while following the highway to La Jolla. He was the president of Fleming Builders, makers of Quonset huts and the like. He and his wife, Helen (that's-what-you-call-her-boys), liked to round up lonely sinners (we-all-are-you-all-know) to come over to the house on weekends (Saturdays-we-take-them-to-church-with-us-wasn't-a-soul-with-us-yesterday) and there were three daughters to be met. Now, they were going to like his fillies, but just to tell them apart, Wanda was the oldest, Grace the prettiest (but-they're-all-beautiful-belles-boys), and there was Shorty Dot, the tomboy of the family. They lived in Beach House, a right nice spread on the oceanfront and built by himself. With the good Lord's help, of course, and the foreman and carpenters of Fleming Builders. Jordan and his companions sank lower in their seats.

They sped past strands of beach littered with empty soda bottles and rusting beer cans and studded with oil rigs, past yellow and green houses on the bluffs. Pink haciendas with white stucco walls flashed by. La Jolla dozed under the ubiquitous palms of Southern California, which were growing too tall to remain real. On the outskirts of the pin-neat community, Gus slowed, turned off the main highway and onto a short private drive. Beach House was a showplace. A thick lawn of magenta-flowered ice plants blanketed the dunes; behind was the ocean, plain, unblemished by ships, islands or clouds.

"Hit the deck, boys!"

They got out of the wagon, stretched and were escorted around the double garage, four cars full, to the rear of the mansion. Helen Fleming was at the family room door. She was peroxide pretty, with pompadour hair fluffed high atop her small head. Her smile was genuine, though she scanned each guest with a jeweler's care. She had her own motives for these weekend soirees: She hoped to snare husbands for her girls. Her notice was specifically worded to attract wholesome boys; the-war-couldn't-have-started-at-a-better-time, nor-ended-either, because-the-whole-yew-nited-states-of-eligible-young-men-was-passing-through!

"Welcome! You-all-welcome! The girls are in their bathing suits and I expect you want to be the same."

They were shown to a laundry room where they could change. "She's not a bad looker, maybe the girls will be okay." Undressing, the boys looked leggy and scrawny, unlike fighting machines at all. They walked from the room self-consciously.

On the outdoor patio, the Fleming daughters were selecting records for an electric phonograph. Each wore a robe, and each had a towel twisted into a turban over her hair, which was removed when the guests appeared. Nobody was disappointed. The young ladies circled like wranglers and cut selections with precise charm. When the pairings were made, the Marine was with Dot. She towed him to the machine and began a dance marathon to the trumpet arpeggios of Harry James; in the wings were Benny Goodman, Glenn Miller, the Dorsey brothers, and the Andrews Sisters, who would beg them to hold tight.

Jordan liked Wanda. She was as fair-haired as he—a mixture of grownup child, sister and mother. "Thought Adventists didn't go in for dancing," he said.

"We go to movies, too."

"How do you square it with the pastor?"

"We don't tell him." She brought him to a table for lemonade. It was poured from a glass pitcher, crystalline with ice. They sipped and admired each other. "If you want to get a tan, you should take your undershirt off." He'd left it on, for some reason she didn't understand.

"I ... you wouldn't like that."

"Why?"

"Just ... you wouldn't."

"Are you shy?"

"No, I'm still healing ... my scars haven't cooled down."

She offered soothing apologies and said anxiously, "Let's sit down then ... if you're not well."

He dismissed her concern airily. "I'm fit as a fiddle, so don't worry. You can pour me more lemonade."

She did, and they went to a bench overlooking the sand. Her father was a few yards off, tending a bed of coals and scampering from smoke following him tenaciously wherever he took a stand. Grace and her sailor joined the dancing couple, and the music got louder. As Gus hacked in an enveloping cloud, he urged everyone to have a swell time. Wanda said, "Do you want to dance, Jordie?"

"I don't know how."

"You're kidding."

"No, I didn't get around to learning."

"Everybody knows how to dance!"

"Not me. Maybe I would have been taught by my sister but she died when I was little. Had a brother, too, but they had diphtheria."

"Didn't you?"

"No, they had shots for it by the time I was around."

"Poor Jordie. It must have been lonely to grow up without them."

"I don't know. My folks made up for it."

"Bet you were spoiled."

"No...but I didn't feel lonely." She looked like a *Saturday Evening Post* cover...the girl next door. Not his next door...this was a far cry from Manhattan tenements.

"Want me to teach you how to dance?"

He was a seabird, flinching from the cage of land. She wanted to hold him.

"No. I like sitting here."

She let her elbow brush his arm. "You said you lived in New York."

"Yeah...that's right."

She waited; he didn't continue. "I've never been. What's it like?"

"Oh...big, crowded, million things to do and see. You'd like it."

"Everything I read about it sounds so glamorous!"

"That's what everybody there thinks about Hollywood."

"But this isn't Hollywood...it's La Jolla."

"That's how you pronounce it—lah hoyyah?" He grinned. "I always said it like it was spelled."

"It's Spanish for The Hollow—the j is an h and the l's are y's."

"That's too dizzy for me."

Grace and Dot changed partners and records and the

75

dancing continued full blast. Helen brought ice cubes from the house to add to the lemonade. She waggled her fingers at them and went back inside to toss a salad. She was wearing a halter and shorts now, just another of the girls.

"I'd like to see New York someday."

"Yeah? I'll take you with me when I get discharged."

"Wouldn't I love it! What are you going to do when you get home?"

"Go to school. GI Bill will pay for it."

"What do you want to be?"

He shrugged. Her father abandoned the smoke to return to the patio, smelling of charcoal and starter fluid. He gawked at his daughters lovingly. Jordan could tell the man was content with life. "I guess I'll be happy to do whatever gives me a family and a nice place to live."

She teased, "You'll need a wife for the family, Jordie."

He smiled into her eyes. Blue, like his. "You'd make a good mother for my kids." She blushed and glanced away.

"I suppose your girl is dying for you to get back."

"Nope."

"Don't say you don't have one. Sailors!"

"There's just Mom and Pop waiting. I didn't have anyone special when I enlisted."

She ran her eyes over him slowly; he was too interesting to have been overlooked. "Don't say you haven't found one since, Jordie. You must have found a girl somewhere you liked."

He didn't reply. He couldn't say anything about Yukiko because she didn't count the way Wanda meant. Wanda was talking about a girl in the States he could marry.

"Haven't you?"

"How could I? I've been overseas."

She accepted the answer. Everything about him attracted her. His solemnity and quick smiles. His romantic scars, or they would be if she were to see them. His face was remarkably young, unlined and responsive to his thoughts; traces of city streets were in his speech but tempered by accents of men he'd served with on the ship. And an intriguing trace of foreign accent, too, she thought. "Is your family Dutch?" she asked.

"No, we're Polacks. I would have been born Jordan Asieczkarny if Pop's name hadn't been changed for him when he got off the boat."

"Whew, I won't even ask you to spell it for me!"

"I'd get it wrong, anyway," he laughed.

"Where do your folks live in New York?"

He was reluctant and then let her draw him out about the slum district he knew but didn't want to live in again. She was fascinated, not seeing the Lower East Side for what it was because her point of reference was her own town. She thought of poor Poles entering the Land of Opportunity as taught in uninformative textbooks. They arrived; they settled; they prospered. *Veni, vidi, vici,* or whatever they say in Polish. Listening to him gave her clues regarding his intense determination not to follow his father's footsteps. Jordan wasn't going to be a janitor stoking coals from a bin into a furnace for the rest of his days. He painted a better existence in the offing for himself. He'd become successful and have plenty of money and live happily ever after.

"With four kids and you'll come to California for your vacations!"

"Yeah, if my chores let me."

"You talk like a farmer sometimes."

"Oh, I get that from Dave. He was my asshole bud ... excuse me. He was my best friend on the *Bulman—* that was my ship." He was mortified; Navy slang wasn't fit for polite society. She wasn't bothered by the slip.

"Well, hang on to this address and you can bring your family here one day and Daddy will fix his barbeque."

"Fat chance. You'll be married yourself by then ... and bringing your kids to New York."

"Then I'll expect you to put us up at your house and you make the barbeque."

"Yeah. I can just see it. We'd have to be on a roof or something."

They smiled at each other. She said, "Okay, it's a date."

"Your kids and mine will have a hell of a lot of fun."

She sipped at her lemonade quickly. He had said she would make a good mother for his children; it excited her physically and the reaction wouldn't leave. Helen swept onto the patio terrace with a platter of ground beef patties. They couldn't talk privately any longer. Everyone mustered on the beach to cook their own food over the coals and they helped each other spill catsup and grease into

77

the sand, ate gritty burgers and drank more cold lemonade. The music played throughout, *Hold-tight-hold-tight,* and Wanda didn't leave Jordan's side until he went into the laundry room to get dressed. She was at the station wagon window when he was ready to be taken back to the base.

"Will you come out to see us again next week?" she asked.

He was there every weekend.

Indian summer ended. The weather's anniversary gift to the Occupation was a freak early snowfall dusting the Inland Sea from Wakayama to Shimonoseki, which placed the fishing village under the brunt of it. Dave fumbled with packages in his arms, his footing slippery. He looked forward to sitting beside the firepit in Yukiko's house to have hot sake served him. The family was good about that; every Japanese was overly careful to repay the slightest of obligations. He hadn't been welcome when he began to bring them things from the ship, but they hadn't known him as well as they did Jordie. It took a while for him to overcome the coolness. Hell, it was still there but they didn't seem to mind him so long as he didn't stay longer than to drop off cans of chow and cigarettes and have one cup of sake. Ooba-san was one mean devil, though. Had she ever been pleasant to Jordie? And why didn't Jordie write? Probably too busy turning civilian. He should have written himself, but he had nothing to say. Jordie wouldn't want to know about the tedium of Occupation duty, and Dave didn't want to tell he'd been looking after the little family for him. He had taken on the extra task as payment to Jordie for saving his life; it just took the time to deliver the stuff, be social a few minutes and then he was free to chase up the mountainside to a more hospitable place. He'd eyed Yukiko once at the start, entertaining thoughts of shacking up, but it was out of the question. She was prettier after Jordan was gone, filled out and womanly. But he couldn't get to first base. She was a respectable girl;

would make some gook a fine wife. Had she married and not told him? It would explain her absence from the household these past months.

When he arrived at the house, Ooba-san was seated on the veranda. She was wrapped in a heavy padded cloth coat, steam puffing into the brisk air from her nostrils with every breath. She had developed lung difficulties of late and the short bursts gave her a deceptive quality of liveliness. Ooba-san seldom moved, being content to occupy each territory she claimed for long periods. He hadn't expected to see her outside the house, not in this weather.

"Hey, Ooba-san," he called familiarly as he halted before her, "you trying to get yourself pneumonia?"

She didn't reply. More than that, she looked beyond him as though he weren't there. He couldn't figure it out. He waved a package at her.

"You're going to crap when you see what's in this can. One gallon of stewed prunes. Make you loose as a goose."

Because she couldn't understand his words, he amused himself frequently by saying outrageous things to her. He waited for a reaction. Usually she demanded to see what was in each bag or package he brought and could not wait to open them; Ooba-san couldn't live without the fruit and pounds of sugar and Luckies he supplied. The damp wind worked into his pea jacket. Stepping to the veranda, prepared to remove his shoes, Ooba-san stood, rising with one swift effort. She coughed angrily, a cough which was forced and meant words she could not speak in his language. It was an impolite cough, directed at him and not covered with a hand or scrap of cloth. Satisfied to have been thoroughly rude, she turned her back and entered the house. The sliding door slammed shut. His mouth sagged. Her meaning was unmistakable.

"Okay, I can take a hint. I don't know why you're pissed off at me but I'll try you another day." He set the packages on the floor of the veranda, pushing them to the wall under the eaves to keep them from the snow. Then, hands in pockets, collar pulled up, he started to leave. Closed windows, closed doors; they didn't want to see anybody today. It would have been nice to have a nip; why'd she run him off?

"Wait!"

He stopped on the path leading to the mountain roads.

79

Glancing back, he saw Yukiko at a window. It was open a crack to keep the wind from blowing in at her. He was delighted to see she was home.

"Hey, Yukiko! I left a bunch of goodies on your porch."

"Arigato gozaimasu, Dave... always *arigato."*

"Be sure to tell your Oto-san or Oka-san about it. The old broad is sore at me today."

She paused; a village conference her parents were attending was called because of herself. "They are at the *hanashiai* now but I will tell."

"Where have you been keeping yourself? I haven't seen you in a coon's age." He stepped closer to the window, brushing snowflakes from his cheeks. "Every time I've been by, your mother or father tried to tell me something but I didn't know what they meant. You go somewhere on vacation?"

"Iie... not. I have been here."

"Why didn't you join us whenever I was in the house? It was murder trying to be company without you to translate for me."

"I was..." She glanced uneasily into the room. He realized she had been whispering and was talking to him against her family's wishes.

"What's the trouble, Yukiko?"

"Nothing! I'm not permitted to leave this room. I was sorry to miss seeing you but could not."

She looked lousy. Maybe they restricted her because of ill health. Tuberculosis was rampant in Japan.

"I hope you haven't been sick," he said. She surprised him with a radiant smile. "You're okay now?"

"Hai... okay!" She checked the room behind herself once again and asked mischievously, "Shall I show you?"

"Yeah... go ahead." He was puzzled as she disappeared momentarily. She returned to the window with a bundle to hold up for him to see. She parted a fold of cloth over a wrinkled doll's face... except it was alive. "Jesus... a baby!"

"Hai," she exclaimed happily.

"You know, I was just this minute thinking you might have gone and gotten yourself hitched and..."

Her giggles of pleasure interrupted him. "Joe-dan-ash," she repeated over and over again. "Joe-dan-ash...Joe-dan-ash..."

He stared. The baby had strands of black hair and obsidian eyes slanting upon its pale features.

"You hear from Joe-dan-ash?" she asked.

"What? Oh, no. I haven't been writing. Neither has he..." He stared at the baby again. It moved its head to nestle deeper into the soft blanket for warmth. "Hey...you better get your baby away from the window so it won't catch cold."

She agreed and was gone for another instant. Returning, her eyes danced. "I have a son," she announced.

He swallowed; indecision beleaguered him as he thought of Jordie back in the States. Was he still in the service? "What did Jordie have to say about it?" he murmured uneasily.

Her face saddened. "He doesn't know I have a son...his son."

"Doesn't he write you? I thought you'd be the one person he'd write, Yukiko. You remember, I said he'd be bound to drop you a line after he got well." The words stubbed each other lamely. It was evident she hadn't heard from Jordie, just as he had not. He'd have to try getting word to him. "I'll send Jordie a letter right away, Yukiko. I'll tell him about you and the baby."

She shook her head anxiously. "Tie...you mustn't! I must be the one to tell of his son's birth."

"Why haven't you done it yet?"

She was chagrined. "I do not know his address. Do you?"

"The last I had was the hospital ship. But that would be all right."

"Will you write it for me?" She held out a postal card, one with a colorful photograph of a Buddha on its face. "My sister brought it from her travels. It is perfect for this joyful news."

He pointed to the divided space on the back of the card. "You don't have much room to put down everything, Yukiko."

"Honorable Joe-dan-ash," she recited, "you have a son." Then she laughed softly. "What more can I say to his father?"

Miserable, he didn't want to say anything to make her feel badly. He agreed it was all the message she'd need and said she would hear from Jordan, though it would be a long wait since the card had to be forwarded from the hospital ship. He wrote: Jordan Asche, TM 2/c, care of U.S.S. *Mercy,* Fleet Post Office, San Francisco, California, U.S.A. He wanted to add her message but she protested.

"I will write it, Dave. It must have my hand upon the words to give them gladness. I will write very beautifully and with infinite care. It shall be painted to give it pleasure along with knowledge."

"Can you do that?" he asked with concern, meaning could she write it in English.

"Hai. I have been practicing and when I am ready, I shall use my finest brush."

He passed the card and pencil back to her. She held the card daintily, exclaiming over the address he'd written. She was lost in her contemplation of it, seeing the completed card in her mind's eye. Sighing, she looked at Dave. He was shifting from one foot to the other, not with cold but impatience to get on with his own affairs.

"Joe-dan-ash will answer?"

"You bet. You're going to set him right on his honorable ass but he'll write. Jordie's a good Joe. He'll write."

She put the card to her bosom and covered it with both hands. Yukiko bowed to Dave. It was only a bow with the head but filled with gratitude. He left her, assuring himself that Jordan would surely write in answer to her news. He didn't know what Jordan could do about the baby but he sure as hell wouldn't ignore it. Dave considered sending his own letter and changed his mind. No, it was Jordie's move. After he sent his response, they could work something out. Dave went up the mountainside, and as the snow obliterated his tracks, Yukiko took up her brush and ink.

..."we taught the sharks to come like dogs to a whistle...every time our guns or depth charges sounded, the thuds and bangs must have telegraphed all over the Pacific because the sharks showed up. It was like a crazy kind of dinner gong for them and they learned to collect and follow us..."

Wanda, snuggling against Jordan in the front seat of her coupé, listened without comment lest he stop talking; Jordan was most precious to her when he was vulnerable like this, when he was more child than battle-scarred man. They had been parked beside the highway for the past hour at a usual stopping place where they necked before she drove him the final few miles to the naval base. The eucalyptus grove shading them from a rapidly descending twilight rustled in the wind.

"Porpoises did that, too," Jordan continued wistfully, as if speaking of lost companions. "The porpoises liked to play around our ships, but they were gone when we were fighting. Isn't that funny? If we were attacked, the porpoises disappeared and the sharks would come. Boom! Blam! And the fucking water was filled with fins." He adjusted his position, squirming to make himself comfortable and said apologetically, "I'm sorry, I have to stop using dirty words. We said them so much aboard ship, they didn't mean anything." Across the strip of beach beside them, the surf tumbled regularly and beyond it rollers moved toward shore darkly. The ocean looked empty. Jordan watched it silently, saw something and nothing vanishing on the horizon and mused, "I wonder how long the sharks will do that? I wonder if they'll forget it after a while..."

Wanda tightened her arm about him and hugged him hard to herself. "Oh, Jordie. That's so terrible."

He laughed lightly. "No, it isn't. That's just the way it was."

"Well, they're going to forget it, Jordie—just as you will."

"I don't even think about them. We had worse to worry about then. You never knew when something would drop out of nowhere to try to get you." He scanned the sky automatically and studied the trees overhead. "Whew!" he exclaimed, changing the subject to escape the seriousness. "Those smell like cat pee!"

That was another thing which endeared him to her; would he ever tell her how awful the war had been for him? Tantalizing bits spilled from him upon occasion only to be capped immediately. She wanted to hear all of it...she wanted all of him. "They're eucalyptus trees, Jordie. The damp brings out the odor. People string their buds and use them as flea collars for their dogs."

"Poor dogs."

"When it rains you can smell eucalyptus everywhere you go."

"You mean it actually rains in sunny California?"

"Oh, my, yes! But the season isn't till February."

"Oh."

She sensed his mood drop and pressed her head against his cheek, murmuring, "What's the matter?"

"I won't be here then."

She caught her breath. No. He wouldn't be. He'd be out of the Navy and across the continent. Jordie would be seeing other girls; she'd see other boys...and none could hope to arouse her as he did. Upset, she turned to put her mouth over his. They kissed as if parting.

"Hey...I'm not going right away," he protested.

"Why do you have to go, anyway?"

-"What do you mean?"

"You could live out here...couldn't you?"

"No, this isn't where I belong, Wanda. I couldn't stand to live on the West Coast. Everything's so dragass...so what do you call it? Oh, *mañana*. Even if New York weren't my hometown, I'd still want to go there to start civilian life."

Extravagant visions of the city crowded into her thoughts. The tall towers were castles outlined with vermeil, a skyline embroidered by fancies films and romantic magazine stories had given her. "Is it honestly so exciting there?" she asked.

"Why don't you come with me and find out for yourself?"

Although flippantly said, his question sank deeply and detonated within her an overwhelming desire to have him mean it. She turned predator, swam through the spreading inner heat and sat upright to stare into his amused eyes. "Are you proposing, Jordie?" she asked with pretended archness.

His grin wavered. He felt trapped suddenly. Her gaze was steady but filled with pleading. Traffic racing along the highway beside them illuminated her face with headlights intermittently. The effect was hypnotic.

"Are you, Jordie?" she insisted, nudging against him slightly.

There was then a fever upon the land, an infectious disease rampant everywhere, which had been incubated in nostalgic ballads throughout four years of war and currently reaching fruition. Returning servicemen and servicewomen transformed past desperation to live for the moment into an urgent grasp at permanency. The maudlin songs had programmed everyone with pledges of waiting and being true. Those fortunate enough to have survived absences and those newly met gave marriage top priority. Everyone was doing it.

Everyone.

Particularly the youngest, for they believed the lyrical promises and plunged without question into their future just as their elders tried to retrieve what was lost forever. The maimed ones, civilian and veteran, were hidden away, rapidly forgotten because they were sick and dying and it was a time for the living who could heal themselves... or thought they could. Or if not able, were encouraged by one another to think it possible. And out of that roil of emotion, out of necessity to renew life, reason gave way to gratification as thoroughly as during the dark days. Surely nothing was uncertain anymore!

Pressing closer to Jordan, she felt his body's spontaneous response. It was automatic, something they mutually experienced upon touch or thought of each other. And somewhat flawed with a dampening minor restraint, always rendered clinically distasteful for having to use contraceptives... but they could be carefree if he'd commit himself. She'd never again have to worry about being "caught." Hadn't that been the single bad part of sex for her? Yes, Jordie, yes, say yes, and she'd give herself without reservation and when she got pregnant, they'd be happier than ever. Feeling full and already bloated with his child, she pushed more ardently against him and demanded, "Jordie?"

He looked away nervously. The first stars had appeared and light beams seemed to haul the passing cars over the cement track toward the lonely domed glow which was San Diego. He'd be sleeping without her at the base or more likely would lie awake to think of her in the restless barracks. Wanting her. In impassioned moments they had

85

whispered declarations of love, one for the other, and repetition made the obligatory confessions true. Turning to her, Jordan decided he couldn't leave her, wouldn't go home without her. He mumbled clumsily, "I guess so."

"Jordie!"

She kissed him and they devoured each other hungrily, betrothing themselves with their mouths. Then she pushed from him and said impishly, "Okay, now ask me properly."

"Ah, come on," he countered sheepishly. "Knock it off, will you?"

"No," she retorted playfully though with deadly seriousness. "No, you have to ask me nice."

He tried to think of how he'd heard it was done and rejected stilted formal phrases, and with red face blurted, "Okay, Wanda: Will you marry me?"

She squealed delightedly and pecked him with a flurry of quick kisses he returned with relieved laughter. They had hurdled the difficult moment and regarded each other contentedly. At once, there was an intangible difference in their relationship—one of ownership and belonging, one of finality. The ocean thundered at them from the shoreline, rumbling in the night like distant cannons. Unrestricted now, they performed the sly partial disrobing they practiced so often before and accommodated themselves to the cramped space to engage one another, and Jordan was hauled down, down, down below the pulsating lights of the road from which steady ram bursts of traffic underscored blunt thrusts which ended all too soon. Then, wriggling back into silken panties and smoothing wrinkles from her dress, Wanda sat primly secure upon the seat. Jordan took her hand in his and they recuperated slowly, the wind blowing across their damp brows.

And Wanda chortled gleefully, "Oh, Jordie! Oh, Jordie! Wait till I tell Mother and Daddy..."

"You loco, sugar? You don't even know the boy! You call seeing him weekends and maybe a time or two in San Diego knowing him?"

Wanda sat with white lips compressed tightly. She had been stormed at for an hour by both her parents. And all she said was that Jordan asked her to be his wife.

"Now you listen here," her father went on. "We're not going to have some white trash Jew boy for a son-in-law and that's all there is to it."

"His parents are from Poland."

"I don't give a hot tamale where they come from."

"That makes them Polish, Daddy."

Helen hushed them. "You're going to wake Grace and Dot if you don't lower your voices!" A pair of eavesdroppers were agog outside the bedroom door and ready to speed down the hall to their own rooms at a moment's notice.

Gus glared at his wife. "The boy doesn't have a lick of education."

Wanda defended Jordan to him. "He's going back to school on the GI Bill to get what he needs."

"What are you supposed to live on while he's pawing through books?"

"I'll work if I have to."

"Sure you will. Never had to lift a finger in your life."

"Daddy, you're not going to talk me out of this."

"Children, obey your parents! Ephesians six one!"

"The Scriptures also say a girl should get married...or would you want me to go to New York with Jordie without bothering?"

He wanted to read the riot act to his wife, too. It was her doing. All the blasted barbeques and beach parties and that kind of hogwash to attract young men to the house. "Can't you talk sense to her, Helen?"

"I've been praying the whole night," she declared, wringing her hands. "If me and Jesus haven't been able to change her mind, you're welcome to keep trying."

He resumed pacing across the carpet. They had been arguing in his bedroom since her announcement. They gave her everything she asked for all her sweet life and now she was going to throw herself away on a penniless jasper from a cockroach-ridden New York ghetto. "No, I'm not going to let you do it."

"Okay, Daddy," Wanda replied stubbornly, "I'll run away with him."

"Try it and I'll have the law fetch you so fast your head will swim."

Wanda exchanged a pointed look with her mother. "Mother knows I mean it. If you don't say yes, I'll live with him anyway. I love Jordie and I want to marry him. I don't want anybody else."

"You don't mean that, sugar."

"Oh, yes I do."

She wasn't bulling him just to get her own way. And he had a suspicion they ought to be married anyway. It hurt to lose his girl; they'd all be going soon enough. It had been years since she had promised not to marry anyone and live with her Daddy and Mommy forever and ever. A lump formed in his throat. He sat beside her on the bed but she shrank from his touch. She hadn't done that before. "I never thought I'd hear you talk so, sugar."

"I love him, Daddy."

"You do," he echoed. "I thought I'd have your love to myself so long as we lived."

"You're not losing it, Daddy."

Before morning, he surrendered. He gathered her wearily into his arms and while she cuddled contentedly, he said it was okay sugar, he was going to talk to her fella and work something out. Gus had a sniffle or two to hide. Helen was partway into the wedding plans; she didn't have time to waste. The boy was getting out of the Navy within two weeks and she had to know if he'd agree to a church wedding.

He did. Though he wasn't an Adventist, Polish is Polish.

Gus engineered a session with his son-in-law-to-be. They ate supper with the rest of the family on Sunday evening and excused themselves to stroll along the moonlit beach. Carrying shoes and socks, they walked through the tide pools and on the edge of the surf. Wet sand squeaked under their bare heels.

"You're the first to take a girl from me, Jordan," the disgruntled man said.

"I'll do everything I can to make her happy, Gus."

"That's what I was wondering. What are you going to do for a living?"

"New York's got plenty of opportunities. I'm not worried."

"I'll give you a job here on one of my construction crews. You'll get good pay and plenty of chance for promotion."

"That's kind of you, sir. I'd rather catch up with my schooling."

"Yeah, that's what Wanda said you planned to do. What will you study?"

"I liked chemistry a lot...something in that line."

"I don't see how you kids will get along on the money you'll have."

"We're both willing to work. We'll manage."

"If you take the job I'm offering, you and Wanda could live in town here and we'd be handy to look after you when you need help."

"No, sir. We'll live in New York."

"Just what the hell is back there that's so goddamned good?"

"It's my home."

Gus mentally told Jesus he was sorry as hell and walked without a word for a while. When he was calmer, he said, "You intend to live with your folks?"

"No, sir. They don't have room for us, anyway."

"You should have waited till you got yourself on your feet before proposing to Wanda, boy."

"We talked about that."

Gus grumbled gloomily, "Yeah, and didn't have the brains to see it was the smart thing to do."

"I'm going home right away. We didn't want to be separated."

"Nothing wrong with waiting when you're in love." They walked in step, the same number of them between each crash of surf. "Three daughters," Gus moaned. "You'd think the good Lord would have given us one boy among them. We should have somebody to carry on the family name. That's what it's all about, Jordie. Helen and I would have kept trying for a boy but I didn't want to risk it. I don't know what's wrong with that woman of mine...oh,

89

that's not to say I don't worship the little fillies she gave me... but you'd think *just one*. Just one!" He laughed self-deprecatingly. "I had to be rich just so I could pay for the weddings!" He glanced at Jordan sideways. "Don't you make the same mistake, boy. We're going to expect a grandson soon as you get around to it." His deep chuckle boomed into the night. "It's about time we got menfolk into the Fleming clan again." After a few more crunching steps in the damp sand, he asked lightly, "Say... would you object to taking our name instead of yours when you marry my Wanda?"

"Yes, sir, I would object."

"Oh. People have done it, you know. To keep an old family name alive. Flemings have been Somebody in the Southwest since before the Civil War. You wouldn't want to be a Fleming, though." It was an observation rather than a question this time. "Well, with two to go, maybe one of them will get a fella who'll do it. Say... that name of yours, I thought all you Polacks had tongue twisters for handles."

"Pop did but I told your daughter how it was changed when he got to America. I don't think he'd want to see it changed again."

"Well, at least it ain't one of them tongue twisters, eh?" They had reached the limit of their walk and were now heading back to the house. Gus made up his mind to like the boy. He threw his arm over his shoulder and thanked Jesus for small favors. Wanda Asche. Could have been a lot worse.

Along with multicopied paperwork done to present Jordan with his embroidered ruptured duck, a distorted eagle emblem worn on uniforms to show termination of service, he also got an argument regarding his future naval status. He refused to sign up for the Reserves. There was a subtle threat of slowing down his separation procedure but he remained firm. His request for honorable discharge on the

West Coast was approved; a severance payment was issued, equivalent to train fare to New York City. It was spent on a set of rings for Wanda in a San Diego pawn shop, rings he didn't think worthy of her but meant to be replaced when he could afford better. Wanda agreed, knowing she'd never part with them. They were irreplaceable to her. While Jordan sweated his discharge at the base, her parents corraled caterers and lit rockets under their Seventh-day Adventist minister, who didn't like being stampeded. There wasn't time to send out invitations. Everyone was notified by phone.

Jordan turned in the bedding, mattress, pillow and hammock issued him at boot camp and carried with him at every transfer. He collected his official documents, then was surprised to receive a last piece of mail: a post card forwarded from the *Mercy*. He looked at the picture first, a big green idol like the pig-iron incense burners sold in Five and Tens. He guessed it was a card from Dave and turned it quickly to read the message. It was brief, brushed on with black ink and composed of elegant mysterious Japanese characters. He smiled. Yukiko. She must have thought of him after all this time and wanted to say hello. There wasn't an address for her—a card sent to the village would reach her—but what the hell. What for? Since he'd gone past the nearest trash can, he stuffed the card into his ditty bag and it was there when Wanda unpacked it for him in the room the Flemings gave him to use until the wedding.

"Hey, Mister Civilian, what's this?"

He was squinting at his reflection in a full-length mirror on the door. The double-breasted suit, hastily purchased off a rack before leaving Dago, made him look strange. It was gray, in spite of advice from Helen Fleming to get a dark blue one to be married in. He didn't want that color again for a while—not until he got used to being free. "What are you talking about?" he said, angling to see another side of his image.

"This card with a Buddha on it."

"Oh, that. I got it when I checked off the base."

She brought it to him from the dresser, cocking her head over it with curiosity. The careful lettering looked so feminine. "Who's the girlfriend, Jordie? You didn't tell me about her."

91

He was uncomfortable. "There's nothing to tell."

"You're blushing, Jordie."

"No, I'm not," he denied, feeling a flush upon his cheeks. He tried to take the card from her but she hid it behind her back.

"Who is she?"

"Nobody. Come on, honey, don't start thinking things."

"Then why are you upset?"

"I'm not upset," he protested, getting redder.

"I know sailors have a girl in every port, Jordie. You can tell me who this card is from."

"How should I know?" he lied. "Jesus, we must have met half of Japan when I was running around there. My buddy Dave and I got to know lots of people."

"Somebody liked you enough to keep track."

"Could be anybody."

"Uh-hmmm."

"Honey, I can't even read the damned thing."

"You said you learned some Japanese."

"I could say a few sentences but not read any."

"Doesn't the picture bring back memories for you?"

He took the card from her and admired it at arm's length. "I sure didn't run into that bugger." Then he threw it carelessly to the top of the dresser. The Daibutsu of Nara, survivor of typhoons and earthquakes and chosen for his strength to carry Yukiko's message, fell face down on a litter of travel brochures he and Wanda had studied when making honeymoon plans. Jordan drew Wanda to himself and they kissed, losing interest in the card and what it had to say. He didn't miss seeing the card again; he had time only for his future, which was approaching with such rapidity it erased his past.

The big news was that Gus would foot the bill for a week in Acapulco, a sleepy resort recommended highly for newlyweds. The Flemings had their way with every arrangement but one: Jordan's parents couldn't be persuaded to fly West for the ceremony. They refused politely, saying they looked forward to meeting their new daughter-in-law in New York. Jordan felt he'd be lonely at the church among so many strangers...there wasn't anyone at the base he'd asked to attend...Dave would have been ideal. But Dave was in Japan. He wouldn't see him again.

The minister of the church gave Jordan an engraved

marriage certificate and an invitation to join his flock; his new female relatives smothered him with kisses; Gus and Helen presented a check for a thousand dollars beyond the expenses he was to run up in Acapulco. So much wealth being unbelievable to Jordan, he let Wanda handle it. She banked the money, shooed off her sisters, put the document in her hope chest and got herself and Jordan aboard the plane for Mexico. She didn't believe anything either till they were seated on a balcony below the border, margaritas in hand as they watched an idiot fling himself from a cliff into a rocky channel of seawater a hundred feet below his launching pad. Maybe it was eighty. Maybe fifty. It wasn't important.

Hotel el Mirador's stucco collection of intimate rooms had as prime attraction a diving show put on by local boys foolish enough to risk lives for the few pesos they scrounged from *turistas* afterward. Men watching the plungers admired their reckless courage; women saw the sheen of sunlight on brown muscles arched sexually into the flight of a bird. Jordan didn't care for them. He thought they were suicidal, like the kamikazes of the war. He wasn't in Acapulco for them, anyway, and he and Wanda did what every honeymoon couple practiced with mutual dedication.

When they weren't industriously attempting creation, they left the confines of their room to wander through the sweltering town. It was growing in popularity and there was a demand for more hotels. Buildings were being constructed everywhere. At the bottom of the hill upon which the Mirador stood, an outdoor market sprawled, dedicated solely to the sale of souvenirs. Colorful junk, exquisite embroidery on cheap cotton which wouldn't last, painted plates and porous, useless jars glazed with shellac, necklaces of seeds and berries soon to shrivel and crack off the string were offered in bins and stalls by stoic dark women, muscled and moustached and bursting from their loose dresses with Amazonian bodies. They were short; beautiful as Aztec calendars and painted saints, marzipan skulls and Mayan glyphs. Wanda insisted upon buying a sample of everything from the Indians to take home. They got wood carvings and clay animals and sombrero hats. They gave money to the poor on the steps of the cathedral. They treated grimy ragamuffins to paper cones filled with finely ground chips of ice with acid-colored fluids poured over them. Warding off flies, they ate enchiladas and burritos and frijoles and cooled the chilis with glasses of tequila. And they returned to the hotel to make love, forgoing siesta hours during the heat of day when the sweat of their bodies rendered the act one of interminable movement sliding to and fro of its own volition. "We'll call the first one Pedro," promised Jordan, "in honor of all these refried beans." And Wanda broke rhythm and wind simultaneously and was unable to control her laughter. He thought of Yukiko later, long after his wife slept. It would be fun to send her a card from Mexico. The idea was forgotten by dawn.

In La Jolla, cleaning out the accumulation of the past busy weeks, Helen came upon the Japanese card. The Daibutsu of Nara smiled enigmatically at her. She clucked at the heathen idol disapprovingly and consigned him to her trash.

Yukiko trembled, fearing to lose her child. Another *hanashiai,* that which is a talking over, had been convened. The villagers were condemning her again. For her son, the baby she gave the foreign name. Joe. To them a name without meaning, a name they called the long-noses. The scandal of having the bastard of the *hakujin* had become intolerable; her father was bowing to them many times with mortification, agreeing to their demands. He threw enraged glances at her and the unacceptable son and assured the leaders of the community they should be satisfied. Mr. Nakatsuru needed most convincing and it prolonged the length of the meeting before it was concluded and the irate crowd could stalk away in groups, declaring this matter had taken overlong to settle. She was left to face her father's wrath.

Oto-san indicated she was to go into the house. She held the boy close and entered timorously. Oka-san and Oobasan sat numbly in the center of the room, eyes fixed upon the tatami. She sank to her knees and hugged the child possessively as her father closed the door.

"You have heard the *yoryokusha*. They will not have your son defile our village any longer."

She cringed beneath his anger "I have kept myself and my son apart from everyone."

"It is not enough. We are without face before everyone."

"How may I lessen the shame?"

"You know how."

"What are you asking of me, Oto-san?"

He drew himself up haughtily. "A woman has five weaknesses. You may be one with a temper or of a jealous nature, have an empty head or wag a slanderous tongue ...but the worst you can be is disobedient."

"What are you asking of me?"

"You are useless to yourself and the hamlet now. Mr. Nakatsuru doesn't want you. No man would be so foolish as to marry you. None would have the child for a son. You must get rid of him."

"What are you asking of me?"

He wavered. She had choices she could make, though none truly suited him. It was simpler to have her leave the village and take the child with her. "I will not keep you and your *ainoko* under my roof."

Oka-san's head bent lower; there was no other sign of her sympathy. Neither mother nor grandmother would intervene on her behalf. "Where can we go, Chichiue?"

She had called him Revered Father, proclaiming the depth of her love for him. "Go among the barbarians in the cities," he commanded roughly. "There is work for women among the Occupation troops and you will not starve."

"I could not sell myself to soldiers."

"And why not? It's a profession like any other."

He had settled the question. She would be gone from the village and, like gossip, be forgotten after seventy-five days. They would strike her memory from their thoughts; shame would be made more bearable by her absence.

She had little to prepare for her departure. She packed a few articles into a rattan case and stole from the house before evening. A slow launch which made regular stops at the village carried her and the boy to the mainland, a tedious voyage requiring the night and much of the next day. It was frightening to be on her own, the more so to be thrust abruptly into a huge city like Osaka. The change was nearly inconceivable to her; she was deafened by the bedlam of the bustling metropolis. Where to go? Leaving the launch, holding child and suitcase for dear life, she followed the flow of traffic into the city proper. Joe was delighted with everything he saw, unaware of his mother's fear. He crowed at dozens of military vehicles they had to dodge, and he could not get his fill of exciting sights. They passed an extensive shipyard which was slowly being repaired of bomb damage. Workmen clambered over new frameworks everywhere. The city was recovering rapidly from the ravages of war, aided by the very forces who had leveled it. Yukiko was impressed by everyone's energy, evidence of the purposeful lives they led. No peaceful village atmosphere here! People ran, shouted. Stores and buildings were of a size she'd not seen before. It was impossible to take any direction without being shouldered aside or pushed from behind or carried along by a determined group.

She arrived at a main thoroughfare in which a pleasure district had been established; soldiers and sailors of the Occupation moved restlessly in and out of garish grog shops. What is it that pulls the strays of Earth unfailingly to their destinations? Knowing she belonged, she saw herself among a new breed of Japanese women. They had discarded timid habits and wore heavy makeup; black-market wares had dressed them in imitation of their American counterparts. They were brazen women, daring to speak openly to men on the streets and to drag them into bars or sign-posted doorways to their dens. Youngsters of escalating age and superb assurance were visible everywhere, making yen by the fistful in their dealings. They sold or bought everything. Stole anything. They were the *daimyo* of the district and ran it well. It was one of those lords who spotted Yukiko and her son. He ran up, money ready in hand.

"Have you something you want to sell?" His avid eyes seemed to rape the contents of her rattan case.

"Iie . . . I have nothing," she said, backing from him, but he had caught her arm. Having heard her village accent, he knew her plight at once. He became her master without delay.

"I will take you to a place you can live. But it will cost you a percent."

"I have no money."

"You will have."

He led her to a side street where rows of abandoned buses had been refurbished into dwellings. The buses were formerly burned out shells, remnants of bombing raids; enterprising citizens had turned them into housing by cleaning them and covering shattered windows with curtains or oiled paper and furnishing them as best they could. He took her to one of the buses and knocked arrogantly. A slattern opened the door, cigarette drooping from her lips. "You're in luck," the tough informed her. "Here's someone to help you pay your rental fees."

The whore inspected Yukiko and the child in her arms. "Have you registered with the *junsa?*"

"We've just arrived in Osaka."

"You can't do anything until you've been to the police."

Yukiko was alarmed. "What would they want with me?"

"You'll be issued your license and they'll want to know about the baby. Is it yours?"

"My son."

"Where is his father?"

"In America. I have a letter looking for him there."

The whore sneered. "Oh...an *ainoko*...the *junsa* will want to register him as well."

It was baffling to Yukiko that police should be contacted, but she had to carry out any instructions this woman gave her; she represented the only future there was. The whore stood aside to permit her to enter the bus. It was three mats long and contained a confusion of bedding and domestic furnishings. An iron stove at the far end sat atop the only remaining seat and served as heater and cooking utensil. The interior of the bus was sour with unwashed clothing and stale towels.

"You can sleep and work over there," she was told, directed to a particular spot where the mats were worn thin. She stepped over a torn *futon* and put her child on the tatami.

"Is there a place to bathe?" she asked.

The whore grimaced, then went outside to discuss the newcomer with her pimp. Yukiko looked around at what

97

was to be her home for many years to come. It's not our home, she thought, only where we'll live—and she sank to the tatami beside her infant son. The mat was damp beneath them, no fault of his. She swept him into her arms again to press fiercely against her breasts. *I don't want to stay!* During the journey from the village she had been obediently passive. Taught submissiveness as a child, as a girl, as a woman from generations of submissive women, she didn't know how to fight against her imposed fate. Her lessons had been instructions for unresisting and patient acceptance, identical lessons taught to identical female Japanese harking back before the ascension of Jimmu Tenno, the first Emperor of Japan. The lessons deadened the outer aspect and sorely contained what was within. They were her rules; she had broken them once and would not again.

She placed a palm flat upon the tatami...felt the cold of its woven reeds...and the chill entered her flesh and enfolded her till she felt naked upon them. And how was she to submit to the men? How? Yukiko wept softly, hugging the boy closely, but his bantling warmth failed to comfort her.

The whore stamped up the short flight of metal steps into the bus, wheezing as she exhaled smoke from her cigarette. Yukiko hadn't stirred from the mat.

"The pimp is bringing us soldiers he has waiting at the traffic circle. You'll have to get ready."

Yukiko was unable to reply. It was upon her, this new life. Rushing at her in a billow of dust as the whore dragged *futons* into place upon the tatami, end to end with a space between for privacy. Litter was pushed aside on the floor, water poured from a pitcher into a large bowl and a towel dropped next to it. Another bowl was filled and shoved toward her. Because it wasn't touched, the whore was irritated.

"Well...am I to do everything for us? There's a towel

behind you. It hasn't been used, has it? But it's not soiled."
She waited. Yukiko waited. "Have you gone deaf?"

"No..." So small a voice as to have called from
afar...far as the village and mother and father and wise
old grandmother. *Oh, Ooba-san, is not the fan in autumn
put by for another season and saved again and again until
it has broken? I shall surely break now, and I don't want
to be broken.* But Ooba-san was not there to answer...and
there was no escaping what was to come. What was the
whore shouting?

"You want us to lose the business? No one will wait for
you to prepare yourself after they've arrived! Put your
bastard aside and remove your clothes! A man hasn't time
for fastenings when he's paid good yen for your miserable
body."

The woman's clothing dropped to the mat; sharp bones
jutted through skin which was bruised across her thighs
and hips. Yukiko wanted to flee but couldn't find strength
to lift herself and the boy from the floor. A thin kimono
was clawed from a drawer and the whore hung it about
herself loosely; then, arms akimbo, she stood over her.

"What's the matter? You're not a virgin, so it can't be
that. What have you to put on instead of those togs?"

She shook her head. Though her mouth formed words,
nothing was heard. The whore tore open Yukiko's rattan
case impatiently and rummaged through it. She found
nothing suitable. In disgust, she kicked its contents into
a heap.

"Well, then. You'll have to be as you are today. Take
off your underpants if you have them and loosen any but-
tons. Who knows? The man may be entertained to see you
in something he's not accustomed to seeing us wear."

Yukiko didn't know what to do with the boy; she kissed
him, tried to smile into his eyes—so wide, so open, so
trusting. The whore threw hands to the air and decided
the stupid villager was hopeless. The pimp could see to
her. Why hadn't he found a lusty girl to help her? It was
a wonder this one had a child.

The pimp arrived with seven soldiers. Laughing, sucking at bottles of cheap Japanese beer, they stumbled
against the side of the bus. A friendly argument was in
progress: Who goes first? One suggested rolling dice, and
Yukiko heard their buoyant curses as they bent over little

white cubes bouncing in the dirt of the lane. Too soon the shouts of triumph. As the rest played on for what they termed sloppy seconds, the winners appeared at the door of the bus. They were unsure which man was to take which woman, and both were uncomfortable to see the one on the floor clinging to a small boy. The whore made their decision for them by taking one soldier by the belt and pulling him down upon her *futon*. She helped with his clothing, taking it off with practiced speed. They were so occupied, they didn't concern themselves with how the other soldier was faring.

This man thought Yukiko was going to set the child aside and tend to himself, but she didn't. He had to lean down to remove the child from her inert fingers and found a nest for him beside the wall of the bus. He was puzzled she sat so still. It was like taking a doll, except her clothing came free of a soft body...shivering and unresponsive, it was true...and more exciting to him as a result. In his heightened urgency, he didn't bother to strip off his uniform but opened his pants and entered her roughly. She was so pained she writhed and struggled against him, attempting to pull clear. Thinking she did it to improve the act, he plunged harder and bit her small breasts and slender throat; his woolen Army pants rubbed her tender skin raw. There were clouds forming in her mind. She didn't want to do this and could do nothing to stop. His weight held her; his breath nailed her cheek to the rumpled bedding; the ghost of Joe-dan-ash masked his face as an unexpected pleasurable sensation surfaced past her resistance. She cried out his name but he was gone, was again the stranger grunting at her ear...and through the slits of her eyes she saw her son watching without understanding.

He watched twice. And again. The other whore took the lion's share.

For Mrs. Jordan Asche, the city was too exciting to over-power or stifle her. The sheer size of New York and its high noise level were stimulating. After exclaiming over the ambitious skyline, she admitted being disturbed by the filth coating curbs and sidewalks. But the messy streets of New York weren't an abomination to its restless commuters; it was an overlay they were accustomed to seeing and because it continually renewed itself, no one suspected it shouldn't be there. Squares of fresh cement were undefiled patches each time a repair was made, only to be daubed with wads of chewing gum and dog slides and sooted over into an even patina. Where people did not skate suddenly upon their heels, they could be seen in brisk motion anyway. Crowds didn't walk anywhere, they were too frantic. Asked if they were running from some-thing, Jordan said it was the other reason: They had to get where they were going as fast as they could.

The cab taking her and Jordan to his parents drove into a sad grid of congested, gloomy tunnels. It was where he was born and raised, so he saw it differently. The familiar ethnic mulch of Middle European nationalities and life-styles was an integral part of home to him; rich odors held ready identification of the same place he left to go to sea. The Block. The street everyone moved from after growing up, leaving parents behind. There were too many elderly folk tousled in windows and doorways and bragging upon the stoops. Just as in villages of the old country. And there, resemblance ended, for each building was its own com-munity without distance from the next; each division of streets, its own nation. The territories weren't marked. They were established by tradition and yearly migrations, often only the shifting of tenants from one floor to another. This neighborhood, he informed her, was predominantly Jewish and Polish. The next was where the Russians lived. And beyond was a beginning of the Irish tribes, whose country stretched to the Bohemians and the Germans and who supplied patrols to the very borders of the five boroughs. Italians were across town on the West Side and seldom seen here. They would have been exotics, like Harlem blacks or blank Chinese unable to root on Mott Street and camping one family to a neighborhood in exile, operating chop suey joints or steamy singeless starch laundries. Wanda's passport into this land was to be the bashful embrace she'd receive from her in-laws.

Casimir and Katarzyna Asieczkarny, Americanized to Casey and Katy Asche by immigration authorities, had a feast waiting for their son and his bride. Food was heaped upon serving platters: juicy spiced sausages and boiled cabbage and black bread and potato salad and a fifth of Polish vodka standing uncorked beside a wide-mouthed jar of volcanic red horseradish. Highly polished silverware and plates and water glasses were arranged on a handmade tablecloth, with matching folded napkins piled neatly in front. Casey and Katy were old country in manner and speech, paired like a stocky wagon team. They didn't see her at first, although they knew Jordan had brought her. They had eyes only for him. The man on their threshold. Where was the boy who'd crossed it years earlier to go to war? This couldn't be he! And was. In his letters, he had not aged nor grown. They had been prepared for everything but this stranger assaulting their affections as his due. It bordered upon disappointment! They looked at him with awe.

"Hey!" Jordan bellowed. "Aren't you going to ask us inside?"

And it was done with tears. Crying, crying to ease happiness. A flood of welcome engulfed them. She was included and swept along to laugh and weep with them. When the excitement subsided, she was introduced and taken into their arms. They were shyly hospitable, anxious to please the young California girl in the smart clothes. So like pictures of girls they saw in magazines! Whenever Casey tweaked the ends of his moustache or Katy bobbed her smiling braided head to speak, Jordan had to translate most of what they said. They had learned little more than was necessary for naturalization papers and for jobs as janitors of the building. They were dressed in church finery, that suit and dress which is not worn but for Sundays

102

and other holy occasions. The deportment was that which was in force on every day.

Wanda was charmed by the formality and courtliness of her new relatives. And grateful there were not more to meet with their hard-to-decipher accents. She was given a chair wiped free of nonexistent dust and handed a water tumbler with vodka. The *naz zdrowie* heard before each searing sip as the couple toasted the newlyweds sounded like battle cries, and it wasn't many minutes before they attacked the meal. A plate was put before her which could not be emptied; her glass of vodka had a permanent level. She bore up bravely, listening while Jordan talked to his parents in a language with a melody of its own. He unintentionally isolated her by speaking in Polish; the rises and falls of the words were meaningless. Wanda's smile solidified and finally faded altogether. Her attention drifted to an inspection of her surroundings.

The three-room apartment was on the ground level of the building, situated directly above a furnace in the basement, which accounted for the warmth of the floors. This room, the living room, was not intended for much. It had a sofa, three straight-back chairs, and a flower stand containing a potted rubber plant. The rug's faded design was dissolved into uniform color by age. Through a doorway beyond the kitchen's scrubbed linoleum, she could see into a tiny bedroom. One large brass bed and a massive wardrobe closet filled it. A curtained window behind the bed opened onto the dank airshaft of the building. Depressed by it, she looked out the window of the living room only to be confronted by an interested examination of sidewalk spectators, who showed no embarrassment about watching the party. They looked like a scene from a grainy film.

Katy turned on the radio during the meal. Polkas and long-winded, unintelligible announcements added to the clamor of the visit. Though Wanda was unable to contribute conversation, she wasn't ignored; she was subjected to a constant secret appraisal. Jordan's mother, effectively concealing possessive jealousy, made an intensely critical survey of the girl. That expertise universally granted mothers of sons allowed her to appear to accept Wanda wholeheartedly ... but the truth was Katy felt cheated and blamed her for it. Katy had thought to regain her baby and resume the cozy life her family once led, but that

103

dream, so prayerfully nurtured throughout the war, was now denied her. It was this girl's fault, this California girl. The stealer of her son's affection and presence. It was the girl's fault and it was hard to be saddled with a daughter-in-law. A small sigh escaped Katy's lips, and she smiled brightly at the girl. The smile returned was that of a confident rival. Well, it was life's way, wasn't it? What was done couldn't be undone and Katy would try to make the best of it.

By evening's end, Wanda was struggling to subdue a rising feeling of resentment toward them all. How different Jordie was with his parents—relaxed and animatedly foreign. He'd fallen into speaking Polish so exclusively she was forced to imagine the meanings of the words and even attempted to learn one or two without success. When a phrase was repeated, it seemed to undergo change by inflection and she failed to follow the thought. So she maintained her blank amiability, occupying herself by thinking of having Jordie to herself later on. She leaned against him from her chair, just able to touch him in that silent oratory they had come to know and share. It was a gesture Katy noted, a gesture like the planting of a proprietary flag upon a battlement. Both women's eyes met briefly. Again they smiled.

Eventually the vodka was gone, the food intimidatingly reproachful upon the table for not having been consumed, and Wanda fought to keep her eyelids open and stifled yawns with her hands. Jordan saw the signals and began their departure by getting their coats. His parents wouldn't hear of it; he had to make several attempts before they agreed to let them go. Katy pressed food upon them, packed into jars and wrapped in cloth napkins and loaded into a big paper sack. Casey hugged Wanda, bussed her with his stiff moustache and they had to be escorted to the street corner to whistle down a cab. Returning to the hotel was also part of the visit, as the smell of the food they carried had the wizened driver sniffing hungrily over his shoulder. They hurried through the lobby of the hotel, hiding the sack between them, and were on their own floor when the dozing desk clerk sniffed a trace of the banquet's passage and wondered where it came from...and where it had gone.

104

"We're in the middle of nowhere, Jordie!"

ELMHURST AVENUE ELMHURST AVENUE ELM-
HURST AVENUE repeated itself on signs along the platform. The subway train had emerged from underground
tubes into the upper air of Queens to make stops above the
rooftops of low buildings and family residences which were
clad in gray and green asphalt shingles. He grabbed her
hand when the doors slid open and hurried her out. The
train hissed at them, closed its doors and raced on. Walking to the exit, she saw trees below, growing out of sidewalks. There were few people on the streets. Strolling! He
led her down an enclosed stair from the elevated station
and across a boulevard to a penitentiary block. Wide, bleak
façades of new brick and identical grids of windows
stretched before her.

"Jordie..."

They went into an entrance of one of the buildings, then
ignored the elevator to walk up a short flight to the first
landing.

"Jordie, where are we going?" she complained.

He urged her along, pushed open a fire door, and took
her through a windowless corridor to the far end, where
he halted before the last door and opened it with a key.
She hesitated, then followed him inside.

The rooms were small cells of plaster without bars, each
with a window facing solid brick vistas a few yards away.
She walked slowly through a room to a kitchenette and
bath. A skimpy closet was cut into one wall.

"Jordie, we can't live here."

"Wait a minute. The ride from the city wasn't so long.
Lots of people put up with it. You'll get used to it."

"Okay, maybe I'd get used to it. But this?"

"You can't expect La Jolla."

Poor Jordie. He was doing his best and she was spoiling
it for him.

"It's not a big rent... and this will be snapped up if we don't keep it."

"Keep it?"

"Yeah, I paid the key deposit. It's all set unless you say no."

She went to a window and craned her neck to see to the top of the buildings. There weren't any tops; they went too high. "I can't see the sky, Jordie. I've always seen the sky."

He pulled her from the window and held her. His heart was thudding faster than it should.

"Jordie, we don't have to be stuck with this. Daddy will lend us money for something better."

"No," he answered quickly. She thought it was pride. "I think we should live here. We have to make a start somewhere."

"Not here. Why do you want to live in such a cubbyhole?" His reason was instinctive and bizarre, and not manifest. He had been looking for shelter for them. A *shelter*. It wouldn't have occurred to either that there was a connection between this vault he'd found and the war; the Bomb was only a remote and familiar image sandwiched between commercials on television screens and rather beautiful when seen in slow motion and color. "Oh, Jordie," she said, locking her fingers behind his neck. His hair had grown; she liked to toy with it. She looked into his eyes appealingly. "I hate it."

"We can't afford the hotel."

"No, we can't."

"So let's move in."

"Is there a choice?"

"No."

Heads together, they laughed. The sound ricocheted from the bare walls. "You know it's awful, too, don't you?"

"You can make any place nice for me—just by being in it."

"Promise we'll move the first chance we get."

"I had to sign a year's lease."

"Jordie!"

"It was a surprise for you."

"Thanks a lot."

"And I didn't want it to get away."

"Who told you about it?"

"The real-estate office. We owe them twenty bucks."

106

"They should pay us for taking it."

"Want to go back to California?"

She kissed him. "No."

They decorated the apartment with temporary furniture made of wooden frames and webbing and foam rubber cushions. Early Halloween, she called the style. She curtained the dreadful view with pastel shades and flowered drapes, and while he enrolled in school, she landed a job with Brentano's on Fifth Avenue as a salesclerk. They became accustomed to living at the bottom of the shaft. The sun that she missed they found in Central Park when meeting for lunch on pleasant days to sit at a table in the small zoo's cafeteria. They enjoyed watching children there... and chose those they admired most as models for their own.

La Jolla was voices over the telephone: Grace was getting married! They couldn't make the wedding but sent love and a gift. Gus was building tract houses now, business booming. Helen had her hair restyled... and as the tie to the Flemings was relinquished, a circle of friends accumulated, most residing in quaint apartments in Manhattan which looked exactly like theirs in Queens. New York was everything Wanda was told. What Jordan took for granted, she considered personal discoveries. They visited museums and galleries, attended recitals and plays. Sundays remained reserved for suppers with his parents. Two years evaporated without distinction.

And one afternoon, as Jordan browsed through a secondhand bookstore on Twenty-third Street, a student selling his collection of textbooks told him of an apartment he was giving up. It was on the next street and they went to the building together and Jordan became the new tenant. Wanda was exasperated not to have been consulted again, but soon was delighted. The building was off Eighth Avenue, one of a row of four-story brownstones which were tied together with romantic iron balconies and porches, set back off the street. There were planter boxes and pots of geraniums clinging to the window ledges which amused her considerably, for they were a far cry from the lush gardens she had known. The apartment was smaller than the one they left, a single large room with a bath. The kitchen area was disclosed when sets of shutters were drawn aside, revealing a tiny sink, a cupboard, and a two-burner stove. The oven took an hour to clean.

It was a wonderful change. The sun burst in upon them daily, since they were on the top floor, and Wanda didn't feel California's loss as before. Neighbors were young couples like themselves. On the way up. Raring to go because they were doomed to be successful. Jordan's career wasn't in doubt. He was at the head of his class; business concerns were showing an interest in him. One firm, Polychem, manufacturers of plastic products, guaranteed him a position upon graduation.

They celebrated the assurance of his future by splurging for seats to *South Pacific,* the biggest hit in town. They were wrung by its humor and its tragedy. Walking from the theater, she asked why he lost touch with everyone from his past Navy life.

"There was only Dave... he was my only buddy, Wanda. He might be anywhere now. He didn't know if he was going to stay in the service or not."

"You'd find out if you dropped him a line."

"No. What's the point? We don't have anything in common anymore."

"Don't you want to tell him how well you're doing?"

"No. And I don't think I'd want to know how horseshit Navy life got to be."

"Some great pals you must have been. You don't even write each other."

"What about you? I don't see sacks of letters going to your friends in California."

"I send cards at Christmas."

"Well, I don't. And nobody sends me any." The ingenue of the show had recalled Yukiko to him. Yukiko... she had sent a card. Whatever became of it?

"You want to have a snack here?"

Wanda had stopped before the doorway of a small bistro, La Petite Couvée. An Irish tenor was singing inside. An aroma of sauces and wines was irresistible. They entered, to be met by a pint-sized charmer with an accent, who ushered them past a maudlin man singing at an upright piano.

"You listen to the radio?" asked their host as he seated them at a table.

"Sure. Why?"

108

He brought a lit candle to it, brushed crumbs from the checked cloth. "The man singing—'e is my friend. My best customer."

They accepted menus. "Oh, is he on a show?"

"No, 'e used to be. Once very good 'am *acteur*. All the shows went to the television but did not want 'e, so 'e 'as retire. *Bon*. I have the entertainer for La Petite Couvée!"

"Didn't you say he was your customer?"

"*Mais oui*—'e sings for nothing, and I feed 'e for nothing!"

He took their order and scurried to the kitchen. The tenor sang some more, asked for requests and seemed to know them all. The meal was good; the wine, too. Their host turned out to be the owner and named Jimmy. He sat with them during dessert, eager to recite his favorite little joke—"'ere comes the 'appy bouncing flea...you cannot tell the 'e from she...the sexes are alike, you see...but 'e can tell...and so can she!" Naturally, it called for wine on the house. Going home afterward, Jordan and Wanda repeated the poem and claimed they, too, could tell easily and proved their knowledge in bed. Lovers, they were receiving love from everyone they met.

Smoking cigarettes in the darkness, they imagined what was to be...talked of homes and travels and children...and imagining further, she cuddled a pillow between them, saying when they had their baby it would sleep there...safely between them...and it was warmed by their bodies, crushed by their nearness to each other. Jordan removed it gently, smiling as he said, "Hey, you little bugger, that's no place for you. You're not supposed to keep us apart. Don't you know anything yet?"

"Say it! Say it! 'Hey, Joe, you want fuck, want suck?' Say it!"

The whore shook the little boy roughly. Why wouldn't he repeat anything she said? His stubbornness and lack of fear added to her fury. Flinging him aside, she got to her feet. The day was stifling, not yet the noon hour. She reached into the open doorway of the bus to get a cigarette from a package lying on the top step. Flicking her lighter, she sneered at the toddler. He had no trouble talking his head off about his own childish interests, she mused. It was time he started to earn his keep. His stupid mother wasted too many hours going out in search of business when the pimp was forgetful. Her brat could bring customers to them; he would snare soldiers easily with his charm. She'd have to keep at him until he obeyed her. It meant more money if he cooperated; they'd be able to drop the erratic service of the pimp. After all, the child wouldn't have to be given a percent.

"What is it? What's going on out here?" Yukiko had awakened and was at the door. She held her thin robe together as she secured it with a safety pin, tossing disheveled hair. It now hung to her waist; she had learned men liked it worn long.

"Nothing. I was just talking to your son."

"It sounded as though you were scolding him." Yukiko held out both arms to the boy but he wouldn't go to her. It would have required brushing past the other woman and he didn't want to get near her; she pinched and was cruel to him.

"I wasn't doing anything of the sort. I was trying to teach him something."

Yukiko bent to help herself to a cigarette from the package. The whore passed the lighter to her and she lit up, enjoying the first of too many cigarettes she'd smoke that day. "He's bright," she said proudly. "He's quick to learn anything."

"He's not much help to us."

"He's only a baby, not five years old yet. What do you expect him to do?"

"All he does is eat and get in our way."

Yukiko darted an annoyed glance at her. "I could say the same about you."

"*Hai?* I pay my share of the rent."

"So do I. Don't make complaints about my son until I can't."

"I was merely thinking he should be bringing soldiers to us so we don't have to walk the streets like tarts."

"That's what we are."

110

The whore sniffed indignantly. "They expect us to be geisha when they come to us."

"Oh, yes," Yukiko shrieked with laughter, "I have heard you singing and playing the skin flute on your mat! You are very accomplished!"

The whore bit her lip and was silent. Yukiko was far busier than herself and could afford to make jibes at her expense. Men preferred Yukiko and thought her prettier...if you cared for that village-girl quality. Well, she had lost freshness, and turned upside down, they must both look alike. But it was getting to be tiresome to march along boulevards without being approached immediately. Men were beginning to look younger. The fools. The whore was forced to be bolder with them or they wouldn't make the first effort. Feeling in the right, she muttered, "Nevertheless, it wouldn't harm him to start to bring men here."

Yukiko eyed her son. He was squatting over an insect as it tracked across the dirt. What to say in reply? It was true he could be useful, but he was so young! She didn't want to launch him upon that business until he had grown older, yet it wasn't any more than other children of the district were doing. When? She didn't know. It would have to solve itself. She looked at the cloudless sky. "It's going to be hot today."

Scratching a heat rash, the whore replied, "We could spend the day at the shipyards. It's bound to be cooler there with the breeze from the bay." And hotter under watchmen and shipfitters, who weren't averse to stopping work to dally beneath a pier if they could spare the yen. Of course, they didn't spend money as readily as Americans, but she had never lost her distaste for the odor of foreigner bodies...so feral. It would be a vacation to bed among her own race for an afternoon.

"No, I don't want to go," yawned Yukiko. "I have wash to do. It's a good day to hang out things to dry." She stepped from the bus to take the handle of a bucket, one of several tucked under the axle of the vehicle. "Do you want to get water with me?" The whore grumbled but picked up another bucket. Yukiko cautioned her child not to wander and the two women went to the nearby water pipe at the end of the lane. Everyone living in the converted buses got their water from the same source. It was a place to gossip and pass idle moments; the women would have

111

missed the fun of it if they had access to water in their dwellings.

The boy hadn't observed their departure. A beetle tractored to a crevice, compressed itself out of sight. How stately it had walked! Like a lacquered nobleman en route to a castle on his horse. Sitting squarely upon the ground, the boy noticed the whore gone and was pleased. He didn't like the strange words she rasped at him so often. They sounded bad. It was clear she wanted him to become friendly with strangers and invite them home. Why, when there were already so many visitors and plenty of gifts left behind in the box on the bus? The thought caused him to scamper into the bus and he pawed through the contents of a paper carton near the door to pick out a chocolate bar. The uniformed men seemed to have an inexhaustible supply of such treats. The box was filled with packs of cigarettes and chewing gum, Hersheys and cans of white rubber rings which could be unrolled and blown into powdered blimps. Life couldn't be happier unless the whore would stop pinching and nagging him. He jumped from the steps to the ground outside and tore the wrapping from the chocolate bar. It tasted wonderful, as always. He sauntered along the lane without purpose.

The drop-off for men from the military base was known to Americans as Piss Alley. A dusty half acre where trucks and jeeps could make a turnaround after depositing their passengers, it was the hub of spokes branching into the pleasure district. Surrounding building walls reeked of urine, since the men used the area as a latrine upon arrival and while waiting to be picked up once more to return to barracks or Liberty ships. Usually the section was deserted. No one hung around unless in need of a lift. When the little boy got there, a tipsy soldier was in residence, seated cross-legged in the dirt with an empty bottle at his side. The soldier saluted him.

"How ya doin', Tojo?" he asked pleasantly.

The boy wiped his sticky mouth. His tongue was too thickly coated with chocolate for speaking. He grinned at the man. The soldier grinned back.

"I'm a general, too," he said. He exhibited his chevron and declared, "General Private Johnny Levecque. Only trouble is nobody's got respect for a general private." He snickered, "Except for the ladies," and began crooning softly, "Oooh, Johnny, oooh, Johnny, how you can loooove..."

His acrid alcoholic smell made the boy blink. They all stank of it and vomited the liquid from their bottles. Why did they drink anything so awful? The soldier poked at his bottle to give it a bleary, sad inspection. An ant was staggering at the rim of its mouth.

"Shit...look at that. My lil' old jug is *kaput*." He looked at the boy. "*Kaput*. Bet you don't know what that means. It's Heinie talk for finish... *owari*... that's you guys, too. Jap and Heinie *owari*."

He winked one eye solemnly. Then the other. Off and On light signals. The boy tried to wink one of his but both shut. A finger was needed to close one singly. The soldier repeated his performance. Left, right, left, right. He and the boy smiled broadly at each other.

"Hey, you know who else does that? The King of the Ants." He raised two fingers in horns at his forehead and waggled one. "When the King's got his troops hustling bunny balls up the hill, he parks his ass on his throne and jiggles his left antenna and everybody has to push to the left." The left finger wiggled. "And when he jiggles his other antenna, everybody has to push to the right." He played it out with one finger and the other for a moment. "You know what happens when one of the ole bunny balls gets away from his troops and starts rolling down the hill at him? He goes like this..." Both fingers waved frantically. "Know what that means, Tojo?" The boy was too entranced to reply. Private Levecque manipulated his fingers wildly with a sham shout, "STOP THAT SHIT! STOP THAT SHIT!" and then subsided into a friendly contemplation of his small companion. "Whaddya think of that?"

"Shit."

He said reproachfully, "Hey, you don't want to say that, Tojo. Shit's a dirty word." Their smiles grew wider. The boy held out his hand. Private Levecque grasped it and stood shakily. With trust and warm amiability, the little boy began to lead him home.

Wanda's sister Grace was pregnant. It was irritating to hear. Wanda and Jordan had been getting the same triumphant announcements from a majority of couples in their clique. It seemed almost every woman Wanda knew was swollen in sympathy with another and she had to send amusing cards of congratulations and attend baby showers given the victims of the epidemic. Jordan was working for the plastics firm; they were mad about him. She had gotten a raise and had more responsibility at the bookstore. They should have been content but she'd caught him looking at her waistline slyly and glancing away before she'd notice.

"Jordie, why don't I get pregnant?"

He laughed. "You want to know in the middle of Central Park?"

"Be serious, Jordie."

They still practiced the habit of meeting for a hot dog lunch and beer at the zoo. Having heard the seals bark and the lions roar, they had left the melancholy animals in their inadequate cages and walked to the children's playground on the next block. Loitering beside a cement parapet, they watched kids on slides and swings; some were feeding ducklings in a pond. Jordan leaned upon his elbows as he asked, "What's your big hurry?"

"Well...everybody we know either has or is having a baby."

"So what?"

"We should have had ours by now."

"Well..." Too noncommittal, she could tell.

"You don't know how many times Mother and Daddy ask about it...and so do your parents."

"Gus and Helen have Grace to keep them happy."

"Oh, that's not enough for them. They won't be happy till Dot is married and we all have children."

"Margaret Sanger should picket Beach House."

"Jordie...I know you want us to have a family."

"Sure. But I'm not worried we won't get around to it."

114

A long silence. She said, "Maybe one of us has a problem."

"Don't be silly, Wanda. We're healthy as horses."

"That's not always sufficient."

"Honey, we're perfectly all right."

"Then why don't I get pregnant?"

He tucked her arm under his. "I'm doing the best I can. But I'll have to practice more, no?"

She refused to be kidded by him.

"We should have a checkup, Jordie. I mean it."

"But there's nothing wrong with us."

"I wish I were sure of that."

"Okay, come on home and we'll prove it." He nuzzled her neck but she drew away, unwilling to be demonstrative in public.

"I have to get back to Brentano's."

"And I have to get back to the salt mine. I came in from Long Island to get the research reports on the cellulosics. The company is going to branch out."

She sighed. His work was a mystery to her, filled with impossible names and magical new applications. She wouldn't be surprised if he said the moon was made of plastic. "Jordie...think about this, will you?"

"Sure, honey." They walked to the Plaza fountain before parting, she to continue along Fifth Avenue to the bookstore and he to catch the subway for the Island. Using a mock growl as his farewell, he promised to see her in bed. She returned to work faintly reassured. It was months before the situation changed.

They hadn't discussed the subject since that day in the park. It came up again out of the blue, when she was being treated to a drink at Cherio's, a place with a "name." Jordan had been elevated to an executive position and wanted to celebrate. They were served by Mario, a talented bartender featured in columns, and his martinis were very dry, very strong, and very large. The olives were intriguing. They tasted like cocktail onions.

"I know how he does it, Jordie." Mario had been smug about the unusual flavor and refused to divulge his secret.

"What do you think he does?"

"Easy. He soaks the olives in jars of juice after he's taken the onions out. I'll bet he made a mistake one night and put his leftover olives in the wrong jar."

115

Jordan arched his eyebrows at her. "Excellent deduction, my dear Holmes."

"Elementary, Watson, elementary." She tapped her glass with her wedding ring. When Mario looked over, she raised a toothpick. He collected a few olives on a paper coaster and brought them to her with a flourish. "Thank you, Mario. We can't resist them." She flashed her choicest smile to prevent him from knowing that they knew what he thought they didn't know. The martinis were affecting her.

"It's not my problem," Jordan said into his glass.

"What?"

He repeated the words slowly, thoughtfully, as if making up his mind. "It's not my problem, Wanda."

The change in him was confusing. What happened to the smile and the bantering tone? "What are you talking about?" she asked innocently.

"Dr. Sorenson says I'm okay. I can father a child if I want."

"But that's what we've been..." It hit with a sledgehammer blow. In her middle, in the deepest reaches of her body. Low. Where the soft dark waits. Panic took over. If he was all right, then she was accused of being less than whole. Mother of his children was a pedestal she'd firmly owned since they met. And he was taking it from her with this subdued revelation, slipped in unexpectedly and under cover of his better news. She couldn't be less than a woman...and, aching, she asked him to say it was not true. "You saw Dr. Sorenson without me?"

"I didn't make a specific appointment. It just happened one day when I was near his office and I thought what the hell, I may as well find out about myself."

Not that way, Jordie. Not that casually. But to see about those sons and daughters you were promised. To find them. To make sure they were there. And that's why it shouldn't have been done alone. Alone, to leave her alone. She stabbed at each pitless olive on the coaster, spearing them into a row savagely until one split to show its emptiness...and pitying it and herself, she dropped the rest to the bartop. "So," she said resentfully, staring at the broken halves, small, hollowed-out cups of nothing, "so...it's my fault." The worst part was feeling so guilty.

"Don't start jumping to conclusions, Wanda. For Christ's

116

sake, we haven't the slightest idea there's anything wrong. I'm just saying I got checked and now it's your turn."

Unconvinced and defensive, she snapped, "Doctors have been looking in and out and up and down me since I was born and none have said a word about my being unable to have a baby."

"Listen, you were the one who said we should get a once-over."

"I can't be at fault!" she protested with anguish. "My sister didn't have a problem, so why should I?"

"Nobody said you did!"

"You're saying it!"

"I'm not!"

A disapproving query of a look from Mario was ignored. She flinched from Jordan's touch. He said, "We're having a fight, Wanda."

"I know we are."

"I don't like it. Do you?"

"No." Her security disintegrating, she began to tremble. "I love you, Jordie. I don't want to fight with you."

"Then let's stop."

"Oh, Jordie," she pled unhappily, "Jordie... it can't be me." Intuition said otherwise.

"Honey," he soothed, "that's what you'll find out, just like me. See? I found out I'm all right. So will you."

"Yes, Jordan." She clammed up tightly, thinking, that's how it is: He's all right, I'm all wrong. Jordan called for his tab and learned Mario's martinis were also very expensive. Jordan left a tip and they went outside. New York was indifferent; she expected it to have changed somehow. They walked rapidly to the IRT subway stop on Lexington Avenue and rode to Grand Central, where they switched to the shuttle for West Side trains. It was easier underground; the thunder of the trains numbed her. A falling away inside returned, thorning and twisting into a widening uterine chasm. Larger than outside. Invisible. Heavy as lead. Jordan was all right. All right. All allrightallrightallrightallright. Words always formed out of the rattle of the wheels on the tracks. But it was a rotten game now. The words wouldn't change. It was frightening.

They said little at home while she prepared dinner. Without appetite, she forced herself to cook and serve the meal, giving herself a portion to congeal on her plate.

117

Jordan said with maddening offhandedness, "Sorenson asked when you'd be in for your examination."

She answered tersely, "I'll see someone soon."

"Not Dr. Sorenson?"

"No. I want a specialist. So give me a chance to ask around and find the best one."

Everyone was asked. All her friends. Those with babies and those without. Names were given; a choice had to be made.

And she put it off week to week because she was afraid to know the truth.

Snow drifted over the bus, mounding upon its roof in a thick layer which served to insulate the interior against the cold. The stove inside steamed the windows behind their doubled shutter of matting and beside it sat the child and his mother and the whore. Each was busy with something: the six-year-old boy eating a hot bowl of boiled rice, Yukiko mending personal clothing, and the whore painting faces on a row of slender dolls. The only sound was that of *hashi* scraping the sides of the bowl and an occasional hacking cough the whore would not cover with her hand. She cursed when spittle fell across the dolls; it smeared the paint and she was obliged to cleanse any spoiled face entirely and begin anew.

Seeing the boy set aside his bowl, Yukiko reproved him. "You haven't finished eating."

"I want a chocolate," he replied.

"You ate the last bar. There's none left." He regarded her suspiciously. She pointed toward the paper carton near the door. "See for yourself. We haven't been given any in days."

The whore shifted in place uneasily. Next, the woman would be telling her son that *she* was responsible! It wasn't her fault there was a shortage of men these days. It was this abominable weather. And she hadn't been eating chocolate. The men lost the habit of bringing it with them at every visit; after all, it wasn't the brat they sought for company. A cough wracked her and she bent to one side to direct it toward the floor. The row of tiny faces smiled at her optimistically.

"Tell me a story," demanded the child of his mother.

"You haven't finished your rice, Joe."

He swept his bowl to his chin and looked at Yukiko eagerly. She knew so many wonderful tales! He offered to eat an additional bit for each sentence she gave in exchange.

"Well, then...but I won't act it out." She had danced hundreds of roles for him, becoming a plum tree or a goddess, a mad cart man or an evil spirit, or cantered like a warrior riding against demons. It couldn't be done with needle and thread in hand. He raised some rice to his mouth expectantly.

"Are we going to hear about your famous Joe-dan-ash again?" carped the whore scornfully.

Yukiko retorted, "Perhaps. At least he's not imaginary like the others."

The whore's tongue protruded as she painstakingly brushed a set of delicate eyebrows into position upon a bald white forehead. "He may as well be."

"You know nothing of Joe-dan-ash, so you cannot speak against him."

"Did he pay you? Does he send money? You had best learn another trade to support you in your old age...as I am doing."

"I don't have to take in extra work for myself now."

Joe's piping voice interrupted their squabble. "Tell me about Joe-dan-ash!"

The women relaxed. The whore really didn't mind listening to Yukiko's fanciful stories when occupied with the dolls. Hours flew faster when thoughts were diverted from present concerns. She would have listened to their raucous radio had it not failed when the storm began. It merely buzzed when she tried the knobs. *"Hai,* let us hear about the father of your son."

"Well, then. Before Joe-dan-ash sailed to Beikoku, we spent much time together exploring our island forest." Stitch, stitch, stitch. She sewed the path to the waistband and stopped to tend the knot. Biting the thread to sever it, she bethought herself of another knot...which she had

119

undone so quickly, fearing the drawstring would need breaking if it did not slip loose... and it came free and she had brazenly taken the hand of Joe-dan-ash and looked her fill upon his nude body... Yukiko brought her knees closer together.

"And one day, we found a dark cave we hadn't seen before. There was a ghost guarding it to prevent anyone from stealing a treasure hidden there. Joe-dan-ash wanted to get the treasure for me and started a big fight with the ghost. Oh, how they raced from tree to bush and leaped from one rock to another! I was frightened and hid myself under some leaves. I could see how furious the ghost was and I was very afraid Joe-dan-ash might be killed."

"Oh, Joe-dan-ash could never be killed!"

She urged the boy to have another bite of rice. "You and I know that," she agreed, "but the ghost didn't. Well, then... the ghost roared and waved his swords like a horrible samurai and tried to cut off Joe-dan-ash's head! Your father had to be quicker than a tiger to escape. Then, because Joe-dan-ash was clever, the ghost was led closer and closer to the edge of a deep ravine. So deep it had no bottom! I thought they would both fall into it but Joe-dan-ash tricked the ghost into charging at him and stepped aside at the very last instant and the ghost plunged over the side!"

Joe cheered, his eyes large and shining. "Joe-dan-ash always wins," he said with pride.

"Always," Yukiko answered. "That's because he's different from other men. We don't see his like here..." And she fell into a reverie and thought, I miss you, Joe-dan-ash. Where are you, Joe-dan-ash? Where are you? It was the tug at her sleeve which brought her back.

"The treasure. What happened to the treasure?"

"Ah... it turned out to be... a lovely crane, made of purest ivory, and when Joe-dan-ash touched it, the crane sprang to life and flew far, far away." She patted her son and took the empty bowl from him. So many tales about Joe-dan-ash had been invented to tell the boy... and though they were sometimes repetitious, they kept the image of him alive. She and the boy had glorified Joe-dan-ash into their own hero. As for seeing him again—well, such an affair takes time to arrange. Was her poor message still seeking him? America was so huge and half the world away...farther than the flying crane of her story.

The whore examined the sewing Yukiko had done and remarked upon the daintiness of the stitches. "You would be good at this work I do," she observed.

"You think I might be?" Yukiko was flattered to have her simple domestic skill admired.

"Hai. If you like, I'll show you how to paint these doll faces and you could sew some of their clothing."

"Oh, it would take too long to instruct me. I know you must have them ready for the merchant to collect."

"You're quick. Look how well you've been doing at your English lessons. None of the rest of us know as much." The whores of the district hired students to tutor them in the language of the foreigners. It was considered a business expense for most; Yukiko did it to be ready for Joe-dan-ash.

"You're too kind," Yukiko replied. "I'm not a scholar."

"Let me teach you this."

"It won't be a bother?"

It would get part of the whore's work done for her. She said, *"Iie...,* I'm bored and it would give me pleasure to explain how it is done. Should I need help, you'll be able to paint a few and sew. Think, together we'll have the work finished when the merchant arrives!"

Yukiko hesitated. Joe was entertaining himself with discarded condom cans and foil. She moved nearer to the whore. "Is it not difficult?" Yukiko asked. The whore gave her the paintbrush and guided her fingers over the outline of a mouth. It was alive at once, richly red and curving slightly upward at the corners. Yukiko begged to be allowed to do another. And putting aside their usual resentment of each other, the women sat like two loving sisters conducting a festival of dolls.

121

In a room she hated for its deception, a room painted pink and light blue, papered with fiddling cats and moon-straddling cows, Wanda was restrained by a cheerful nurse with hands of steel, held down while a fluid was forced and an implosive cramping agony was traced by an unfeeling fluoroscopic screen. The nurse insisted melodically it would soon be over. But it wasn't. It hurt more after they stopped and the technicians left to give her moments alone to recuperate; and hurt even more after the nurse, her manner funereal as they prepared to make the verdict known, returned to ask if she was ready to see the doctor again. And she dressed fearfully and went into his office to sit facing gold-trimmed tableaus of his children lined above the desk.

He said she couldn't have any.

Their images tumbled into tears where lullabies start and end. Gone were those she imagined, gone daughters and sons; gone the family promised, gone love's exquisite proofs and proud exhibitions. She wouldn't fulfill whispered giggling sessions of dreams spun with her sisters, wouldn't call Jordie and parents with great excitement and pleasure, wouldn't choose names from lists of names, wouldn't buy small blankets and powders and diapers, crib or carriage, wouldn't nuzzle at a soft body and kiss each little limb, knead it lovingly with oil and feel the sensuality of taking care of a form she'd made, another human bright with newness...a baby. Their baby.

Wouldn't.

The doctor said she couldn't.

She didn't remember leaving the office. Jimmy and the entertainer were eating omelettes at a table near the door when she entered La Petite Couvée. The bistro was dim, lit by one light behind the bar. Both men stood, napkins in hand, wondering what she was doing there so early in the day. Folded clean tablecloths were piled on a chair between them; the luncheon crowd wasn't due for another hour.

"Hello, Jimmy...Frank." She knew the actor's name now. She and Jordan had been by a couple of evenings; they were old friends, as New Yorkers go.

"Madame Asche...you wish the lunch?"

She imitated his accent to seem light hearted. "No, Jimmy. I wish zee drink." Raindrops dripped from her coat in a circle around her sodden shoes. She had walked to the place.

The men didn't know what to do with her. Politeness indicated she should be asked to sit with them but she looked too strange. Ill, perhaps. When she pulled her coat from her shoulders, Jimmy took it from her to hang on a hook on the wall.

"Thanks. I've been..." Dazed, she waved at their table and continued with another sentence. "I'd like to sit down."

Frank hurriedly removed the tablecloths and she flopped into the chair gloomily. Their unfinished meal made her gag.

"You don't have to stop eating because of me."

"I get your drink," Jimmy said. He took a step, then paused to ask, "What you like...cocktail?"

"Anything. Oh...not anything." She began to cry and said, "Yes, get me a double Scotch or something."

Hesitant, Jimmy went to the bar. Frank reached toward her but she spurned him. "Mrs. Asche...it's none of my business, but..."

"It's none of your business, Frank." She'd like to have crept into his arms for comfort but he wasn't Jordie...and if he had been, she couldn't tell Jordie yet...couldn't tell yet and wanted to be heard.

Jimmy brought the whiskey to the table in a large shot glass, along with a tumbler of ice cubes, a paper napkin, and a stirrer. He put them before her, saying, "Something else, madame? Something from the kitchen?"

The double Scotch spilled as she picked it up. The trembling hadn't stopped, had remained since Jordie said he was all right. Jimmy patted the wetness with his own napkin. "You don't have what else I want, Jimmy..." Almost telling him. She drank, making a face over the liquor's rake, then set the glass down. "This will do for now."

The men resumed their seats slowly. Frank took up his fork to eat while Jimmy watched her fish a handkerchief from her purse. A hand mirror smirked at her as she

dabbed her eyes. "God," she wailed, "I look like shit."
Frank ate. Jimmy watched. She drank again. All of it,
without the grimace. The Scotch went down, pulling hurt
and condemnation after itself to the soft, useless dark inside.

"It's not a nice day," Jimmy observed tactfully.

"No. It's not a nice day. In fact, it's a very, very rotten
day. May I have another of these, Jimmy?"

He leaped up, trotted to the bar and was back with the
bottle. He sat, filled her shot glass and said, "It will rain
till tomorrow. I don't think we get the business today."

"I did," she said and began to laugh. "That's terrible.
I don't feel funny. Frank, know anybody who needs a few
bad jokes?" She picked up her drink to swallow a small
amount. "That's me, bad jokes unanimous."

"What's the matter, Mrs. Asche?" He had the plump
cheeks of an Irish squirrel...or a confessional priest...and
she wanted to be heard.

"I've been..." The searing weakness was felt. And the
degrading stirrups. And the hurt which needed expunging.
"I've been to see a highly recommended gynecologist.
You'd be amazed how many of my girlfriends swear by
him. I don't know why they like him...his fingers are
cold."

Frank pretended not to hear and ate faster. Jimmy's
reflection and hers in the bar mirror excluded the actor.
They could have been alone; Jimmy, dapper in his three-
piece suit, leaning upon an elbow toward her solicitously,
gray wings at his temples, and herself scrunched into an
abject bundle...Freud through the looking glass.

"Madame, nothing is so bad it does not get better. You
are not well?"

"Do you have children, Jimmy?" she asked.

He smiled and tugged at a breast pocket. "Ah, *voilà!*
I show you!"

"Please don't. I don't want to see them. I thought maybe
you'd be able to understand what it is to be told you can't
...have...can't...have...any."

"Oooh, madame..."

"At least he doesn't think I can. Or I don't think he
thinks so. Have you ever listened to somebody and not
heard what they have to say because it's too important
and you don't want to hear what you don't want to hear?

124

Words are like knives, *oviducts* and *pelvic* and *Fallopian* and none of it meaning babies to me. He went into a very detailed description and I listened *so* hard! I don't know what he said, Jimmy. I don't know. But it meant I couldn't have a baby."

She cried again. Frank cleaned his plate, got up and carried it to the kitchen as the rain stampeded before the wind outside, splattering on the sidewalk wildly as applause, hurriedly as his exit. It made her laugh crazily, and she blew her nose. Jimmy nodded at her solemnly. "Does your 'usband know you are 'ere?"

"No." *He does not know and he does not know.*

"You wish to call him?"

"No."

"*Bien.* But you should."

"No."

Frank didn't return. She supposed he was lurking in the kitchen, waiting for Jimmy to get rid of her. It was kind of him. Usually a crowd gathers to see the disaster.

"I will call your 'usband for you, yes?"

"No."

"What can I do?" he asked courteously, knowing there was nothing. And accustomed to diplomatic compromise, he suggested, "There is always the adoption."

Her glass made wet circles on the bare tabletop. A phone number was inked into the ugly round of cheap plywood, the words CALL ME underlined beside the digits. Would it be like Alice in Wonderland and make her a different size if she used the number? No, it should say DRINK ME. She drank.

"It is a solution, madame. A child can be adopted."

The glass blurred watery ovals on the soft wood. It wasn't a solution. It wouldn't be hers, not the child which was a blend of herself and Jordan, not the grandchild expected by her parents, but some teenage slut's discard with God knows what awful hereditary traits. The mistake of one female substituting for the defect of another. It wouldn't work. If she couldn't have Jordie's baby, she didn't want any ... *didn't want any* ... words she'd shrieked under that torture because it seemed to be like giving birth and was too much to ask of anyone and she didn't care if she never had children—and it came true.

"I want my own baby."

125

"Is it possible there 'as been a misjudgment, madame? Per'aps *monsieur le docteur* is wrong."

A farfetched lifeline. She clung to it, needing it for Jordan as much as for herself. "He could be, couldn't he?"

"Oui. My Corinne did not 'ave babies right away and then, poof, she could not turn them off." He was proud of himself. "Even now, we use the birth control."

"What did she do?"

"Oh, it was Corinne's *docteur!* Madame, it is not for me to discuss these matters with you. Would you like to talk to my Corinne?"

"You say her doctor is very good?"

"Madame," he beamed proudly, "we 'ave four children."

"How may I reach her?"

He gave her a card from a vest pocket. "On the left...my 'ome telephone. She is seldom out, unless to come 'ere."

"Thank you, Jimmy." The card went into her purse, handled like a relic.

"Madame, 'e is not a young man, this *docteur.*"

She was able to smile. He watched her make herself presentable with the mild interest of a man with none for her. No one was lovely as his Corinne, who wore no makeup at all.

She rose. Fetching her coat, he helped her into it. When she attempted to pay for the drinks, he waved the money aside. At the door, he asked if she wanted a cab. They were inching by in jammed traffic, filled to capacity. She refused, unwilling to wait, and ran into the rain to begin her relentless journey from one doctor to another. He thought sorrowfully that she should have discussed this with her husband...but saloonkeepers' wisdom taught that everyone goes to the dispassionate ear with intimate revelations. Husbands, wives, lovers, *papa* and *maman* were displaced by professions of listeners, those wearing the skirts of *le bon Dieu* or adorned with doctoral degrees or, more often, tending bar. Well, there was a child for her somewhere. She had only to see it.

Yukiko had learned to call the private Johnny. As his visits increased, tiny responses flickered within her body. It may have been because Joe was sent outside whenever the two women had company, or when men arrived at late hours, Joe was asleep. She didn't think Joe knew exactly what took place in the bus beyond thinking it a game similar to the wrestling bouts she sometimes played with him. He was outside now, rattling the calm of twilight with running after children in the lane. The whore was being discreet, sitting upon the steps of the bus with her back to Yukiko and the soldier. A column of cigarette smoke spiraled above her head to waft toward them and the heat of the stove, which kept the draft at bay. Johnny lay contentedly upon the *futon* while Yukiko washed herself. As she slipped into a robe, he caught her ankle.

"What would happen if you took the rest of the night off?"

She combed her hair with long strokes of a brush he had given her. "Oh ... I would study. My English is getting *ichi ban*, yes?"

"Suppose you put it off."

The brush stopped, then went on. "I must learn! Much better, so I may speak as you do!"

"Better, I hope. Your kid's talking like me already."

"Yukiko thinks she's going to America!" The whore blew smoke over her shoulder as she interrupted the conversation.

"Yeah? No shit."

"Maybe," Yukiko corrected quickly. "Maybe someday."

"I hope you're not taking off right away."

"You make fun of me, Johnny."

He stroked her anklebone lightly with a finger. "What I'm trying to find out is if we can spend the rest of the night together."

"You have yen, you stay!" the whore exclaimed at the door.

127

"Please to mind your own business," Yukiko retorted.

"If I had any, I wouldn't be sitting here with nothing to do..." The smoke curled lazily and made her cough. Her chin dug into her sweater. She hadn't been with a man for an entire night for a long time, she sulked. They didn't seem to want to pay the cost.

Yukiko removed her foot from Johnny's hand and gave him his clothing. He sat up to dress. "I don't think you want to stay all night, Johnny," she said considerately, knowing she had to ask a high price.

"You can let your partner there know I've got yen—but not the kind she's talking about. I have a yen to take you somewhere...just like a date in the States."

It was a mystery! "Where do you want to go? We do everything here."

"No, I don't mean more screwing around. I want to take you out. We can go eat in a joint you like, okay?"

"You're hungry? Ah, now I know! We have food here."

From the door, "You pay, you get!"

"Blow it out your ass," he retorted good-naturedly. As the whore cackled, he resumed his explanation to Yukiko. "You don't get it, Yuki. I want to go eat...then take in a show, just like Stateside. That's what we do on dates back home. Take our girl out and have a good time."

The women were fascinated. They stared at him, darted glances at each other and stared at him again.

"Well? What do you say?"

"But I have to be here."

"Shit, the other broad can take over for you, can't she?"

It was too strange to contemplate without smiling. She consulted in whispers with the whore. "May I go with him?"

"It's not worth your while."

"I would like to go."

"Then go! It's your loss...but I won't look after your *ainoko* for you!"

"Hai." She kept her smile when she refused the soldier. "My son can't be left behind."

"That's no sweat. We'll take Tojo with us." Standing, he towered over her. She thought it over, then decided yes. Feeling he was eager to start, she moved to the doorway but he restrained her with a hand. "Whoa, Yuki, you can't waltz into a restaurant dressed like that." She was flustered. What had come over her? Murmuring apologies, she changed into a dress and warm coat, then stepped barefoot into a pair of shoes.

"Okay like this?" she asked.

"Itchy-bon-bon," he drawled. They went outside, raising the grumbling whore from her roost. Yukiko called into the lane for Joe. He was there immediately, flushed with chasing anyone who'd run from him.

"Come," she said. "Johnny is taking us on a date."

They ate in a dingy restaurant in the theatrical district. The place was dark, smelled of kerosene from the lighting, and the service was slovenly done. Johnny put one of the lamps in the center of their table; the glow turned his guests more golden than they were. He tried without success to imagine himself on a date back home. Giving up, he enjoyed what he had and devoured every course without seeing what it was, mostly tasting of salt. Yukiko liked being waited upon; it was possible to feel upper class. Thirsty, Joe was given sake to drink from the warm bottle on the table. The strength of the wine went to his head swiftly. The meal was finished all too soon.

A movie down the street beckoned with neon tubing around its sign. They strolled to it, the boy skipping ahead to pore over displays of pictures and posters in front. He danced with excitement to see men in armor and bowmen on horseback engaged in combat. Yukiko and Johnny stopped to look at the photographs, too. It was evidently a bloodthirsty presentation.

"Hey, you don't want to see this, do you? Tony Curtis is playing not far from here."

"Hai?" Yukiko was fond of American movies, which were dubbed into her own language. She was willing to go but Joe wouldn't hear of it. They had to restrain him from dashing into the theater without them.

"Okay," laughed the soldier. "Shit on Tony Curtis. I can't understand him in Japanese anyway." And he paid their admission and they groped into the dark interior, waited for their eyes to adjust and found seats near the screen. Action tumbled across it; swords, blood spurting, heads rolling, confrontations every other frame. Powerful men with scowls and styled hair growled at each other; fragile women shrieked and submitted to rape through a gauze filter. It was standard local film, with nothing new

129

to recommend it but an athletic young leading man. Jihei Segawa was making his debut in films. Johnny bent to Yukiko's ear. "Think he's better than Tony Curtis?" She nodded yes vigorously. She thought him handsomer than the American actor. Oiled pectorals and biceps straining, nostrils flaring, Segawa had just dispatched his sixteenth rascal and was stalking his next opponent.

"Joe, do you like him?" she asked. And got no response.

Joe had fallen asleep beside her. The sake and stormy film had done him in. They allowed him to sleep till the showing was over, and Johnny carried him back to the bus in his arms. She was beset with unsettling thoughts on the way. This man was kind and didn't behave like a customer. He wanted to be more. Did she want him to be more? She often substituted the face of Joe-dan-ash for his during their intimacies, but it seldom remained. This man was swarthy in feature and had dark brown hair. He confused the memory. Yet she liked him. What had gotten into her? His gentleness, perhaps.

She continued to be troubled whenever he saw her again. It made her do things to please him which were not done for other men. The other whore thought they were courting.

It was another Sunday and Jordan was at supper alone with his parents. His pensive mood bothered the old couple. During strained gaps in the intermittent conversation, they eyed each other and wondered if they dared talk about his wife. His absent wife. They could not help feeling she thought herself too good for them since she preferred not to come to supper these days.

"You're not hungry?"

Jordan replied, "You always give me too much, Mom."

Katy said with unabashed love, "I couldn't give you enough of everything I want for you."

They were a family portrait at the kitchen table: mother, father, and son. A shred of the traditional family they desired. Casey was done with his plate. Reaching for his pipe, he tried to be casual. "Well, here we are. As we used to be when you were a boy. And here we are again, with God's blessing."

Jordan stiffened. He'd run out of apologies for Wanda's absences and was afraid they were going to criticize her again. "Gus is trying to give us money again," he said in English. It was his means of being defensive; by discarding their language he aligned himself more with his wife.

"That's not the practice of a rich man."

"Pop, he heard my company would let me buy into a partnership if I could swing it."

"Is that what you want to do?"

"We'll be in a boom bigger than you ever saw soon. Everything is going plastic. I could become rich if I own a piece of the action."

"What will Mr. Fleming get out of it?"

"Oh, I'd pay him back with interest. He's doing it for Wanda's sake."

"You're going to take his money, then?"

"Nothing was definite. They just hinted at a deal. I'd have to find out how serious they were."

"Well, they thought enough of you to hire you straight out of that school you were in."

"I've done a lot for the business in the past couple of years."

"Why can't they just make you a partner if you're so valuable to them?"

"It's not done like that, Pop."

"Well, what do I know? In the Old Country you couldn't get a commission in the military without buying it. It must be the same here."

"Not quite, Pop. They don't make room for you unless you've got the talent. I'm the best around."

"Then they ought to just make you a partner." Casey lifted himself from the chair and went to get a humidor from a cabinet above the sink. Standing there, he filled his pipe, lit it with a wooden match and leaned against the drainboard to enjoy the aromatic smoke. He knew Jordan was trying to lead them away from the subject uppermost on their minds. Katy was too quiet. What was she thinking?

131

She was blunt about it. "Why is your wife always at the doctor?"

"Nothing to get excited about, Mom. Wanda is getting checkups."

"She has cancer."

"Oh, my God, no! Where'd you get that idea?"

"Nobody goes to a doctor so many times for what you call the checkups."

"Look, we're trying to have a baby."

"The doctor doesn't make the baby."

"Okay. It hasn't been wham, bam, thank you, ma'am, so we're having her looked at to find out what's wrong."

"I tell you what's wrong: She doesn't want a baby."

Jordan got angry. "Why the hell would she go through those examinations if she doesn't?"

"You know she has examinations? You go with her?"

"I don't have to go with her."

Katy was triumphant. "There! How do you know she goes at all?"

"Because I get the damned bills and have to pay them, that's why!"

"Don't shout at your mother, Jordan," Casey reprimanded him. "I can still give you a clout you'd remember."

"Sorry. She got me hot."

"Watch your tongue."

"Okay, okay. Sorry."

The blows of her words were meant well, just as the leather strap had been for his own good years ago. Katy continued, "We think she prevents herself from becoming pregnant."

"It's not so. She's going through hell just so we can find out what's wrong."

"Maybe she should try another doctor."

"Mom, she's seeing more than one now. Get off my back."

The disgruntled pause of people injuring each other in spite of themselves settled upon them, but an insidious urge drove Katy on. "What happens if you find out nothing can be done? What then?"

"It won't be the end of the world."

"You don't care if you have children or not?"

"Christ, I care! I want kids just like everybody does. You want me to dump her and find somebody else?"

"This problem wouldn't exist if you had married a Catholic...a Polish girl."

Oh, balls, he thought. They hadn't gotten over his marrying in a different Church...and that led to more and more...and he wasn't going to try to reason with them. He decided to go home. When he got up, his mother pulled him forcibly back onto his seat.

"No, we aren't saying you should leave her. We know you love the girl and maybe you aren't able to believe she wouldn't want to bother with babies. Not even for you."

"Not Wanda. We've been dreaming about a kid from the day we married. Longer, in fact." Yes, longer. From the first day. When she asked to see him again and he knew he'd see her waking and sleeping...and had no doubts about the outcome. "Mom, she loves me...she's doing her best. It's not her fault she's not pregnant."

"Then forgive us for holding evil thoughts about her. But we wanted you to know how we thought it was."

"No. You forgive me. I shouldn't have lost my temper. This whole month has made Wanda and me jumpy and that's why she hasn't been coming to supper with me. She's sure she's lousy company and she doesn't want to talk about her problems."

"If not us, in whom can she confide?"

"She calls her folks in California, or they call us. How do you think Gus found out about the company's offer? Look, she has somebody. She has me to talk to about it." She hadn't said much to him. Only that she was going to have his baby, come hell or high water. "Please...give the doctors a chance to see what they can do."

"I pray for their success." Katy crossed herself several times and kissed her thumb. Casey, puffing thoughtfully, recalled another thing from his past.

"When we lived in the Old Country, it sometimes happened that a woman proved to be barren..."

"Pop, knock it off. Wanda's going to be okay."

"Shush. I'm merely telling what we in the village did. To bring joy to her family and to ease her misery, the woman was given custody of one of the children from an abundant family to have live with her and to be raised as her own. Of course, there was no question the child belonged to someone else, but she would be content and her

133

husband was content, and someone had one less mouth to feed and was also content."

"Pop, this isn't the Old Country."

"No, but you can do something on that order. You could adopt children."

The silence could have been cut with a knife. He looked at his wife. Was it wrong of him to say such a thing to their son? He returned his gaze to Jordan.

"Well, you haven't said anything. It's not a dumb green-horn idea, is it?"

Nervous, Katy erupted. "Don't call yourself names, you booby!" He didn't reply. He was waiting for Jordan to say something. Anything.

Jordan squirmed on his chair for a moment. "Listen. It's too soon to talk about anything like that."

Anything. There was Casey's anything and he didn't like it. "Why too soon?" he demanded.

"We haven't given up. Wanda would hit the ceiling if I said a word about adoption now."

Katy got up to clear the dishes from the table. She meticulously scraped leftovers into bowls she'd store in the refrigerator. Excuses again, she thought. If the girl couldn't be approached to take in a child, she didn't want one at all. Surely Jordan must comprehend the obvious. That's what one gets for marrying out of his own. He didn't speak Polish anymore but talked with them in English. It wasn't right. Their son was forgetting his heritage.

Puffing his pipe, Casey made room at the sink for his wife. Having had the thought, he was dandling a child on his knees already and convincing himself it was truly of family stock. What's an orphan or abandoned child but what you make of it? "I would give it a try, Jordan."

"I don't think so, Pop. She's not...not open to suggestions these days."

"Suggestions? You refer to something so important as a suggestion?"

Wearied, Jordan said, "Pop, if I did ever bring it up, I'll have to find the right moment, the right day."

"And how will you know when that is?"

Jordan refused to answer. Nothing more was said on the subject until after he went home. They kissed him good night and were sorry to have upset his evening. He said

134

he wasn't upset and would see them the next weekend. His step wasn't jaunty as he left.

Katy put her dishes away; Casey sat smoking at the table. When she seated herself beside him, she was peeved.

"He won't talk to the girl about it."

"I bet you."

"Then he'll find out she wants nothing to do with babies no matter what."

"I tell you, that's doesn't enter into it."

"Oh? And why not?"

"Because a man wants his heir. After all, what is marriage for?"

"These modern boys and girls marry for companionship, not heirs."

"Nobody troubles a priest if they want to tickle and slap for the fun of it. A man marries to beget sons and daughters. You hear him? He's going to be a partner and make money. He needs an heir to claim it."

"In that case, he married the wrong girl."

"No, I believe as he does about the doctors. And we must believe she wants a child."

Katy agreed only to keep peace between them. He could never understand a woman's instinct. He was as foolish as his son. How could she show them the truth about the girl? "We'll have to do something to help our son."

"What can we do? We can't speak to the girl for him."

"We've been at fault, Casimir. We should think kindly of her and express our love and accept hers in return. We'll have to coax her into joining us on Sundays again—no, we'll beg her to do it—and then not a word of criticism or adoptions."

"And how are you going to get onto the subject of children if you don't discuss that with her?"

She smiled fondly at him. Men and their straightforward thinking. "Leave it to me," she said.

Reaching the top-floor landing, Wanda caught her breath sharply as she saw a silent figure rise from the steps leading to the roof. It was Katy, serene with purpose, purse under arm, braided hair tidily fixed into a bun at the back of her head.

"Oh, my God, you gave me a scare!" Wanda exclaimed. She leaned weakly against the stairwell wall to recuperate, then asked, "How long have you been sitting there?"

"I not wait long," Katy replied in heavily accented English, smiling with the timidity of a stranger.

Wanda reached into her bag for her key. Her hand trembled badly, partly from the experience and partly by the confrontation with this uninvited guest. Struggling with the lock on the door, she was reminded of the unused ones at home. Home? Why was California always home and not New York? Keys weren't used at home, no, never, and anybody walked in and out without worry. Biting her lip nervously, she pushed the door open and said, "Come on in." They entered quickly, the girl shutting the door while the woman gave the room that intimidating wicked inspection one housekeeper unfailingly makes of another's domain. Wanda said, "Make yourself comfortable."

"Dziękuję, pani."

Katy was hesitant about choosing a seat. The bed doubling as a couch repelled her; a low cloth hassock positioned before a television console was too informal. Wanda solved her dilemma by unfolding a hardwood slat chair for her use. The women shared a disavowing shrug over it.

"Well, it's practical. There's a set, four chairs and a bridge table. They come out if we have company or if we eat here, and they go back into the closet after breakfast." With a wry grimace, Wanda added, "There are days I wonder if we're ever going to own any real furniture. The only decent pieces are the bed and the matching nightstand we moved over from our first apartment."

"Is all right," Katy reassured her as she sat, meekly

resting her callused palms above the purse on her lap, one hand cupped over the other as if holding a small thing captive.

Wanda agonized that she hadn't straightened the room earlier. Nothing was put away. The sink looked like a garbage can. She edged toward it to block it from Katy's view, knowing it had been seen anyway. "May I get you anything...?" Wanda asked, leaving the sentence hanging. She never knew what to call her mother-in-law—not *Mother*, not *Katy*, and *Mrs. Asche* was what people called herself. So Wanda didn't use any name when speaking to her, just left a little blank space at the end of her words for the woman to fill in as she pleased.

"Dziękuję, nic."

Wanda understood that much by now. The first word was "thank you" and the other meant "no" or "nothing"; negative, anyway. Slyly closing the screening shutters to conceal her kitchen, she apologized lamely, "Excuse the mess. I had to rush out to an appointment this morning."

"I know you not go to job today."

"Oh? How did you know?"

"My baby say."

The reference to Jordie as baby was irritating. No; stupid. When would they let him grow up?

"My baby telephone, say you see doctor today."

"Why did he do that?"

"Just talk. You go?"

"Yes, I did." She went to the window to hide her feelings by fussing with the geranium plant on the sill. Well, of course they talked about her! Everybody talks about everybody. Plucking a dead leaf from a fuzzy stem, she said, "Nothing to worry about." The leaf smelled of dry dust and she shredded it into an ashtray beside the plant. "I've been going fairly regularly."

"You sick?"

Sick, yes. "No, I'm not. Just a slight problem I'm having treated...oh, let's not discuss it, okay? Tell me," she continued lightly, "what brings you over? This is such a surprise."

The reply disconcerted her more.

"You know I pray for you."

Wanda didn't want to ask why. She averted her face to watch traffic on the street through the window; the grime

137

on the glass was another mortification. "Oh, do you?" she said bleakly, thinking how stolid her mother-in-law's faith was, like that of the olive-skinned Mexican women back home—see, back home!—with crucifixes dangling from their sweating throats as they cleaned gringo houses and were nursemaids to gringo kids. They, too, didn't question their God—none of them did—didn't ask why their own went untended. They docilely accepted what He doled out for their lives and what their priests proclaimed was their lot. Threatening messages from her childhood surfaced with a vengeance—a minister promising retribution and hellfire for the commission of sins.

All of them. Spelled out in such exciting detail, she had to rush out to lustful boyfriends to try some.

That was before Jordie.

She had already been collecting guilts before then.

Katy opened her worn purse and took from it a rosary to show her. It was the identical chain of polished beads the devout display no matter where encountered. Fingering them skillfully, she held them before her with reverent regard, saying, "When pray, God gives. Sometime God not listen, you go to church, ask saint to talk for you." Her gray-blue eyes shifted from the silvered cross to the girl's stiffened back. "You don't go to church."

"No...I don't anymore." How could she when she blamed God for everything? It was all his fault.

"You like to go? I take. Always open, always priest to listen."

"I'm not Catholic."

"Yes, but you need somebody listen, no?"

As Katy replaced the rosary, Wanda chanced a look at her. There was a forced kindness emanating from her like an aura. She was attempting to make peace in her peasant way, but the rivalry between them was too strong. Katy's suppressed rejection of her as Jordan's wife had been growing more obvious. Subtle, yes. Nothing to point to when it was done. If anything, small attentions were magnified to disguise true feelings. Yet Jordan's mother was offering herself as confidante. It wouldn't work. Apart from the language barrier, they saw life differently. Wanda wished she could fling herself at Katy's feet, rest her head against her knees and cry out her resentment at being plagued by God for past misdemeanors. Oh yeah, that's what was behind it: Girls who sinned and didn't want a baby were punished by getting pregnant right away; and she was being forced to wait for hers because she wanted it so damned much.

Oh, God, I need somebody I can complain to about You! But there was no one.

No, not any of her coven of friends, not even the closest would do. They were vixenish practicing seers in a shopping-bag world, more concerned with conjuring bargains from Saks or Bonwit Teller than listening to her woes...and if they did, one drew forth astrological charts and horoscopic calculations to prove her stars were disordered, or another declared it was a result of diet and exercise and rhythm and pointed to her own swelling womb. As for the mechanical collegiate girls she knew at the bookstore, each was copy to the next, same exterior jacket, same interior substance, same disappearance act at lunchtime and closing—single girls, childless, who'd never get the aloof stone library lions to roar.

So there was no one. Not Jordie, not his mother. And not her own mother, who'd righteously remind her that, after all, though dear Jesus knows Jordan is beloved by us Flemings, it was a marriage Wanda blackmailed them into permitting and she had to suffer God's sure punishment for defying her parents and giving up her Church and Bible studies afterward.

To counter Wanda's introspection, Katy raised her voice, "When I go see Saint Antoni...sometime he not listen and I have to scold! I shake my finger at him and I say I not buy candle next time! He know when I pray, I light one candle, two candle, how many I need...because I want he listen good when I pray." She saw a flicker of impatience in Wanda and stood to conclude with mild justification, "Saints like candle, many candle." The girl said nothing; it was time to leave. Whatever she hoped to accomplish by this call could not occur. Having promised not to bring up the subject of children, she had thought to get Wanda to do it of her own volition, but like most modern girls, this one was cold. Unbelieving. And untrustworthy. That was to be seen in her avoidance of discussing her medical appointment as women of a family should have done; indeed, could not have done otherwise. Katy tucked her purse under her arm.

139

"You want me to walk you to the bus stop?"

"Dziękuję, pani." Thus declining, Katy walked to the door. Wanda remained at the window, staring, wondering what she had been after. Pausing at the threshold, Katy promised, "I gonna talk Saint Antoni ... ask he make you better ... and maybe you come my house again." She studied Wanda intently. "You come?"

Wanda stirred uncomfortably. Had she been wrong about Katy?

Katy smiled, wishing she could speak her own tongue instead of this heavy-going business of assembling the few words she knew of the girl's language—always so inadequately and sounding quite foolish—but she persisted. "You not come see us long time, I say to Casimir, I see you, see if you all right, see if you not mad on us."

"Oh, for heaven's sake, why should I be mad at you?" Wanda retorted quickly. "Come on, you're kidding, aren't you?"

"We worry you not come my house no more."

"Well ..." There wasn't an explanation she could tender gracefully. Eyes brimming due to a sense of overwhelming isolation, Wanda suffered a foreboding of worse to happen. "You really want me over?" she asked with a tremor.

"You come, yes?"

It was an evasion and Wanda said insecurely, "Okay. Sure. You don't have to bother your saint about it. I've just been so busy, that's all."

Katy's scrutiny wavered. Had she opened her arms wide only seconds sooner to invite Wanda to unburden her heart, the distressed girl would have run to her. But she hadn't. Deciding it a tiny victory, their duel could be carried out upon her own field after this, Katy was content. "I pray for you," she repeated firmly and let herself out.

As the door closed, Wanda gritted her teeth. Fighting off self-pity, she directed her annoyance at the ceiling. "That's all right, God!" she cried. "But I didn't do it for me! I did it for you. I have to show up at her boring suppers again or she'll burn Your church down with her damned candles."

And with a choking short laugh of resignation, she went to the kitchen enclosure, pulled the shutters aside and searched the shelves of the cupboard. There was a little cooking sherry left. It would do to seal the bargain.

Sometimes when Joe enticed several men to follow him, two huge fellows might take each of his hands into theirs and walk with such long strides he had to run to keep pace, and sometimes they'd lift him into the air and he'd laugh with glee as he soared over the ground. But arriving at the bus, the whore would order him away and lock the door behind the men. Or if it was his mother telling him to remain outside, it was a gentler command, yet it amounted to the same thing. He was immensely intrigued to know what they did in there.

He made a plan to find out. Behind the bus was a grid covering the rusted engine. He knew he could climb on it to see through the wide window, which needed an opening prepared in the oiled paper masking the glass from inside. It seemed he would never be able to do this without being caught; each time he loitered atop the seat at the rear, his mother thought he was playing with the stove.

"Come away from there, Joe," she said, losing patience. "You'll burn yourself and I'll have to take you to the clinic."

He stepped from the seat, but was bold enough to tear a corner of the paper as he did. Looking guiltless, he walked to stand at her side. She and the whore were packing a box of dolls; they had been quarreling about them since awakening.

"The merchant will be furious I've brought these to him," the whore lamented.

"I don't want him here to get them while I'm with Johnny. It is his last visit."

"You know the merchant likes to fuck after he's paid me for the dolls!"

"He can do it in his shop."

"His shop! Are you mad?"

"You don't have to sprawl across his counters."

"You don't have to see your soldier so early in the day."

"He asked and I agreed."

The whore slapped Yukiko's hands from the box, scorn-

141

ing her aid to continue the task herself. "You thought by granting his slightest wishes he'd be a replacement for Joe-dan-ash, didn't you?" she said meanly. "Well, don't buy your wedding kimono, because he's finished with Osaka for good. What a pleasure it would be if you'd trap some fool and leave me as I was before!"

Yukiko slid a glance at her son. Joe wouldn't see Johnny after today; his tour of duty was at an end. Had it been likely, would Joe have accepted the soldier as a father? He was fond of the man... they shared silly games and looked forward to seeing each other. But it was over. Johnny had not proposed. The ban upon marriages between troops and the Japanese was to be lifted; marriage could be possible for a man and a woman in love. But she did not delude herself. Johnny did not love her, nor she him. He was her poor substitute for Joe-dan-ash. Who did she represent to him? Oh, Joe-dan-ash, what has become of you? I miss you, Joe-dan-ash, as if it were yesterday....

"There. I'm done. The least you can do is have your *ainoko* help me to carry this."

If a look could kill! Yukiko had warned her before not to use the term. She wanted to shield Joe from it if she could. "I have an errand for him myself," she spat. "Shall I give you money to hire someone?"

The whore said nothing, thereby assenting. Yukiko got her money can and handed her a few yen. She stuffed them into her purse without thanks and picked up the box of dolls. "I'll be delayed getting back but if I should pick up a customer, you'll have to let us in. Your soldier won't like me kicking at the door while he's with you."

"The door will be open, but please don't return so soon."

She smiled disagreeably, then left the bus. Yukiko said to her son, "I'll bathe now. You can go wait for Johnny. Don't bring anyone back with him."

"I know. You told me." Joe sneaked another look at the torn oiled paper and ran to the door. He jumped over the steps, landed safely, and was one of those new jet planes zooming down the lane.

Waiting for Johnny had its drawbacks. As each young pimp checked Piss Alley for customers, they tried to intimidate the boy into leaving. Being quick, he eluded them and fled through the surrounding maze so adroitly he was again in Piss Alley within moments. Every truck and jeep got eager scrutiny. Finally, there was his friend.

"Hey, Tojo! Are you my escort today?"

"Special favor. Even if you know how to go."

"I got something special for you, too. Good-bye present." Johnny tossed him a bottle of Coca-Cola. "It's still cold. Fresh out of the PX machine."

What a treasure! Joe shook the bottle, watched the bubbles cloud inside, then secured it under his arm. Later, the cap could be pried off to drink from it but it would be fun to play with the bottle for a while. Maybe show it to his fickle playmates. Maybe not. They'd want some, too.

Johnny and the boy ambled from the traffic circle companionably. The man said he was going to miss him and was sad to be going away. He explained he had no control over his destiny, just as no one had. He had to do as he was told.

"Why? Why must you?"

"Because I'm only General Private Johnny Levecque, that's why." He had a higher rank now but they hadn't changed his name; a man must live all his life with the name he is given.

"If you were somebody else, would it be different?"

"Shit, yeah. If I was somebody else like MacArthur."

Joe thought about it. Then he said, "I'm not somebody else, but I'm different."

"What do you mean?"

He walked straighter. "I'm half American. Someday I'll go to America, too. I'll ask Ojiisan MacArthur to send me. Then I'll see you there!"

Johnny didn't want to disillusion the boy. Shit, calling MacArthur his grandfather! "Yeah, you ask him, Joe." They had reached the bus. Paper flowers were taped to the top of the frame, and the door was ajar. Johnny smiled, then knocked gently. Yukiko called a greeting and he went inside. Joe shook his bottle again. How the bubbles foamed! He almost forgot his plan. Remembering, he walked to the back of the vehicle. It was going to take stealthy climbing in order not to give himself away. He put the bottle on the ground and slowly worked himself up the grid. So slowly...sooo quietly...the metal was cooler than the bottle had been.

The highest rung of the grid placed Joe level with the

143

window; he had to sidle along it to get to the corner where he hoped to see through the tear. His curiosity was mounting. What did they do in there? Twisting awkwardly, he located the tear and pressed his eye to the window. Cold glass. Everything was cold today. What were they doing? After a few seconds, he discovered he'd been looking too high. They were closer to him and lying upon the matting before the stove. The *futon* was in place and the comforter...no, that wasn't the comforter, it was something moving. Moving...moving...moving...moving rhythmically and was General Private Johnny Levecque hurting his mother! She was open-mouthed, her eyes shut, and the man was hurting her! He was supposed to be a friend! Joe couldn't cry out, his throat stricken with shock. Pushing from the window, he fell to the ground. He scrambled upright and ran to the door of the bus, shoved it open completely and bounded inside, where he flailed at the soldier vainly. Johnny spun, caught and held him against his bare chest. Yukiko, alarmed and not seeing at once what was happening, covered her own nakedness with the comforter at her side. When she and the man had the boy well in hand, they tried to control his fury. It took shouts and shakes to get him to subside. In tears and bewilderment, Joe sat shackled by Johnny's painful fingers while his mother said she was neither hurt nor unhappy. What he saw was only what other women did, too; all women; and he would do as the soldier when he was himself a man. Joe hated the thought. Hated Johnny. Hated his mother. Hated himself. He shut his eyes tightly and plunged from their grasp. Outside, he hesitated. The Coca-Cola bottle crashed against the side of the bus as he raced from innocence.

"Mom's talking to you, Wanda."

"What? Oh...I'm sorry. I was...well, you have to tell me what she said anyway, Jordie."

It was ludicrous. The old couple spoke in their language,

144

he answered in English, and if they directed words at Wanda, they needed translation. It was a long, stupid process. She knew Katy and Casey could speak English very well but pretended they couldn't. The French are guilty of that, too. Everyone who'd been to Paris said they were...she didn't have to go that far. Jimmy's wife, the mousy Corinne, with the ancient *docteur* who was no good...she'd needed translating, too. Oh, God, wasn't there anybody worth seeing to help her? She had sat for hours in offices with women she didn't know and didn't care about, hearing their advice concerning doctors for her to see. She met those same advisers again as they also switched medicine men, beat upon other medical doors. Two years. Two years to be convinced doctors were charlatans. Her friends clucked and said she was chasing around for nothing. If they could do it, she could have babies, too. Relax, Wanda. That's when it happens. Relax. And in the meantime, enjoy. Enjoy! Relax! She couldn't without the help of a bottle. The damned things were beginning to accumulate under her sink. One after another. Empty bottles. Empty Wanda.

"Mom wants to know if you brought pictures of your sister's baby."

He didn't know how frantic she'd become. How impossible to live with herself. He didn't understand what it was to be incomplete.

"What?"

"The pictures. You were supposed to bring them."

"Oh, they're in the apartment somewhere."

"Jesus. It's only one big room. How could you misplace them?"

"She's seen them before, Jordie."

"Not Grace's baby. She's talking about Dot. Dot's baby."

"Tell her I forgot."

The Sunday suppers weren't working out. She wasn't able to please his parents; they were too sweet to her. She didn't need a scorecard to tell which team she was on. Their Slavic suspicions were loud bugle calls in their studied avoidance of her inability to get pregnant. Instead, there was heightened interest in the latest Fleming marriage, the latest family addition; more than it deserved. Pictures. Show pictures. The evening was interminable. Her nerves were giving way. Katy had served her standard hearty meal; the scent of stuffed cabbage was a suffocating canopy over the table. Sauced with tomatoes. Wanda couldn't get it down.

"Mom doesn't think you like the food."

"I'm insane about it, Jordie."

"What's the matter with you?"

They liked to play the same broken melody, like that Cracow bugler she'd been told about, the one shot in midnote by enemies attacking his town. Every Sunday she was there. The babies. Shafting her. How gracious. Polacks. They're everything people say: You don't need an enemy if you've got a Polack for a friend. Or a relative. Oh, God, she berated herself, I'm prejudiced. The whole idiotic world is prejudiced. Everybody has it in for somebody, and only because we feel so damned inadequate we have to jack ourselves up by looking down on everyone else. I hate them, I hate me, I hate—no, I don't hate you, Jordie. The drink she had at home had worn off. If she asked for one here, they'd be up in arms. Booze was for holidays and weddings and deaths and births... birth. She wasn't drinking with her former cronies, either. Their weighted breasts and creased stomachs and sniveling brats were anathema to her. None of the old gang had time to spare for leisurely lunches at Schrafft's or a stop for a cocktail somewhere. She walked the treadmill of her days alone. She shouldn't have quit her job when Jordan bought his partnership. Now that doctors were useless to her, she was bored with nothing to do. Bored to death. Without being able to give life, she was bored to death.

She stood, not caring what they thought. "I'd like to go home."

Instead of consternation at the table, the others stared at her. Jordan was angry; he didn't offer to take her to the apartment. She clamped her mouth together to keep from shouting obscenities about baby pictures and got her coat from the hook on the door. They watched her struggle into it, said nothing when she opened the door and went out. She couldn't find a cab; she had to walk blocks before she did.

When Jordan got home, Wanda was in bed, slightly tight. He made lots of noise in the room, calculated to irritate her. He watched television for a while; the laugh-

146

ter was a series of identical inane bursts. He switched channels, setting her teeth on edge with the wait between. At last, he turned the set off. She tensed as he switched off the light, listened while he removed his clothing, felt the bed jounce as he got into it. Not a word. Wouldn't he make up? She sulked. His breathing was even but not that of going to sleep. She threw an arm in his direction only to have him move out from under it and turn on his side. Away from her.

"Jordie," she said.

He smelled the whiskey and wouldn't forgive her for the evening. That was why he was keeping still.

"Jordie...I couldn't help it."

Sirens outside. The city always burned at night. There were sometimes shots in the streets but nobody found out what they meant. Or a lone voice yelling meaningless sounds. Help! Help! Nobody knew what those meant either.

"Jordie...it was only because I'm sick of talking about my sisters and their damned babies."

Somebody running outside. Why? She had never been so keenly aware of sounds. Please make up, Jordie.

"Jordie...I love you."

He stirred. "You should have behaved yourself tonight. You acted as if you were doing them a favor by being there. Oh, fuck it."

"I'll be better next time."

"Sure."

"They upset me. I have the feeling they're after something and I'm supposed to guess what it is."

One...two...three...four...he sighed. "You know what they want? They want me to find out if you'd be willing to adopt a baby."

Five...six...seven...eight...nine...ten...zero. At last, she said, "I don't want to talk about it, Jordie."

An hour ticked by. She knew when he fell asleep; his body went limp. Steam in the radiator hissed wetly. It was winter and the seasons of her life were ebbing without stop. The phone rang a fourth time before she realized he wasn't going to answer it. She reached over his head to take the instrument from the nightstand. "Hello?" she said, wondering which of their friends had thought to call. The voice said things for a long measure of held breath

147

after she confirmed her identity. She listened, then said, "You'll have to repeat all that to my husband." She shook Jordan awake and gave him the phone. After he had it firmly in hand and held to his ear, she sank deeply into her pillow. She felt ill.

Jordan told the caller he was listening. An official, uncultured twang replied with brass-buttoned impatience.

"We need somebody to make a positive identification, Mr. Ashe."

A as in air. "Yes?"

"We got two bodies here the neighbors say are your people."

"Yes?"

"We had a fire here in the building and they got killed in it."

"A fire..."

"Yeah, the apartment was gutted. The furnace in the basement malfunctioned. One of them was by the window in the bedroom and the other on the bed. I guess she tried to cover herself up."

The wide brass bed of their loving and the smoke rising through the airshaft chimney.

"You can come down here or see them at the morgue."

He didn't want to see them scorched and skinburst. His ravaged heart unraveled over his cheeks and downturned lips. Wiping his mouth, he tasted salt. Once more a five-year-old, he was shaken by a ghostly elevated train caterpillaring through multistoried vistas of undershirted parlors and unmade beds and steamy kitchens and window-framed wan not-as-happys who sometimes waved back...and he rode to the wide park meadows and tree-shaded strands of Pelham Bay. In his mind's eye mother, father, and son waded and swam and danced at a fire on a muddy, rock-strewn beach, so happy then to pry hairy mussels from piling and stone, crush crackling clamshells and smash jellyfish to gelatin smithereens...and held sticks to blacken potatoes and frankfurters over flames...heat heightened by sunburn, and they ate together, tasting the sea and the sweat and the charring...there was always grit in the mouth, sand and salt tempering enjoyment to perfect it. He yearned for their embrace. They had held him, kept him safe and loved him and tried to hold all of him again each time he saw

148

them...so ordinary a gesture he had forgotten to declare his own love's return. It needed saying aloud to those ears. And he would say it.

"I'll be there...at the building...in a few minutes," he promised after clearing his throat.

"Sorry, Mr. Ashe." *A as in ache.*

"Thank you."

He replaced the phone receiver upon its cradle and sat up to throw the spread from himself. As he swung his legs to the floor, he was too weak to stand. His hands fell open at his sides; his body, nude, was that of a man, as far as it could be from childhood. Being left behind was the curse of living when loving was so full; his faith was broken. Parents meant to be forever, never gone, always present, now were gone forever and no longer present and without a hint of it when last he saw them. Someone, Something, should have given them an omen so they could say good-bye. He shivered. Wanda had touched his burning back with icy fingers.

"I'm so sorry, Jordie."

"I know."

"I feel terrible...so guilty."

"It's okay, Wanda."

"No. I should have seen more of them. I shouldn't have been a bitch. I should have...oh, I should have...I haven't done anything right for you!" She was crying and thoroughly miserable.

He took her into his arms to comfort her. "Don't cry, Wanda. They knew you were going through a rough time."

"What's to become of us, Jordie? I haven't brought you the happiness you wanted, or the children, and I don't know why you just don't leave me."

"I wouldn't leave you, Wanda. I love you."

"I can't forgive myself about your parents. How can I make it up to you?"

"Shhh. Don't think like that, honey. This isn't something for you to feel guilty about."

"I'm...so...sorry...we were...angry with...each other...tonight." Her sobs released words sporadically.

"So am I. But I was to blame, too."

"Oh, Jordie!" She cried into his shoulder bitterly. He caressed her, combing her hair with his palm. His own eyes were dry. Casimir and Katarzyna were no more; van-

149

ished as no alias could have erased their being. He placed his wife gently back upon her pillow.

"I have to go across town."

"I'll go with you."

"No . . . no, there's no reason for you to be there. If you want, heat up some coffee for when I get back."

Then he dressed and went out into the friendless streets to look after his dead.

The shortest distance between a boy and home is mapped with pitfalls and side trips and delays. Joe had been away from his mother since early morning; Yukiko fretted when he disappeared for so long. Exhausted from men she'd served the night before, she was finding little desire to tend to her quarters, but it had to be done. She took pride in the bus and its contents now that it was inhabited solely by herself and her son. The whore was gone; there had been a providential scene about dwindling contributions toward the rent, and the woman was forced to leave. All to the good. The bus had order in it; men were more comfortable to visit. Yukiko's reputation was excellent, being known as trustworthy and without diseases. A man wasn't robbed in her bus of more than his proper fee for her services. But where was the boy? He could be carrying water buckets for her. What was he doing?

Joe was riveted before an exhibition. In an illegal shop called Karadamonya, the Gate of the Body, humanity was adorned skillfully by a spry artist enjoying his labor for the pain it created as much as for its beauty. He was a tattooist and could depict anything upon the skin of his willing victims. His name was Tadanobu and he had hundreds of drawings which plastered his walls and were stored in chests. A man or a woman could spend hours poring over them before making a decision. He liked to decorate the whores of the district, closing his shop discreetly for the time it took. They had fanciful notions, meant to delight and excite their customers erotically. A whore might wish her inner thighs colored with gradually deepening shades of pink until reaching the mons veneris, which he then transformed into a peach or the spread wings of a butterfly. The influx of Occupation forces brought less refined requests for designs. The women occasionally wanted copies of what they'd seen on the forcigners: a mouse fleeing to the anus; ship's propellers centered upon each buttock with the legend TWIN SCREWS KEEP CLEAR. Tadanobu executed the work but was repulsed by it. He could put up with anything, however, so long as he had body suits to do.

A limited number of men asked for such intricate and expensive tattooing; a woman, rarely. The body suit was fashioned from shoulders to knees, open at the throat with unmarked flesh the length of the chest in a strip falling to the crotch but carried across back and rump. The work ended above the elbows and seldom touched the genitals, though there had been instances in which a man of fortitude, rendered insensitive by sufficient drugs or alcohol, allowed the head of his penis to be disguised as a rose. It was a hazardous undertaking, any of it; infection could ruin a piece or escalate into serious illness, sometimes fatal. The skill and past record of the artist raised his price into ten thousands of yen, and he parceled out his efforts into a multitude of sessions to lessen the risk. As a result, his contoured canvases were restricted mainly to those most able to afford both time and money: the *yakuza*. They were the gangsters of the city, sleek men in Occidental clothing, the elite of the criminal world. Whenever one was to be found upon his couch, head hanging over the edge to bite a towel when the agony rose, Tadanobu was sure to have a spectator peering over the banners of his window to watch. Lately, this same small one.

Joe loved the blaze of colors across the walls. The pictures were dramatic: samurai and carp and hawks and flowers and insects and dragons and ocean waves! And he was engrossed by the shopkeeper's scribing of the same designs upon a man lying undressed beside him. Tadanobu pricked lines on the man's back with a sharp instrument, a constant quick stabbing which drew blood, and then color was pressed into the wounds. Black, green, yellow, blue and red ... the blood welled over the pigment, obliterating it until Tadanobu wiped with a cloth and a thin indelible mark remained. There was no response from the man on the pallet, only slight movement when his hand adjusted the towel between his teeth. Tadanobu stopped his concentrated torture as the man grunted.

"Well, then...are you restless?" he asked, hoping conceit would say he was not.

"I have to be about my business. What is the hour?"

"It is early...the flies haven't risen."

The man rolled aside and sat up. He mopped sweat from his face and forehead. He looked drained; a sickly aspect made him seem smaller than he was. "We'll continue in a week or two," he said bravely. Tadanobu was dejected. He kept the tools in his hands, reluctant to part with them while skin was before him. "How far have you done this session?" he was asked.

"The claw below the sword."

"I want to bathe now to set the colors."

"You are welcome to soak in my tub."

"Iie... I prefer my own." After being swabbed with astringent, the man dressed glumly, pulling his undershirt gingerly over his back. He spied the boy at the window and frowned. Joe was too awed to vanish; he recognized the man as one everybody in the prefect respected, even feared. The receiver of rents and fees. The man was soon garbed in his double-breasted pinstripe suit. No one could suspect the suit beneath. He stamped to the entrance of the shop and surveyed mackerel clouds above as if they were debtors. The wounds throbbed beneath his clothing, smarting from the bite of the liquid the artist used to stem further bleeding. His fine shirt would be stained, he knew. The blood always seeped along the thin weals, cut through his undershirt, and always made slight tracks somewhere...enough to soil the material.

Joe eyed him shyly. What he would not give to be a *yakuza!* To be tattooed! A sinuous snake with sharp fangs battling an eagle in a thunderhead would be the very thing. The *yakuza* was regarding him balefully. Joe placed his palms flat at his sides and bowed.

"You're one of the bus people," the great man said.

"Hai."

"I know you, *ainoko.*" Because the recipients of pain are unfulfilled unless they give it, the man scarred him as surely as Tadanobu might. "Your mother should have

152

strangled you with your umbilical." He sheathed his contempt and strode away. Joe was stunned. The man should have been pleased with his admiration; if not wanting to be seen under the artist's hands, he should have driven him off. But he had not. Why did ho say such a thing? Each day Joo seemed more despised for being the son of an American father. It was confusing. He was not unlike other children he knew; nothing distinguished them from himself. It always returned to Joe-dan-ash. Joe-dan-ash, the father of fathers according to his mother's words. A great man and Joe would be a great man one day, too. Did not his mother prophesy it? Handsome as his father, she said. As clever; as bold; to become the talk of men. Surely to make a name in the world. So why did the *yakuza* say what he did?

Tadanobu had come to the doorway to look at him. Joe hung his head; he was not wanted here. He would return to the lane where he belonged.

In the midst of housekeeping, Yukiko heard a clamor of children and went to see what aroused them. A limousine was easing into the lane. She was intrigued since cars were unknown here and could only mean an important personage had arrived. The polished length moved slowly past the buses and stopped at hers. They must be lost. She went outside to assist them. Shouting children clambered over the fenders until a chauffeur emerged to scatter them. He looked at her expectantly. Before she could speak, he indicated his passenger with a jerk of his thumb. Looking inside, she was astonished to see a foreign woman sitting on the rear seat.

The woman was examining a sheet of paper with many notations on it. She was primly severe: thin lips, unpainted cheeks, mouse-colored crinkly hair covered with a cloth bonnet tied beneath her chin by a wide ribbon. She looked dowdy, yet was one of those women who talk through a smile always, showing a set of dentures like polished rice squared off into flat porcelain teeth. The mouth of a doll, Yukiko thought, unreal and too perfect. The woman's piercing gray eyes left the paper she studied to fasten upon her.

"Hello. I'm Mrs. Kritzky...Major Kritzky's wife. Can you tell me where I can find a lady named Yukiko Shimada?"

153

"I am she."

Shimada. She had not heard her family name since registering with the police.

"Oh, wonderful!" The woman leaned toward Yukiko, placing a leather-gloved hand on the window ledge of her car door. "I'm here about your son."

"My son?" She stifled a surge of panic. The woman was smiling, so whatever she had to say about Joe could not concern an accident or something similar. "My son?" she asked again with firmness.

"Yes. The major and I are in charge of the mission's home for unwanted children and I was given your name and the boy's by the Regional Police Bureau." Yukiko stared blankly. "Did you not tell them he was a burden to you?" No answer but a negative shake of the head. "You didn't send a friend to do it for you?"

"*Hai* . . . I did not."

"Well, somebody reported it!" The woman spaced her words and pronounced each more distinctly, as people do when confronting persons of another country; they seem to believe speaking louder and slower clarifies meaning. "My dear, I'm here to talk to you about taking the child off your hands."

Yukiko backed from the car, glanced at the Japanese chauffeur but saw no help there. She wouldn't give up her son to anyone! The woman opened the car door and emerged, becoming formidable. She was tall, with a girth suppressed by a girdle beneath clothes like a uniform.

"I know you may have reservations about how your son will be looked after but we want you to see our orphanage. You will have no fear for his comfort."

"Joe is not an orphan."

"Of course not. We can shield the poor boy from much he suffers as a result of his birth and you'd want that, wouldn't you?" The smile beamed at the alley and its rows of buses with distaste. Whores had appeared to watch; they caused the chauffeur to assume a nobler bearing. He puffed out his chest, flattened his stomach. He hoped he was admired.

Yukiko stammered that the lady must be misinformed. It was not true she wanted the boy taken from her, and the lady could please to forget the matter and not trouble herself further.

154

"My dear, I can't force you to part with your son but look at the life he has with you." Her smile scorned everything about them. "It's un-Christian and debasing. Come with me and see what we have to provide instead." At that moment, Joe arrived. He slipped behind his mother and peeked at the white woman and her shining *karuma*, the like of which he'd not seen before. Its sleek black streamline and bright metal fittings was transportation fit for the Empress. But this was not she. "Is that your little boy? Why, he's beautiful." He liked her musical voice. "Come here, child." Joe went to her, thinking to solve the snap of her bulky purse. She wore neither jewelry nor perfume. She couldn't be rich if she couldn't afford those for herself! She was speaking nicely to him, saying, "Do you understand English? Yes? Then how would you like to have a short ride in my pretty car? Your mother will be with us. Would you like that?"

Of course, he accepted with alacrity. He had ridden in Army vehicles but not such a magnificent automobile. He tugged at his mother's dress. She didn't want to go, yet finally consented. The chauffeur held the doors for them to enter the car. Both women sat in the rear while Joe was enthroned beside the driver's steering wheel. The limousine drove from the lane cheered by children running alongside, every one of them dying with envy because the *ainoko* was inside.

The trip was longer than Yukiko had been led to believe but Joe enjoyed it immensely. The unfamiliar luxury of tanned leather seats and music from a dashboard radio seemed unreal; no wonder the wealthy did not walk! He smirked at peasant pedestrians. See me? Most did. None smiled. And the car was driven to a dilapidated structure in a wretched section of the city.

"Here it is!" trilled the major's wife. She didn't say this shelter was limited to Occupation forces' bastards, children tinted brown and black and pink; a piebald muster

155

nobody wánted. The chauffeur remained with the limousine while the women and the child went into the building.

They entered a cramped, airless room where the small residents were seated upon an earthen floor. Cut-down ammunition cases formed tables which had partially filled bowls of rice upon them. Sets of *hashi* were lined precisely beside each bowl and the children seemed gripped by an odd stillness. There was none of the giggling or pinching which is normal, and Yukiko held Joe's hand tighter in her own. A white woman greeted Mrs. Kritzky. The white woman must have been in charge of the kitchen, for she wore an apron and carried a ladle. Upon signal from the major's wife, she proceeded to lead the children in song, conducting with the utensil in her hand. They sang in English *Jezuzluvzme, thizeyeknow, becuzthebibletellzmezooo*. The song ran several verses. And then the children were permitted to eat. They lunged for their *hashi* and bowls and ate as quickly as they could. Yukiko did not see one laugh nor smile, nor see the least interest in the visitors. The music of the song frightened her. It contained meanness she failed to comprehend. Everything in the building conveyed the same: lines of foreign cots, chamber pots near them fouled with use, and a lack of toys. There was a blackboard attached to a wall; chalk dust haloed it. And for decoration, a picture of the hairy man with nails driven through hands and feet, sacrificed like the holy bears of the Ainu in Hokkaido in the North. All of it done for goodness.

"You haven't seen the other members of our staff but they are eminently qualified to look after the little one. You saw how well-behaved the children are, how well they've learned what is taught them! The religious training they receive molds them forever to walk in the paths of righteousness."

The road back to Yukiko's bus stretched agonizingly. Had it been so long before? In the front seat, Joe clapped hands happily. "Go faster!" he urged the chauffeur. "Faster, faster!" The speed remained steady. He wanted to see pedestrians skip from their path. He would have asked to work the horn but the man was too grim. Joe could tell he'd gladly chuck him out of the car had it not been his duty to do as his mistress demanded.

156

Mrs. Kritzky still chattered through her smile at Yukiko. "I'm sure you'll want to sign the necessary papers when I call upon you again."

Squirming, Joe slipped over his seat to join his mother. She reprimanded him but he felt better under her arm. The American lady had a smell he couldn't label. Dry, like burlap. She needed a pimp to get business for her and then she would have everything, he thought. Was the large house really hers and did she always invite so many children to play there? Too bad the chauffeur was unfriendly. Joe would have been glad to give him important tips on how to make the major's wife have a more productive life.

Released from the clutches of the foreign lady at last, Joe fled to join his comrades. Yukiko resumed housecleaning. The children watched the limousine depart and began to play *jan ken pon*. In the bus, Yukiko smiled to hear their chanting trebles as they displayed hand signs to each other representing the stone or scissors or paper. The game was an amusement even among adults, who used it to settle choices in ordinary activities. It was pleasant to hear young voices and laughter each time a round was concluded... and Joe was being diverted from his perpetual questions. Always asking about Joe-dan-ash. When was his father to return? Why had he not written as she promised he would? When would they go to America to see him? What did Joe-dan-ash do in America? Tell me again... tell me. Poor child. She could not blame him for clinging so tenaciously to the tales she told him. He had no one else for comfort. None of the older folk of the area would have anything to do with him... and the children, sometimes. A boy with mixed blood was not acceptable to the Japanese. She didn't need the major's wife to tell her that of all the castes in the nation, his unacceptable breed, the *konketsuji,* had been thrust below the lowest rung. The Occupation government tried to alleviate the problem but couldn't overcome the enmity of the people against those like her son. The best offered was to separate them from the populace by placing them in foster homes with foreign families... or worse, gather them into orphanages like that she had just been shown. Who could have said she wanted to part with Joe? Never. She would not surrender him to the lady with teeth like grains of rice.

Her musing was interrupted. Someone had been hurt,

was crying. She ran from the bus to find the playmates had become a mass of arms and kicking legs. She burrowed into the fight and pulled her son free. His nose was bloodied and he struck at her, eyes shut so he couldn't see. "Stop, Joe!" she cried. She wiped his face and hugged him. Whimpering, he sank gratefully into her soft bosom. She scolded the other children angrily. "What are you picking on my son for? He was playing nicely with all of you."

They chanted the tune of their game at her, nastily substituting the word *ainoko* for each climax. One of the ruder boys made a speech about the worthlessness of a boy with impure blood. She lifted her son and took him into the bus. He resentfully submitted to being washed with a damp cloth.

"What's the matter? Are you unhappy with me, too?"

"Everyone is mean to me," he said plaintively.

"It was just a squabble among you, Joe."

"No. They have always been mean..."

"Nonsense. They were jealous that you rode in the beautiful car and they..."

"No! They hate me. Everybody hates me."

"What a thing to say about yourself. I don't hate you...and your father doesn't hate you...."

He cut her off with a wail of anguish. "I don't want to hear about him! I don't want to know about Joe-dan-ash anymore!" He twisted from her grasp, sobbing, "Good-bye, Joe-dan-ash, I don't want you anymore!" and curled into a ball on the floor.

All right, she thought, looking helplessly at him. She wouldn't speak of his father again. To what purpose had been the studies of Ei-go? She was not going to see Joe-dan-ash again; she was not going to America with the child. Everything she had said over the years about Joe-dan-ash had been to make Joe think well of him. The stories were all that gave the man substance, not only to the boy but to her. Well, she was done with it. Done with sitting with other whores in a class to learn what she could; done with inventing dreams of a dream...*iie,* it wasn't a kindness to continue the practice. She wouldn't speak of Joe-dan-ash again.

But she would think of him.

Wanda looked up from her drink as Jordan entered the Oak Room. A rosy glow lent her welcome more than it needed. He slid into the booth beside her and dismissed a solicitous waiter, saying he didn't want a drink.

"I'm starving," she said. She didn't appear to be. Wanda had accumulated weight during the past couple of years. Her diets were defeated by alcoholic calories. When she handed him one of two menus brought her from the dining room, he looked at it listlessly.

"See anything you like?"

The menu duplicated those they became accustomed to seeing since his rise in financial status. Having money was pleasant but after getting used to the convenience, life wasn't much different. Bills were larger, friends changed. Birds of a feather and that crap. He wasn't interested in social pursuits and left them to Wanda. She talked about relative strangers to him now, people he met over and over and couldn't remember other than having met them before.

"I'm just going to have a salad," she said predictably. "And maybe another drink." Also predictable.

How many had she ordered while waiting for him? Not more than one, he decided. He hadn't been late.

"I'm not hungry, Wanda."

"You've got to eat something."

"None of this seems appetizing."

"Then have the salad. That's what I'm going to order."

"Why couldn't we have met at home for lunch?"

"That's no fun. Only peasants eat at home."

He kept his focus on the descriptive lines in the menu. They had spent less and less time at the apartment. It was a place to sleep, nothing more, growing smaller with each occupation. His wife seemed unable to rid herself of disappointment. After telling him she was through seeing doctors, she became distant, refusing discussion or comfort. Her drinking worsened and gave her an unattractive puffiness. Couldn't she see that in her mirror? Comments about it could be explosive and did no good. Time should have eased the hurt for her...if she would let go of it.

"We're always in a crowd," he muttered.

"I love people, Jordie. And so should you. There's nothing stimulating about keeping to yourself."

"I don't need gin mills for that." Her annoyance warned him to veer off the subject. "I suppose I'll get the salad, too."

"Did you find anything this morning?"

"I would have said so."

"Oh...just asking. Why are you peeved?"

"I wish you'd take over scouting for another apartment for us. It's impractical for me to take time from work."

"You know I hate running around with real-estate agents."

"You used to bitch about me finding a rental without your approval."

"That was when we were poor. I doubt if you'll get anything in our price bracket that would be a disaster."

"We'd solve a lot of problems if you'd agree to live on the Island...or Connecticut."

"No. I'm not moving out of Manhattan."

"Christ, do you know how impossible it is to find an apartment in the city these days?"

"That's why you're doing it and not me."

"We're registered with half the brokers in town and they all have the same listings." He pushed the menu across the table and under the one at her elbow. "Too bad that damned loft didn't come through for us." When he was searching in the quainter neighborhoods surrounding Sheridan Square, a converted loft slipped past by a hair. Pubic, as it turned out; the scheming competitor paid for the key with a few gaudy nights. Real-estate channels leak *all* the details. "It was big as a house...could have been remodeled beautifully."

"It would be marvelous if you found a house for us."

"There's not a brownstone in the city we can touch."

"Do the brokers know we'd be interested?"

"It could be years before one was available."

"But are we on a waiting list?"

"We can be." If he wasn't careful, she'd lose her temper.

And so would he. Which was stupid, since they wanted the same thing. The West Side apartment had been outgrown.

"Before we married, I didn't know what an apartment was. You might be a little more enthusiastic about a house, Jordie."

"I could be if it was out of town."

"We'd be at the mercy of train schedules. What have you against a house in the city?"

"Do you realize the cost? My God, apart from the down payment, the mortgage and upkeep would be astronomical."

"Haven't you confidence in your future?"

She wasn't asking for a reply. His firm was among the top-rated successes in the state. The loan from her father had been repaid almost immediately.

"The future has nothing to do with it," he grumbled. "What do we need a house for? There's only the two of us."

The remark stung badly. She felt threatened and gulped her drink. The room tightened about her; noisy men stood three deep at the bar and the waiter was a covetous irritant nearby. She looked for escape out a tall draped window to Central Park. Pigeon fanciers dropped peanut shells on the walks. A pony ride paraded tired cavalry beside the path to the zoo; children with balloons and toys on leashes and pinwheels revolving on sticks defended the ramparts. She retreated.

"Do you know," she said, draining her glass, "I'm having a devil of a time finding a dress I like. I've been up and down the Avenue but there's nothing in my size."

The waiter hovered over them. "Ready to go to the dining room?"

He was trying to ease them out to make room for some-one else.

Without checking with Jordan, she snapped, "Not yet."

Unruffled, he asked with bland assurance, "Another drink, then?" She gave him the glass to take to the bar, where he was given a fresh old-fashioned to bring back. The chit was left on the tray as a hint. When it wasn't touched, he withdrew by turning his back and standing within earshot, knowing customers hated it.

Ignoring him, Wanda lipped past an orange slice to sip at her drink. "Where were you this morning, Jordie?"

161

Lighting a cigarette guiltily, he answered, "Lower Broadway, near Grace Church. It's quiet down there."

A choir school for boys was buttressed at the corner of the chapel and the school playground invited distraction by softball or soccer games according to season. Scholars in navy blue shorts and turtleneck woolen sweaters rammed out of a gothic doorway to gambol over the slag cinders of their field. Tall and short, fat and thin, hair curled or straight, golden or jet black or shingled muddy brown or carrot...and not older than a son might have been if Acapulco had been the start. There was one youngster, hair clipped short over his head, scooting around bases like a deer...with bluest eyes. Jordan's hour for looking at apartments was spent clinging to the wire fence till a stern headmaster lined the sweating daydreams beside the building and marched them inside and sealed them in with a heavy wooden door: the wind assaulted its carved panels with dust devils...with his wish for a running boy.

"If the neighborhood was so depressing, I'm glad you didn't find anything there."

"I'm not depressed!"

"What are you thinking about?"

"Nothing." He rubbed a thumb over an imperfection on the table. The highly varnished wood grain was polished smooth from constant use. Why not ask about adoption again? She wanted a house; why not a family, too? They could be looked for at the same time, but this was a lousy place to bring it up. Solitude was needed, if not that of home, where there was too much of it, then...the park? She used to like meeting him there. They could walk, find a secluded spot near the pond and have lunch afterward, as they did when they were happier and in love. That bothered him. He wasn't sure he was in love with her anymore.

"Wanda, how about doing something silly today? Let's have a bite at the zoo cafeteria and look at the...animals and everyone..."

Look at the children. Both had the same thought. And she replied carefully, "No, thank you. I gave up hot dogs and beer."

"We haven't been there in ages."

"I've already reserved a table for us, Jordie."

162

Okay. The subject would have to be broached here. He began obliquely. "Hear from your sisters?"

"Constantly. They're a bore."

"Gus and Helen haven't called lately."

"They don't have to. I send them cards."

"How come?"

"Well, they expect scraps of news about us, Jordie."

"I meant, why haven't you been talking on the phone as before?"

She put a cigarette to her lips, and the waiter was there with a match instantly. "Thank you." She waited for him to turn his back, then explained, "Mother and I had a squabble."

"Oh..."

She blew smoke at him crossly, saying, "Don't accuse me of fighting with everyone, Jordie. We simply had an infuriating routine going and I put a stop to it."

"Is that all you want to say about it?"

"Oh, for God's sake. Mother can't resist needling me about not having kids like Grace and Dot. I got fed up and hung up on her. We haven't communicated directly for months."

"Bragging about grandchildren isn't needling."

"May we talk about something else, please?"

He wished the waiter were a mile away. "Wanda, we could have a family."

Precisely the conversation she ran from and didn't want to hear. She mashed her cigarette out in the ashtray. "Don't ask me to take on somebody else's baby."

"Give me one good reason why not. Just one that makes sense."

"This is the wrong time to go into it."

"It always is. So it may as well be now."

"All right, damn it, you want an honest answer?"

The waiter's head twitched. "If you can lower your voice," Jordan cautioned.

Always in the wrong. Always. She hissed at him heatedly, "Every time I'd see it, the baby would be a reminder of my personal failure. You think I need that? I thought you married me for myself. I wanted to give you your babies but it didn't work out. I still love you. If that's not enough and it's babies you want, then leave and find yourself a prize hen. You're free to play cock-a-doodle-do wherever you want."

The outburst shamed him. Heads were turning in their direction. It was a mistake to have asked her. He shrank lower into his seat. "Why do you have to be so irrational, Wanda?"

"What's irrational? I told you the truth."

"Why can't we talk without this kind of reaction from you?"

"We touched on this before and I thought it was settled."

"We didn't discuss it!"

"I don't want to discuss it!"

"Sorry," he said, subsiding. It was so easy to take on her tone. "I hoped you were over feeling hurt. I thought you could consider an adoption now. Everyone we know has children in school. We don't fit in with the younger set and we're out of step with our old crowd."

"Are you keeping up with the Joneses, Jordie? Is that it? Or am I hearing things?"

"People are looking at us, Wanda."

"Screw them." She glanced at the others in the room, whose interest pitied her behavior. Their disapproval incensed her. "Is there a sow here that appeals to you, Jordie? Let me pick one. We can have her start a litter for you."

He stood, knowing he wanted to strike her. "I'll see you when I get home from the office," he said icily and stalked from the table.

She straightened her back, composed her face to conceal misery. She had been dreadful to him. How do you cope?, all you empty ladies, she thought, feeling herself the center of attention. How do I cope? Idiotically. He shouldn't have been taunted about finding another woman. How do I cope, ladies? A woman at the next table smiled and looked away. Someone like that could take Jordie. There wasn't much to keep him if he hadn't become resigned to the idea of not having children. But life wasn't the ball everyone imagined it to be, and people learn to adjust to their limitations. She had adjusted. Her parents had adjusted. What was the matter with Jordie? She reached for her purse to pay the bar tab.

Jordan walked into the park purposefully. He wanted to see what it would have been like had she agreed to lunch there. It made him miserable. Kids were everywhere in captivating elfin shapes and poses. She couldn't have failed to have been influenced by their charm. He circled the seal pool and couldn't bear to remain. Crossing Fifth Avenue, he averted his eyes from F. A. O Schwarz. Enough is enough; the toys in the windows hurried him past. He continued down Fifty-ninth Street, getting away from Wanda's stamping ground. She used the smart shops as a private club, meeting friends and wasting days with fittings and deviling salesgirls. She didn't buy anything...or seldom did. It was a pastime shared by idle women. Head down, lost in thought, he collided violently with a woman turning the corner. He grabbed her instinctively and held her, apologizing profusely.

She was small, the duplicate of the actress in a movie from his past. He'd seen Teresa Wright with exactly that expression on her face when Joseph Cotten had her in his clutches. "You're Charlie," he said with wonder. Her eyes widened.

"I'm not."

He stammered, feeling like a fool. "No...sorry." He released her. "I mistook you for someone."

"I hope you don't greet her as forcibly whenever you meet." Her accent was crisp as cucumber. British. He didn't want to stop hearing it. She was puzzled yet friendly. "Who did you think I was?"

"An actress."

She laughed. And instead of dashing away, she remained in place. It was like another meeting, part of the same confusion. "Did you really?" she asked. They were in a vacuum, oblivious to the people pushing by. "I'd be enchanted to learn who it is you think I resemble."

"I'd be enchanted to tell you." He imitated her accent unconsciously, astounded to know her so well he expected her affirmative reaction.

"My name is Vikky. Victoria Cooper-Heath."

"One of those hyphenates," he grinned.

"And you?"

"Jordan Asche."

"How do you do?"

"How do you do?" He looked around; nothing but a Nedicks nearby. "If you can spare a few moments, I'd be glad to apologize with an orangeade."

165

She agreed negatively. "I've a better suggestion. I'm bruised and I'd love to sit down to a refreshing tea."

"Wonderful. We'll do it."

"Shall we go to the Plaza? I was heading there till you bowled me over."

He rejected the suggestion. Wanda was sure to be there yet. "Let's go to one of those Gypsy tearooms near here. We'll get our fortunes told at the same time."

She adored the idea. They went arm in arm, talking like old friends while they found out about each other. In the tearoom, he explained about the movie aboard ship during the war, admitting to harboring a minor crush on the actress at the time. "But it was the only film I've seen her in. I was afraid she'd change." Victoria was flattered, relishing being a vicarious part of his Navy life. As for Jordan, he was stimulated by her and full of conversation and wit. They got around to admitting they were married, she to a member of a British import firm and he to Wanda. They discussed their spouses as they would with anyone, hiding the flaws and describing what good marriages they'd made; their eyes held each other throughout that bit, telling another story. The gypsy flounced to the table, had her manicured fingers crossed with dollar bills, and she forecast long lives and a happy marriage together. She could be forgiven for assuming they were man and wife. They looked right together. Victoria hesitated before giving Jordan her private phone number but did. He saw her to a cab, pleased with the encounter, not imagining he'd see her again.

Not really...yes, really.

The boy was ten and an accomplished storyteller regarding his origin. To shed the stigma of being the bastard of an American and somehow gain indirect respect, he claimed to be the child of a Luftwaffe pilot, presumably a fugitive from the German collapse. It was accepted with reluctance by those of easy gullibility but met with open derision by his fellow pimps, who promptly dubbed him Heinie Joe. The name stuck. He thought it added credence to his fable and gave him a romantic edge other boys didn't have. The name was something of his own; therefore he treasured it.

Life's patterns were well established for him these days. His mother didn't begin work till the latter part of the afternoons and could spare his presence. Heinie wasn't able to associate with the youngsters of the district because they scorned him; there were no card games to pass the idle hours; no pimp's council asked for his attendance. Time and money available, he sought escape at the movies. He could be an ordinary child there, lost in the fantasy of films. The theaters showed a few American movies, which he avoided, preferring those made by his own countrymen. He was addicted to samurai adventure epics, each a gory tale of swords and honor. He indentified with heroic dedication to Bushido, the Way of the Warrior. Slumped into his seat, eating tangerines, he suffered every agony and relished every triumph. The great actors were those in leading roles. Hana Hanabi seemed to play all the women's parts. She was ageless; producers fought to get her for their pictures. Namboku Ichikawa was a favorite. The antagonist in most of the lurid plots, the broad man could be counted upon to die prodigiously. He was known to be an egotistic drunkard off screen, which was forgiven by an adoring public and his personal ontourage. Heinie Joe was also a fan of the finest actor in Japan, the incomparable Jihei Segawa. Within the past few years, the actor had extended his reputation beyond the Asian world and was appreciated as far as Paris and Berlin. It was said he might become known in America, too. Segawa had an extraordinarily muscular body, which he developed with gymnasium workouts, and spoke in a guttural tone, an accident of vocal chords, giving every phrase he said the bark of command. Women and young girls commented loudly and favorably whenever he appeared on the screen.

There were others seeking entertainment during the day, furtive men with odd habits. Heinie Joe changed his seat to evade their hands. Though wise in many ways, he had no experience of them and wanted to be left alone to enjoy the films. It took the persistence of a lanky balding American corporal with calf's eyes to introduce him to the

167

mysteries of homosexuality. Having seen Heinie Joe a number of times, and having brought chocolate bars for him to eat during a show, the corporal dared one afternoon to trust dimness and scarcity of audience to permit him his way with the boy. They scuffled silently below the level of the seats, Heinie half alarmed and half involved. He was astonished. Presented with a royal payment of yen, he added the sport to his repertoire. It was another thing of his own, over which he had full control. In no time, he learned it gave him power over those who desired him.

He would have liked more influence over his mother. The films imbued him with wanderlust; he wanted to visit some of the historic settings he saw on the screen.

"Himeji is not so far from Osaka," he insisted on one of his plaguing days.

Yukiko agreed, "Hai, it is only the other side of the bay."

"If you won't take me, give me permission to go myself. I can get rides on the road."

"I'm afraid to have you go anywhere so far alone."

"I wouldn't be alone at the castle! Hundreds of tourists are there! And movie companies! I'd be able to see where armies stormed the hill and forced the big gates. Do you know they are covered with iron sheets? And there's a little door to let friends through but the enemy has to use battering rams."

"You're certain anything is left for you to see at Himeji?"

"Hai! Weapons rooms and dungeons and apartments for the daimyo, and there are trapdoors around the balconies to drop boiling oil and stones on attackers' heads."

"You know it so well, you don't have to see it."

"Oh, but I could show it to you!"

"I'm not going. And neither are you."

He begged to no avail. She kept him in check to keep him comparatively safe from harm. He'd be at the mercy of those thinking him an ainoko; if not loved by any but herself, he wasn't being beaten by his peers in the district as before, because of her popularity among the troops.

She listened with mild interest when her son described opportunities to be found in other cities. It was part of his campaign to have them move to Tokyo, see the palace of the Emperor and that of the imperial man named

168

MacArthur, the supreme commander of the Allied powers. Or they could travel to Kyoto to set up shop. It was re-knowned as a pleasure center and could be less raucous and uncomfortable than the seaport they were in. All convincing gambits. She replied patiently that the Occupation forces were everywhere; it made no difference where they lived, but she was content to remain in Osaka. Heinie Joe chafed at her control and bided his time.

In explorations beyond the boundaries of the red-light district, he skimmed the surface of the sedate Japanese world. Average citizens with regimented lives carried on without smothering beneath the foreign presence. Below the massive shoulders of the GI horde were to be seen the smaller multitude, not in amount but stature, for they outnumbered the Americans. The compliant people of the nation worked to repair ruins around them and took up the same ambitions they subscribed to before the surrender. Heinie Joe envied the students, the future leaders of Nippon. He would be less than any of them. His learning came from the streets and the servicemen; it made him bilingual and clever, but he was denied entry to formal schooling. The serious students in dark uniforms angered him; their self-abnegation was exhibited with intense pride. Shit on them. He would not trade his freedom for constant study. Anyway, they were like everyone else. They hated him.

Because Yukiko told him much about her elder sister's family of actors, Heinie Joe was drawn to the legitimate theaters in Osaka. There was the Nohgaku-kai, which gave performances every third Sunday of the month. Here players in masks performed on a square platform projected into the audience, unlike proscenium stages as found at the Kabuki or those modern plays given at the Naka-za or Kado-za. The Dotonbori district was far more elegant than that in which he lived, so he felt he was among people of a better class. They were no different, actually. Other than dressing in finer clothing, the prey and predators had the same passions. He was able to make casual friends of musicians and actors, those being outcast as he for their professions and disorderly lives. A night he didn't return home panicked Yukiko. He was to do it again. She didn't ask what he did; the knowledge wasn't truly wanted, wasn't to be made reality. Gifts he exhibited without explanation were shared, as they had shared everything.

A postman came bowing, tortoiseshell eyeglasses slipping down his nose each time.

"Miss Shimada, *hai?*"

"Hai."

"I have not had occasion to stop at your door before." He would have given her the contents of his bag but offered a single letter.

"Arigato gozaimasu." Her heart leaped to her throat, but the stamps were not American.

"I hope you get many, many more letters, Miss Shimada."

"Hai."

He left, walking stiff-legged. She sat upon the steps of the bus and tore the envelope open. It was alarming for being the only one she had received from home, though she had sent several.

"What does it say?" Heinie Joe demanded. She drove him mad with reading it twice through before looking up. He was dumbfounded as she burst into tears.

"Oh, Joe..." Is the ability to cry never lost? She had not done it for years. She handed him the letter and he traced the characters with a finger.

"Ahhh...your Ooba-san..."

"We'll burn prayers at the shrine for her."

"Old people drop dead all the time. You shouldn't cry."

"Ooba-san taught me to sew. I learned my childhood songs from her."

"Everybody knows those."

"She was everything I've missed since leaving home to live here."

"I didn't know you missed anything."

How could he not? He should have guessed from the detailed stories she told him about the village; he had learned every path and turning from her descriptions of the gentle life she led as a girl.

"Haven't you missed the village, Joe? Don't you remember anything about it?"

*"Iie...*nothing." A zephyr of a glen or stretch of sand came to mind, not a picture to pin down or identify as places she took him to escape the remarks of neighbors. Ooba-san meant little to him; he had no recollection of the

170

woman, nor of the one Yukiko called Mother, nor of the dour man who would not look at him. If only he had seen his father! He still had that buried within him. Joe-dan-ash. He wouldn't say the name or speak of him but the specter couldn't be pried from himself. Her unhappiness about Ooba-san made the bus cheerless, and he left Yukiko to deal with it on her own. He went to the movies and accepted a patron's invitation to have dinner with him. He'd be away most of the evening but by then his mother would have dried her tears.

Yukiko was careless of herself that night and not inclined to examine customers before they took her. She was visited by two sailors, some soldiers, and an Army officer of low rank. He was out of his element in this area, a refugee from the stuffiness of the Osaka Officers' Club and its overpicked bevy of imported American secretaries and service wives. He brought more than his boredom with him; he had signs of a venereal infection to which he wouldn't admit. It was the source of many miseries before Yukiko was cured of the malady. She was subjected to visits from the *junsa* and medical inspections by the score. She had to account for everything in the refurbished bus and for the hours her son spent away from her. *Hai*, he was always within call and never out of her sight. *Hai*, it was so. One would have thought she and Joe criminals instead of honest whore and pimping son. The attitude toward her profession was changing, just as the district seemed to be deteriorating. Both had the air of becoming uncivilized.

"You think I drink too much, don't you, Frank?"

He poured tomato juice over vodka and put the glass before Wanda. She let it sit. Everything was fine when she knew it was there and didn't have to wonder if she'd left it on the piano top or in the john or at someone's table. The regulars were noisy as ever; there was seldom room for outsiders at the bar. She had become one of the gang

171

this past summer. After moving to a Washington Square South address, she was sorry to find the improvement didn't extend to her collapsing marriage. It gave herself and Jordan the option of retreating to other rooms when arguments or bad feelings were intolerable; at worst, anger could be walked in the park or piddled away browsing in bookstores on Greenwich Village streets... which is how she began reading yards of paperback romances having identical plots. She read them, one to the next, without stop. In subways, cabs or buses, she was sure to have a book or two in her bag. They permitted her to coast through the days supported by pages and glasses of oblivion. Taken in tolerable dosage.

"You're just having a good time, Wanda, like the rest of us."

Frank was right. She'd quit like a shot if she couldn't handle her liquor. Besides, she didn't drink because she liked it. She drank because she wanted to drink and knew when to stop, which was about now, so she could get home to scare up dinner for Jordan.

"When are you going to play and sing again, Frank?"

"No chance till after the rush. I promised Jimmy I'd help tend bar until the mob clears."

Patrons were a stacked daisy chain, thrusting arms past to give Frank or the bartender a glass; somehow, each knew what drink was desired. She liked the crowding. The hubbub. Even the thick gas of cigarette smoke and alcohol and malt. Mens' clothes gave off a titillating fustiness of spent energy, and their women, doused with Shalimar, had sloe-eyed anticipatory faces and spoke slower than they had during the day and weaved knees and thighs and breasts like temple dancers. Wanda wished she weren't just a spectator. She didn't have Jordan with her. It was kind of Jimmy and Frank not to mention his absence whenever she dropped in, but domestic arrangements must be too intricate for them to follow among their clientele. God, it had grown enormously over the years! Past six o'clock. If she went home immediately, there was time for a shower unless Jordan was there. But he wouldn't be. He was keeping later hours at the firm. She left change on the bar as Frank's tip and twisted on the stool to leave.

"You're not going? We didn't get a chance to talk."

A tie with subdued stripes. Button-down collar. Hair a trifle overdue for tomorrow's barber appointment.

"That's too bad," she said curtly, and wasn't able to stand. He was too close to her. "Do you mind?"

He didn't make room. His charm waxed as though adjusted by a switch. Madison Avenue glamor. "I'll buy you a drink if you stay."

"Big deal," she smiled and tramped his foot with a heel as she swung off her seat. He winced but didn't back off.

"Please stay. I had to wrestle a guy to get this spot."

"Buy him the drink."

Windsor knots and Hart Schaffner suits slowed her. The intentional obstruction wasn't offensive, being a manifestation of appreciation, closer than street-corner whistles ... they pinch in Rome, so far not in La Petite Couvée. Jimmy called a farewell and she was outside, already at a half run to match the pace of the other pedestrians. She got lucky, stepping into a cab as its rider left, and was driven downtown behind a gaseous bus. It was Thirty-fourth Street before they could scoot around the dreadful fumes to race to Washington Square, one block at a time, catching every stoplight.

The Arch was a plaster model scrubbed clean by a maintenance team; troubadors in jeans serenaded the empty circular fountain behind it. A turn. Another. And she was deposited before the entrance of her building. She paid the fare and went into the foyer chewing Sen Sen. The slithering descent of the elevator took forever. Entering quickly, she threw a look over her shoulder to the menace which follows every unescorted woman to her door and punched the button for her floor. Keys. Locks. And no one there. The message service said Jordan was going to have a bite on the Island before coming home. He'd be late then. So there was all the time in the world. She could do as she pleased ... which didn't please when there was nothing to do.

She went into their bedroom to drop purse and clothing haphazardly across the chaise and bed. The figure ignored in the mirror was unstuck, quivering in places it shouldn't; the damned new diet had to be improved. Showering was over quickly. It used to be wonderful, making the day seem to start over again; but time didn't need extending now. There was so much of it, getting through each day was a

triumph in itself. Toweling, she thought disdainfully of
the ego booster in the bistro. He was necessary to feed a
faltering vanity. Couples without families raise battles
instead; such tempests might be stimulating to some, but
love had shriveled between herself and Jordie into indifferent responses to physical need. In dawn hours, aroused
by pressure on his bladder, he sometimes moved to her
and they thrashed in bed for so long as it took, without
passion and without pressing mouths to each other. Since
he failed to seek solace in her arms, she suspected he went
to others. It was important to know she was attractive to
men, though she wasn't tempted to be unfaithful. She was
only for Jordan—there was no one else. Just thinking of
the flattening scars on his back was weakening.

Dressed in bathrobe and terry-cloth scuffs, she retrieved the latest paperback sensation from her purse.
Another hysterical historical concocted of harmless por-
nography to spice the long evening. In the kitchen, the
morning newspaper was scattered over the counter. As she
assembled its pages, an ad intimidated her, one of those
calculating foster-children appeals, scrawny legs and arms
dangling and huge round eyes, all pupil like Bambi. She
turned the paper face down. She didn't want to be home.
The movie listings were dull, except for a new film at the
Trans-Lux: *End of the Wheel*. She hadn't seen it. A review
raved about the leading man, one with an exotic name:
Jihei Segawa. Reading further, she found it was a film
with elements of the unreal romances she read—and that
was enough for her to decide it was something to do.

One whore panicked and tried suicide; many continued to
entertain men in defiance of the new law. Licensed prostitution was declared illegal throughout Japan. The *junsa*
created consternation in the district with each disruptive
sweep. A new man was their overlord, demanding adher-
ence to law with feudal ruthlessness. His subordinates
were in awe of him. They trod lightly in his presence and

were aware he had gained his elevated post through distinguished military exploits in Manchukuo. For them, Chief Superintendent Shugo Hidenori of the Kinki Regional Police Bureau in Kansai Province was *Nihon* personified. For Yukiko, he was Authority ordering her to pack up and go home.

Heinie Joe was overjoyed at the prospect of leaving Osaka. He wanted to go at once but there were a few debts to be paid, some bribes to be dispensed, and they had to make a final visit to the *junsa*. It was a tedious hour and a half. Dossiers were examined. New sets of fingerprints and photographs were made of each and attached to their records. Over fourteen, he looked younger; his mother's pictures seen side by side showed her to have aged much. She was instructed not to take up her profession again and the boy was regarded with suspicion. Nothing was said to him; his path would inevitably cross that of the *junsa*. When all was done, Yukiko and her son sold the bulk of their possessions to the next tenants of the bus and went down to the busy pier at the foot of the shipyard to buy passage on the Inland Sea launch.

Carried from stop to stop at a snail's pace, Yukiko suffered more fear than at her son's delivery; in a sense, she was delivering him again by attempting to return home with him. But he was too big to strangle now, and not without worth. He could work in the paddies with her family—her parents were old and needed strong, young hands. And if hatred existed among the community, it wasn't so large a number to be borne; she and her son had survived that of the city, where there were tens upon tens for each one of the villagers. Life might be painful, yet they would be home. Not the bus of existence... home. The word had healing in it. She would willingly exile herself to the cubicle if her father and mother would accept her again. Accept her and the boy. The blades of apprehension sawed at her while she tried to sleep that night.

Morning brought them to the stone wharf of her childhood. Walking past the ramp and along paths leading to her father's house, they were not recognized immediately; they were a woman and a boy with a suitcase, to be observed casually, then discussed with vigorous alarm. At the sight of the veranda, Yukiko paused with thudding heart. Love washed over her at the same instant. She walked closer, with Joe marching smartly at her side. They arrived before the step, removed their shoes, city shoes which looked incongruous beside the wooden *geta,* and she called a timid announcement into the doorway.

Her mother was astonished. Oka-san ran to the door, mouth agape...ran forward uttering sharp cries of welcome...then stopped, aghast at what she was doing. Daughter and son, mother and daughter stood transfixed with distance, none revealing the turmoil inside.

"Did you get the letters I sent, Oka-san?"

"Hai, we got them...and the yen with them."

"You didn't answer."

"It wasn't necessary, was it?"

"But you wrote about Ooba-san."

"Hai, only then...without your father's knowledge."

"We have nowhere to go, Oka-san. The *junsa* gave us permission to return here. I cannot practice my profession now, it is forbidden."

"Your father is in the rice field. He will come home when he hears of you. It would be well if you left before then."

Oka-san admired the boy secretly. How grown he was! How much of her daughter was in his face; it was a pity he was not fully of their blood. She turned her back upon them lest they think she would accept the *ainoko* into the family.

He didn't need more. Heinie Joe lost his joy of the trip; fury possessed him and he threw down the luggage. "I can still catch the launch before it leaves."

"Stay, Joe! Give me time to win them over."

He glared at his mother. "You don't need me anymore." He grabbed his shoes as he leaped from the veranda.

"Joe, wait!" Opening her purse, she removed a bundle of yen to extend toward him. It was everything; her savings and the money left from what was sold in Osaka. *Hai,* everything! For everything was sold in Osaka! He snarled at her, jamming his feet into his shoes.

"I don't want it."

"You don't have anything. How will you live?"

He snatched the bills from her, took a third and dropped the rest at her feet.

"Where will you go?"

"Everywhere."

"Will I see you again?"

Hurt, he ran from her. Down the streets they used to get there, hearing curses of villagers who were silent before. Nobody wanted him, he raged Nobody. Not so. There were those on Honshu willing to take care of his needs if he took care of theirs. Why was he crying? He didn't care about anyone. Why should he cry? They didn't want him. The family of his mother didn't want him. The village of his birth didn't want him. He didn't care. And the tears seared his cheeks.

Heinie spent the next hour waiting impatiently for the launch to get under way...and was unable to stifle the hope that his mother would appear upon the wharf, carrying the suitcase and hurrying to leave with him. She didn't. The cargo for the village was unloaded and the launch pulled away without taking anyone else on board.

In the village, Yukiko was given a grim reception by her aged father. She was taken in like a leper...but she remained.

The launch stopped here and there and crossed to Shikoku, then dropped cargo at short hops along the coastline and picked up cargo and passengers. The tedium itched Heinie's feet. He roamed over the vessel as trapped boys will. They were on the lower Huichi Sea when he discovered his loss. The money was gone! In that inexplicable robbery which occurs to those most careful. He searched the decks frantically, retracing every step and inconveniencing new passengers by scrabbling at their heels and turning their baggage side to side. They pushed him from their possessions, outraged. A sailor asked what he was doing. He said he lost his money. The sailor wasn't convinced it could have been more than a couple of yen and roughly told him to mind his manners or be put ashore as a nuisance. He made another desperate circuit of the launch, taking care to keep his distance from everyone. It was gone. No one looked sly. No one looked richer. It was gone.

At Imbari, he was thrown off the launch for being too suspicious. Complaints made to the captain accused him of looking for things to steal. If one of the crew was too eager to get him ashore, he did not note it. Heinie was stranded. Townsmen on the waterfront chased him from the community. The calamity was being where nothing existed, as it did upon the mainland of Honshu; it was too primitive here for the life he knew. He struck out upon the road, hoping it would lead him to salvation.

He became employed by mingling with a group unloading wood from an old truck beyond the town. Bales of split logs were piled into rows beside the road. The workers were a woman and her stocky daughters, six uneven copies of a man supervising them and tallying each load upon an invoice. Heinie pulled wood from the truck and fell into line as though it was his job; no one deterred him, none spoke. When the truck was empty, the man took the slip of paper into a warehouse nearby. He returned, counting yen. Heinie and the others, still strangers to one another, were squatted in the dirt before the woodpile. The woman and her daughters got up to climb into the back of the truck. Heinie was more obvious for being deserted. The man looked up from his money.

"Who are you?"

"Joe. I need work."

"Jōō." He mouthed the name as if to find the end of it. Spitting it out, he said, "I'm not looking for help."

"But I want to get back to Honshu."

"Oh...you're from there." The provincial finding fault with the sophisticate. He got into the cab of the truck to start the engine. Heinie scrambled to his feet and hung at the window.

"You only have girls to work for you!"

"Any of them could crush you with one blow."

"Please, if only for a day or so till I find something."

"We live in the mountains. You won't find anything there but trees." Gears rasped into position. "From Honshu...you've no home?"

"Hai."

The truck percolated forward, then slowed. The man peeked out the window and shouted, "Climb on!" Heinie leaped onto the tailgate and sat against it. The females were sullen; he could have been a twig flattened across the slats.

They were driven from the warehouse into the hills, which were mountains soon, covered with woodland. From one road to another, wheels channeled rutted trails used by the same family over the years to bring wood to the carpenters of Imbari. Joe was uneasy entering so natural a district. He missed the vast carpet of black heads bobbing over humanity on the run; the quiet was awesome. Only later did he hear birds and insects harping the air. At the cottage they reached, there was no talk of salaries or even of being hired to work. He was assigned a pallet outside with the hens, under a roofed and burlapped pen. The man was a woodcutter. His wife was mute. The girls talked among themselves and treated Heinie as a stray animal who wouldn't be allowed to stay. After being fed a bowl of stew, the man led Heinie into the woods and to smoking mounds tended by yet another woman, turned black with ash and cinder. The mounds were of newly created charcoal and the black woman saw to it that the fire didn't erupt; she circled and tramped over each one to dampen the sod cover and prevent flame from destroying her yield.

"You want me to work with her?" Heinie asked.

"Tie. It takes skill to do what she does. You will cut logs for me and watch what she does. Maybe you will learn her trade." He handed him a serrated blade and showed him where trees had been dragged. The labor had been done for years, as could be seen by the amount of saplings growing where their forebears had been cut down. Only the mounds had been immovable. Rebuilt ever on their own rifled ashes, they had grown taller than the black woman stood and each was more than fifteen feet wide. She patrolled across them with the sensitivity of a bat, walking featherlight to keep from breaking through the crust to the crimson death inside.

"The charcoal burner won't harm you...and she won't have anything to do with you, either. Here..." He gave Heinie a shove toward the fallen trees. The thick trunks lay with limbs askew like wooden whores. "Trim branches from those until dark, then follow the path to the cottage." He took three or four steps before cautioning, "Leave the hardwood for her. She'll make charcoal of it."

179

"How do I know which is hard and which soft?"

The woodcutter laughed heartily. A threshing of leaves and then nothing of him was heard. Heinie looked at the black woman. She had flitted to another mound and was sprinkling wet charcoal dust over an evil yellow plume. The smoke turned gray and she moved to another hot spot. The smoke hung over everything; scorched; thick with restrained heat and explosiveness.

Heinie learned all wood was hard to the novice.

For the next week, he lived in pain. His hands and muscles were agonizingly sore. Blisters broke on palms and fingers. There was no comment from the cottage. Bowls of food; water to drink and bathe. The girls in the forest chopping and hauling and sawing with the woodcutter every day from dawn till night. The charcoal burner, always active when he arrived, didn't tire. He was afraid of her.

He was resting one afternoon, tending his torn hands, when a fairy music lilted through the trees. It was unlike bells, yet metallic and tuneful. A bearded hermit poled along the path, using a slender staff with rings on it for support. He was merry-looking and middle-aged. Warm clothing was fastly secured at ankle and wrist; he had white fingerless gloves; an eboshi, a black lacquered hat, tilted from his forehead and was precariously though firmly held in place with a string tied under his ears and behind the neck. He walked to Heinie with a smile and halooed at the black woman. She steamed in another yellow plume without answering. The man found Heinie's canteen and drank from it.

"Covetousness has no zenith. With water to be found under every fern, I cannot get my fill."

"You are welcome to drink it all."

"I've been watching you since you arrived."

"I come every day."

"*Hai*. I've been watching every day."

"Ah..."

The hermit sat beside him and produced some wild berries. He passed a few to the boy. "You are new to the forest."

"*Hai*. I'm from Honshu...Osaka."

"Your future is on the mainland."

"I can't get there swimming."

"Did the woodcutter buy you?"

"Iie ... I work for him."

"Hai ... but is he your master?"

"My master?"

"If you don't want to take her place when she dies, you'd be wise to go home." The black woman flew from the top of a mound and circled out of sight behind it.

"I don't want to go back to Osaka."

"Please forgive me. I mistook your state of happiness."

"Oh, I don't like this work!"

"Then why do you do it?"

"They feed me and I have a place to sleep."

"Would none do it in the town?"

"I didn't try there." No reason to say he hadn't been allowed to stay.

"From my eyrie, I see tankers and cargo ships on the sea. There's one anchored today off Imbari ... they will go to Kure next. You might be allowed to work your passage there." Heinie and the hermit saw the black woman clamber over the top of the mound, hunched and skittish. "The woodsman won't apprentice one of his daughters to the charcoal burner and no one from the town will apply. She's paying him for your keep."

"Ahhh ..."

The hermit dipped his lacquered hat at Heinie and clink-clinked into the brush; the staff rowed above it and disappeared where trees twinned and tripled and became woods again. Heinie tongued a shred of berry from between his teeth. It was tart and dry. Raising the canteen, he discovered it empty. He couldn't continue to work without water. He didn't refill it at the woodcutter's cottage but ran down the mountain, followed the turnings of the road, and didn't stop until he was at the waterfront again. The hermit was right: A freighter lay off the land, its hoists creaking to take on nets of goods. Heinie didn't have any trouble getting aboard.

Jordan dialed. He wasn't sure his call would be welcome...and didn't want to add the rejection to his negative existence. But the phone number had been saved, transferred from old wallet to new, and he should use it or throw it away. The clicks of each digit ended in a *jirr* at the other end of the line. Once. Twice. Three was the one to hang up...and she answered. He begged, "Can we meet?"

"Of course." She didn't ask questions. It was as though they met yesterday. Her readiness to see him lightened his depression.

"I can get away for part of the evening...if you can."

Victoria's voice was even and clear. "After dinner?"

"Yes. If you can."

"I won't be kind to the gypsy if we're to meet at the tea room."

He suggested they meet at the foot of State Street. They could talk on the ferry, which took an hour to sail to Staten Island and back; they'd renew their friendship and could extend the meeting if they wished by repeating the ride.

Dinner with Wanda provided one bad moment for him. The meal had been ordinary. They ate over gossip about friends and employees neither knew in common; names had become acquaintances through repetition. She complained of having read everything in the house.

"There's television to watch, Wanda."

"There's nothing on I care to see."

"You could run out and pick up a book, you know."

"Thanks. I was hoping you'd take me somewhere."

"Where?"

"Anywhere! A show. Dancing. I'd like to go out for a change."

"I'm going back to the Island after dinner. I've got work to do at the plant."

"Can't it wait till tomorrow, Jordie?" she wheedled, trying to change his mind. "You used to love going places with me."

"I'm too tired at the end of my day to go on the town."

"But not too tired to go back to work?"

Any reply would have been the wrong one.

"Do you know when you took me out last?"

"For dinner?"

"For anything."

"I don't know. I don't keep a diary."

"What am I supposed to do with myself while you're at the plant?"

"Whatever you always do. Don't you and your friends like to get together to play canasta?"

"What do you think we did all day?" She got angry and gave up. "Okay. I'll get myself a book to read."

Jordan was afraid his nervousness would show but she didn't detect it. They concluded their meal and she continued to be aloof as she cleared the dishes. He was grateful; more questions would get him into trouble. She might have asked why he shaved again or why he needed a clean shirt. She was rattling dishes in the sink when he was ready to leave. "See you later," he called.

He didn't think she heard him go out the door, and doubted she'd note the marvelous sky overhead. Summer was often clouded with electrical storms banging bolts at the Empire State Building, but tonight the cumulus masses had tumbled into New Jersey and beyond Atlantic City. Stars were actually visible above the city's belligerence of windows. It was going to be beautiful in New York Harbor. Cooling. He and Vikky would have the best of both views: the skyline and the spattered heavens above it.

She was waiting beside the entrance to the terminal, a sheer print dress clinging to her trim figure. She called to him cheerfully, "Isn't it a glorious evening!" Fare paid, they went aboard the ferry. The vessel was shabby, stinking of oil and engine exhaust. But there was also the sea smell and a vague rocking motion underfoot. He and Victoria commandeered a portion of the railing at one side of the stubby bow. Tugs hooted to each other or into the tenement forests. The Battery was enshrined with towers lit bottom to top; behind them, the city blended into night through a yellowed aurora. Liberty held her beacon steadily over the bay, lighting her stride to nowhere, a green goddess crowned with thorns. The ferry filled with trucks, cars, a bus; passengers sat reading tabloids in the tacky vestibules port and starboard, or nodded into their chests. Some adventurers moved to the railings to feel the breeze and to watch water drift by with its sargasso catch of garbage.

"I'm sorry I didn't contact you sooner," he apologized.

"I don't know whether or not it's complimentary to be remembered after several years go by."

"Not after. During, too."

"Really..." She had thought about Jordan after their accidental meeting and had all but forgotten him until he spoke over the phone. The attraction was still there. The curve of his mouth as she remembered...

"You still look like Charlie...the girl in the movie," he said.

"I'm surprised a film made such a deep impression upon you."

"It wasn't just that one," he denied. "Didn't movies do that to you when you were a kid? In my old neighborhood, we went to the pictures faithfully every Saturday. We believed every bit of them."

"Hmm. I think I was partial to Andy Hardy then."

"He gave us the fits. All those yes, sirs and no, ma'ams and pleases and thank yous. But we thought we were the same as he was. He lived in a white frame house...rose gardens and wide green lawn...and we went back to our cold-water apartments thinking we had what he did."

"The actress I admired most was Deanna Durbin...she was such a lovely girl."

"They all were...those girls we saw."

He was off on a tangent she hadn't expected, talking from a far place. "Yes? What about them?" she prompted.

"They were very real to us on the ships...our girls back home. They were the ideal girls next door. We were going to marry girls like that and have families."

"Did Andy Hardy get married? I can't recall."

"I don't think so. I don't think he went to war, either, or if he did, he was probably heroic. We didn't get those kinds of films. We were past believing them. Men at war aren't heroic; surviving is. Whether us or the enemy. When the war ended, we didn't find the enemy in Japan, after all. It was amazing to find out they were just like us."

"Was there a girl in Japan?"

An Asian face opened a small mouth at him from the wind off the bay. An alien face. What was her name? He had forgotten.

"How long were you there, Jordan?"

"A few months. Not as long as I would have liked. I was happy then... and not lonely."

"What is this about, Jordan?" she asked gently.

"What I haven't got. The afterward hasn't proven to be better."

"What seems to be wrong for you?"

"Well, till now I was doing fine... resigned to the life I've been leading with my wife. Is it all right to talk about this?"

"Yes."

"Maybe I can explain another way. There's a building I pass sometimes. A broad gray mass. Windows screened over with heavy wire netting like a prison. It is one: an orphanage. Broken panes here and there. I see a child watching me from a window under the rooftop once in a while. Small face. Looking the way I feel."

"We can't help becoming sad about orphans, Jordan."

"But I identified with the kid. I was suddenly aware that I was an orphan, too. Adults don't recognize that ordinarily; they lose parents and for some reason don't consider themselves orphaned afterward. An adult doesn't say my mother just died, my father just died, my parents are gone and I'm an orphan now, so it must be because there's an ongoing family to sustain bereavement. To take away the pain. It's very lonely not to have a family."

She was at a loss. The night's promise of diversion had crumpled. They weren't supposed to talk seriously; at least that should have been the unspoken agreement. An assignation is meant to be fun.

"I'm so sorry for you, Jordan."

"But I don't want you to be," he replied defensively.

"Good heavens, you've left me little alternative."

"It wasn't my intention."

"You were leading up to something?"

"Yes."

He was impossible to read, suddenly smiling under her thoughtful regard. She asked, "Why did you want to see me? Really?"

185

"I had to talk to someone."

"So you chose me, a stranger."

"We should have met years sooner than we did."

"But we did. And you didn't take advantage of the meeting to continue seeing me."

"Can we remedy the error?"

"I don't know. What are you after?"

"It involves divorcing your husband...my wife...and we'll run away and live happily ever after."

She cocked her head at him pertly. "You're mad."

"I suppose I am...really." His smile faded. "That's your word. Really."

"Jordan, even if you were serious, I wouldn't dream of giving up my husband." A broken crate floated by. A gull, balanced upon one leg, slept clutching the peak of a corner. Round and round went the crate, spinning lullabies with the sucking sound of the ferry's passage. "There are also my children to consider. They'd never forgive me!"

He knew what they'd look like but asked to see her snapshots. They moved closer to the light from the passenger vestibule to go over her collection. A daughter and son in their teens. Fair, and as he had pictured them in his fantasies. He touched each with a finger, caressing the shiny pasteboards. "They could have been my children, Vikky." She put the photographs back into her purse and they returned to the shadowed ferryboat railing. "What are we going to do?"

"Nothing, Jordan." Regret tinged her voice. "I won't see you again."

"Please don't say that."

"This has to be good-bye." She put her hand over his but felt no response. He was storing another hurt somewhere. "Oh, Jordan," she continued with wry humor, "you've ruined everything. I was prepared to flirt with you for a decent interval before agreeing to go to bed. I'm not a wicked woman, just as I don't believe you to be a philandering husband. I'm weak enough to succumb to an impulse, and you were one. But I think you want something I'm not prepared to give you. We can't resurrect the past and twist it into working for you today. I'm not your girl in the movie. Is that terrible of me?"

The light from the vestibule showed her to be other than the image he imposed upon her. She was suddenly herself: a pleasant, thirtyish Englishwoman. Comforting. Tender. Someone who'd kiss you good night from childhood ever after. "You're not terrible, Vikky. I'm in the wrong and I apologize with all my heart."

She squeezed lightly and removed her hand from his. Tugs trumpeted in the distance. "If you're having such a miserable time of it, why haven't you left your wife?"

He hadn't asked that of himself. "I imagine I pity her."

"I don't understand."

"Rather than accept being unable to have her own child, she's blamed everyone and everything else for her guilts. It turned her into an ugly person...but she was beautiful and lovable once."

"Do you still love her?"

"I don't know. We aren't getting along."

"It's not too late for you to find what you hoped for with another woman, Jordan."

"No. Do you think I'd find someone exactly like you?"

She laughed, and he was able to join her. "I hope not," she said emphatically. "You want someone who's free for more than one visit to Staten Island."

"We're not going to ride the ferry for the second trip, then?"

Smiling, she refused. "It wouldn't do to prolong anything so nice. I'll remember having been at sea with you now."

They didn't kiss when they parted. He remained aboard at her insistence, but was glad to get off when the ferry returned to the slip.

Without a destination, he walked along the deserted streets of the financial district. His steps retorted from brick hemming him into the narrow streets. As he passed each lamppost, his circling shadow worried at him. Ridiculous. He was an ass. The Englishwoman triggered wartime longings in him through her vague resemblance to an actress and he'd blown everything out of proportion. His initial purpose in phoning had been to indulge in exactly the purpose she had considered. That's what the evening really should have meant to him...her word, he'd said...really. Real. He should learn to practice reality himself. The grotto of a subway station presented itself and he went down its stairs to go home.

* * *

187

Wanda was curled up in an armchair when Jordan let himself into the apartment. Waiting.

"You weren't at the plant," she accused.

"No."

"I phoned to find out what time you were going to come home but no one answered."

Jordan hung his jacket inside the hall closet. "Well, I wasn't there. I've admitted it."

"Where did you go after dinner?"

"Wanda, it doesn't matter," he said wearily and started for the bedroom.

"You've been with another woman, Jordie." She was sober and in a mild panic.

"Yes, I have."

"You've never been unfaithful to me before."

"I wasn't this time, either."

"You're going to be."

"I don't know."

"Are you in love with her?"

"I was. She's not in love with me."

"How long have you known her?"

"Forever." He would have left but the next question made him pause at the door.

"Will you see her again?"

He was tired. She hadn't known Jordie to be so tired...of her. He said, "She doesn't want to see me again," and went into their bedroom.

In Kyoto, the illustrious actor, Jihei Segawa, was hoping to honor his country's leading *onnagata*, the equally eminent but older Shichisaburo Yoshizawa. The arrangements for the Kabuki player to be his guest took the delicacy of preparing as if for marriage, using a go-between, for this *onnagata* liked to maintain the fiction and habits of being a woman even off stage. The go-between was necessary in case the invitation was declined; neither distinguished artist could afford to be subjected to a direct confrontation which might give cause for offense.

A maid of the household kept watch for the mailman each day, and at last he had brought a perfumed envelope of finest rice paper with leaves embedded within its thin layers. She hastened to her master's room, stopped to compose herself and tapped for admittance. He gave permission and she entered.

"The letter is here!" In her excitement, she neglected to address him properly. He seized the letter from her and tore it open. He was delighted when he read the acceptance.

"The *onnagata* will come," he announced. The maid rejoiced with polite cries and he began to pace nervously. "I must summon my other guests at once. Only the cleverest and most handsome . . . this must be a perfect evening in which all the senses are gratified." She twittered agreement and he ordered her to have the servants scrub his expensive house till it gleamed. They were to prepare for the important event as for a visit from the Imperial Family. She bowed, scurried from the room to carry out his commands. Segawa went to his study to phone preselected guests. As he talked to each, they accepted hastily, promising to be prompt though some had many miles to travel. He had trouble reaching one person.

"Can't you raise anyone at the theater, operator? Of course someone's there! Meijin is directing his new play. What's that? Who's this? Good, I wish to speak with Meijin. I know he's occupied! Tell him to come to the telephone . . . fool, do you think I'm calling long distance to be told to call later? Get Meijin immediately! Do you know who I am? This is Jihei Segawa! Yes, himself! That's better. Now run tell Meijin he's wanted. . . ." Segawa drummed his fingers on the mahogany desk top for an interval. Framed award certificates and statuettes were interspersed with signed photographs of celebrities on all sides of the room. One picture was of himself with Meijin, taken at Cannes two years before. Meijin looked ill. He hadn't written or directed *End of the Wheel;* it was a congratulatory pose. Perhaps his name should have been removed from the list. He was impossibly pretentious, had noble aspirations, unpredictable talent, and produced nothing but political plays these days; however, the *onnagata*

189

might be amused by him. Someone rattled the phone at the other end. "Ah, is that you, Meijin?"

"I was staging my fifth scene!"

"It will be brilliant. But listen, I want you to come to a party."

"In Kyoto? That's miles away!"

"You don't want to miss this. Shichisaburo Yoshizawa is my guest of honor."

"So? How did you manage it?"

"He writes, and I quote, 'I have long been an admirer of your virile samurai portrayals in films and look forward to exchanging social courtesies.' Isn't that a charming note of acceptance to send?"

"You'll notice the old dear says he's been seeing your films for a long time."

"Age does not wither, Meijin."

"You'll find his makeup wrinkled, Jihei."

"Have you met him socially?"

"*Tie*...but I've watched him in a thousand performances."

"Well, then. I'm having a selection of interesting friends in to meet him and you must be here, too."

"I'm flattered...but busy."

"You can get away for the weekend, surely?"

"What would my actors do?"

"Have them rehearse by themselves. It will give them a chance to learn those lines of yours word perfect."

"Well. Who else are you asking?"

"Come see for yourself."

"I realize you're spreading your finery for the *onnagata* but I don't wish to travel so far to spend the weekend alone."

"Bring someone with you...whomever you like."

"I don't like anyone at the moment."

"Well, then. You may choose from among my friends."

"You're too generous."

"Naturally, there is an exception."

"Naturally."

"Shall I see you then?"

"*Hai*. But my play needs guidance."

"As we do. I promise you'll return to Osaka refreshed. *Au revoir*, Meijin." Segawa hung up with a smirk. So much

190

persuasion! Meijin would go anywhere for fear of denying people the benefit of his intellect.

It was on the following day that Heinie Joe set foot in Osaka, having fled the dreariness of Mihara, the town he lived in after trying Kure, which he disliked. Mihara was a dud. He knew everyone, had tired of showing tourists the castle and moat and cement works. Anyway, it was too close to Hiroshima, which was constantly exhibiting its sores. He was thinking to pass through Osaka to go to another city but a harsh singing overhead gave him pause. A solitary goose, neck outstretched into the wind it followed, flew low in the sky above the shipyard. It was deserting limitless horizons for clustered forests of antennae and buildings and honked mournfully in triads of sound. Straight on its course the goose went, wired to the line which runs ever out of somewhere to the next destination, hoarsely crying into the wind bearing it—the same wind slanting across the boy's cocked head as he watched the bird wing effortlessly on its certain journey. Heinie envied the bird's return to its flock and familiar haunts. Would it change the song then? That sound ached in his own throat and deepened the hollow he felt. Seeing the wild bird devoured by rooftops, he entered the maw of the city himself.

He walked automatically to the pleasure district, taking the path his mother found years earlier. His absence had altered his relationship to the city: Population and streets were out of kilter; invisible barriers were across lanes and alleys, pushing him, urging him to pass without stop. The *junsa* seemed doubled in quantity. MP patrols rode herd upon gray-faced soldiers with Panmunjom eyes and mouths slit into vacant smiles. The racing bustle of Osaka carried Heinie faster than he wished to move. Where? Where, before it took him to... No, there was no home. No bus for him to enter unannounced and unbidden. There were gates across everything. Hands fisted into his jacket pockets, he felt the flesh of his rib cage softly resistant to the pressure. Himself. Himself, touching himself. He warmed with the friendliness of it; flushed angrily with the loneliness of the gesture. This person he inhabited *was* wanted by someone... could be fed and sheltered by someone... he had only to find a patron or patroness. The question of which didn't trouble him; he had long since wrestled with confusion and given up. Taunted, avoided, even attacked...in the company of strangers, he could receive tenderness and acceptance. True, it ended when hungers were sated. And then he was turned out in the embarrassed departure such partners make one from the other without a backward look, though sometimes there was a final, regretful glance. The warping of dreams was one of the legacies he and his duplicates were heir to in their pariah lives; their common dream was to yearn for security in a perverted coupling, as was available with luck to those upper-caste misfits with unclouded bloodlines.

"Where've you been?"

He ceased to resist the sudden grasp of a strong hand when he saw its owner. Tadanobu looked like a man surprising himself.

"How did you know I went anywhere?"

"I saw you and your mother leave. I thought it was permanent."

"I was happy to go."

"And your mother?"

"Why do you ask? You were never a customer."

"She's not with you."

"Tie. I'm on my own."

"You've returned to stay?"

"I'm just passing through."

A grunt which could have been laughter. "There are no train stations on this lane, *ainoko.* You came looking for something. What is it?"

"Nothing. I'm passing through."

"I've watched you grow. You have beautiful skin."

The pressure of the man's fingers increased. Stubby. Thick. Tendoned with the strength of hours of concentration.

"How would you like to stay with me?"

Tadanobu wasn't a man to take another male into his bed. Heinie became uneasy and asked, "What for? I'm on my way to Tokyo maybe. I don't want to live here again."

"No matter where you go, you'll have a chancy life. I can give you food and a *futon* in back of my shop."

Karadamonya. The Gate of the Body. But what was he after? "You don't want me as an apprentice?"

192

"You'll live a life of ease."

The fingers were a vice now and he had to strain to twist from them. He rubbed his elbow with annoyance. The man hurt him and was speaking of providing for him. Ah, was that it, then?

"I won't interfere with you, *ainoko*. I have a woman for that."

The surrounding street gave no clue. People went about their business as they would ordinarily. He and the man could be seen by everyone, the man an object of undisguised interest by those knowing him. "Why do you want me to stay with you?"

"I want to make flowers grow." It was a dread sentence. "A masterpiece of color." Lovingly said, it held intangible threat.

"I've no time to waste," Heinie said nervously. "I want to see Himeji and other places I've heard about." He started to move but was gripped once more by the artist's talons.

"Wait. Isn't it tempting to you? You could never afford a body suit. Think of it! I could create what has never been attempted." The inks were poisonous. He had not dared use them as he'd like upon clients. With such a boy, he could risk anything; a dead *ainoko* is of no consequence. "But then," he sneered, "perhaps you like the suit you wear now. Everyone admires you."

It was cruel. Heinie Joe was torn between becoming the owner of an exquisite design or running from the danger he sensed behind this proposition. It wouldn't add to his own worth to become a walking advertisement of the man's skill. Whatever was done to his skin could change nothing for him... nothing.

"What's the good of wandering, *ainoko?* Stay with me."

Heinie wrenched from the iron hold and stepped back with a negative shake of the head.

"You're chasing after the wind," Tadanobu jeered.

"Hai, that's what it is." The wild bird died into a design in his thoughts and Heinie stood still. He waited for the man to go into his shop. Tadanobu sat on the couch, regretting having spoken to the boy and having been noticed doing it. When his eyes lifted to the window, Heinie was gone.

He had run down the lane to the row of buses. How old

and rusty they were! He pulled up short, breathing hard with exertion. Why so fast? To see if the bus was there and as he remembered? It could never be...not without his mother. Not even if he regained possession of the vehicle and restored every article taken from it. A child near the steps eyed him. Small boy. Shirted, with bare bottom hunched over grimy heels. Guarding the territory as though born to the hearth. A tear leaked from a corner of Heinie's eye before he could catch it. Blinking rapidly, he mashed the gathering wet with a thumb and blurred his sight of the usurper in the dust. The child's sister came out of the bus at that moment, saw Heinie and frowned. She was pretty, he thought. They were the same age but he felt infinitely older; she didn't know shit about life. What he could teach her! She snatched her brother bodily from the ground and lifted him into the bus to watch Heinie from a window pane. Were they happy there? Not lonely there? Someone shouted at the end of the alley. Pimps, shaking fists at him. They wanted him out of the district. He swallowed dryness in his throat and turned obediently. Retracing his steps, he passed the shop named Karadamonya with bowed head.

Tadanobu listened to the shuffling drag of Heinie's feet. The tempo picked up and he heard the boy run again. Running. Running. And it was fainter and fainter until he was beyond thinking of his beautiful skin.

A corner of a house hid him. Heinie Joe coughed up phlegm, spat and then smoothed his hair. He must be presentable to cruise the districts. He'd have one last good meal in Osaka before leaving the city for good. But the respectable streets looked more formidable and he gravitated toward Dotonbori, thinking to run into a friend from one of the theaters. And he was discovered by Meijin en route to take the train to Kyoto. Heinie was shadowed for a hundred yards. He acknowledged his follower by slowing, and was caught up and accompanied until they were strolling along together.

"Boy...what's your name?"

"Heinie Joe, sir."

"You're not in school?"

"Iie...I'm already a genius."

194

Meijin chuckled. "So am I. I write plays for my living. What do you do for yours?"

"I steal and make love to anyone I meet."

"What ancient practices for one so young!"

"I'm past sixteen."

"I'm old enough to be your father."

The boy disliked the remark and started to edge away. Meijin walked faster. "Oh, does that have some significance? *Hai,* I see...you are one of the GI bastards."

"You can eat shit for all I care." Heinie tried to outpace him but was matched.

"I'm wise to your sort. You won't trample me underfoot while I hope you'll be nice to me."

Heinie halted and faced him. "Are you interested in feeding me and putting me up for the night or not?"

"I have something grander in store for you. How would you like to attend a congress of giants in Kyoto?"

"What do you mean?"

"I'm going to a party given by Jihei Segawa." The boy's eyes grew large and his jaw dropped. "Ah...I see you know of him."

"Who doesn't?"

"Would you like to meet him?"

Silence. Disbelief.

"And his worthy friends?" His snicker was peculiar but Heinie didn't care. He was too impressed by the possibility that such a thing could be true.

"You don't mean it."

"Hai. It pleases me to learn what so many hawks will do to find Ishmael in their midst."

"You're talking riddles."

"Let's solve this together. Will you go with me?"

"Now?"

"To Kyoto."

He studied Meijin. He had nothing to distinguish him; that is to say, he looked harmless. Heinie's instinctive alarms had not sounded. Smiling. There was worse than humoring a madman with a smile and if his offer was a true one, it could be the greatest experience of a lifetime. *"Hai,* let's go," Heinie said, and they linked arms and hired a sedan to take them to the train station.

The house of Jihei Segawa was situated upon a quiet street with similar residences on both sides of the cobbled road. The solidly built white stucco structure had to be approached through a bamboo gate and across a charming formal garden. The cobblestones of the exterior were repeated in smaller form here, pebbling a path sentried by a large ceramic badger. Illuminated by a lantern behind it, the animal stood upright; a sake bottle dangled from an arm and the other carried a stuffed bag. Enormous testicles spread rudely over the lower limbs to provide a firm base. A wide conical hat was tied to its head with hempen cord to shade the droll brown face, yet candlelight flickering from the lantern enlivened the painted eyes. Stronger lights filtered through thickly woven drapes at tall French windows on a portico facing the entry. In place of a traditional *fusuma,* the sliding door, an imposing wooden slab lacquered orange and studded with metal points was hinged into a frame in the Occidental manner. A provocative door knocker was at its center, made of brass and polished to a high gloss by use. Handling it, a visitor aided a cormorant to sodomize a gleeful dwarf.

Social rumblings could be heard as Meijin escorted Heinie Joe to the door. The boy was sparked with lightnings, already impressed by the neighborhood and the sheer elegance of the actor's property. The two new friends added their shoes to a platoon of shining leather lined two by two at one side of the portico. The playwright ignored the door knocker and rapped imperiously upon the wood beside it. "I remember when he got this plaything as a gift," he informed the boy. "We had to argue at length before Jihei would have it installed; now the dwarf never gets any rest." A housemaid opened the door. Meijin plucked a personal card from a card case and gave it to her. She bowed, admitted them and led the way inside.

They were ushered to a parlor decorated with authentic Victorian furniture. The couch and tufted chairs, occupied by a score of intense men and youths, revealed coverings of patterned white damask. The company turned heads like a nest of owls to assess the newcomers, then resumed their adoration of the royal pair in the midst: the actor and the *onnagata*. As Meijin and Heinie Joe waited for the maid to present the calling card to Segawa, the boy absorbed everything he could see in the room. The opulence was seductive; bibelots of silver and Dresden miniatures adorned shelves and end tables; paintings in ornate gold frames looked down their noses at a carpet fashioned by hand in the Near East which swallowed his feet as though to conceal the poor cotton of his stockings; overhead an effervescent Austrian crystal chandelier flashed rainbow darts of color. He had not known people lived like this. He saw how naturally the other guests accepted it all, and he coveted everything about them.

The maid accomplished her unobtrusive errand; her master smiled broadly as he read the name on the card. Excusing himself from those nearest and in particular the *onnagata*, he stood and went to greet Meijin. "You're late," he accused urbanely.

"I'm not. You've had eager sycophants arriving before me." The actor barely glanced at the boy. Meijin introduced him. "This person is named Heinie Joe. I assume it's an alias, but we can relish the mystery while we get to know him. And please forgive him his inappropriate wardrobe. We left Osaka so precipitously to oblige you, he didn't have time to change."

Heinie cringed. He was wearing black-market GI castoffs, his Navy peacoat shining at its edges with hard use. As the ubiquitous maid took it from him, he rued its shabbiness and surveyed the room. The others were sartorially correct, displaying garters and gold watch chains, buttoned vests and four-in-hand ties. The hair of their heads was clipped short; his was unruly and growing. He looked at Segawa with a hangdog expression... a captured poacher before his liege. Segawa seemed not to have heard Meijin's remarks; he courteously invited them to join the party.

"While my *jochu* prepares your drinks, you must meet everyone."

They were presented to the guest of honor first. The tranquil *onnagata* was modestly sibilant, forming his mouth small over pomegranate words. A soft silken scarf

197

tied to his neck in lieu of a cravat was the only feminine touch, though Heinie thought Yoshizawa resembled an old woman in a man's tight suit. As for Meijin, he was amused to note the *onnagata*'s makeup was indeed showing cracks upon the aging features. Nevertheless, Meijin bowed with respect, and the boy at his side was duly appreciated by a lift of painted eyebrows. The *onnagata* received their obeisance as his due, at the same time catching Heinie's evident worship of their host. Segawa then introduced them rapidly to the other guests and space was found for them to sit. The maid brought strong drinks of imported whiskey and mix in cut glass tumblers reflecting the gems of light from the chandelier. The company adjusted to the new situation; several were thrilled to have the irascible playwright at hand and possibly living up to his eccentric reputation. Imagine, bringing a street pickup to Jihei Segawa's house! The younger men were disconcerted to find Heinie a rival; he had stolen their pre-eminence by being a leopard among angoras.

Taking advantage of a lull, Yoshizawa observed to the boy, "In years past, you would have been a fair candidate for the Wakashu Kabuki...how sad it doesn't exist in our day." Everyone hushed. He struck a pose out of habit to limn himself upon the minds of his audience as he would have done from the stage. "The Youth Kabuki took their handsome players from every strata of society to ensure a flood of patrons...exciting boys like yourself." Heinie grinned at the compliment. It wasn't one; Yoshizawa was instigating closer inspection to identify him as an *ainoko* to those with less discernment.

Meijin pooh-poohed the statement. "Exciting boys! Exciting enough to have authorities suppress them for immorality, *Sensei*. They were no better than their predecessors."

Addressed as teacher, the *onnagata* was mollified but defended himself. "The audience can't resist falling in love with those playing female roles, Meijin. But you can't point to us for instilling base instincts in men. We followed custom, didn't we? Blame the women! You, of course, know the art of Kabuki was introduced by Okuni, the Shinto priestess, to improve dances she performed while striking a gong and singing Buddhist chants. It was women who furthered that drama! Courtesans danced and acted scenes with men before the populace! Idolized and sought after, those *ladies* created uproarious scandals and were rightfully banned from theatrical life. For three hundred years and more, their roles have been taken by boys and men...and though women may act now in Japan, they cannot return to the modern Kabuki. Blame the women, Meijin!"

"Then let us talk of men, *Sensei.*" The *onnagata* was about to have his trapdoor pulled open beneath him. Meijin dearly loved wresting a conversation from anyone people listened to with concentration. He felt an egotistic liberty to make the substitution without so much as an "excuse me."

"I love to talk of men."

"Let us talk of men's instincts...which you mentioned. Those are to rule, not be lumps of concretions masturbating under a roof as they watch pretty boys prance across a stage in imitation of their sisters." Yoshizawa put hands over his ears in protest.

"You're not going to introduce your political nonsense, are you?" interrupted Segawa with a woeful grimace at the rest of his guests. Meijin was being absurd; but, then, that was expected.

"I call it a cry for independence, myself!"

Yoshizawa chided him softly. "You talk like a revolutionist."

Meijin beamed. "A nationalist, *Sensei.* A royalist, if you will!"

"We've had a sufficiency of bloodshed in our lives. It's time for peace and dancing."

"Not to the tune of the barbarians. They've given us a legacy of weakness to follow. Look at us here—not one in uniform!"

"You prefer to have men march off to die again? It's a waste. They have more to offer living. It can't be what you want."

"I want my Emperor back. Lord MacArthur made a pet gardener of the ruler of my country. These young boys you coddle should be men of Bushido! They should rise in proud armies to regain our former standing in the world."

Segawa said, "You'll be having the Americans intervening with us as they are doing everywhere else, you *gunjin.* You want the Occupation reinstated?"

199

"I defy them to try!"

"*Gunjin, gunjin!*"

"That's right. I *am* a military man. I would gladly throw out my typewriter to take up the sword."

"The sword," mocked the actor. "That's my weapon."

"What you do with it is make-believe. I'm talking about reality."

A few of the company smiled behind their hands. The *onnagata* was irked at being led off the track. "But we were discussing art..." he protested.

"What is art?" demanded Meijin. "When what you do is popular and successful, it is art. Have diminishing audiences and you'll soon see how much art is involved. I'm after something which will be successful and popular forever."

"How you twist words and subject to suit yourself!" Yoshizawa complained. Deciding the playwright had been too mischievous, Segawa jumped to his feet and suggested everyone mingle and not tire the guest of honor with foolishness. The group stirred, stretched their legs as they walked around the room to converse. A boy came forward to speak cordially to Meijin.

"You may have missed my name before. I am Shiro Nakayoshi."

Heinie Joe looked him over calculatingly. He was of the same age; heavier, he couldn't be considered fat. Living the soft life. The scrubbed look of a scholar and an oval Buddha face undone by lips permanently shaped into a kiss. Obviously at ease; possibly a relative of the host. Shiro was offering to conduct them through the house to see the decor.

"I've been here before," said Meijin, disappointing Shiro. During prior moments, the young man had visualized the playwright at the forefront of battle, leading a battalion of dedicated students against the barricades. The last thing he wanted to hear was, "Permit me to renew my acquaintance with the other gentlemen while you take my friend on your tour."

Shiro was obliged to go through with his comedy. He hadn't intended to show friendship for Meijin's street boy but had trapped himself. He took pains to be amiable as he led Heinie Joe from the room.

"Been to Kyoto before?"

"I've been many places."

"I'm here to study at the university."

"Kyoto's not your home?"

"Iie...I live with my uncle's family."

"Well, that's almost the same thing."

"These cabinets contain canisters of film...everything Jihei Segawa has done. He doesn't show them, however." He swung a door aside to reveal rows of round, flat cans stacked on shelves. Tape listed their contents on the edges—titles of films Heinie had seen. The door was shut. "And the shelves there store his record collection. Do you like music?"

"Hai...anything."

"I like American music. It is my hobby. That and discussing politics. Do you like coffee shops?"

"Anything..."

"There's nothing like a brisk argument with your fellow students!"

"Hai...it is so."

"I could talk politics day and night!"

"Ah..."

"And you...what do you think of Meijin's ideas?"

"I think he's full of shit."

Shiro objected. "You don't know the man. He's the rage on every campus."

"I know all I want to of him. He doesn't compare with Jihei Segawa."

They walked along the hall in silence. Heinie traced the texture of a tapestry to feel a unicorn's horn, caressed the shade of a Tiffany lamp without knowing its value. No one he'd known lived like this. "I'd like to stay in Kyoto and see how I'd do," he announced, "but I'll have to get money together before it's possible."

"Did Meijin bring you from Osaka?"

"Hai...that's where we met."

"Ah..." There had been speculation about it in the parlor.

"Why do you ask?"

"No reason. What business is your family in?"

"None." Then Heinie chuckled apologetically. "I'm alone now," he admitted.

"Ah...are you at boarding school?"

"Iie. I've never attended a single class."

Shiro slowed to look at him askance. "You can't mean it."

"I was too busy."

"Doing what?"

"I pimped for my mother before the whores were outlawed."

As it had been an ordinary and legal profession, his answer was matter-of-fact. Shiro now knew the whispered guesses he'd heard when Heinie and Meijin arrived were accurate. This was the first of the *ainoko* he'd met personally...and was liking his honesty. Indeed, it was quite easy to be kind to him!

"What's behind those doors?"

Shiro wanted to become friends with Meijin; he could do it through Meijin's friend, but not if they continued inspecting the house. "I think we should get back to the party. Everyone is anxious to talk with you." Heinie allowed Shiro to rush them to the parlor, where the boy turned him over to the other guests. Heinie was promptly surrounded by the older men, fussed at like some unique find in a flea market. It was plain his mixture of beauty and roughness overcame his origin temporarily to make him the third major attraction of the evening.

Housemaids passed through regularly with hors d'oeuvres and replenished drinks without being asked. Heinie Joe took each glass handed him; he'd learned not to refuse anything since he was a child. The evening promised intrigue, for he searched out Segawa while Shiro followed Meijin; then they exchanged partners only to return to the chase again. Yoshizawa watched with inner mirth. He delighted in seeing the youngsters vie with each other. How he missed the passionate days of his youth! Ah...the playwright with the atrocious manners was hurrying to defend his claim. What was he saying to the *ainoko?* The *onnagata* knew without having to hear.

Having maneuvered Heinie Joe to one side, Meijin hoped to deflate him. "Don't cut off the end of what is already short."

The boy was light-headed and enjoying himself hugely. "What's that you say?"

"Having brought you, I expect you to leave with me."

"Hai, but what was the other thing you said?" Heinie

held Meijin's arm familiarly, thus embarrassing the man since they were in public view.

"It meant you won't always be young. Once you've lost your youthful appeal, you will have lost everything. Beware of growing old. That's when you'll have no one caring about you but yourself." He left Heinie to mull it over and didn't speak to him again until they were seated beside each other at the long dinner table in Segawa's dining room.

The guests were treated to an elaborate European dinner of numerous courses, served precisely as it was done abroad. Copying Meijin, Heinie Joe solved the sequence of using knives, forks and spoons. He gulped his wines, to Meijin's horror, and ate everything to prevent himself from getting drunk. This was the style, he told himself; these fellows know how to get the best out of life. Smiling at everyone, he saw their eyes shine at him in the light from centerpiece candles. He sensed love around him. Where better for it to exist? Fine crystal and Sèvres plates whisked before him and vanished without letup. It must have cost a fortune to provide so much fancy food!

After dinner, Shichisaburo Yoshizawa pleaded a headache and asked to be taken to his residence beside Lake Biwa, some miles out of the city. Half the table responded but he said he would be content if one of them, a bashful department store manager, did him the favor. They were sent off gaily, everyone savoring the fun of learning who captured the *onnagata*'s fancy. When they were gone, the group spent more congenial time in the parlor. Segawa played symphonic records and was seen to yawn behind his palm. The hint was obeyed. To the music of Stravinsky, each guest made his departure, bowing very low, embracing the host and each other with optic affection, bowing more and eventually backing out the door. Segawa suggested to Heinie Joe privately that he return within the hour. The boy was pleased to agree. He went into the night with Meijin but escaped shortly in the darkness, leaving the playwright to condemn all *ainokos* to their demons.

Shiro was another matter. He had not left and was reclining upon the couch, listening to the music as he sipped the last of his brandy. Segawa dismissed the household staff for the night, then turned to his friend.

"I'm exhausted, Shiro."

"So am I. It was something to meet the *onnagata* but I tired of so many people trying to be brilliant at the same time."

"I think I shall go to sleep early tonight."

Shiro sat up, drained his goblet and said, "Very well. I'm sleepy, too."

"No...I mean for you to go home, Shiro."

Shiro stared. "You don't want me to spend the night?"

"Iie. I'll call you in a few days after I've settled some business about a new film I'm to do."

"You didn't tell me you were going to be working so soon."

"It came up this morning. A call from the studio. You know how these things happen."

"Hai, I know." Shiro had witnessed the quick communication between the actor and the boy the playwright brought. He didn't have to guess why he was being sent home so abruptly. "I'll bid you a good night, then." He meant it. He wasn't unhappy to be replaced, nor to owe a debt to Heinie Joe. His release from Segawa gave him leave to contact Meijin. Not this very evening, but eventually.

The actor was relieved to have something end gracefully. *"Oyasumi-na,* Shiro. A good night to you as well."

He saw the boy out and waited till he had left the garden before dousing the lights in the parlor. He was waiting in the dark beside the window when Heinie Joe returned.

Sedate the moon...

The mottled orb hovered hazily between obscuring clouds. Anyone hoping to sing praises to *meigetsu* was sure to have given up; the weather was too foul. If it would rain! That could relieve the heaviness over the Inland Sea. Yukiko preferred downpours. Neighbors stayed indoors then and few were encountered when she had to leave the house, not that she went out often. She restricted her errands, her needs so limited she could purchase enough to last through a week or more. Sitting in the dusk beside the cold fire pit, she heard the clatter and piping of villagers with sharp clarity, knifing the oppression cloaking her. A woman's voice curdling with argument. That would be Mr. Nakatsuru's termagant, an imported woman from Kyushu who'd outlived the octogenarian and took his place among the leaders of the community. She was as vindictive as he had been. Though she hadn't known Yukiko until her return to the village, she made certain Yukiko was kept ostracized.

Was it after Oto-san's death that they attempted to oust her from the village again? So hard to separate the parts of a continuing pain. The Nakatsurus, husband and wife, teamed to force the issue during Oto-san's illness. Mr. Nakatsuru went to sleep at a meeting of the *yoryokusha* and didn't awaken. Elaborate arrangements for his funeral ended the effort. So one death was a loss and another a gain. Then Oka-san became feeble, as though the passing of her man slipped strength from her, as the quill is drawn from a squid. She suffered helplessness for months. Waited upon hand and foot, she shriveled tinier than she was and Yukiko could lift her from the *futon* easily—so easily she knew the weight of her mother's life was no longer in her hands or within her power to keep it with her. How the broth, fed drops at a time, dribbled at her lips...her wizened face was that of a hatchling, pointed and eager, and unable to control the sucking desperation of a hunger which could never be appeased again. Oka-san didn't want to die; she left life complaining of death.

The house crushed Yukiko. Its emptiness and fullness crowded upon her. The moldering deterioration of tatami and other furnishings, interior and exterior, could not be stanched. There were no people to turn to for repairs; there was no tearing down and rebuilding fresh to duplicate the original. She sought refuge in memories of the few joys she had known, finding each wrapped with sadness. There wasn't money to spare for just one persimmon to place upon the shelf for the moon. But she had made small dumplings of rice flour, as was customary, and put them there, sorry not to have composed verses, as was customary; and then she took the dumplings from the shelf and added them to the iron pot over the fire pit. It was this thinking of another moon-viewing which had stopped her from lighting the coals. How long had she been sitting, doing nothing? It happened so often; seasons changed without notice with so much thinking, events of the past filching those of the present. There was one good feature about it: She could be a girl again with the thinking.

Joe-dan-ash walked in upon her in the person of his son. In through the open doorway, casually as could be. He had a paper box under his arm.

"Where are the old people?" he asked loudly. "Nobody is working in the fields."

"You're back, Joe."

"Iie ... till the launch stops by in the morning." Belligerently, he continued, "Will I be permitted to stay the night?"

"This is your home."

"Yours, not mine."

"Where have you been, Joe?"

He dropped the box beside her and sat. He wore a new windbreaker without its lining, and he was taller ... and older. He opened the box to give her cigarettes and sticky candy. She could not take her eyes from him to see the gifts.

"You went to Osaka?"

"Shikoku. I lived in Imybari for a while."

"Hai? I did not think you went to Shikoku."

"Well, that was where the launch went that morning and I wanted to be somewhere and that was as good as any. I worked chopping wood for a man until a *yamabushi* said my future was on the mainland."

"How would a mountain hermit know? You were making a living honestly and shouldn't have given it up."

"It wasn't for me. I was getting calluses and there was nothing exciting to do."

"Hai. And then? Where did you go?"

"I let a cargo ship decide. I took one which stopped near Mihara. That was very good. I had a good life in Mihara."

"You could have seen me before you went there."

"I was still angry. Did your mother and father think I would come back right away?"

"They didn't speak of you."

Loudly, looking to the doors. "Well, then. Now they will."

"Iie. They're dead." It was too dark to see his face but she heard him laugh.

"All that worry for nothing," he said with relief. "I was so fucking scared to come because I thought I'd be driven away. Then I thought, I'm bigger now and nobody can do it. And then I wasn't going to bother. And then I wanted to see you so I hitched rides to the coast."

"But you said you were living in Mihara."

"Oh, that was before. I came from Kyoto."

"Kyoto!"

"Hai. I go everywhere now."

"I missed you."

He groped in the gloom to find the cigarettes and ripped open the pack. He pushed it into her hands. "Hey, aren't you going to smoke these? French cigarettes. I stole them from a rich friend." *Gauloise.* The tobacco was stale. Segawa's souvenirs of Cannes had been an accidental discovery when searching the mahogany desk for yen. "The package won't be missed. He has dozens."

His voice was deeper...older. How it could have filled her silence!

"You want to light a lamp? We can't see shit in here."

She scraped a match above the fire pit and touched it to the wick of an oil pot lacking its chimney glass. Shadows sprang at them and staggered with the flame till it settled. Then she lit another match for the tinder prepared for the coals; she nursed the fire, blew life into edges of charcoal and spread the red glow into the ashes. The iron pot was swung into place. "We'll have something to eat when it's ready," she said. Now the cigarette. Taking one, she offered the rest to Joe.

"Iie. I don't smoke. You know I don't smoke."

She looked at his arms but the sleeves of the jacket covered them.

"Iie. I don't take drugs, either."

She chose a stick of charcoal to light her cigarette. The ember flamed hotter as she inhaled. Like a small sun. *Where flamed summer's sun.* She replaced the charcoal carefully to let it do its work in the pit. "I'm glad. You're growing into a fine man, Joe." He looked ruddy in the light...son of the moon and the sun.

"You look bad," he said. "Why don't you leave this dump and go to the mainland with me?"

207

"What would I do there? Here I have this house and a plot of ground to dig."

"We could make a fortune in Kyoto. It's like Osaka without so many *junsa* around. But there's lots of soldiers from Saigon looking for action."

"You're not pimping, Joe? You'll be put in prison."

"*Tie*, I'm not pimping. Who would let an *ainoko* move in on them? The only way I could do it is if you go back with me."

"Give up that life, Joe. Get another job cutting wood or learn a trade that is honest."

He tossed his head angrily. "Shit."

"Your hair is too long. Shall I trim it for you?"

His head tossed again. "It's the style. Nobody wears short hair anymore."

"Soon it will be like mine when I was a girl."

"Leave me alone about it. You want me to be angry?"

"Ah, Joe..."

"You don't know shit on this island. Everybody's like a hundred years ago." He got up restlessly and automatically cased the room. "No television? Shit, you don't even have a radio!"

"There's no money for them."

He returned to sit beside her again. "You need money? I don't have any."

"I wasn't asking."

"Hey, you still sew? You still know how to paint dolls?"

"I could."

"I met a man in Mihara. He has a shop below the castle and sells to tourists. You want to work for him?"

"I won't leave my village."

"Okay. I was trying to think of a way for you to make money."

She lifted the lid of the iron pot. Though thin, the mixture wasn't heating yet. "He wouldn't hire me anyway. I'm not young anymore."

"Oh, he's not like the merchant we knew. Let me look him up when I get back on the mainland. Maybe he will hire you."

"*Tie*. I won't leave here."

"Well, shit. I'll tell him to send you the junk and you do them and send them back. You can do that, *hai*? You won't get rich but you'll have a few yen for cigarettes, maybe buy a television set. Battery is extra but you need it since you don't have electricity. I'll talk to the man." His smile was Joe-dan-ash bringing luxuries. "He'll do anything for me. I used to guide tourists to his shop... and there are other favors he owes."

She was quick to see an advantage. "If you work for him again, Joe, it would be simpler for us."

"He would like that." Heinie brayed in a manner she would not question. "I've outgrown him now, anyway. But I'll talk to him before I head back to Kyoto. He'll send you work to do."

"Do you think you will live in Kyoto?"

"Till I get bored. Then someplace else."

"I wish you could stay with me."

It would hurt to answer. Heinie Joe laughed instead, saying, "Remember Tadanobu, the tattooist? He says I chase winds."

"Ah, you were in Osaka, too?"

"Hai. You wouldn't know the city."

Someone threw a rock at the side of the house. It sounded like a shot and both were startled. Yukiko put a hand out to stop him from going to the doorway. "It's nothing," she warned.

"They do that all the time?"

"No, I'm not threatened. No one cares about me now."

Another stone thudded and someone skipped away as Heinie ran to the veranda. Dark as shit out there. Fog was filling in where the clouds left off. The moon wasn't even a sick shimmer anymore. He slid the door closed and padded back to his mother. Looking past her head to the cherry red of the fire pit, he said, "Shit, what are we going to do the rest of the night? No fucking television. Not even a radio!"

She heard his complaints contentedly and voiced her own about what he was doing with his life. After he returned to the mainland, he kept his promise to speak to the merchant of Mihara and she was less destitute but still did nothing to correct the lack of modern conveniences in the house. Change would have made it too strange; within the old walls, time was stationary until the boy was there again. Only then did she see that another season was over, another year marked on his young face.

And when he was gone, promising to return, she talked

of him to the man they did not mention. Talked to Joe-dan-ash in the embers of her hearth or the clouds of her skies. Told him what little she knew of their son.

Fabrications.

For herself. To give substance to what she loved.

It wasn't gloomy in the basement. The walls had been repainted warm pastel colors and the furnace area was remarkably neat. Windows at the rear looked out upon a small enclosed backyard Jordan and Wanda thought of as a patio. A sturdy ginko branched above high walls; it spread fan-shaped leaves toward the blue hole man allowed it. Sections of the ground had been seeded and planted with ivy and grass and flowers but the earth would support only the tree. Rusting metal chairs and a round table were stacked beside its trunk. They hadn't been used since Jordan bought the house. A marauding cat balanced precariously on top of the wall between the branches to pick its trail among broken shards of glass embedded in the cement to deter larger prowlers. Jordan hoped the fool tabby wouldn't leap down today. He was tired of carting it out the front door to release it again.

He finished checking his furnace. They would have to order their allotment of oil soon. The autumnal days were cooling and the house would shut down its air conditioning to wear the pinched shawl of winter. He didn't like that weather anymore; it kept him indoors. He couldn't say he was going for a walk, to remain away for an hour or more while his wife read her books. They were still at an emotional standoff but it fluctuated. She had regained her youthful figure despite continued drinking, which she had under her own system of control. Never drunk. Never quite sober. She thought the method kept her wits at their peak. He had given up mentioning that it would ruin her health for she had only to preen herself in response to show how well she looked. She worked at her face, figure, and coiffure with the drive he put into becoming part owner of the plastics firm. They had everything now. Everyone said so.

He turned off the light and started for the hall stairs, passing an unused room, a room with a walled-up fireplace and its own bath. Ideal for a guest ... or one of the family. They had no use for it and seldom went in other than to see if it required dusting. The windows had a view of the street, which was above eye level. Parades of legs and wheels; a dog cocking his leg at the curb. A child would have loved this room. He took the stairs two at a time, switching off the light over them before shutting the door. It was full day up here; the large kitchen and its dining alcove caught the reflection of the sun from windows opposite their building. The rooms were unpleasantly hot unless shades were pulled against the glare. The coffee was perking on the stove. He turned it off. A cup stood ready at the sink. He poured some of the brew into it and set it aside to cool. The woman they hired to stop in each week had left the kitchen immaculate. He could hear her running the vacuum upstairs in one of the bedrooms. A Puerto Rican woman. Leticia Valdez. A name and Social Security number. She didn't disclose more of her personal history and carried out her duties without emotion. He didn't think she cared for Mr. and Mrs. Asche particularly; they were the source of her dollars, that's all. Whenever he tried to be friendly, she got busier. She acted as if he wanted to brush up against her, but he knew she had mouths to support and all he wanted to do was talk. She could be someone to talk to in the house when he heard its emptiness too loudly.

He went into the front room to see what the morning paper was bannering. Kids in helmets piling out of helicopters in Viet Nam. President Johnson was committing more American troops and the Far East was getting hotter. Jesus. What the hell did the man think he was doing? We can't take over all of Asia and tell them what to do. It was going to end in another stalemate like Korea. They didn't know how to fight wars anymore. Not like the big one. Two? The hell with it. He tossed the paper aside and went up the next flight of stairs. If he'd known owning a house meant running up and down all the time, he might have insisted upon a penthouse apartment. Leticia was lugging her equipment from Wanda's room to his. They weren't

211

sharing the same bed now; his wife liked to read most of the night and he had to get up early each day to make it to Long Island. He couldn't sleep with a light near his bed: It made a red glow through his closed eyelids. The arrangement wasn't all that bad, though. Each time he did go to her bed, it was like a renewal of what was lost. But when they had spent themselves, he returned to his room. They were a convenience for each other.

Seeing Jordan on the landing, Leticia seemed perturbed. She thought he'd be at the plant. "It's okay, Leticia. I'm not going in there." She plugged in her machine and turned her back. Jordan climbed the final flight to the living room. He loved this room best. It had wide slanting studio windows, constructed of many panes of glass locked together with lead and metal frames. People across the street could see into the room from their own puny windows but he refused to have these draped. The ceiling was fifteen feet above him, and the fireplace in this room worked. The large area was decorated with soft stuffed chairs and low couches. A flat rib of varnished redwood burl served as a rustic coffee table. The television was buried among shelves of books and turned on for the news or sometimes as a source of sound; zealous commercials interrupted by interchangeable actors and episodes weren't considered entertainment.

His briefcase was on the window seat. Work ought to be brought home in duplicate, he thought. One briefcase could be kept up here and another downstairs; these flights shouldn't have to be climbed every morning. As he picked the bag up, shadow streaked the building across the street. Stark as a Georgia O'Keeffe. A checkerboard of sky mirrors, except where the bones of humanity peered through square brick and glass holes like a Punch and Judy show.

The phone rang.

"Hello...yes, this is Jordan."

"I was to catch a plane to London but missed it when I didn't get to the airport on time. Could you keep me company till the next?"

Victoria Cooper-Heath. He couldn't help smiling, couldn't help teasing her. "It's very complimentary to be remembered."

"I deserve that. But we weren't going to stay in touch...and I'm leaving, so you're safe and I'm safe."

"How did you guess you'd find me at home?"

"I didn't. Your firm was kind enough to tell me where to reach you."

"London. Going on vacation?"

"No, we've moved, bag and baggage. The children are to matriculate in France and it will be convenient for us."

"How shall we get together?"

"Can you come to the airport?"

"Yes, no trouble."

"Will you be able to find me?"

"Is it BOAC?"

"Yes."

"I'll find you, Vikky."

They hung up and Jordan hurried downstairs. He paused to speak to Leticia. "If Mrs. Asche should phone or get back from shopping while you're here, please say I decided to go to work today, after all." She nodded at him over the drone of her machine and he sped from the house.

Victoria was having tea at an airport cafe when he found her. "You'll not get your fortune told here," he said by way of greeting. She laughed and invited him to sit down. She pushed a cup to him and filled it from the small teapot on the table.

"It's good of you to come to my rescue. I don't like traveling alone and it's horrid to wait in this terminal by myself."

"Why are you?"

"My husband's taken the children on ahead to see relatives in Bath before we lose them. The children, I mean! Children...great lumps they are now. At any rate, I was permitted to beg off this time."

"I've been wondering what led you to call me. You weren't going to see me again."

She regarded him steadily. Still the gentlewoman. "I thought of you because of the war news in the newspapers," she replied sadly. "Those young boys...it made me think of what you told me of yourself." Then her eyes twinkled mischievously. "I do recall most of it, Jordan. Even after so long a stretch."

"Too long. We should have remained friends."

"We did. Are you still with your wife?"

"Yes." Planes on the runway coasted into position for

213

takeoff. He didn't want to discuss Wanda with her. "What time does your flight leave?"

"Two hours from now. Is that too much for you?"

He grinned. "It's longer than you gave me last time. You're very generous."

"Not really," she laughed.

"Yes, really. And you could have called someone else to see you off."

"I could have...but I didn't."

They drank their tea and time went faster than they wished, winding down as they had begun, with casual mention of the husband and wife neither could leave. He saw her to the departure gate, accepted her farewell kiss regretfully. She started to go, then returned to say he had lipstick on his cheek. He didn't have a handkerchief and she took one from a bulky purse to give him, leaving it behind when they heard the call for passengers to board. He waved at her with it and wiped his face clean.

I could have...but I didn't.

It applied to both of them, he thought forlornly. Despite his unsatisfactory life with Wanda, he hadn't been able to take up an outside affair. Oh, the urge flashed into life occasionally but was doused because he lacked the deviousness and perhaps the courage to begin a surreptitious existence needing lies and evasions to sustain it. Victoria was the nearest he'd tried at straying and represented the fantasy he first discovered in the screen actress of long ago. He could never be unfaithful to Wanda but would always cherish the Englishwoman hereafter without feeling guilt.

I could have...but I didn't.

And walking to the taxi stands to hire a ride to his plant, he put the handkerchief into his pocket, where it became a talisman to be transferred affectionately from one suit to another.

Because he was now past eighteen and in danger of growing old, Heinie Joe spent the entire day driving Kyoto shopkeepers mad by howling in their doorways. He'd made the discovery that each alcove produced a different tone and he had the fine pleasure of examining elaborate window displays at the same time. A casual entering of a glass-lined cubicle; a moment to take a deep breath. And he'd throw back his head, long, shaggy hair sending gooseflesh down his spine, and yodeled that soul-satisfying cry from the depths of his gut. The pretty objects in the windows quivered with sympathetic vibration. Short, angry men and women charged forward to shout at him. And stopping under garishly colored cheap cotton banners, they watched ineffectually, hands clenched and wavering in threatening gestures, looking about hopefully for a policeman. As usual, the *junsa* were nowhere to be seen.

He regarded them foggily through thoughts and eyes that would not remember the episode well, and wondered why they did not appreciate the curious phenomenon which so delightfully caused each doorway to change the quality of an identical howl. His fingers, thin and blue with cold, distorted his eyelids, already slanted from birth, and he mimicked the complainers nastily, whining, "Who are you? Stop that racket! Get out! Who are you?" The repetition of the question burned into the haze of his confusion and he broke into angry laughter and fled. The street was wet with the aftermath of a decaying flurry of almost snow; he slipped dangerously on the slick pavement as he brushed aside passersby with flailing elbows. Behind him, the shopkeepers denounced him agitatedly to a disinterested officer of the law. Another tough, the policeman agreed. A *garentai;* probably drunk or doped. The officer was decked out trimly in a military uniform and offered calming remarks. These kinds were all alike, all doomed to similar endings. You say he was an *ainoko* and howling like a dog? How interesting.

215

Gion, the pleasure quarter of Kyoto, glittered harshly in the night. No longer the haunt of thousands of bright geisha, it displayed substitutes: bar hostesses in inappropriate miniskirts; sly women far more painted than their predecessors ever were. They slouched indolently against doorjambs, bars and tables, and clung deceitfully to men they sought to fleece. Heinie Joe trotted past the warm openings of their dens without being accosted, his figure glowing alternately red and green and yellow beneath twisted overhead neon tubes. He had festive crowds of civilians and troops to contend with as he ran but they were tolerant of a boy who might be trying to shake the chill from his lightly clad body by jogging to his destination. He had not eaten all day. Had he yesterday? Tantalizing aromas spurred him from lantern-lit wagons, whose intent customers sat upon stools to gorge upon frying snacks with no awareness of his hunger. He decided to go to the Lock Society, a coffeehouse frequented by *ronin,* those footless students unable to pass the examinations for the university this year.

A fabric awning protected the shop entrance from the weather. Music blared from speakers at the door. Raw. Occidental. Savagely tearing at the ears with its masturbating beat. The atmosphere was clouded with a thin drizzle now, a penetrating sheath of dampness. Gasping, holding his fingers under his armpits for warmth, he stood under the canopy to peer through dusty sign-papered windows. The place was jammed with exuberant youngsters. Very radical; inclined to be democratic. But not with an *ainoko.* His stomach spoke to him as he inhaled the attar of bean curds and fish and fried foods above the stench of urinated beer permeating the alley. Assuming a fawning, humble attitude, he went inside.

He saw the face he sought immediately and forced a path to Shiro through the students. The table was crowded with handsome boys in tailored brown uniforms, tipped with military tabs and brass, but Heinie Joe squeezed himself onto a bench beside his friend. Shiro was eating a simple meal and barely acknowledged him.

"Phew, you're drunk again."

"I've been drinking but I'm not drunk. It's too cold outside to stay drunk."

Shiro glanced at him shrewdly. "You're hungry?"

216

"Hai."

"Eat. I know you'll help yourself anyway."

Heinie plucked a set of hashi from the tumbler on the table and wolfed food from Shiro's plate. Shiro was a lifesaver. The round-faced student, though imposing in his musical-comedy uniform, was an easy mark for Heinie. It was a puzzling friendship but he accepted it. Shiro could have ignored knowing him after meeting him but hadn't. Learning he often took his main meal of the day in the Lock Society, Heinie had evolved this effortless routine to cadge something to eat when necessary.

There was sorrow in Shiro's voice as he pleaded, "Heinie, why don't you go home?"

"Where I live is always the best home. Anyway, I've been there again."

"You have? Why didn't you stay?"

"Trade what I've got in Kyoto to work in a rice paddy or carry boxes of dolls for my mother? They'll have you in a straitjacket soon."

"What did your mother say when you left this time?"

"She nagged. I have to sneak into the village each time to see her and she lectures me on my loose life. I don't listen to what she says."

"That's where you're wrong."

"Shit, she always lied to me. I didn't even know what to expect from the villagers. When she took me there long ago, I didn't know they were going to hate us. Well, it was me they hated. And I was so stupid I thought they wouldn't. Can you imagine? My own grandmother turned her back on me that time! I showed my heels to her."

"How do you avoid her when you visit your mother in secret?"

"Ah...the old woman is dead. Her husband, too. My mother was living alone before I got her the deal with the doll merchant in Mihara."

"What did you have to do to get it?"

"My mother didn't ask, why should you?"

"She needs you, Heinie."

"Kyoto needs me."

"You're foolish to live from hand to mouth in Kyoto...or anyplace, for that matter. You can't subsist on charity and pickups all the time."

"It's a good life so far."

217

"Go home, Heinie." Shiro leaned closer to him and added earnestly, "Let your Oka-san look after you and you her."

Chewing comfortably, Heinie Joe smiled. "You know what, Shiro? You're an asshole. My mother doesn't want me around. She's happy as hell when I stay away. Everybody in her village is happy as hell and nobody throws rocks at her house."

"Who are you calling names?"

"Sorry. I was just being friendly." He wiped a trickle of soya from his chin. The music in the smoke-filled shop was becoming a din everyone surmounted with shouted conversations. Another course arrived and the two young men ate again from the same plate, pointedly ignored by the others at their table. Heinie challenged Shiro by saying, "You've wanted to see the last of me since the night Segawa gave his fucking party."

"Not so. I thought you did me a service."

"Hai? What did I do?"

"I got to meet Meijin."

"I didn't bring him. He brought me."

"Still, I felt obligated...and I'm returning it by my concern for you. You'd be better off with your mother."

"It was different when I was younger and she needed me to bring soldiers to her. She can do without my help now."

"Don't you care for her?"

"Certainly! I told her she could make a fortune here with the R and R Americans from Saigon and she said no."

"Prostitution is illegal."

"Don't let the women of the *iromachi* hear you."

"Red-light districts don't exist today."

"Hai...in Kyoto we go to the Gion!"

"You're hopeless, Heinie."

"I can't help it if I got corrupted in the big cities."

"Living like a stray cat gets you a cat's life. Is that what you want?"

"Tie, I've no choice, Shiro. If I were you, I'd dream of being a tiger or a lion. But I'm luckier than you. Not having self-respect, I'm in no danger of losing it."

"You can't call the life you lead a pleasure."

"Is yours? You and this gang marching around with

that crazy playwright like toy soldiers...no wonder your studies suffer."

Shiro reprimanded him haughtily. "Don't talk of things which are over your head."

"I know all about it! You want to revive Old Nippon and turn back the clock." Saddened to think of it, he mourned, "If only you could. I wouldn't be born." Pitying himself, he glanced sidelong at the students at the table before asking seriously, "Shiro, why must an *ainoko* be hated?"

"Don't be stupid. Everybody knows the reason. You're not even a citizen."

"It's not fair. Dope addicts get better treatment than I do."

"For the public's defense. Dope addicts are a menace to society and must be cured. You can't be."

"Am I a menace? I'm not a professional criminal, Shiro!"

Shiro's eyebrows lifted. "The *yakuza* wouldn't have you for their night soil carrier."

"It's not fair. My mother used to say I'd make her proud someday."

"All mothers do that."

"It isn't fair," he repeated angrily. "If my father was Japanese, I'd be a citizen. If nobody knew who he was, I'd still be a bastard but I'd be a citizen. It isn't fair."

"That's life. There's nothing to be done about it."

"Don't quote fucking adages at me."

Shiro squinted at him with annoyance. "You're lucky I talk to you. My companions have reprimanded me many times."

"Some of them like me." His meaning was missed by Shiro, who assumed he was referring to the *ronin* at the table.

"You are an amusement to them; a monkey on a string. An example of how our nation is being contaminated."

Insulted, Heinie ate with smoldering, vengeful looks darting at the students seated with them. Their smiles were actually smirks, the turds. Little did they know how silly their uniforms were...fucking chauffeurs.

"When will you go home, Heinie?"

"When will you?"

"Don't compare us. You know I'm boarding with relatives in Kyoto."

219

"Oh? I thought you were living with Meijin."

"Not so loudly."

Louder, in order to be heard. "Is it a secret...your friendship with him? How could it be?"

"I live in Kyoto to be here for the exams. It has nothing to do with Meijin."

"What about his political group...you and the rest of your gang? Queer as bedbugs. It's not all flag-waving with you."

"I told you not to discuss that. I'm just interested in passing my exams. I may even pass them next year."

"Maybe you'll settle for *seppuku* instead."

Shiro reacted with alarm. "I'll never kill myself! For what? I can pass the exams if I apply myself."

Heinie belched outrageously. "I never got the chance to worry about that shit."

"Well, you can't help what you are."

"Shit. If old MacArthur didn't clear out when he did, it might be another story. That tough old prick looked after his own people."

Shiro cleared his throat noisily. "So why should he have helped you?"

"He would have!" Heinie shouted heatedly. "I got a half interest in his fucking country! Of course he would help me!"

Even students at nearby tables looked over to snicker at his outburst. Flushed with embarrassment, Shiro tried to calm him. "Look, Heinie, you can't believe such a thing."

"I gotta believe it!" Swollen with rage, he tossed his head to clear the tousled hair from his face. "You got your fucking Emperor to believe in. I gotta have something, too!"

"Forget it, Heinie Joe. God is dead, remember? Old Mac-Arthur died. He can't help anybody anymore. Not himself, not you...not ever."

"So what's the use of anything? How do I make my name in the world? What good am I?"

They stared at each other. The answer on Shiro's face ended their friendship. The music and crowd roar dulled their ears. "Go home, Heinie," Shiro urged again. "Go on home."

He considered his next move resentfully. "I'm staying," he muttered.

220

Shiro sighed. Neither advice nor criticism made an impression. He was sorry to have been introduced to Heinie Joe. He made life uncomfortable; the *ainoko* should seek out his own kind among the *senmin*, pariah groups delicately referred to as the "water trade"—nothing to do with the upper classes. "Segawa's been looking for you."

"He's been here?"

"Hardly. He sent a messenger to ask me to keep a lookout for you."

"What does he want?"

Large red spots peaked high on Shiro's cheeks. "I was too polite to ask."

Heinie combed his fingers through his hair thoughtfully. Then he asked, "Can you put me up for the night, Shiro?"

"You know I can't."

"You mean you won't. That's okay. I'll see what the Gion provides."

"You'd do better to head for home."

"Lend me some money."

"You don't pay back what you owe."

"It's hard to make a living on the streets."

"Try a real job for a change."

Annoyed with Shiro and having cleaned his plate, Heinie Joe stood up. "No one will hire me...not for what you're talking about. And stop worrying. I'm not going to steal your fucking Meijin from you." Without waiting to see if his guess was right, he pushed through the mob to the exit. Shiro was upbraided immediately by his tablemates for insulting them with Heinie's presence but he was prepared for them. He ordered a round of beer. *How did the bastard know?*

It wasn't raining when Heinie emerged from the Lock Society. As he stood beneath the flapping awning music raged around him, popular rock rhythms which gave the establishment its name. Wind bit at him; he had to see what he could do about a place to sleep. He didn't want to go to the actor's house, not wishing him to think he was so easily available. Just thinking of him made Heinie giggle. Imagine what the world would think to find out the most vicious samurai in films became a woman in the privacy of his room. Well, if nothing turned up, he would have no choice. It was better than no woman at all. He'd

221

get to snore under the man's *futon* for a little pretense of depravity.

The mouth of the alley opening onto the main street darkened with the forms of *boryokudan,* a brotherhood of criminal youngsters. They ruled the area according to their whims, sanctioned by the *yakuza* to whom they reported. Looking identical, heads framed in stylish masses of teased hair and wearing the latest in Western dress: skintight pants and patent leather jackets. Their arrival worried Heinie. He didn't have anything they could possibly want but they might attack him merely for the sport. He rejected the thought of asking if they knew where he could stay. He'd be under an obligation to them if they helped. Ignore the plea of the accident victim who is a stranger for fear of a lifelong involvement.

Strutting down the corridor toward the shivering boy, the hooligans refused to recognize his existence. They shouldered by roughly and entered the noisy coffeehouse to be greeted at once by an obliging manager with money in hand for the protection fee. The door swung shut upon the agreeable meeting. Heinie bored his fists into his pockets and fought the wind as he left. The Gion was alive with teeming throngs of pleasure seekers. Ambling from the alley, he mingled with them. There were searching looks but he hoped for better, perhaps that dream of dreams, the accommodating American lady who'd become his paying mistress. Oh, for the luxury of a tourist hotel! He walked around for a long time before the cold, clinging wetness drove him to the actor's house.

When Heinie knocked, enjoying the action of the brass figures, music was playing inside. One of the actor's cultural records: *Petrouchka* or some such crap. Heinie rammed the cormorant harder against the dwarf. The music was switched off. A moment, and the door opened. Segawa dipped his chin slightly and stood aside to permit him to enter. The actor was nattily attired in a pearl-gray

222

suit minus jacket. His vest was buttoned over an ecru linen shirt; a striped Old Etonian tie slipped loose at the knot and an open collar exposed his corded neck. Heinie glanced around quickly.

"No maids?"

"You know I dismiss my servants when I am expecting you."

"You're ashamed of me."

"I like to wait upon you myself." Segawa gestured for him to be seated and the boy sank onto the couch against the wall. His unkemptness seemed a stain upon the expensive material but the actor merely clucked his tongue softly. "You're drunk, aren't you?"

"You like me that way," replied the boy brusquely.

"That isn't so. I prefer that you didn't drink at all." The rasping voice made more of the words than he meant. The boys were always more amenable when tipsy, of whatever class.

Heinie Joe crossed his legs as he swung them above the couch, guffawed at the actor's dismay, and checked his feet in time to slip them from his shoes, prying each off in turn with the opposite stockinged toe. His feet stank. "I won't hang around if you don't give me something to drink."

Segawa went to a portable bar cart and began to make a whiskey and soda. He breathed heavily, stimulated by the commonness of his visitor—a vulgarity the boy wouldn't have if allowed to live with him, which was out of the question, though it made each of their meetings uncertain.

"You might tell me how Shiro is."

"Don't you ever invite him when I'm not around?"

"I've not been with him socially since you and I made our acquaintance."

Heinie accepted the drink, savoring the flattery. He talked of Shiro with a sneer. "He fucks around with Meijin. They are very close now."

"Ah...the playwright turned university agitator. That won't last; they've been together too long. Almost three years..."

"You're wrong. Shiro and Meijin have formed a political unit with student demonstrators and they've designed fancy dress uniforms for themselves to strut in everywhere they go."

223

"Well, it's still playacting and part of Meijin's professional interests, so there's nothing to worry about."

"Why should anyone worry?"

"Meijin is unbalanced, I think. He gets carried away with his inventions and begins to believe them. That's what makes his plays fail. A play must only imitate reality or no one can enjoy it."

Bored, Heinie Joe rolled to his stomach, spilling drops from his glass. He thumbed them into the white damask.

"Shall I play music on the machine for us?" asked Segawa, displeased with the smudge on the cloth.

Heinie sipped greedily before answering. "Let's watch television instead."

"There's nothing you'd like."

"There must be sumo wrestling."

"I said I'd take you to see those at the arena one day."

"Shit. You said you'd take me to Himeji but you didn't." He was probably one of few in Japan not to have gone to Himeji, where its castle was revered as a symbol of invincibility. His mother hadn't taken him, he'd missed seeing it on his own, and Segawa didn't like to appear in public. Not with him. "You make lots of promises you don't keep."

"I've been busy filming."

Heinie eyed him from beneath half-closed lids. "You should take me to the studio someday."

"That's not permitted," the actor lied, refusing to be seduced. His colleagues in the film industry were not to see him with this boy. Not with an *ainoko*.

"Well, do you want to go to a movie?"

"The hour is too late."

Heinie sat up, pouting. "So what are we going to do?"

"Have you eaten? I hoped you'd be here sooner. There's food set aside for you."

"I'm not hungry," Heinie replied, draining his glass. As he held it out, Segawa refused to take it. "You want me to go?"

"Iie."

"Then don't be so stingy."

"You'll get drunker and fall asleep."

Heinie grinned. "I'll stay awake long enough for you."

"You've had plenty to drink."

"Okay, then." He scooped his shoes from the floor and

224

started for the door. He was turning the knob when the actor stopped him.

"I'll give you one more drink. But you must take it into the bedroom with you."

Heinie considered going back into the wintry streets but he'd had his fill of them. The actor mistook his hesitation.

"I'll take you somewhere tomorrow, I promise."

"Shit you will."

"The Fuseiro! For luncheon. How's that?"

The Fuseiro was a legendary restaurant, famed since the seventeenth century and still specializing in serving terrapin from Lake Biwa, the source of the finest snapping turtles in the world. It catered exclusively to the upper stratosphere of society. The boy relinquished his hold on the doorknob. "You will?"

A secluded table in a private alcove. *Hai,* it could be done. "I'll make the reservation before we retire."

Heinie sniffed close to his own armpit. "I need a bath," he announced.

Mixing a fresh drink for him at the bar, Segawa replied, "In the morning...that's soon enough. Please go into the bedroom and I'll make my call and bring this to you."

"I'll take it myself." Heinie grabbed the glass and walked into the next room. It was more civilized, done Japanese style. A large *futon* was ready upon the tatami. Translucent rice-paper windows shut out the cold night air; charcoal gave off heat from a brazier beneath a metal flue, but very little light through the coating of ash. He undressed with one hand, using the other for his glass. He heaped the jacket and shoes and the rest of his clothing upon themselves in a corner of the room. He sat on the *futon,* with the thick comforter thrown back, to drink slowly, watching dots of fire glisten and fade atop the brazier.

When dawn tinted the room palest lavender, Heinie Joe sat up blearily. The actor lay beside him, mouth agape and snoring; their quilt covered his legs partially, having been cast aside during sleep. Segawa's body was a compact accumulation of muscle, kept in superb condition by constant classes of kendo and exercise; a man portraying the epitome of swordsmen must work at it. His lean face was spoiled by a covering of rice powder, part of last night's parody. On a stand hung a woman's attire, so breathtakingly embroidered it should have been the feature of a museum exhibit. An elaborate wig had fallen to the mat floor, raped by decorative pins in disarray. Heinie glanced to the charcoal brazier: a dead white film of ash. His empty glass offered nothing, either. It was glacial in the room.

What could he steal? If he left for the final time, he should take something with himself; a present, so to speak, to send him happily on his road. He wondered if the thin doors of the wall closets could be slid aside without disturbing his host. Clutching a portion of the quilt about his nudity, he pondered his chances. If the actor wakened and caught him, he'd get a bad beating. Yet...there were such treasures in the house! Valuable swords. Costly carvings. Silver frames, boxes...a cigarette lighter or two. Paintings which would fetch a good price anywhere. Money, *hai*...but he'd steal that as a matter of course. How he reeked of the sweating nonsense of last night! A long soaking *furo* would cleanse him and ease his tiredness.

A hand caressed his hip through the soft quilt. Over his shoulder, he found the actor's face close to his own, reptilian with desire. Segawa said good morning sleepily. At his tenderest moments, his voice was violent and menacing. Insinuating himself closer to Heinie beneath the quilt, he worked his body around until they were facing each other, enclosed in the cotton batting cocoon. His legs closed around the boy above his crossed legs and he held

Heinie with strong arms. Heinie yawned. He wondered what was on television at this hour...

When the *futon* and bedding were stored, Heinie Joe and Jihei Segawa scrubbed each other in the actor's specially designed bath. Like the rest of the house, it was a mixture of traditional and novel ideas. Plumbing supplied a square tub having ample room for several bathers, and the tile floor sloped to direct suds from wash buckets to flow toward a drain. After thorough cleansing and a shower under fixtures set into one end of the room for the purpose, they stepped into the steaming bath to soak for a long, refreshing interval which was not without its playful moments. Heinie lost much of his lethargy and felt hungry. "Are we going somewhere for breakfast?" he asked. "You've no one to make it for us."

The actor rested his elbows above the rim of the tub. "I will do it."

"You're a rotten cook."

"Well...I can't be good at everything."

"We could eat at the Fuseiro."

"What, terrapin for breakfast?"

"Hai...and champagne, too."

The usual token extortion levied by these types. He regretted last night's impulsive promise. He'd run the risk of meeting an associate at the Fuseiro...though unlikely at this hour. Well, then, the boy would have less reason to complain of broken promises. "We can do that," Segawa agreed. "But I want you to wear something of mine when we leave."

"What for?"

"Your clothes are disgraceful."

"You bought them."

"You mistreated them."

The boy roiled the water and got out of the tub, piqued to be criticized. "I'll wear what I've got."

As he toweled himself fretfully, he was soothed by the actor. "You shouldn't be seen in such a famous place looking like a street tramp."

"I don't care."

"I care."

"Your clothes don't fit me."

"Not enough to notice."

"Shit, if they don't notice that, they won't notice what I'm wearing in the first place."

Unable to refute the logic, Segawa gave in. After all, they would be eating out of view. The boy was dry and prancing into the bedroom before he could get out of the water. Pity. There was a satin texture to the *ainoko*'s skin after a bath and he would have stroked it. Heinie Joe tended to be elusive with him; that was his attraction, too.

Of course, the great actor was recognized by everyone in the establishment. Segawa was sure they were being polite about his guest; gourmets had been served here since 1620 and they could not have entertained so disreputably dressed a person in all the intervening years. Even settled in a private alcove, he was discomfited and could not do the meal justice. Terrapin for breakfast. And champagne. It made him disagreeable.

"Why don't you cut your hair, improve yourself? You look like a hooligan."

Heinie studied his plate intently. The actor was going to bore him with a familiar litany.

"You'd be far more handsome if you took pains with your appearance."

"Oh, that shit again."

"Behave yourself."

He looked up to snarl, "Why do you think I stay away from you so often? Just to avoid that reforming shit."

Stiffening, the actor glanced to see if their waitress had taken notice. She was not in the alcove. "You mind your manners or I'll have no more to do with you."

"You think you're the only faggot in Kyoto? There's a thousand like you on the Gion!"

Idiot. They all begin with that idiocy. Thinking themselves untainted; thinking themselves normal males. Paid today, tomorrow paying. Well, this one had no tomorrow; he'd never amount to anything. "Why are you so hateful to me? Do I not treat you well? Why are you so cruel?"

"Maybe I don't like you."

"Then why bother to call upon me?"

The boy shrugged callously. "It's better than sleeping in somebody's parked car."

Leaning toward him, the actor smiled icily. "If we were

228

not in this public place, I would box your ears. I don't have to endure abuse from a nothing."

"I'm somebody! I'm somebody..."

After that outburst, they ate without speaking. The waitress entered noiselessly to refill their wine glasses and left them again. Segawa admired the downcast boy secretly; the urchin was attractive. A deplorable embarrassment, but attractive.

"Let's not quarrel," the actor rasped at the conclusion of the breakfast. "I thought you might care to see a performance at the Minami-za this afternoon. They've set aside a seat for you." The boy didn't respond. "You'd like that, wouldn't you?"

Heinie shrugged once more. Irritated, Segawa was tempted to strike him. He laid down his *hashi* and drank a final sip of champagne.

"Very well, I shall attend the theater in your place." Segawa stood, ready to leave. "If you haven't found yourself a convenient car, I shall expect you after nightfall." He waited. The boy said nothing. "Try not to be late. It's offensive to be kept waiting for someone. Nobody likes to be lonely."

At last, Heinie looked at him, winging back in a forlorn glide from nothingness, and he said remotely, "No shit? I thought that's the way it was supposed to be..."

...announces that by no means does this imply change of policy...

Heinie tore the newspaper page carefully into even squares. One thing could be said for the *Asahi Shimbun:* It was excellent sanitary paper. The American President was bombing and pouring more troops into Viet Nam, getting everybody excited. That explained the influx of more GI's turning up in the cities again. The whole fucking country was beginning to look as it did in '52 just before the Occupation ended, when he was six and learning to talk

229

English from men he brought home to his mother. Too bad she wasn't here to take advantage of the boom. Heinie Joe was squatting on the third story of an unfinished building, heels apart against the cold concrete of the floor. Around him rose steel girders riveted together into open geometric patterns. A view of the city lay before him; even a portion of Yasoka Pagoda was visible beyond a perpetual-motion neon billboard.

Once, he tried sleeping up here but the wind was raw and the damp concrete made his bones ache. Moisture insisted upon penetrating his clothing and whatever cover he could manage. If the laborers had done a little more work on this building before giving it up, he might have had walls to protect him. From below, a whiff of woodsmoke and *udon* boiling in a pot let him know the watchman was preoccupied. Heinie could sneak down safely and be on his way. Had he been foolish to refuse the actor's gift of a theater seat? The show would have been better than farting around Kyoto by himself. He finished his business, adjusted his clothing and decided to cruise the pleasure districts again. Soiled paper squares kited in the air above the street long after he was gone.

The Gion was challenging in daylight hours; crowds were more sedate, less inclined to pursue sexual amusement openly. Still, he knew the predators were there in force, automatically thinking of himself as a victim. He had only to saunter and be obviously available, and he was certain to be approached. It wasn't smart to become the actor's guest again tonight...the Fuseiro was a mistake. Reputation and soft meat without bones was all the place was. And since he hadn't been pleasant and kissing his ass for taking him, the actor would want him to make up for it. *Hai,* a special favor would be expected. One of Segawa's *productions.* Fuck him.

Heinie risked much by being independent; he could be replaced by another protégé. Segawa didn't like appearing in public with him, though the actor's aura seemed to brighten visibly when he was noticed. His calculated stride grew pompous and his eyes flashed with pride, all the while insisting upon walking a pace or so ahead of his companion to maintain superiority, which was galling to Heinie and made him feel degraded. As it was meant to

230

do. Fuck him. There had to be someone else with whom to spend the night simply.

He sidestepped an aggravation of businessmen departing from one of the many restaurants. They were tipsy, or behaved so through politeness toward their friends. They had convened for a lavish expense account meal unaffordable on their meager salaries and were returning to their offices. They barked laughs, bowed low, faked slight staggers...just so much as needed to indicate unsteadiness but not to embarrass. More low bows, angles implying the degree of respect given. Many more farewells. More bows and smiles and farewells and bows again; a flock of costumed pigeons pecking the walk except that each backed subtly to a parked car or was absorbed into the pedestrian stream.

A woman passed. She was smartly dressed in the Western mode, even to wearing a pair of short white gloves. Matronly; widowed. Pearls and a fur-trimmed coat. Assured, she had a hunter's smile playing about her painted lips. Heinie Joe's infallible instinct led him after her. She slowed to pause at a shop window. When Heinie stood beside her, neither looked at the other. They admired the display for a few moments. Television sets. Air conditioners. Clock radios. Wristwatches. Prices in yen.

He dared to look at her boldly. Averting her powdered jowls, she spoke to him in a low voice, and it affected his behavior at once. He drew himself up and tried to appear debonnaire. The woman fell in next to him primly as he turned to walk down the street. They began to converse like old acquaintances: Could one inquire where the lady lived, and what brought the young gentleman to the Gion without a friend? She purchased a bottle of sake from a vendor before hailing a sedan. She wouldn't inspect her masculine trophy closely until she got home, choosing to prolong her pleasure. He sounded a trifle crude, but that was ordinary. Young men are unintentionally careless in manner and speech, *hai?*

In her apartment, Heinie Joe was garrulous. She hadn't taken him into her bed immediately, but he was in no hurry. Shadows outside her windows hadn't yet lengthened into twilight and he was bragging about himself, taunting her deliberately with his origin because he thought she wanted to wallow.

231

"There are three thousand, two hundred and eighty-nine," he boasted. "We're a very special group. The authorities have kept an exact account of us."

She sat stiffly, her fingers plucking lackadaisically at the strings of a koto, the polished length of the musical instrument lining her knees as a wall between herself and the boy. She had been listening to him for an hour, interrupting to offer more rice wine or singing as she played to drown him out. She was decidedly fat, had too much money and preyed upon the student population of Kyoto with the honed avarice of one accustomed to indulging herself. This boy had been an unfortunate slip; after initially being attracted by his good looks and allowing him to think he was making the conquest, she was mortified to discover he was one of the Occupation leavings. Her plan was to get him drunk enough to push out the door without submitting to him. There was yet time this afternoon to visit the Gion to find someone suitable.

"You know what that means? Three thousand, two hundred and eighty-nine? That many fathers didn't give a shit about their sons and daughters." He was having a fine time telling the truth to stir up her blood. She wasn't such a beast after all; maybe she'd pay him well.

"You mustn't think so," she said without wishing to encourage him. "Who knows the circumstances? Perhaps your father was prevented from returning to your mother."

Grimacing, he emitted a rude sound. *"Hai,* so she said. I used to bring her ten, fifteen, no...twenty GI's a night when we were in Osaka! Sometimes repeaters! No civilians; just Americans in uniform." He added thoughtfully, "She always stared at sailors and had to know the names of their ships before she washed their cocks." He rocked back and forth on his heels, crooning with remembrance, "Ooohhh, my Oka-san was a real *ichi-ban* whore!"

The woman sniffed uncomfortably. "Well, there were some of us who would not collaborate with the enemy."

He giggled maniacally and fell back on the mat. He exasperated her but she thought she could turn him out shortly. She demanded, "What is so funny? Why are you laughing like this?"

He sat up to regard her owlishly. "Half an enemy is like none at all," he snickered. "You want to see my weapon?"

She rose grandly and indicated the door. "It was good of you to pay me this call. I'm afraid I must ask you to leave now."

He sobered somewhat. "You don't want me to stay?"

"I have another engagement."

"But I don't have anyplace to go . . . I mean, I was all set to have supper with you . . . give you a happy evening!"

She waddled to her door. If necessary, the neighbors would come to her aid. "That is not my concern."

He pulled himself to his feet, felt the impact of too much sake and waited for the room to steady itself. "Well, I could drop around later, if you like."

"My evening program is filled."

"How about tomorrow?"

"I shall be engaged. Be good enough to lose your way here."

He could hardly ignore the disdain in her tone. Straightening, he stumbled to the door. She threw it open and stepped aside, as if shunning contamination. He couldn't permit her to feel she was in control of the situation. "You know something?" he said seriously. "I would have to charge you double." Smiling amiably, he left her apartment and stumbled down the flights of stairs like a marble falling.

On the quiet street outside, tourists from a nearby inn strolled about the residential neighborhood. The afternoon was near its end and he'd already been through the Gion; last-chance scavengers would be the prowlers encountered. Alley bums. While everyone else was dining, he would have to wait for the night crowd and compete with the whores. No point in going there now. Shit. It was true. He really didn't have anyplace to go.

Watching a pair of airborne helicopters, Chief Warrant Officer Bell crossed the runway threshold of the flight deck. Sikorskys hovered over choppy seas, flattening circles of water with the powerful downdraft of their revolving blades as the *Intrepid* pitched up and down in the rough Atlantic, holding course. The helicopters advanced unevenly; 58 leading, then 57. The word passed to the ship's company said *Molly Brown* splashed down sixty miles short. A twenty-knot wind whipped signal flags rigid on the bridge superstructure as they ran up the rigging. The hoist was two-blocked at the yard. A blinker light flashed.

"Execute!"

The flags dropped and were stowed with machinelike precision. The carrier's speed shifted to Ahead Flank, its stern furrowing a slate wake into a boil as the recovery fleet raced after the helicopters. It would be a while before the Gemini astronauts were reached. Dave leaned to compensate for the list of the deck as the big ship heeled in a great arcing turn; destroyers off the beam making the same arc dug into waves which swamped their bows and gun turrets and burst over their bridge wings. They raised nostalgic memories. The tin cans were getting too large, looking more like cruisers with every modification . . . not like the *Bulman*, waiting for resurrection in mothballed silence somewhere up the Hudson River. Just the same, they were exciting to see in action, even though changed. As he was. Uniform changed, ships and shore stations changed as his duty assignments were changed since the big war, one ocean changed for another . . . and he was calling it quits. One final change.

"Cup of java, sir?" An Aviation Ordnanceman invited him to enter a hatch on the island where a huge electric percolator kept flight deck crews supplied with coffee. A mix of ratings lounged inside with mugs in hand, unperturbed by the pigsty. During the pressure of recent hours, no one kept house; magazines, papers, empty milk cans, and candy wrappers were underfoot.

"Thanks," he said, taking a filled cup. He didn't add any of their sticky Carnation Milk to it; they used gallons of the stuff. Kids. Ate more damned sugar and candy. It was a wonder the Navy entrusted sophisticated weaponry, ships and planes to them.

"What's the score, Mr. Bell?"

"We'll soon find out."

"The copters will pick them up before we get there."

"Just so somebody does before they drown in their own puke."

"Too bad we couldn't have done a spacewalk, too, while they were at it. Fucking Russkies are leading us in everything."

Wind blew into the hatch as the ship straightened from her turn. The deck leveled. "We'll catch up...don't want to kill anybody by rushing."

"You must be glad this exercise is over."

"I will be when we hit port."

"Where are they mustering you out, sir? Florida?"

"No, I asked for New York. Better plane connections."

"Gonna miss us?"

He smiled at the destroyers, bounding in line like shallow diving porpoises, streaming white wakes into one another's track. "Nope...I don't think I will." It would all go with him; he wouldn't miss any part of it.

"We thought you were good for thirty."

"So did I. But my folks are turning over the farm to me. Couldn't pass that up. My wife and kids think it's their home, anyway."

"What do you grow on it?"

"Wheat."

"Is that all they do in Kansas? Plant fucking wheat?"

"Got a better idea?"

"Jesus, I'd plant fucking rum trees and beer bushes and raise cunt for eating."

The foulmouthed AO looked like a choirboy, with clear blue eyes and a wide smile from ear to ear. *Jesus.* What Jordan Asche always used to say; they hadn't been any older than this punk in those days. "I thought you'd be sick of rum by now."

"Hell, no! If they'd lower the fence at Gitmo, I'd drink Cuba dry from Santiago to Havana!"

Drink Cuba dry...young swabbie making liberty at Guantanamo Bay would get pissed just sucking on sugar cane.

"Bet you're going to celebrate when you get off this bucket, sir."

Celebrate. Drink it dry. More than a resemblance. Is it more than coincidence to see the same faces repeated in the same professions? Celebrate. Jordie with tears in

235

his eyes saying we got to celebrate and drink all the torpedoes dry...

Why the hell had they lost touch? It would be worth trying to look him up again. Yeah, by God, he'd look him up...

"Is that what you're going to do, Mr. Bell?"

"What?" No, the snot wasn't a mind reader. He wasn't talking about Jordie. "Yeah, I'm going to celebrate. Probably whoop it up by taking the family to a restaurant somewhere and think about you Kilroys out here."

"Kilroys? What the fuck's a kilroy?"

He flicked the dregs from his coffee cup into the breeze, where they zipped aft to stain the bulkhead. Damn. He was a half-assed civilian already; he knew better than to do a dumb thing like that. He stepped from the hatch to hike along the flight deck with his head lowered into the wind. The kid didn't know who Kilroy was. He felt a hundred years old.

Kyoto contracted in the dusk. As streets and buildings merged into obscurity, yellow and blue-white lights gleamed; first here in the recesses of a house, then over intersections where bright circles defined the limits of civic influence. Beyond were ground-swelling glares bursting into customary evening debuts in the business districts and the Gion. Heinie was angry. The aging ugly behemoth had insulted him and he wanted revenge...if not upon her, then upon anyone. The dismal fog settling down was freezing; if it didn't lift, the dew would skin everything with a crackle of ice. Roaming stealthily in narrow lanes of Ikazaki, another part of the suburb, he tested wooden gates before quaint gardens and homes of weathered wood and old blue tile. Rice-papered windows hid the interiors from inspection and he wasn't able to tell which homes were occupied at the moment. There were fences where dogs hurled themselves at him, snarling through the cracks; he had to melt away swiftly lest anyone question his loitering. Once, he opened a gate and was at the sliding door when a cur sent him vaulting over the high stake fence. Animals are such a pestilence to a thief! Breath blowing before his face visibly, he savored the woman's sake again—it would wear off if he didn't get more; he should have asked payment from his hostess in advance. They sometimes agreed. He could have been rich now. He kicked a gate maliciously and was in the act of passing as it swung open invitingly.

It was too easy. Instead of a dog barking, a kennel stood empty. Behaving as though well known to the residents, Heinie marched to the house and knocked loudly. If a person answered, he was a mistaken schoolboy thinking to find his pal there. No one responded and he slid the *fusuma* aside without hesitation. He made a fast tour of the rooms, every sense alert. Drawers were pulled from chests and dumped; closets were flung open. He found a flat purse with yen in it, which he confiscated. A wedding picture papered to a wall along with dozens of other snapshots and a black-bordered photograph of John F. Kennedy looked at him with smiles and squints and frowns. Beside the walleyed late President, the bride's powdered face mourned under a tinseled headdress. She sat stiffly upon a cloth-covered bench, her husband in yukata and splittoed white socks standing sternly at her side. He held a closed fan ostentatiously in his right hand...didn't he know it should have been his left? A man is thought wealthy if he holds a wine cup with his right hand and flutters his fan with his left. Well, there was no wine cup to be seen in the photograph. But was there a bottle in the house? Heinie tore a calendar from another wall to see if it concealed a shelf. Nothing. He searched through cabinets and achieved success: a package. Tissue wrapped about it was pasted over with many labels. When he shook it, liquid gurgled. Delighted, the boy ran to the door and left as boldly as he had entered, clowning at the gate to bow a farewell to the house.

He was soon far off and tearing the paper from the box to get at the contents. Sitting out of the wind in the elbow of a hedge, he drank his prize. It was excellent sake, though cold. As its heat spread in his stomach, he thought about the house he'd plundered. They had everything there. They had everything and he had nothing and they would be furious to have lost anything. Well, what was he to do?

237

Nothing was his unless given to him or stolen by him. He couldn't hope to work in a factory in a blue jumpsuit and a badge on his cap and accumulate possessions and family as the owners of the house did. Not that he had such ambition. He preferred his unfettered existence: He could live without steady employment and regimentation and security and responsibility so long as others were willing to buy his companionship. What was happening to the sake? Was there a leak in the bottle? It drained so quickly! Perhaps it had a false bottom, a hump of glass inside to displace what should have been there. The foolish homeowner got less for his money than he thought! At least, Heinie had not paid for it. *Hai,* why should he pay for anything when it was to be gotten by making calls upon people or their unattended households? And why couldn't he have what everyone else had? His anger grew, enforced by envy of his countrymen. No, not his. He was not considered a national. He had to live among them like a parasite. Unwanted. They scratched ferociously whenever they became aware of him. The sake wasn't fighting the chill as he thought it should. If he didn't get indoors, he'd be sniffling and hacking soon.

Heinie got to his feet with a stagger. With no place to go, he knew of a place. He wondered dimly when it was he had begun to dislike the hospitality of the actor. The grand mansion had lost its allure. Always so clean. Always a showpiece. Like the man himself. There were lanterns being lit at every gate now and the dogs behind each were passing Heinie Joe on to the next to take up the alarm. Don't worry, I'm not stopping here. I'm not stopping anywhere . . . except to piss.

The dogs went berserk, howling and barking en masse. Heinie put two fingers to his forehead like horns and wiggled them at the sounds.

Heinie Joe stopped to steady himself. The lanterns were at fault. They were fogged over though the night had cleared. He wanted to shout to everyone indoors to come out and tend to them. He started forward and pitched into a fence. There. The fools would cause an accident by not keeping the walks visible. He wouldn't say they were exactly in dark shadow but they were definitely deceptive. Each step was treacherous and required care. His concentration upon the placement of his rubbery feet dissolved when he came to the badger. It looked into his eyes resolutely. Smiling. Friendly. Welcoming. Heinie Joe patted a hard ceramic cheek . . . it was wet . . . and wandered along the path to the portico. The door opened before he could touch the cormorant.

"You're here."

"*Hai*. Are you going to let me inside?"

"Take off your shoes."

He kicked off his shoes and was helped into the house. Segawa chose not to remark upon his condition.

"You missed a rousing performance at the Minami-za."

"I had a pretty good time anyway."

"*Hai?* What have you been doing?"

"Same old shit. You wouldn't be interested."

The empty bottle was removed from his fingers and he was guided toward the bedroom. "I'm sorry your day didn't turn out well."

"You're not angry with me?"

"Should I be?"

"I'm drunk."

"That's nothing."

"You're not angry?"

"Not at all. I'm happy you're here. I took the trouble to prepare . . . to make our evening more amusing."

"I'm laughing . . . you always make me laugh." His voice trailed off because he felt sorry for himself. The man was so sure of him, he had watched for his arrival. Segawa left him and went to the closet. The coals in the brazier were cherry bright, throwing color over Segawa's back, and then across his face as he turned from the closet with something in his arms, which he offered with a broad grin.

"I want you to be an American Marine this evening, freshly arrived from the battlefield."

"What battlefield?"

"Any. Choose for yourself. Pleiku—if you want it to be the present—or imagine one."

He tried to see the uniform clearly, slipping on the tatami as he stepped closer to examine the material in Segawa's extended hands. It was camouflaged, spattered with leaflike shades of green and brown upon a khaki background. And there were darker stains, stiff and evil to the touch. "Where'd you get this shit, from the morgue?"

"Don't let that bother you. It's only the blood of a hen. For effect, that's all." He put the cloth to Heinie's nostrils. "See? There's not much odor to trouble you."

"You're crazy, you know that? I think I'll go back to the Gion."

"Please don't."

"You want to fuck, you want to suck, we don't have to play with this shit."

"Humor me."

"What for?"

"Because you have no place to stay tonight."

"I'm going."

"Don't! Please, don't." Segawa went to a cabinet and poured wine into a glass. A small amount. As he handed it to him, he said, "You'd be cold wandering about the Gion now...and it's warm here." Heinie Joe drained the glass and stared with distaste at the bloody uniform.

"You're crazy."

"Go on. Put the uniform on. Mr. Yoshizawa loaned me a beautiful kimono for this game. You remember the *onnagata*? I'll get dressed and you can pretend to attack me."

"Shit, I don't want to get into no fucking uniform. I don't want to make believe I'm a stinking Marine."

"It's a game. Think of it as a play—that you are an actor playing a part." He was eager, apprehensive of being turned down. Smiling, he held out the uniform and pleaded some more. "It isn't the real thing...you will not be hurting me. Please. Play this game with me."

240

The messages were a murky irritation. What power to wield over someone to make them grovel for his assent! Segawa wanted him to play a game...just get into a uniform and attack, attack, attack! *Banzai!*

"*Banzai!*" Heinie shouted.

The actor expelled his pent-up breath with relief. Thrusting the uniform into Heinie Joe's arms, he rushed to the closet to get his feminine apparel. The kimono was a glorious stage costume, blazing with rich color and embroidery. Both undressed then, the boy drunkenly and careless and the man with anticipatory precision. When they were ready, their street clothing lay upon the tatami at the sides of the room.

"Hey, aren't you going to stick that makeup shit on your face?"

Segawa raised a nervous hand to his cheek; it really would not do to proceed without it. In spite of mounting desire, he disciplined himself. "*Hai*...I was about to attend to that. You may have some..." He hesitated; the *ainoko* was in no need of more sake. "You can have a rest before we start. Relax and think how it will be." He knelt before a low dresser and opened a drawer.

Heinie Joe watched him daub himself with the solid, plain colors of a geisha. The room was reeling, whirling constantly and slowly; Heinie felt in a continuous fall...it was hard to remain upright without falling. Shrinking from the texture of the uniform and its grisly additions, he sank to the floor. Propping himself upon an elbow, he couldn't snap out of his funk. The woman at her toilette was weird; he knew there was something...very wrong with her. And there was a reflection of a GI in her oval hand mirror; he must have brought another one home for her. Why did she keep nagging at him? She was surely the *ichi ban* whore of the whole of Osaka...the Hole of Osaka was what she was! He giggled, and it grew into uncontrollable peals of laughter. She hissed at him with surprise and anger. Finding that funnier, his sounds grew more raucous. She sprang to her feet to advance upon him, crying out in fury.

"Stop that, you stupid boy! Stop that! You know what you are here for. I don't have to put up with your ridicule!"

She leaned over to pummel him with her fists. How it

241

hurt to be beaten by a woman! He curled from the blows and she flailed at him without letup.

"You ungrateful bastard! You're supposed to entertain me. Stop this behavior!"

How could she mean to have him service her? That's what the man was for. He couldn't find the GI and realized she intended for him to cover her as the others had. Where was the GI? Standing, Heinie tried to get away but she kept beating him, raising welts where her knuckles raked his face. He retaliated. He struck her wildly and she almost swooned with joy. She grinned at him in a terrible fashion; they thrashed at each other in a frenzy. He shouldn't be striking his own...why was she so frightening? Heinie fell heavily against a wall, spun to his side and went through the flimsy papered fretwork of the closet door. Grabbing at clothing hung in rows, he bore them down as he went to the floor. A black-lacquered case fell apart at his head; a short sword etched with gold nested inside on yellow velvet. The details were so vivid, so intensely clear. He seized the weapon with both hands and shook it free of its scabbard. Rocking to his feet he lunged from the closet with the shining blade upraised. The woman cringed, long sleeves covering her head. There were purple clouds and white cranes and gray-winged geese with long necks stretched into the winds; silver, red, blue, black, gold...

Attack, attack, attack!

That's what she wanted him to do, and he chopped down with all his strength.

Seated upon the blood-soaked tatami, Heinie looked miserably at the slashed corpse. The actor seemed posed, as if from one of the Kabuki plays when action is stopped for the audience to contemplate. Segawa was lying serenely on one side with both eyes shut upon his calm painted face; the elaborate wig was neatly in place on his head. Only the stunning iridescent brocade of the kimono was disarrayed. The obi had been cut asunder and rents gaped redly from shoulder to knee. The blade Heinie held was immaculate, showing not a trace of its labor. Seeing his hands were spattered with blood, he dropped the sword to wipe them on his damp uniform. Worse. Gore was added to his fingers from the cloth. Jumping up, he ripped the uniform from himself.

It was incredible that so much fluid was contained in that delicate blue tracery lurking beneath the actor's skin. Segawa's bowels had given way, thickening the hot scent of the rest. Blood smelled; in quantity, it smothered. Naked, Heinie entered the bathroom. The air steamed with heat rising from the tub; it had been made ready in advance by the actor for their use. Unable to go near it, the boy fled to the kitchen of the house. Here he tried to wash at the sink. The water from the tap was icy and made him shiver as he worked. It took a long while to feel cleaner. Somewhere outside, drunken shouts rang through the street. They had been sounding for some time, occasionally joined by a chorus of answering voices, and it seemed to him he'd heard them during that eternity when he emerged from the nightmare to a realization of what he was doing. In this house, there had been no sound but the awful thunk of blows...splitting melons made that very noise...

Dish towels dried him; then he returned to the bedroom. One outflung hand of the actor clutched the boy's other shirt on the floor. He disengaged the beautifully manicured fingers from the cloth and slipped into it. His tattered shorts were next, followed by the worn Levi's and his skimpy black student jacket. As his socks were steeped with blood, he didn't think to wash them out to wear. He left the sodden things where they lay and ran from the room. On the portico, he donned his scuffed shoes and waited a second to inspect the lane, wondering if he was being observed. The residents of this exclusive street were accustomed to the actor's visitors and seldom ignorant as to their identities, though none went so far as to offend by being openly inquisitive. Stepping from the veranda, Heinie crossed the patch of garden to the bamboo gate. The ceramic badger's enameled eyes glistened at the boy as he passed—glistened, as did those of another watcher from behind curtained windows next door.

It was fortunate he'd taken the yen from the untended

house in the Ikazaki district. Heinie Joe was able to purchase a train ticket to Osaka, where he might lose himself. It was sensible to go to the very threshold of the Police Bureau, he reasoned craftily, for they would scour all of Kyoto before looking elsewhere. Additionally, it was the morning rush hour, and its human lemmings would be perfect cover. He shoehorned into the packed train with an assist from a station attendant; open windows were inadequate for ventilation, being sealed solidly by the crush of travelers rendered locust-eyed in the constriction. Yammering upon uneven tracks, the train vibrated the multitude through a countryside they could not observe. Road, river, field, stream and mountain flashed by ignored by commuters intent upon exiting when they reached their destination.

It was raining in Osaka. Heavily. After arriving, he had to inch from the station, street by street, dashing from shelter to hall to little avail. He was getting soaked to the skin. He huddled under a theater marquee to wait for the rain to stop; hundreds of yellow light bulbs socketed into the overhang gave him small comfort. Whenever someone passed, he tried to look personable. It was no good. The rain made everyone hurry; no one was in search of company. Behind him, on display in glass-covered frames, were dozens of glossy photographs of the film being shown. He didn't want to look at them. The samurai of the story was lying dead in Kyoto. Or maybe they'd found him by now and sent his body to wherever his family lived.

A policeman's boot heels gaveled the wet pavement. He thought the boy had stood there long enough. It's these kinds who are the troublemakers. The ones to nip in the bud before they flower. Gloved hand resting on his holster, he strode to the hooligan.

"You. What are you waiting for?"

"Just waiting. I don't want to go home in the rain."

"So? I suppose you've seen the movie and it was raining when you came out. Is that it?"

"*Hai*. That's it."

"Don't give me such impudence. I've watched you here for more than an hour."

"Well, it's been raining."

"I must be a fool not to have noticed. Won't you be missed at home?"

He didn't answer and tried to appear inoffensive; these *junsa* got rough as hell when given the chance.

"Go home! Quickly!"

Go home quickly, indeed. Where was he to go? He sidled to the limits of the marquee's protection. Rain poured down.

"What are you waiting for? Go! There must be someone wanting to know where you are."

In Kyoto, another policeman wrote rapidly in his notebook. His uniform was immaculate, sharply creased, with short sword and pistol encased in creaking leather on his belt. The neighbors of Jihei Segawa craned their necks at the gateway, absorbing as much of the tragedy as possible before being ordered away. At the moment, the *junsa* took depositions from them and wrote down every word. A photographer systematically covered the house with brilliant flashes of light while other men prepared the body for removal. The neighbors were reluctant to volunteer information they knew to the representative of the law; it meant involvement. It was one thing to live close to so famous a public figure, another when he has been the victim of a homicide. What a stir would rise throughout the nation! And the scandal! What was commonly known on this circumspect street would become general knowledge now. The lies of how well we knew him would become the truths we seldom spoke.

"You say a boy was a frequent guest?"

"Perhaps."

"He was or he was not?"

"Well, then: the most recent of many before himself."

"How recent a friend was he?"

"Well...a year or two...perhaps three?"

"That's an old friend. He had to be familiar to all of you."

245

"Iie! None of us met Mr. Segawa's friends!"

"Do you know his name?... Well, then, was he here last night?"

No one spoke; they eyed exhibits being tagged on the portico and packed into boxes: the sword, the wine glass, a pair of bloodied socks and an equally revolting uniform. A man brought stained towels from the kitchen to add to the collection. He beckoned to another associate to say he'd found signs of blood and prints on the sink. A small equipment case was taken inside to lift whorls and loops and palmprints the murderer had left in his haste. A wicker basket was used to carry the late actor to a waiting hearse.

"Well, then, has no one any more to say?"

The neighbors splintered from the gate with their secrets. It was up to the *junsa* to find out for himself. The lady from next door hesitated, then went to her own house to stand behind her curtained windows. She watched the policeman as the hearse drove away. Tucking his notebook into a pocket, he glared at the street with suspicion, marking one house after another with a long inspection. When he looked at her windows, she shrank from them. He gave her a most distressing sense of guilt.

Naranu kannin suruga kannin. The proverb inscribed in flowing calligraphy upon the *kakemono,* a pure white rice-paper scroll hung in the alcove of the spacious room, observed: *To bear the unbearable is truly to bear.* It seemed to point up the spoiled flower arrangement below it where a vase lay tipped over and a spray of dry branches littered the shelf. To bear the unbearable. It was originally dedicated to the occupant of this room but came to represent the world outside after invading Allied forces established themselves throughout the land. The foreign rule was over now; the fortunes of the country flourished. The nation was sovereign once more. But the room's occupant remained the same.

Hichiriki Hidenori should have been a grown man by

now. Unfortunately, he was born brain-damaged, and his gross, immature body, fat for lack of exercise, wore the wondering, exquisite face of purity given to infants. He was confined here permanently, with access to a patch of ground out of doors where he could pull up stray blades of grass or feel sunlight or touch snow. The name chosen for him was that of a flute but he was speechless and his needs had to be guessed at by the nursemaid assigned to his care...and by his family, whose brief visits were a mystery to him.

The old nursemaid was always present, sleeping within the same *futon* at night to keep him company. She was not bright and both found a silent, loving comfort to share over the long years. Whenever a member of Hichiriki's family appeared, she scurried to one side, nervously upset over not having kept the room meticulously tidy. His mother remained the shortest amount of time during her visits, being fraught with shame about him. Only the birth of her second son had preserved her from total despair. She looked in upon Hichiriki daily as a duty, never touching him and addressing herself to his timid companion about his welfare. His brother, a successful electronics factory employee with an obedient wife, stayed longer when he came but thought of him as a baby and brought simple toys. Hichiriki liked the toys but gazed at his guests with a tolerant recognition that they were harmless and would soon leave him to play with his adored attendant. She was his sole object of complete affection but for one: his father.

In the privacy of his home, a dwelling undistinguishable from other prosperous but lesser households in the suburbs of Osaka, Chief Superintendent Shugo Hidenori lived a sedate and regulated life based upon tradition. Having adjusted ably to every circumstance throughout the demeaning surrender and retreat from conquered territories till the present, his pride remained. The appropriate words of the scroll had sustained him during those travails. He had painted them shortly after the birth of his firstborn son.

Hidenori was with the boy when his wife scratched politely at the edge of the shoji. She did not enter but knelt on the polished floor of the hall and waited, unseen, for his acknowledgment. She regretted to inform him of an

247

urgent telephone call and begged him to say if he would listen to the instrument. Hidenori grimaced. He disliked the necessity of having the modern convenience in his domain but could not be without it. Having banished it to the farthest reaches of his property, he took calls by presenting himself in the section of his house given over to servants as their own quarters. No one dared to trouble him with such a summons unless it was of grave import, and each incoming message was duly submitted to the judgment of his wife before being transmitted to him. Considering that she brought word to him personally, Hidenori curtly replied that he would accommodate the caller. A whispered *"hai"* and she was gone from the door.

His son stared at him expectantly. Hidenori didn't agonize as he once had upon seeing him and cherished the artless exchanges they made here. Love was given and accepted openly. With a smile. With a tender stroke of a hand. Long ago, the man avoided such gestures because it was like petting a groveling, dumb animal. There had even been an occasion when the boy bit him, out of pique for not receiving attention. The boy. It was hard to think of him as anything else, in spite of his flabby muscles and large bones. Standing, he would have been taller then his father. Standing. Standing was beyond him; Hichiriki lived upon his knees and buttocks and elbows and the palms of his hands. Only when he was asleep or prone upon the floor did he remotely resemble a man.

The nursemaid took that moment to attempt to put the vase and dry branches in order. Hidenori was distracted by the movement and read the scroll above her head. The baby could have been strangled mercifully when its condition was discovered, but his unhappy wife defended it fiercely. Hers was the motto lighting the shadow which had befallen them, an ordinary *kotowaza*, such as is heard among every level of society. He thought her courage remarkable and it added further distinction and respect to their marriage. Sighing, Hidenori reached down to tug gently at Hichiriki's ear and received the caress of his son's cheek against his hand in return. They smiled into each other's eyes once more and the superintendent bowed slightly to the nursemaid and walked slowly from the room. Behind him, he heard the scuffling, muffled sounds of pursuit. They stopped. The old woman had caught the child-man and was soothing him with teasing laughter. Hidenori continued on to the offensive instrument; the servants vanished at his approach. The closet in which the telephone was imprisoned stood open.

"*Moshi-moshi,*" he growled into the mouthpiece. After listening, his attitude was less aggressive. It was indeed a matter of urgency. A tragedy, in fact. He was respectfully informed of the sudden demise of Jihei Segawa. A murder. There were substantial clues and mention of a possible unnamed suspect. Assuming full control of the investigation, he said he would fly to Kyoto immediately to participate. Had routine procedures been observed? Excellent. He would inspect the grounds and house of the illustrious victim himself and wished to study the reports of the recording *junsa.* And please arrange for interviews with the actor's peers in Kyoto and elsewhere.

Hidenori replaced the phone upon its cradle. He frowned at it, felt uneasy and switched off the light. Then he shut the closet door upon the hated object to condemn it to the silent darkness again.

Osaka was slowly being strangled by reproductive expressways which soared everywhere above abandoned canals. Worming through the city, the Yodo River once provided uncountable water routes, creating an Oriental Venice. It was surrendered to industry now, the new fanaticism. As the city spread and stretched into ever more polluted heights, the canyons of its streets and corridors became gutters of neon, stench and humanity. People living in such proximity are alienated and are antisocial as a defense against their lack of privacy. Thus no one took much notice as Heinie Joe splashed into the old pleasure district under cover of rain.

The lane he'd known with his mother was gone. A broad new freeway slashed through modern buildings and ran directly over the place it had been, so the haunts of childhood were denied him. He shivered again; he had been suffering chills and fever. Cold and wet too long, he suspected he was going to be quite badly off. It was a poor situation for him; he had wagered so heavily upon being aided by the security of familiar surroundings. The entire area had been transformed into a business district, all offices and somber fronts. There could be no respite here; he would have to scout the rest of Osaka and explore new warrens, which must have replaced the old secret places.

The showers drove Heinie beneath shelter wherever possible. At a junction where freeways arched above the ground, he slowed his pace to walk between their uprights, looking hopefully to vagrants hiding from the weather. Some were burning scraps of wood and twisted newspapers in metal drums. They turned their backs upon his hesitant figure; there was little enough heat. Had he joined them, he would have seen that they retained the next-to-last page of the *Yomiuri Shimbun,* which is traditionally reserved for news of crime. This paper carried, as usual, re-served for news of crime. This paper carried, as usual, the most lurid accounts of the latest story; two rival newspapers tried to be less sensational about the murder, but the savage nature of it rendered their coverage into a scenario gory as any Jihei Segawa had filmed. Forgetting the boy passing by, the vagrants read every detail and would not burn the sheet so they could read it all again.

Holding his fingers under opposite armpits for warmth and pressing his elbows to his damp jacket, Heinie Joe plodded on, nose twitching at the acrid smoke. He reached a place where the freeway bridged a canal, rank with contaminated water. Against the last abutment raising the span overhead, the boy reeled and felt the clamminess sink into his shoulders and back. His shuddering threw him to the ground, where perception dissolved. Like a crumpling wet paper doll, he sagged into himself, a waterlogged casualty having no thought or reason or hope.

But someone wouldn't let him sleep. Kept hauling him to consciousness. Bringing him up, up, up to the surface. Listening, he heard without understanding. He would rather sink again into the dark and avoid the disturbance. The ache. His body pained and heat raged all around. Why had the rain turned hot?

A whispery voice spoke as Heinie felt hot broth spilling into his burned mouth. "Although coarse, the net of heaven catches everything. What are you running from, eh?"

250

He choked on the searing liquid. It was inedible, something concocted of the canal's content, dredged up and heated to violent boiling over a rusted grill which teetered upon an improvised stove. When he could focus his eyes, he saw that he was in a hovel constructed of flattened cans and slats from wooden crates. A derelict gazed into his face, fuming putrid breath into the frigid air before his sparse, yellowed teeth. The man had lost an ear, leaving a diseased scar scabbed with pestiferous sores at the side of his temple. The hut stank dreadfully. The only solid place to rest against was the smoke-stained cement of the abutment.

"What makes you think I am running? I'm keeping out of the rain."

"Hai. I could see that. You could not have been more wet had you been a carp." The man spooned another mouthful into the boy. "Don't make such a face. This broth has sustained me for more years than you own. If you are fed poison, lick even the plate." He shook with silent mirth, causing the boy to turn his nose from him. The man nodded sadly, saying, "Well, the *furo* of the canal is not so cleansing as one may desire. But look at it this way: No one bothers me. I am left to my own devices. It's not a bad life. I have shelter, my *furo* brings a harvest... and flotsam finds itself welcome here when it is such as you." He leered evilly.

Heinie Joe felt powerless. His arms and legs were dead; only the ragged heat of the food paining his gullet and stomach made an impression inside his body. Glancing down, he saw his clothing had been taken from him and he was lying upon loose straw, covered with a threadbare tarpaulin. He tried not to think about what had taken place, knowing it was more than likely the derelict had used him.

"What did you do with my clothes?"

The man pointed upward. Above them, on a string over the smoke of the fire, Heinie's clothing steamed.

"Arigato. I'd like to put them on."

"They are not dry."

"I don't give a shit."

"Of course, one gets chilled without apparel... unless warmed by another." He reached a filthy hand to grasp Heinie lasciviously through the canvas.

"Hands off, you son-of-a-bitch." The boy said it weakly but the derelict withdrew his hand. Noticing the man wasn't disappointed, Heinie confirmed his suspicion by asking, "I've been here a long time?"

"Not so long...yet long enough."

Heinie Joe hated him. The man sniffed, then sat back upon his heels. Not whining, he made a complaint. "You've finished most of my supper, did you know that?"

"What do you want me to do, pay you? I haven't money."

"Hai. I know."

"Then what the fuck do you expect?"

The derelict folded his hands complacently. "Nothing. I was just making a comment." He pulled a rag aside from the rickety wall and observed, "It's not raining anymore."

"Good. Give me my clothes so I can get out of here."

"Oh, but they are not ready! It would be your death to leave without resting with me for a few days." Once more he grinned with his sewer cavity.

The boy regarded him unsteadily. It was warm under the tarpaulin and the food was generating a spark of life in his limbs. There was a slight tingling sensation in his toes and fingers to suggest they might revive. The man made a show of being cold.

"It would be friendly of you to share my covering. Without a supper and without my tarpaulin, I am most uncomfortable."

Heinie tore the canvas from himself and threw it at the man. Part fell across the fire and the man rescued it frantically. He looked up reproachfully at him.

"You didn't have to do that. You must understand how depressing my life is. Here..." He covered him again, refraining from touching his nude body. "Keep this over yourself. I won't have your death on my conscience."

After all, it wasn't as though he hadn't already collected for his charity. His face mellowed and he began to sing tunelessly. He waited till the boy shivered himself into a stupor again and then pleasured himself some more.

Preparing to take one of Jordan's suits to the cleaner, Wanda emptied the pockets. A crumpled sugar packet; loose tobacco strands. A book of matches. A handkerchief. Folded flat and gone rather gray. He should have a clean one to carry around. She tossed it aside to be put in the wash.

But it wasn't a man's handkerchief.

She picked it up again and unfolded the dainty square. It wasn't one of hers, either.

Another woman's handkerchief.

With a smear of lipstick. Another woman's lipstick.

She slumped onto the chaise beside the closet with his suit lying limply across her lap, the handkerchief crushed in her palm. Its presence didn't paint a new picture; his late working nights were fairly obvious weren't they? Her humbling compromise of tolerance was chosen because Jordan always came home and had certainly been tactful about his affairs. Was he careless now because he did not care? The women he saw must be younger than she...and there wasn't a family to hold him.

Oh, Jordie.

Goddamn you, Jordie.

She longed for the days of her foolish security, before all that was nice became bad and beyond her control. When the phone rang, she didn't pick it up. One of my friends calling, she thought. I need help, not friends. The phone continued to ring, as though someone had to get through. She answered listlessly to stop the turbulent sound.

"Hello."

"Hi. I'd like to talk to Jordan Asche."

"This is his wife. What can I do for you?"

"I'm an old pal of his. David Bell. We were in the Navy together years ago."

His name, heard before in happier days, improved her mood. She managed to smile into the phone. "I know all about you."

"Now I don't know what to say."

"Relax. Jordie's stories weren't that damaging."

"That's good!"

"He'll be simply thrilled and amazed to hear from you."

"Put him on the horn!"

"I'm afraid he's not home. Won't be till dinnertime. He's at work now."

"Can I call him there?"

"Of course."

"Boy, you don't know how pleased I was to find you listed in the directory."

"Where are you?"

"It looks like cockroach heaven. I'm in a phone booth...a hotel lobby on Times Square."

"Don't tell me you're staying at the Astor."

"God, no. I just stepped in to look through their collection of phone books."

"Well...let me give you Jordie's extension at Polychem." She gave him the number and hung up thinking of the earlier Jordan this man remembered. She clutched the suit to herself with desperation. "I don't want to lose you," she wailed forlornly. And a solution she was to attempt waited in her hands. Her tight grip gradually loosened; the material had been bundled into a small shape, like that of an infant in swaddling clothes. She pondered it ruefully, re-examining a crueler, self-inflicted jealousy she had nurtured throughout the years.

Striding eagerly into the lobby of the Astor, Jordan saw Dave at once. They fell into each other's arms and hugged, then checked to see what the years had done.

"Dave, if you hadn't warned me to look for fancy epaulets, I'd have passed you by."

Dave smoothed his thinning pate and replaced his chief warrant officer's cap. "You look just the same, you old turd bird."

"I had a hunch you'd stay in the service."

"Well, every time my enlistment was up, they sang shipping-over music at me and I signed on again... until now. I've been holding a hot discharge in my hand since 0900 this morning."

"I should have told you to meet me at the house."

"No sweat. It didn't take you too long to get here. Is it all right for you to take off from work like this?"

"Sure. I'm half owner of the outfit."

"That's four oh," Dave replied appreciatively. "I didn't know you turned rich."

"Jesus, I have to be. Nobody can live in New York unless they're millionaires."

"Who are all the panhandlers I see?"

"Tourists. Trying to get back to Kansas or some other jungle like that."

"Smart-ass."

A sofa was available and they sat, each looking at the other's clothing covertly, imagining what might have been had they done differently with their lives.

"Is the *Bulman* still knocking around, Dave?"

"None of those old cans are in service now."

"You must have been through New York before. What have you been doing?"

His stripes of glory bars told the story he dismissed lightly, saying, "I was just a Pacific sailor until my last assignment. Even when I got stationed ashore, it was on the West Coast."

"How'd you get on this side of the world?"

"A slot opened for me on the *Intrepid.* You probably saw us on TV: We picked up the Gemini 3 shot."

"How long are you staying in New York?"

"Till this afternoon, when my plane leaves."

"No, you don't! Cancel the flight."

"I've got a family waiting for me."

"You can't take off without meeting my wife... having a visit."

"Well..."

"Come on. Spend the weekend with us."

"I can't. But I'll switch to a later flight and we can have a few hours to chew the fat."

"Where's your luggage?"

"In a locker at the East Side Terminal. The bus was going to take me to the airport from there."

255

"We'll pick it up and I'll get you to the airport after dinner. I talked to my wife before I left the office, so she's expecting us." He stood, eager to leave. "Jesus, we should have stayed in touch!"

As Dave joined him to go to the exit, he said, "Well, you didn't write . . . so I didn't." There was a questioning behind it which Jordan didn't notice. They went into the street to stand at the curb. A billboard opposite the hotel puffed perfectly round rings of smoke over Times Square. A taxi swerved to them. Sitting inside it, Jordan gave directions and the cabbie drove into the crawling traffic lanes to head south and east, following convoluted routes instead of short, straight lines. The mileage meter beat cents into dollars with a merry, relentless clatter.

"You said your family was waiting, Dave. Got a wife?"

"Yeah, and three kids. Boy and twin girls."

"Must have been rough on them, traveling and moving to be near you."

"Oh, they stayed put most of the time. Lived with my folks on the old homestead."

"That was lucky for them. Service families are usually such gypsies."

"That wasn't for me. I wanted my kids to grow up where I did. Now my Dad's too tired to handle it, and we didn't want to lose the farm. Hell, he had it from his father, and my son wants to keep it."

"That's nice . . . that's nice, Dave."

Again the odd look, and then Dave seemed uneasy. Jordan chalked it up to their long absence from each other. Once closer than brothers, they'd soon quit fidgeting. Dave asked, "How many kids have you got, Jordie?"

He hesitated, unhappy to feel inferior, and answered airily, "None. There's just me and Wanda. I think you two will hit it off okay. She's a West Coast girl . . . California."

"That where you met her?"

"Yeah. It was love at first sight. We were married the same week I got out of the Navy."

"That nice, Jordie . . . nice."

At the terminal, Dave's suitcase was recovered from a steel locker while the meter ticked and other yellow cabs pawed cement behind them. Getting downtown along Second Avenue was a faster trip. When they arrived, Dave thought the street was grubby but was impressed by the

256

three-story brownstone Jordan said was his. A few small buildings on the block were identical—each mildly restored, reflecting an older and steadier generation. Jordan's front door displayed a brass nameplate over the letter drop. A colonial lamp bolted to worn bricks overhead was new. Steps to the stoop had iron balustrades topped with horseheads holding useless rings in their mouths, and outside every window a long box on the ledge was filled with stunted geraniums. The friendly effect was spoiled by the unsavory neighborhood and the number of locks Wanda had to open to admit the men.

The kitchen clock nudged her. Of all days not to have Leticia around! A soapy dish slipped and chipped an edge. Wanda rinsed it quickly and stood it on the drying rack. Her thrown-together dinner hadn't been half bad, considering. And getting it to the table while trying to play gracious hostess could have been less hectic without the difficulty of making up her mind. She had vacillated all day about her decision. Or almost decision. Or not one. Even now, with the handkerchief and its lipstick stains still rankling, she had vestiges of doubt about going through with it.

Jordie was marvelous during the meal, behaving ideally, very like the beginning years of their being together, holding hands across the table and speaking and smiling at the same instant she did...and Dave beamed at them as if a proud uncle. Well, maybe tentatively, but he must have been convinced his former shipmate's marriage was a good one. Dave didn't match his description; he should have been dashingly handsome and irresistible, not a balding old salt. He was dull. American Midwest and boring about his future rural life. Where was the sexy womanizer Jordie claimed him to be? Another example of how men talked a bigger game than they played. But Dave was sweet, polite. Watched his slang and was shy with her. It was work to get him to talk.

257

He had to be coaxed into the mandatory display of his family snapshots. The plastic card-case was filled with color photographs of his wife and children, and she took pains to admire them. The girls were ordinary, duplicates of each other in clothing and pose; the boy resembled his mother, who was the plain Jane seen in every yearbook. The succession of pictures showed childhood and puberty overcome with perpetual smiles, but it was Jordie's smile which troubled her. He handled the photographs possessively, wanting them to be his... she had to take each from him in order to see it. She asked to see the earliest ones again—the babies; it hurt, but she *could* look at them, could feel their sweetness move her. Just you wait, Jordie. She glanced at the clock again. We'll see your friend off on his plane... and then... we'll see...

Upstairs, in the third-floor living room, Dave amused Jordan with ancient history concerning his brief stay in Norfolk, Virginia, where he had been sent from basic training to wait for his first ship. It was prior to their meeting and a story he hadn't told.

"My folks thought I went to church regularly every Sunday, like we did in Colby. But who thinks to find a church in a liberty town where the whole side of a building is painted with a sign saying FIGHT VD? Anyway, I got closer to Jesus than I wanted the day I lost my cherry there."

"I would have sworn you were born without one, Dave."

"You were the only crud I ever heard admit to being a virgin. Hell, I told the damnedest fibs about my shackups at first just to look good, or everyone would have thought I was queer. I finally could tell the truth about my shore leaves."

"Go on: What happened in Norfolk?"

"Another kid and I got steered to a whorehouse downtown. We were both seventeen and on a real sailor's liberty at last; we damned near got seasick on the trolley getting there. The place was next door to a storefront where some religion set up shop and I got pretty self-conscious hearing old-time revival hymns as we waited in line for the girls. It was awful and it was the most fun I ever had. I was scared shitless every second. The beast I got tried to cheer me up by saying if I heard a little prayer from next door when I got my rocks off, it meant I was saved."

"Were you?"

"I was everything else! I never hear hymns now but it doesn't make me horny." Dave grinned impishly. "My wife's crazy about Sundays." He swirled the ice cubes in his glass and was silent. Jordan assured him Wanda would be up to join them when her dishes were put away. City sounds filtered through the windows. "Jordie, why don't you and Wanda have any children?"

Jordan debated answering, then decided he could. Dave wasn't a stranger. "We wanted them. It wasn't possible, that's all."

"Why?"

"We learned Wanda couldn't conceive. It was a hell of a jolt. She took it worse than I did." He wasn't going to say how much had altered between them. "We both counted on having a family. There was lots of pressure on my wife about it. From my folks when they were alive...her own...and me." The word was repeated reflectively. "Me...but I didn't hound her about it the way her own family did. They couldn't help it, I guess. You see, her sisters were having babies every other year...one or the other of them."

When he didn't continue, Dave asked, "What about adoption? Didn't that appeal to you?"

"Yeah, that's supposed to be the drill, isn't it? God says, 'No babies for you guys,' so you say, 'Thanks, God, I'll look after somebody else's'...and then you get one. But we didn't."

Leaving his glass, Dave left his armchair to go to the window. The sky was bleak over the tall buildings outside. The weather was cold and wet. He recalled a stone wharf and his leg aching in a cutting wind.

"Remember the fishing village on the Inland Sea?"

Jordan stopped frowning and replied warmly, "Yeah. There was a girl there...damn, her name's on the tip of my tongue."

"The swabbies on our ship envied you then."

"Yeah. She made a big difference for me."

Dave nodded, seeing another place in the mist of the street below him. "Everybody in the Occupation tried to get themselves a shackup like her for the duration."

"Don't call her that, Dave," Jordan protested. "It wasn't like that for us."

259

"You ever write her?"

"No."

"I can't understand how you—especially you, Jordie—could walk away from a kid in Japan."

"I couldn't bring her home as a souvenir, Dave! What are you talking about?"

"Not the girl, Jordie...her baby."

An abyss opened under him. Dave's stiff back presented no saving handholds. "What baby?" he demanded urgently. He leaped from his seat and strode to Dave to pull him around roughly. "What are you talking about? What baby?"

"You saying you don't know?"

"Know what?"

"The girl had a son. I saw him. Your son."

He blanched. "You saw..." It was nightmarish; Dave's face swam before him accusingly.

"I wondered about him for years. You didn't write after you left the ship. I thought the boy was worth one letter."

Jordan exploded angrily, "How the hell was I supposed to have known about him?"

"She sent you word," Dave answered mildly. Jordan shook his head in denial. "She sent you a message about him, Jordie. I know for sure that she did."

Unmanned, he sank to the window seat. "Jesus...a son."

"Our ship didn't leave Seto Naikai except for escort duty and a couple of runs to Tokyo. We had a going naval base for ourselves in the village harbor and I ran into the girl whenever I went ashore."

"You were there long enough to learn she had a baby."

"We didn't get relieved till a year after you were wounded, Jordie."

It didn't seem possible; shock numbed him. A son. The girl had a son. His son.

Dave sat beside him and continued his report softly. "I took over your habit of bringing stuff to her family, thinking you'd have wanted me to do it."

"That was damned kind of you."

"I felt I owed it to you, Jordie. I'll always owe you for not letting me go over the side."

"You don't owe me nothing."

"Just my life."

"Fuck you, Dave. That's something you never owed me."

They sat quietly. Jordan remembered the timidity of the girl...and himself. Each frightened of the other and daring to touch; and finding how glorious and pleasurable it was not to be denied anything, they had done everything—again and again, drugged with permissibility, granted one to the other to gratify themselves. Not once thinking it might have a consequence. After a while, he asked, "How did you find out about the baby? Did she tell you when it began to show?"

Dave's mouth was dry. He would have gotten his glass but the drink wouldn't help. "She used to be the one to meet me at the door, and then one day she wasn't there. I didn't know what to make of it. The family couldn't tell me. I thought they were saying she was visiting someone. Hell, I didn't learn much of that gook language the way you did. Anyway, I didn't find out about her. It was pretty much the same, though. The old grandmother grabbed everything I brought, and the girl's parents sat me down to drink sake or gave me bowls of soup or rice. I couldn't get out of having to make it a little social occasion each time. You know, I couldn't get to first base with that old broad? She hated my guts to the last day I saw her."

"You were going to tell me how you learned about my son." The word sang. My son. He wanted to shout it.

"I was getting to that. The last day I saw the old woman was also when I saw the girl again. She suddenly popped her head out a window and called to me. I was so pleased to see her! I asked where she'd been and she held up her baby. It was a hell of a surprise..."

"A hell of a surprise..."

"She wanted to get word to you. I thought she'd have done it sooner but she hadn't known where to write. I said the address of the hospital ship would do."

"I got a postcard. It caught up with me in California."

Dave looked at him steadily. "Well?"

"It was just a picture postcard. With a line of Japanese chicken tracks on it. Somebody wrote my address for her in English."

"I did it, Jordie."

That angered him. "Why not her message, too?" he demanded.

"She wanted to write it herself. She said she knew how."

"It was in her own language. I thought it said something like 'Wish you were here.'" Something much more like that. He stared at the floor disconsolately.

"You should have had it translated."

Jordan said bitterly, "Christ, I had no reason to. It was only a postcard. What do you do with a postcard? You look at the picture and throw it away. It was only a postcard, Dave. You'd think a woman would send something more...make a bigger deal out of..." Remorse overcame him. "All I knew was that it was a pretty card from..." The floss silk of her name surfaced to strangle him. "Yukiko...she was called Yukiko."

His choked whisper echoed hollowly, fading into the sound of Wanda ascending the carpeted stairs to the living room. Both men needed a drink. She served what was their last drink together, attributing the depressed atmosphere to letdown friends suffer after exhausting themselves of all remembrance of past days. Dave was edgy, anxious to get to the airport. They soon put on their coats and went down to the street to find a cab. Wanda gave up trying to make small talk on the long ride to Kennedy. Instead, she projected herself ahead...to being alone with Jordan at home.

The derelict locked his door securely upon its outer latch and listened, head pressed to the wood with his healthy ear. It was well; the boy slept and it was safe to leave him temporarily. Everywhere under the expressway, dampness misted the air. Far off was a pale glow; the vagrants had continued to stoke their steel drum with more tinder to tend to their warmth. The derelict was certain one of them would have the medicine he needed for the sick boy...there was always a bottle of raw spirits among such a group. Running on rags he had bound to his feet, he left his hovel to try his luck with the other men. They heard his approach and squinted into the dimness fearfully. The *junsa* patrolled this area and frequently drove them from it with blows of their batons. Seeing who it was, they relaxed and made room for him beside the fire.

"So...you've come out of hibernation."

The derelict glanced at every face. They had seen him pick up the boy and drag him into his abode. "He's very ill."

"You should have left him to die."

"I considered it."

"Aren't you afraid the *garentai* will kill you and take over your possessions?"

"Love has no enemy."

The men elbowed each other and laughed. They well knew how this derelict behaved with anyone he found incapable of resisting his advances. "It's not love you're giving him and you know it."

"I have need for affection, too. I'm surprised you men didn't have your fill of him when he dropped."

There was another exchange of lewd laughter. "You stole him from us. We had begun to decide what to do when we saw you come upon him. We could not have gotten there soon enough to prevent you from barring your door against us."

"You're animals. You would have killed the boy."

"He's not better off with you."

He warmed his fingers over the drum. "Who knows? I may have him to look after when he is better."

"You'll get the same as Jihei Segawa if you try."

"Jihei Segawa? What's happened to him?"

"You haven't heard?" A man pulled the folded page of newsprint from his pocket. "He's been killed by a lover. Not different from the one you hope to have."

The derelict read the article slowly, lips moving as he traced the words. A full description of the murder scene. The chief superintendent of Kansai Province, Shugo Hidenori of Manchukuo fame, had taken charge. And the murderer was known. An *ainoko;* Joe Shimada. His photograph, reproduced from files, was of a fourteen-year-old boy. The derelict looked closer. *Hai*, the same; younger, but the very same! It was the fortune of having two good things in hand at the same time. The boy was in his own hut and not well enough to escape. The derelict saw also a photograph of the actor beside the column of print—a man proud of a prized possession, the sailboat in the background.

"I'm sure the man was killed because he was wealthy. I don't have anything."

"To a boy with nothing, you are a prince. You should have left him out here with us."

The derelict returned the newspaper page to the man and washed his hands in the heat of the fire again. They eyed him enviously but did not continue to tease him about the boy. After a suitable interval, he thought he could make his request. "Is there anything to drink among you?"

"We've nothing left. The night has been cold."

"Ah...I was hoping for a dram to give the boy for his fever."

"You'd do him more good by turning him out."

"It's too late. I've committed myself and we have an obligation between us."

"*Hai?* Then you'll have to take care of it without us."

"Surely there was something left in the bottle." One of the vagrants shifted uncomfortably. "He's sick. You've been sick yourselves. A dose of spirits would do much for him. Was there nothing left in your bottle?"

The vagrant coughed. "I need it myself. You can hear how ill I am."

"I've given you food, even though you cursed me for dredging it from the canal. When have I asked for anything but a drink from your bottle?"

"But you want it for the *garentai.*"

"What does it matter who I give it to? Let me have what's left."

The vagrant looked at his companions but they averted their eyes and would not advise him. He watched the flames inside the drum and stood upon one foot and then the other. It was a difficult decision. In the end, he reluctantly drew a small bottle from his ragged coat and handed it to the derelict. "It's only a swallow."

"*Arigato.* If it shows the boy I mean him no harm, he may be persuaded to stay with me."

"What of that?"

The derelict smiled. "I've shared my food with you, haven't I? I may not be jealous of him after a while." He held the bottle snugly to his chest and ran back to his hut. They stared after him speculatively. It's easy to give before giving. They watched until he stopped before the place, lost him in the fog as it thickened, and when it cleared he was already inside and out of sight to them.

In the hovel, the derelict knelt beside the boy. Heinie Joe was breathing harshly with his mouth open. His temperature had risen. The derelict lifted his head tenderly and uncorked the bottle to tip its contents into Heinie's parted lips. The boy gagged on the fiery liquid.

"Drink. Don't waste it. It's to help you." Heinie accepted the rest and would have had more but the bottle was empty. The derelict set it aside to save and lay the boy's head back into position. He fell into his deep sleep again. "They think out there that I should be wary of you. An inch ahead in time is unknown to everyone...so I may believe as I like. Perhaps you'll repay me farther than you think." He made fast the door and poked the ashes beneath the grill to expose the last of the dying coals. A little warmth was released from them. Then he proceeded to remove his rags. He was anxious to crawl under the tarpaulin and hold the sleeping boy in his arms once again. Imagine, getting as good as Jihei Segawa got!

The ride home was frustrating to Wanda. In a mood of growing elation, she tried to engage Jordan in conversation. She observed she should have arranged for Leticia's services; no hostess likes to miss chunks of an evening, not one so special as this had been for them. Jordan grunted and remained uncommunicative. She did her best to lift his spirits, taking care not to require answers. Obviously he'd been affected by seeing his friend after so many years. But why was he glum? When they returned to the house, they went upstairs to the living room for a nightcap. She wondered how to begin.

"What was the matter, Jordie? Old Navy days too nostalgic to bear?" She tried to tease him into good humor. "I can't imagine what you men said to each other up here. Have a fight?"

He left her restlessly to light the remnants of logs in the fireplace. The wood was delivered from a nearby florist's shop, neatly split and tied with red ribbon like a gift; for the exorbitant price, it deserved the extra trim. Flames snapped cheerfully in the hearth. Jordan muttered, "Nothing happened up here. We just ran out of steam."

Wanda stirred the ice cubes in her glass; tiny moons and suns flashed at their corners. "I like Dave," she began again. "I'd forgotten how attractive men in uniform can be. He has a lovely family. Don't you agree?" She waited. "I didn't mind looking at his collection of photographs, Jordie."

He returned to the sofa, hearing her as a familiar background requiring little concentration as he descended the years to Yukiko, seeking fragments to make her real again. Blunders are retained more readily than joys, and good things fade with lessening recollection, becoming ephemeral as she had...as indistinct as mists from the Inland Sea now crowding in to shut out the present and revive his past. But the girl's face remained obscure, her child's impossible to see. His child. A son like himself.

The fire crackled, orchestrating itself to the tinkle of ice in a glass. Wanda leaned against the sofa reflectively, undisturbed by his lack of comment. It helped not to be led off the track before she could lose determination. "I've been unable to look at people's children, Jordie. You've known that. But I really didn't mind his photos." The liquor helped, too; thinking herself stronger and sure of herself, she chattered on, "How I've hated particular words! Women aren't trees or vegetable patches, so if we can't have our own babies we shouldn't be called *unfruitful*. Or *infertile*. We aren't plowed like farmland no matter who's concerned. Even rape needs a certain finesse to accomplish, don't you think?" She sighed, because rambling wasn't the means to her goal, and braced to get to it faster. "They say a woman is pregnant when she's to have a baby. I'm not sure I've liked that word, either."

Her words had a gadfly effect; they fringed at his consciousness without touching. He said impatiently, "Let's not talk right now, Wanda."

She replied quickly, "Don't worry about me, darling. It's not painful for me to talk about it." She relished a tingle of excitement and smiled. "You can thank your friend for showing me how terribly wrong I've been all these years."

"Wrong?"

"Will you come down to earth from wherever it is you are? Dave can't have created such an impact! You'll be making me jealous of him next." The slip was a dangerous one and she continued rapidly to prevent him from analyzing it. "Darling, I'm doing my best to tell you I've changed my mind!"

"I don't know what you're gabbing about, Wanda. I seriously don't. What's gotten into you?"

"Oh, Jordie," her voice wobbled. It was the moment to stop or go on. Once given, her word couldn't be rescinded. "Jordie...we should have a family, too." And having said that much, the rest tumbled after to strengthen it. "I'm not prejudiced against adoptions." She waited vainly, unable to read his expression. "I'll bet you gave up on me."

"What are you talking about?" he responded harshly, frightening her and himself with his abruptness.

Doubtful again, she forced herself to say, "Why don't we?"

"Why don't we what?"

"Let's adopt a baby."

It took his breath away. Meaning yes and no, he said, "It's too late."

"Why? No agency would consider us too old."

"Age has nothing to do with it."

"Right!" she agreed happily. "And if we're to enjoy raising a baby, we should begin right now. If we wait longer, it *will* be too late." Enthusiasm bubbled from her; launched, the prospect improved with each moment. "We don't want to be fuddy-duddies and not able to keep up with a growing child."

Stunned at this reversal in her attitude, he got up to pretend to freshen his drink at the bar. "When did you arrive at this idea, Wanda?" It was a stall for time and a test. He was afraid to believe her.

"It was Dave."

"Dave? What did Dave say to you?"

"It was those pictures he showed us, Jordie. I loved those adorable, sweet children of his. Didn't you love them, too? Weren't you wishing they were ours?"

267

A ship's clock on the mantelpiece ticked and dinged louder than before. He sought between the metallic din for a way to tell her about his son. "Is that how you felt?"

"Oh, Jordie, I found myself wanting a family like his for us...well, one child like his, anyway. Let's adopt a baby, Jordie."

"You're after a little girl you can dress in dainty dresses."

"No, darling, no! We'll hold out for a sturdy boy you can pal around with when he's old enough." Nervous relief made her laugh; she was uncertain of her happiness. "We can even name him after Dave. David Asche is a lovely name for a baby." A log settled into the fireplace grate with a comfortable rustle. Leaving the sofa, she ran to Jordan and brought the aroma of woodsmoke with her. He flinched from it, remembering the village. She said, "You and I need this, Jordie. For us." Her eyes wavered with uncertainty, then she added sincerely, "I want our marriage to be wonderful again...and you need the child for that to happen."

Confronting her squarely, he said, "That's honest of you, Wanda. Do you need the child, too?"

"For you. I want to be a mother for you."

His heart raced uncontrollably. "Are you sure, Wanda? Absolutely sure?"

"Yes, I'm sure."

The woodsmoke was heady in his nostrils. "Yeah...I think you are."

"Well? What shall we do about it?" Smiling confidently, she felt all was well with her world.

"A son," Jordan answered shakily. "I'd like to have my son."

"Oh, Jordie!" She threw her arms around his neck and tried to kiss him, something they hadn't done spontaneously longer than she could recall. She was puzzled when he disentangled himself to hold her off. "What's the matter? Why so gloomy? You're about to become a father!" she cried delightedly. And her joy waned when she saw he wasn't sharing it. "What is it, Jordie?"

"Wait a minute." He bought time to compose himself by going to the fireplace. He crouched to poke embers beneath the logs. Ooba-san wouldn't have approved of this

268

wasteful foreign blaze...she hadn't approved of him, either. What had she done to that poor girl when Yukiko's belly grew large? His wife was waiting. He gathered his courage, then stood and began.

She was misled for a while because he started by telling her how it had been in those days, recounting his friendship with Yukiko haltingly, as of a dream remembered dimly. Each word stung like another thorn. The resultant child, spoken of with awe and increasing possessiveness, inspired a furious envy. Her own proposal diminished in worth disastrously and her optimism and happiness collapsed into anger. "I see," Wanda said grimly. "And I suppose you want to bring it home."

"Not 'it.' Him. Yukiko gave birth to a son."

She itched to slap him. "You were a big stud before you met me, weren't you? Which makes me the naïve one..."

"Don't be like that, Wanda. It might have been different had I not been injured and sent home. I didn't know she was pregnant."

"I didn't know she was pregnant," she mimicked nastily. "You sound like a teenager caught with his pants down." His inference that she was second choice poisoned her further. She wanted to retaliate, to return pain to its source.

"Please, Wanda..."

Instead of attempting to understand, she regarded him dully and went behind the bar to add a large dollop of whiskey to her drink. Ticking. Ticking. The hands of the ship's clock were dismayed at the hour, too late for bickering; when the next bell chimed, they'd be snugly overlapped...unlike the couple in this room.

Jordan begged earnestly, "I want him. Now that I know, I must have him. If we're thinking of adopting any child, it should be my own son."

The logic revolted her. Struggling to defend herself

269

against it, she sought to undermine him. "I'm amazed you didn't stay in touch with his mother."

"That ended when I didn't get back to my ship. It wasn't my fault." He couldn't say anything right. "Anyway, I only care about the boy now."

His involvement with his own feelings had made him overlook others. She found a flaw to exploit. "What makes you think she'll give up her child so easily?"

"He's my son, Wanda. He's mine, too."

"No," she answered with smug harshness. "You're making a faulty assumption. If she's married, I can't see her husband allowing the boy he's raised to be given away like an unwanted kitten."

"Married?" The thought had not occurred to him and she goaded him with it.

"Women marry, Jordie. They wind up as I have, except most don't disappoint their husbands. She could have lots of children by now. You may not get your son in spite of what you want."

The metronome of the clock took over again. Distressed, he knew he'd been thinking of Yukiko as she had been, not as she must be now. Of course she'd have married; it was stupid of him. And he blocked negativity by insisting, "Okay, that's a complication I hadn't considered. It doesn't have to be impossible to overcome. In any case, I've got to see the boy. I want to go to Japan . . . right away."

"Unannounced?"

"I can't depend upon letters, Wanda. If Yukiko isn't living in the village anymore, I have to be there to ask about her. They'll know where I can find her."

His impatience fueled her opposition; the girl of long ago was a new rival, she thought, though they talked of the boy. And why were they thinking of him as a child? "Jordie . . . this son of yours. He must be almost an adult."

"Yes. He's nineteen."

"How exact you are."

"I figured it out in the taxi coming home."

"He's old enough to make his own decisions. He may not want to leave his country."

"He's half American."

"Which doesn't give you license to bring him here. He's not your property."

Jordan argued stubbornly, "Everyone wants to come to

270

America...but it's another bridge to cross. I think my biggest problem will be to convince his family to let us have him."

"And I'm sure Japanese adoption procedures won't resemble ours."

"I'll cable someone. There's bound to be some sort of department there with the information I'll need."

She drained half her glass. Cold sober and sorry for it. "All right, Jordie. What about me? Have you any idea what this does to me?" Despairing of changing his mind, she spat her reasoning at him. "We've been having a dreadful marriage. It's a wonder we didn't split up ages ago. Now there's a chance to regain what we had in the beginning and love each other again—each other, as we once did."

"That's right, Wanda," he interjected. "That's what I've been getting at."

"No!" she retorted. "You've been talking about a selfish desire of your own. You want a big lout you got on another woman's body and you're willing to deprive me of any shred of personal involvement...of my own pretense of motherhood."

"What the hell is this? You want just any baby but not my son? I can't believe you're that callous."

"It's because he's your son! When I couldn't face having another woman's child in our house, it was only that I'd see it as a constant reminder of my own lack. Your son should have been mine to bear for you years ago, Jordie. How much worse do you think he'll make me feel?"

Unyielding, he replied, "He's my son."

"How am I supposed to relate to a half-grown man?" she cried. "Let alone one from an alien culture! I was ready to love a baby I can't produce myself—a little baby, Jordan—not a bastard of nineteen! Just look at it from my point of view."

"There's nothing more important than the fact he's my son."

"Tell me about him, Jordie," she challenged spitefully. "Tell me about someone you didn't know, didn't give a hoot about, and never heard of before this evening. Somebody who's done without you till now and is so suddenly so goddamned important to you."

He let her fury simmer and subside before attempting

271

to speak. He wanted her to help, not fight with him. "I got used to having no one," he said painfully, finding his explanation difficult to put together.

"Thank you. I thought I was someone."

"No...wait...beyond what you meant to me. I wanted something we're denied. The baby you're talking about wouldn't do it, though I was willing to accept that and wanted us to adopt children before. You said I'm thinking selfishly. I am. I couldn't be more selfish if I tried. The boy is my connection to tomorrow, more so than any other baby boy or girl we could possibly find. Does that make sense to you? Can you honestly quarrel with me over this?"

She couldn't, and she gave in, saying nothing.

"Believe me," he assured her fervently, "you'll be happy with him. Our marriage will be okay. This will make it better for both of us."

She gazed at him bleakly. He wasn't going to understand; he was blind to what he was doing to her. If she was half a woman before, he was killing off the rest by bringing the boy into their lives.

"Wanda, think it over...don't close your mind to him. We'll go to Japan. Meet the boy. Get to know him together. You'll see you're wrong to object to having him...and we'll talk to his family. It can be a vacation for us!"

Too ravaged to continue listening, she murmured, "A vacation. I couldn't bear to meet your...Japanese ...woman."

Her prejudice and loathing were undisguised. He entreated, "Don't condemn her. You'll want her to like you, so she won't hold back her consent. We've got to be a team in order to get my son."

How could she argue against so formidable an opponent? His son. Jordan had a son and he wasn't hers. Never could be. Not even through pretense by raising as her own. He was already grown. "I don't give a shit about her, Jordie. But you want the boy. He's not a baby, Jordie. He's not what I had in mind..." Her argument trailed off.

"No. He's not a baby," Jordan admitted protectively. "But he's mine. That's the beauty of it. He was all I could think about after Dave told me about him, and you've made everything possible by being willing to adopt someone for us. It's like magic, Wanda. You'll actually become the mother of my real son."

272

Outraged at his insensitivity, Wanda retorted, "You're such a prick, Jordie," and ran from the room. On the lower-floor level, the bathroom door slammed behind her. Listening to her cry, Jordan remained by the fireplace to watch the embers fade to darkness. He envisioned visas and passports...so many things to do. He wouldn't permit delay. No. The boy wasn't a baby. Those were lost years and he didn't want to lose more.

It was late, close to dawn when he went to her bedroom. Though the light on the night stand was lit, Wanda was asleep. Or so he thought. But he took off his clothing quietly and slipped in beside her. She was warm, smelling of bath scent, her breathing soft and measured. He wanted to be with her, talk with her before calling it a night. Well, she'd be less disturbed in the morning. "Sleep on it" went the old saw. She'd had her cry and would be rational again. He switched off the light and shared one of her pillows with a sigh. Poor Wanda. She had been so angry with him. Hearing about the boy had stunned her as it did him; he could forgive her reaction. Nevertheless, they had been discussing the same thing. She'd see it eventually. He couldn't resist touching her. His hand moved over her waist, caressed the mound between her thighs. His fingers stilled and she moved to him urgently and their mouths met. She kissed hungrily, demanding his response; when he took her, she matched his lovemaking with something stronger. She wanted to prove she could be complete, could bear his son for him herself, could conjure from her barrenness the child they hadn't been able to create together. He went along with it, for he was there to do the same. They whipped the fantasy with their bodies and each achieved an orgasm which was a prolonged draining, refusing to let them part. Panting, glued to each other with the sweat of their exertion, they kissed the kisses of their first couplings. Jordan knew they were all right again. They were going to be happy, as he had assured her they would be.

Wanda was not so mistaken. She could not set aside the age of the child they made that night. For the sake of keeping Jordan, she was forced to bend to his will, loving him, but unable to love his son who was not hers. She turned from him and found a pillow; he rolled on his side, falling asleep at once. In the street outside, a fire engine

273

rumbled by, shaking the foundations of their building with the powerful throb of its engine. A flashing red light illuminated the room, and the wailing siren carried the blush and the alarm to a distant street, where it was too faint to hear. She wanted complete silence to enclose her but there was noise everywhere, that of the city and the reverberation of what had been said...and left unsaid.

I wanted to buy back our lost marriage, Jordie, and everything has its price. I've been ambushed by my own scheme for punishment because I truly wanted a baby for us, and it could be another woman's baby because I could love it now...but not this one. Not your almost-grown son. He won't need me and perhaps not need you but that is your affair. He's not a baby, Jordie. Your son will not be someone to hold in my arms to comfort and ease his fears and sing all his hurts to sleep....

And Wanda pushed her pillow hard between herself and Jordan, pushed it with cruelty, where it remained wedged while she waited for day to come.

When a cloud scudded over the gibbous moon, a man entered the shadow it made and drifted to Yukiko's window on bare feet. It had been left open and he was inside without making a sound. A watcher from another house saw him without recognition. A short curse was exclaimed; it must be the *ainoko* to see his mother again. Well, let him depart without fuss afterward. Soon gone, sooner forgotten till his next clandestine visit. The eyes of an island community are always open; the man was fortunate not to have been discovered as himself.

"I've brought *sakana* for you," he said timorously, squinting to see where she was. The fish were his payment and seemed too few for acceptance. They had been culled from another man's catch and hardly worth what he wanted from her. She said nothing but took the damp package from him and kicked the cover from her *futon*. He panted as he disrobed and lay down to wait for her. She was with him quickly, a darker mass in the darkness. The scorched odor of the man's boat hull smoked from his body. He had spent the day ridding his wooden craft of marine borers and brought the vapor with him. She wanted to smile at his anxiety. And at his fear, too. He started at every creak he heard as though they were to be taken by surprise. The village would not condemn him for lying with her...they suspected their men of it and evaded confirmation. What occurs out of sight has not occurred, or so the wives comforted themselves. An ocean and a continent apart from another violent pairing, she submitted with her old skill and walked around in her mind while the man took his pleasure. They were all the same to her now.

Oka-san and Oto-san sat to the right and left...and there stood forbidding Ooba-san. If Yukiko permitted herself to be present at such a time, she feared to see them. Too often had they tried to evict her from the house but she stubbornly fought their shades. Obedience had restored her presence; the wheel turning upon itself had left her childless, as the *hanashiui* demanded years ago. But there was no relenting of scorn for her; no one forgave her, not even these visitors in the dark.

Spent, the man arched from her and stood. He was surly now, no more a man in need. He dressed rapidly and went to the window. The moon teased him by discarding one cloud after another before wearing one long enough to permit him to leave. He scraped over the sill without another word to Yukiko. What words could they share? They hadn't spoken but for what he said about the fish. She remained motionless upon her *futon,* soiled with the salt of his sweat and semen. Her thinking had taken her to Kyoto, which she had never seen. Was the boy well? In Kyoto, that templed center of culture, filled with teahouses and parks and theaters. He had said he mingled with well-known gentlemen...a fabrication, surely. He wanted her to believe Kyoto was a paradise and she could lead a whore's life there as in Osaka before the ban. *Hai,* without risk, he said. But she was content with her smaller trade here; it supplemented the work sent by the merchant of Mihara.

Why did his dolls trouble her?

Small beings; lifeless and rigid. She was learning to

paint and dress them swiftly to be done with them. They went dutifully from cupboard to packing case without protest and were carried to the wharf, from there transported to the merchant in Mihara and would stand before tourists in quiet hosts until purchased and then would be taken to homes of their own. Some were never bought and did not leave the merchant's shelves; some were kept by their owners for a time, admired and then discarded. But always, each stood alone within a fragile glass case.

The La Jolla sun grilled the beach sands without clouds to filter its heat; peroxide youths and platinum girls flirted on the strand, corraled by a hedge of upright surfboards breasting the wind from the ocean. Lapping gently north and south, salt froth threaded beads of clam and abalone shells through the long skeins of kelp it rolled inland; sand dollars were banked among purple-spined sea urchins where rapid sandpipers skittered over flattened starfish in their daylong pursuit of food. The suds of the tide chased the puny birds spur deep and ebbed from them to be chased in turn...and the iodine scent overall was as she remembered it.

Wanda had made Jordan agree to adjust their itinerary to allow for a day's visit with her family. She had declared vehemently that their trip could only be explained by her in person; she wouldn't do it by letter or phone. And now that they were in her parents' house, she found excuses for not saying anything about the Japanese boy—there were the arrivals of her sisters and their husbands and children, and preparations for eating out of doors. Everyone talked so much she wasn't noticed to be listening only...and that with half an ear. Jordan was restless, wanting to be flying west. He kept to himself, waiting for her to get it over with so everyone could share his excitement. Everyone; how large the family had become!

Grace brought a gang of young adults; her husband stayed long enough to show them off and went back to his position at the local bank feeling snubbed by Jordan's aloofness. Easterners and Westerners didn't mix; he thought Wanda's husband proved the point. Shorty Dot could scarcely be told from her lively teenagers, nor could her young husband, Pete, who was the one to accede to Gus Fleming's desire for the perpetuation of the family name. Now legally a Fleming, Pete wore an air of being a fraud among the rest. Writhing to music on the patio with the crowd, he seemed to be dancing by himself: A new record player, plastic, blasted forth rock 'n' roll, and the affection of relatives hopped and bumped and jiggled with bemused expressions to tuneless noise and badly sung cryptograms. Helen and Gus were antique blurs with glazing eyes, yet they were gracious as ever, moving with arthritic vigor and following old customs. Being nearer to Jesus now, they obeyed more of their minister's commandments and had given up meats for a vegetarian diet. Lemonade still showed up in pitchers, with paper cups to one side; dip for chips handy for nibblers. Wanda congratulated herself for concealing a flask in her purse for her private use.

Sensing a lull to come before the food was served, Wanda fled the opportunity by asking Jordan, "Want to walk down the beach?" He had to cup a hand to his ear to hear her; the music was deafening. "How about it, Jordie? Work up an appetite."

He nodded and they left the patio. The loud discordance was gradually replaced by a clapping of gulls beating wings through the sea breeze above the peeping calls of the surf dancers. A steady sigh and crash of water tumbling ashore drowned the high lingering laughter of a running girl as she met the surfers on the beach. Sand crunched underfoot; Wanda shook her hair free of a scarf and scuffed her toes as she walked. She had missed doing it, she thought sadly. Jordan had his arm around her waist, keeping up with her step for step.

"Did you say anything to them yet?" he asked.

"I haven't been able to get them away from the others." She had insisted her father and mother should get the news separately, before informing her sisters.

"You'll just have to take them aside, that's all."

"Okay, I will! Give me a chance!"

She glanced at the surfers on the dunes with envy.

277

Lovers, all. Did they never go into the water? Just wait throughout the day for the perfect wave and lie bronzing at the feet of their boards? This was where her girlhood blanket parties had taken place. Was it chasing grunion she had to thank for landing Jordie? No waiting for waves with him; it was instead done during the traditional Southern California sport, everyone bringing buckets and blankets to the beach at spawning time. Spawning, spawning; that's what made it so popular. So much of the activity took place at night, grunion hunting was suspected of being a myth. He'd been sure of it when she invited Jordan, arriving from the base skeptically to accuse her of inventing the creatures. But they existed. Gleaming silverlings infested each incoming wave to drill their tails into wet sand until the next wave carried them back into the ocean's phosphorescence. The small fish had to be caught by hand, and when a bucket was filled, they were taken to driftwood bonfires to be fried in skillets of butter. And blankets moved farther and farther from the light into dark; she had given herself to him without hesitation. A blanket accumulates sand no matter what. Sand got into everything...everything...

"It's hot, isn't it?" she said, wishing she hadn't recalled that bit of her past. He looked at her oddly. What was he thinking?

"Yeah...you wouldn't believe it was winter here..." *Yukiko had commented upon the heat of the sun...atsuine?*

"It isn't," Wanda replied sourly. "It never is."

A heavy fog bank rested solidly on the horizon...a low cotton bale undone to be lit brightly by sunlight and creeping closer with each hour of the afternoon. It would move ashore at night. Cooling; cold. And retreat in late morning the next day to hatch the beginning of waves again. The fog hid the ocean's end, that fine division of water and sky, blue Pacific sheeting into its own blue exhalation and defying definition. When Jordan picked up a handful of sand dollars to skim into the air, she watched them skip across advancing rollers and sink out of sight. They would return to the beach round and flat, marked with poinsettia shapes on delicate gray skeletons. Inside them were five birdlike chips. A flock of doves, finders said they were. Doves of peace. But the wafers had to be destroyed to see them.

They were back at Beach House. Jordan wouldn't let her stall anymore. She spoke covertly to her mother and took her father in tow to the master bedroom. Helen, atwitter with curiosity, chattered inanely to Jordan as he escorted her. In the confessional of the large room, kneeling on the bed to face parents and husband, Wanda revealed that she and he were to adopt a child. Helen whooped with joy and beaked hummingbird kisses at everyone's cheeks, dashing from one to another in spike-heeled hops.

"Then what's all this about going to Japan?" she chided happily.

"That's where the boy is."

"Oh, they're going to adopt a little boy!" She hugged her husband, nudging him and peering into his face to see if he heard, and looked to her daughter for more. "A boy! Oh, Wanda! Jordie!"

Wanda compressed her mouth, casting her eyes down, and Jordan said, "Yes, he's my son."

"Well, he will be! He will be, Jordie!" Helen smiled widely. "Let's go outside and tell everyone!"

Gus had heard Jordan clearly. "Your son?" he said, and blocked Helen's access to the door. A pall fell upon the room. Gus stalked to the door and shut it firmly. He didn't like the news. As Jordan attempted a rambling answer, he cut him short. "We're not going to come down on you for it, Jordie. Jesus forgives. Had to forgive a lot of our boys leaving babies overseas... and here at home, too."

Feeling injured and misled, Helen asked plaintively, "Why didn't you ever breathe a word, Jordie? How could you keep it a secret for so long?" she demanded querulously. "Why?"

"I didn't... know," he stammered.

Wanda intervened impatiently. "For heaven's sake, what difference does it make? I told Jordie I was willing to adopt a baby and luckily there was one tucked away for me he didn't know about until his dear friend Dave told him."

"Cut it out, Wanda."

She lightened her attitude immediately. "I'm being funny, Jordie. Where's your sense of humor?" His jaw set and she turned brightly to her parents. "And you're not to get upset, either. Haven't you been dying for us to give you a grandchild, too?" Her mother was frightened and clung to Gus; Wanda wanted to cling to both of them. "Just think, when Jordie and I get back from Japan, we'll be a storybook family: Pappa Bear, Mamma Bear, and the... other bear." She sat back heavily on the mattress. A child again in their presence, she found no comfort on their bed. Their shocked silence expanded the alienating emptiness.

"What?" said Jordan to Gus.

The old man opened and shut his mouth, then replied, "I didn't say anything."

"You were about to."

Gus squirmed and shrugged. Then he released Helen's hand so he could walk to the window, where the reflected blaze of sunlit sand deepened the lines of his face and neck. Helen crossed her arms under her sagging breasts. She was a parody of her former self, made up and coiffed as she had been from the hour she ceased acknowledging her age, halter and slacks blousing from prominent bones and wrinkled, dry skin. How old they are, Wanda thought. When did they get so old?

"Mother? Are you going to say anything?"

"It's all right, my dears...but it's such a shock."

Wanda's head ached badly. She wanted to run to her old room, sneak a drink and lie down, but knew she wouldn't be permitted so easy an escape. "It should be fascinating," she said, "to make an American out of him."

"That's right; he's Japanese, isn't he?" Helen directed her next statement to Gus, questioning for his opinion in order to know how to form her own. "He's Japanese, Gus."

"What the hell did you think?"

The surf shook the buried pilings of the house. The structure was always vibrating. Wanda used to lie flat and put her ears to the rugs to feel seaquakes when she lived here; she was more sensitive to the tremors now. "Does it bother you, Daddy," she asked, "that he's Japanese?"

"As a Christian, I know it's not supposed to. That's easy to do when it's somebody you don't have to meet...or anything..."

Helen stood defensively in front of Gus, shielding him from Wanda and Jordan, and scolded them. "Jordie, that boy's people were probably trying to do their best to sink your ship when you were in the Navy."

280

Jordan's hands clenched into fists. "Helen...that boy's people...listen, *I'm* his people..."

There was nothing to be said after that. Wanda and Jordan were treated with studied courteousness afterward. The matter was settled. Helen and Gus pretended nonchalance; oh, go get him if you want...get the alien Asian boy. The implication was evident he'd never be one of the Fleming clan. Impatient to cross the Pacific, Jordan didn't care what they thought. The Flemings didn't say to stop in upon the return trip; Wanda was vexed by the omission, then relieved. She had lost the option of putting things off. Decisions had crowded in upon her with headlong speed. Like that of the aircraft they were to take to Japan, once set into motion, it had to reach its destination or experience the immutable alternative of a disastrous crash.

Chief Superintendent Hidenori shuffled the papers before him carefully. He extracted one, showed it to the man opposite himself and said, "This is the testimony taken from the playwright, Meijin, whose latest work premiered recently. Like his play, this has nastiness in it. He is a mischief-maker and will make a bad end one day." He scanned the tightly written report. "Now then, listen to this: 'Meijin admits to feeling remorse for introducing the suspect originally to Jihei Segawa.' Ha, remorse. There's none of that in his writing. Nor humility, either. I continue: 'He asserts he once brought the *ainoko* to Kyoto as a joke. He meant to upset the sensitivities of the *onnagata*, Shichisaburo Yoshizawa, who was being feted by the film star at that time, along with other important artists.' There we have the playwright in another lie. The guests, we have determined, with the exception of the *onnagata*, were *dilettantes*—snobs, if you will, and of no importance to any but themselves."

He set the report to one side on the low table in front of him. "Meijin accomplished more than he bargained for," he mused aloud. "I may have to close down this play of his." He smiled at his listener. "Have you seen it? No? I can give

281

you a résumé. We have to attend in order to discover how incendiary he dared to be this time; there were students and activists packed against each other like sardines... *hai,* I like sardines, too. We shall have some brought to us shortly. I believe there are several cans from Portugal stored in the pantry... but I digress. The new Meijin play is his old Meijin play. Each time we close it and bar performances, he recasts and hides his lines under another version of how Amaterasu established the Imperial line. Bah! I won't bore you with the play. Meijin will have us believe we are the children of gods and goddesses without informing us why we are so impotent as to have lost a war."

His companion smiled and nodded sagely. Everyone likes to believe an origin of that nature; it is the substance of earliest imaginings and is reluctantly given up with age and experience of the world. Hidenori slid another report from his sheaf of papers. He placed it on the table, frowning. He disliked its elements. The listener didn't interrupt, waiting politely to be told the reason. Hidenori glanced from beneath his brows and said with distaste, "This concerns the schoolboy, Shiro Nakayoshi. I mentioned him to you before. Disgraceful. Instead of toiling at studies to bring honor to his family, he consorts with these types." He hammered his fist slowly upon the paper to emphasize every vowel of the name he read. "Nakayoshi... a good name. The family is respected. I didn't have his relatives troubled by my *junsa* to spare them embarrassment. Anyway, they could not tell more than the boy knows. He has confirmed the *ainoko*'s continued friendship with Mr. Segawa... and if you'll pardon me, also confirmed the intimate nature of that friendship."

"You're not surprised, surely?" Hidenori said, reacting to the other's expression. "These theatrical people—these filmmakers—they manage to rise above their private lives to become objects of quality. You've been seeing the extraordinary craftsmanship of Mr. Segawa on television, I know. There's nothing but his films on every channel since his death—a blessing for those who've missed any of his work..."

The paper was covered by another, a third report. Hidenori said dryly, "And there's always one of these to be found. The snooping neighbor. No one would admit they had seen the boy arrive at the actor's house during the night of his murder. But there are always eyes where there is celebrity. Naturally, this confession was delivered in secrecy to avoid the derision of the neighborhood, though you and I know they are all equally guilty of spying upon Mr. Segawa and his undoubtedly fascinating callers. Shall I tell you who this informant was? *Iie,* I'll keep her name anonymous. She had palpitations as it was to come forth before we concluded our official inquiries. She saw the suspect arrive and depart that night! *Hai,* and was able to provide a full description. He took his time approaching the house...drunk, she said. She was able to see his features clearly by lanternlight when he paused in the garden. There were no other visitors, if you were thinking to ask. Ah, you don't think she will testify to that for us? Be content. This woman has nothing to do and therefore spends hours at her window. Her nights are our days...and she would even be interested in what you do with yourself if she could see you."

Hichiriki couldn't control his body any longer and swayed and fell to the floor. He lay with eyes fixed upon his father adoringly. Keeping upright for excruciating periods was a small price to pay for listening to the kindly voice and being taken into his confidence. He didn't know what was said but felt its importance. The papers were an attractive nuisance; he'd been chastised mildly for attempting to touch them. They made such lovely crumples!

The chief superintendent continued to hold his smile, but his jaw muscles jerked spasmodically. The charade never became reality; his son was never transformed into a normal man sharing his thoughts after a tiresome day at the bureau. Hidenori assembled his reports into one pile and slid them back into his briefcase. "That's enough for this evening," he said over his shoulder to the old nursemaid in the far corner of the room. She unwound from her frightened crouch to be ready to go to Hichiriki. Hidenori stood, looking down at his son affectionately. "You'll have the sardines for your supper—I haven't forgotten mentioning them—but we won't try to dine together. I think you're tired." He reached to his son, almost touched the cheek strained toward him and walked to the door of the room. He eased the *fusuma* aside and left without looking

283

back. Hichiriki started to crawl toward the open doorway but was intercepted skillfully by the woman. She cradled him fondly. Her crooning covered the ugly howling protest he made with a soundless mouth.

From La Jolla to Los Angeles, carrying the albatross of winter coats through California's near-tropic climate, Jordan and Wanda traveled companionably as strangers. Exaggerating concern for her comfort, he took pains to get her the best of everything, be it the choice rooms of first-class hotels or the selection of paperbacks to take aboard the plane. Wanda permitted him to indulge her; she needed tenderness. She capped her inclination to give up and went doggedly through the motions of participating in her husband's quest.

Japan Air Lines used a standard American-made Courier DC-8 but she felt herself on foreign territory the instant they boarded. The decor was determinedly Oriental, insidiously capable of removing ties to home. It was too soon for that. She refused the window seat, saying she preferred not to crawl over him each time she had to go to the ladies' room. Then, choosing her best defense, she escaped by strapping herself in and going to sleep. Travelers filled the rest of the cabin. Talk stilled to expectance. A nervous cough here and there. The overloud "What time is it in Tokyo now?" An engine shuddered on a wing, took hold, added a partner, balanced with another pair, and the plane quivered against the power surge while it eased into position on the runway. Outside, low sunstruck terminals and many planes. Waiting. A hush and roar, more power and they hurtled forward into the takeoff, which seems terribly fast until aloft, where it has a floating sensation instead. Halfway to Hawaii, Jordan remembered to loosen Wanda's seat belt.

The stewardess swayed mincingly down the aisle, kimono sleeve held neatly aside as she offered warm sake from a delicate bottle. The Beikoku-jin were now zori-shod, happi-coated and getting bland on raw fish and young spirits from labeled liquors bearing words they could not read. Professionally charming, the stewardess was an enigmatic hostess. She didn't resemble the Japanese girls Jordan had seen along the Inland Sea. Yukiko was almost Old World, this woman too polished, modern; a bisque geisha gone astray. She smiled at him over Wanda's head but he refused the drink with a negative gesture. She went on to lean over a passenger in the seat ahead and answered questions with a soft, lilting accent... like Yukiko... and not like her. The stewardess was gowned in pink brocade, sewn with designs of white cranes and cherry blossoms. Thinking her too artificial, he looked out the port at the limitless ocean beneath the wingtip. Putting his head against the cool glass, he fogged the view with his breath and had to wipe it away. So blue down there... so fathomlessly blue. Because the sun's angle prevented a glare on the ocean's flat ryme, he was able to detect a ponderous pod of whales moving in slow motion and belying the speed of the plane. Clouds bunching at the horizon sieved sunlight into a fan of rays like the *hinomaru*, the vivid ensign of Nippon, spearing down to the water; the whales were also pursuing their fate.

Jordan wished he could doze off as Wanda had. She did it to avoid talking to him, he knew. Her head was cushioned on a pillow at his shoulder; she looked marvelous ...peaceful and kind. She'd have to use her charm if they were to cajole the boy into leaving for the States with them. It wasn't a foregone conclusion; much depended upon what the boy's ambitions were, what his family wished for him. His family? That was the rough part to brood over. Loving him, they would want to keep his son, wouldn't they? Or loving him, would they want him to have the advantages he and Wanda could provide? But she had said it: The boy was old enough to make up his own mind. They would have to be very persuasive. He wondered if Wanda had been too influenced by the dismal reaction of her parents. Stopping at La Jolla had been a mistake. She was showing renewed signs of resistance, which he could combat only by keeping her on the run and too busy to think. As the stewardess passed again, he signaled.

"Yes, please?"

Like Yukiko, and not Yukiko. He spoke softly past his sleeping wife. "We're interested in going to the Inland Sea. Do you by chance carry information aboard concerning various routes to get there from Tokyo?"

"Will you be hiring a car?"

"Unless there's a faster means."

"There are trains or buses...and we have domestic planes connecting with cities in the South."

"That sounds good to me. Have you schedules and road maps I could see?"

"Yes. I'll bring you them."

When she left, he felt better. There wasn't much he could do about another uneasiness nagging him. Wanda wasn't adept at hiding her feelings and might antagonize Yukiko. It was a dilemma without an answer. He put it aside temporarily to study the material the stewardess brought. It wasn't much but he found what he needed.

The flight was interminable. Day stretched and darkened with infinite slowness. Meals arrived amid countless snacks passengers were urged to accept. Jordan and Wanda took unsatisfying promenades along their cramped aisle. It was preferable to remain seated and read...sleep... or simply dream. Wanda shut her mind to the future, refusing to contemplate anything beyond landing in Tokyo and getting to the hotel. Jordan's anticipation was increasingly more irritating; he even seemed to become visibly younger with each mile they put behind. Expecting a loving reunion, she supposed angrily. He hadn't looked so boyish in years. Everything was hateful: the length of the flight, its iron maiden confinement, and its inevitability. Attracting the attention of the stewardess, she asked for another magazine. Skimming rapidly through the selections shown, she returned them exasperatedly. She'd seen them. Her paperbacks weren't wanted, either; their turgid fiction no longer amused: There was too much of mistresses in them, too much of bastards. She plumped her pillow. She wasn't resting well and so many naps tired her more. Wishing she hadn't surrendered to Jordan, she shut her eyes. If this were home, she wouldn't be feeling responsible for adding to her own misery. Wife and husband fell asleep side by side, twisting a single dream between themselves...

Jordan sat up with a sharp motion, hearing the report

of a loud ringing sound in his ears. Whatever it was had no body anymore. It was the ghost of it which had brought him upright and queasy to peer into the chamber of the plane. When he was a child, dreams of falling had jolted him similarly and he'd found himself twitching violently on his bed, as though it had netted him at the termination of a long drop. Muscular contraction was responsible; he hadn't fallen at all. His mother used to reassure him it was part of the dream he'd had, but in this instance he retained the dread of the current vision as it departed from consciousness. There was a cloying remnant of aircraft fuel in it... and choking diesel apparitions from the *Bulman*. Dimmed passageways receded with helmeted pharmacist's mates working with chemicals to make blood sew wounds into scars.

Wanda adjusted her position beside him and opened her eyes. She looked haggard. He pushed the call button to request coffee. The stewardess was remarkably fresh for having toiled steadily for almost thirteen hours. She hurried away immediately to the galley. Wanda pulled her blanket off and wriggled from her seat.

"I'm going to powder my nose."

She left grumpily and walked down the aisle to the lavatory, clutching her handbag at her side. The facility was occupied when she got there and she waited impatiently. An American businessman edged from the cubicle. Seeing her, he smiled apologetically and adjusted his rumpled happi-coat to execute a mock bow as he hissed, "So solly." Unamused, she called him an ass before storming into the lavatory.

The stewardess brought a tray to Jordan containing steaming cups of coffee and a number of small cakes shaped into flowers tinted white, pink, red, and green. Yellow centers spiraled atop them and their petals were sculptured over leaves. The cakes were made of bean jam... Yukiko had once given him two edible roses enclosed in a special box painted with golden cranes flying over pines; it had been tied with a twisted cord of purest white and scarlet. He'd saved the cakes for a brief time, only to lose them to Dave's gluttony when he hobbled upon them in the torpedo shack during an afternoon Jordan spent with Yukiko. Dave was welcome to them—they

287

were meant to be eaten. Now Jordan nibbled at one the stewardess had brought. It dissolved in his mouth sweetly.

Wanda didn't want anything when she resumed her place. She was neat, having made repairs to her makeup and hairdo. The flask she kept hidden from her husband was emptier. Jordan excused himself and took his turn at the tiny sink in the lavatory. Shaving, he wondered about the man in the mirror: Would Yukiko know him? He couldn't see there was much difference, but it had to be there. He couldn't believe so many years had passed.

At last the passengers were given landing cards to fill in, routine questions detailing information about themselves and the purpose of their visit to Japan. Jordan and Wanda wrote "vacation," and the indefatigable stewardess patiently collected the answers with gullible belief. The activity in the cabin became fitful; men and women busied themselves with personal possessions and shook themselves out of the somnambulism of the past wearying hours. Jordan and Wanda maintained their armistice and waited for the plane to start its descent.

The spirit of Tokyo rises to awesome heights to notify arriving travelers that they have reached an Asian megalopolis. The plane flies into an amber sky which traps the young evening in a clouded bell jar of industrial pollution, and this constant pall overlays an extensive plain of gray and tan, a humble disguise quickly revealed as an unrelieved rooftop sea without a shore nor movement to say it lives—until one discerns pulsing veins of artful electric signs buried in the canyons. It is on the ground that the city asserts its existence, overwhelming itself with a black-haired populace which it attempts to destroy with noise. Clothing is brighter under that mass of dark heads, and so many similar faces become an immediate norm. Everything speaks in shouts, using amplifying devices to assault the hearing till traffic must depend upon doomsday horns to blare passage through inadequate streets. It begins in the airport facilities, and everyone gets acclimatized making their way through customs. Wanda had run short of patience by the time Jordan led her into the terminal amid a barrage of flight announcements from loudspeakers on every side.

"Can't you walk faster, Jordie?" They were following a porter who wheeled their luggage from the customs area. Jordan didn't answer but was more infuriating to her by slowing even more. When he stopped and took her elbow to pull her to a halt, the porter fidgeted patiently, accustomed to the wayward habits of the *hakujin*.

"I've been thinking..."

"Do it at the hotel."

"No. Listen..."

Wanda interrupted him as she jerked her arm from his peevishly. "I'm tired and I'd like to get a decent drink. Do you mind?"

He parried her complaint. "Why do we have to stop here, Wanda? We can catch a connecting flight south and..."

She wouldn't let him finish. "I'm not killing myself just to pander to your eagerness, Jordie."

He looked about desperately. "Let's talk about this."

"In the terminal?" She had to raise her voice to be heard.

"There's a bar over there..." Determined to have her listen to him, Jordan told the porter to bring their luggage along. The man watched them enter a cafe to take seats at a table, where they were served promptly with tall drinks; he sat on an upturned suitcase to wait.

Wanda was in no mood to be agreeable. "I'm not—repeat, not—flying to Osaka tonight."

"It's a short run."

"The hell with it. I'm going to get some rest in a real bed before I go any farther."

"We'd be that much closer to our goal."

"Don't include me in that statement," she protested. He didn't want to start arguing again but had to remind her she promised not to make a decision about the boy till after they had seen him.

"So I did," she said, "but let's go about finding him at a reasonable and civilized pace."

"Please. Don't be difficult now."

She sighed. "Jordie, we've flown halfway round the world and I'm exhausted."

He paused to think about alternatives. "I have another idea."

"If it includes going to our hotel, I'm in favor."

"Suppose you go to the hotel and I continue on myself?"

Wanda put her drink down with a thump. "You're not serious?"

"You didn't want to meet the boy's mother, anyway."

It was like being slapped. She blinked her eyes several times. "What are you proposing?"

"I'll go to the fishing village and present my case. Then I'll bring the boy to Tokyo for you to meet."

"What if he won't go...or they don't let him go?"

"He will. And I know they will." He waited. Waited.

"How long will it take?"

"I don't know. It depends upon whether they're still living there."

"You're mad to think they are."

"People tend to stay in the same area."

Wanda vacillated. She wanted to say, "let's go home. I can't go through with this." Surrendering, still surrendering, she took up her glass again and drank. "I don't relish being alone in a strange country."

Jordan took advantage of her mellowing. "If they aren't in the village and no one can tell me where to find them, I'll get back to you immediately."

"How soon will that be?"

He weighed her patience against her temper. "A week...okay? That's from the time I get there."

"Will you give up afterward?"

"I don't want to discuss that now."

She shrugged, weary of the strain. "All right, take me to the hotel and do as you please."

He smiled delightedly as he stood. "You'll have to go there without me," he said. She was startled. "The stewardess," he explained. "She gave me some domestic airline schedules to look over while you were napping. If I'm to make my connection, I won't have time to see you to the hotel." As she began to sputter, he took her chin in his hand and put his face close to hers. "You're a big girl, Wanda. You'll be fine." He held his breath as he watched her eyes. There was angry resignation in them.

290

"Send me a postcard," she said, but he ignored the barb.

Jordan checked his wristwatch hurriedly, then kissed her cheek. "I'll phone from Osaka. After that, I doubt if I'll be able to...the village was rather primitive." Wanda didn't say anything. "I'll get my bag from the porter and tell him to look after you. Are you all right for money?"

"I suppose so."

He left quickly and she was desolate, barely able to watch him. *My husband can't wait to leave me...to get to his first love without having me tag along...he'll kiss her hello...if she's there. He'll surely want to make love to her again...to relive the first time. God, it's never the same but we like to think it could be. So he'll make believe and then demand to see his son. His and her son. And Jordie will hug them both and kiss her again—oh, never mind her husband, they're always the last to know—and Jordie will be very high, drunk with the exaltation of seeing his son. If he's there...*

Jordan was asking the attentive porter for his overnight bag, giving instructions laboriously, and the man was overly obsequious as he accepted a large advance tip. Then Jordan turned to wave a farewell at her. Too jealous to return the salute, she sat still, and Jordan ran easily into the depths of the terminal. The porter flashed his widespread teeth at her and nodded reassuringly. She took her time finishing her drink.

And ordered another.

Hurrying past a news vendor near Nihon Kokonai Airways, Jordan did not even glance at the papers on the stand. Vendors throughout Japan were hawking life-size posters of the slain actor in the regalia of one of his roles, coyly inscribed: *KATAMI KOSO IMA WA ADA NARE* ...my regret is deeper because of what remains of him. How these wares were produced so instantaneously was a wonder no one ever solved. It was enough that the victim could be carried home at once, rolled up and tied with a bit of string, and having read the details in the newspapers and seen it discussed on television screens and reported excitedly on radio everywhere and every day, one could now envision the horror upon the full-color portrait.

Alas, who could murder the incomparable Jihei Segawa?

Jordan pushed his way among the *narikin,* the affluent who scorn packed trains and buses to ride packed planes instead. Few airports had been rebuilt in Japan; after he was to reach the city in the South, he'd have to find other means of transportation—the village was far from Osaka—and then he thought it would be good to get there by sea again. After minor confusion, he was directed to the right plane. Boarding, he locked his seat belt and sat back to endure the short flight. As the plane took off, he thought fleetingly of his wife. Too sore to wave good-bye at him. She'd be in the hotel by this time, bitching to herself in a tub. That's okay...she had allowed him to do as he wished. Relaxing, he looked out the window past the gentleman sitting beside it. The plane was banking and Mount Fuji turned gracefully in the twilight with a burst of snow nippling its purple breast. Sparks of lights dotted the darkening landscape, jiggling over mountainsides and along roads and waterways. He sat well back into the seat and napped.

It was raining when the plane arrived in Osaka; sleet laced the windows and wings of the aircraft; propellers threw water alongside in a storm. The landing was unsettling. In the shabby terminal, they said it had been raining for days.

Heinie Joe and the derelict were snugly entwined beneath the filthy tarpaulin. The boy wakened slowly. He stared at the man's sleeping face for a long moment with disgust, then cringed and eased from his embrace to leave the warmth of the canvas covering. Standing, testing his equilibrium, he pulled his dry clothing off the string over the ashes and warily dressed himself. The clothes were warm and redolent with smoke.

"Don't leave." The derelict looked at him steadily.

"I don't owe you anything," Heinie said gruffly.

"You are still too ill to be going somewhere by yourself."

"I'll survive."

"We could make a life together if you consented to stay with me." The man listened to the boy's derisive hoot end in a spasm of coughs. "There. You can see how much you need a person to take care of you."

Heinie Joe was contemptuous of him. "I had my pick of the Gion if I wanted to live under someone's thumb."

The derelict raised to an elbow to study the boy. *Hai,* he was stronger now. It would be dangerous to attempt to restrain him: Segawa had been a powerful man. "Ah, then you are from Kyoto," he said meaningfully. Heinie didn't reply. "I can keep you well hidden here."

"Who needs to hide?"

"We all need a refuge but I think you have more cause than most." As Heinie avoided his eyes, he pretended not to know anything about him and nudged him slyly. "I know what it's like to go from town to town...steal a little...eh? What have you done? Eh?"

"Which direction is it to the harbor?"

Iie, he wouldn't risk tussling with the boy. Life was too precious. "You need only follow the flow of the canal."

Heinie nodded curtly. "Thank you. For the care...and the food and shelter."

"Where are you going?" the derelict asked as he sat up. The boy refused to answer and went to the door. As he opened it, the man tried again. "Are you expected somewhere? Is someone looking for you?"

"Nobody's looking for me."

"That's hard to believe."

"Why are you so suspicious?"

The derelict smiled at him knowledgeably. "You're too beautiful to be skulking around the country like this."

"Then go to the *junsa* and find out about me," the boy snapped and flung himself out of the hovel.

The scent of the man and his dwelling reeked in Heinie's nostrils and he was glad of the rain for its cleansing bath. The derelict stood in his doorway thoughtfully to make certain of the boy's direction. *Hai,* he was too valuable to lose without some profit. He would speak to the *junsa* when next they appeared on their rounds.

The unlit section beside the canal was too oppressive. Heinie tolerated it for a hundred yards or so, then veered toward a lighted, busy street. The rain was ending, already intermittent as clouds parted in the sky. He went from street to street; then he came upon one lined with expensive shops tucked into the bases of smart new buildings. A first-class hotel for travelers extended both carpet and awning into the rain-polished boulevard. Unwilling to attract attention, Heinie Joe slowed and pretended to be interested in the many shop windows. It was consoling to see people in numbers again. He wondered if they could detect the stink upon him, and he drew aside from any who came near. He was sidestepping someone when he jarred awkwardly into a man exiting from the interior of a cab. The man was tall and blond, with creased, tired eyes that held his own unlike any he had seen before.

"I'm awfully sorry," the man said in English. This minor accident hadn't been his fault, but he apologized.

"*Sumi-masen . . . sumi-masen,*" the boy echoed. How blue the man's eyes were, he thought, and he liked the short, twisted smile that was made at him before the man turned to pay his driver. Heinie hesitated. He had apologized; there was nothing more to keep him on this spot. As the man glanced over his shoulder inquisitively, Heinie bent slightly and cried out again, "*Sumi-masen!*" The man grinned at him and completed his transaction with the driver.

When Jordan turned once more, the boy was gone and the welcoming arch of the hotel canopy opened before him. He'd be able to soak in a bath now, and afterward he'd sleep soundly. Then he could make arrangements about getting to the village.

From the concealment of a doorway, Heinie Joe watched the American enter the hotel. Foolish not to have attempted to make friends with the man! There had been something . . . a trace of interest in the man's face. Just think: There might have been the use of an enameled tub and no doubt an excellent meal. Fool. The American was not repugnant, not someone it would have been a trial to please. But that special message was lacking in him; there wasn't that unspoken vital exchange which transmits recognition to another of his inclination.

A van pulled up before the hotel. A youngster jumped from the rear to carry bundles of newspapers to the hotel lobby. Heinie read the doleful heading, outlined in a black rectangle like a formal announcement. How long was it to be featured? And there was his own picture, from the police records—trackers were at large to find him. Would it be like the movies, with racing cars and firing guns? How stupid and careless he had been! Those bloody socks and smudged towels—he should have wiped everything he touched! He should have...

The reflection in the glass beside him glared back with fearful eyes. Of course, they knew everything; he was not unknown now. He was somebody. A perverse pride tweaked at him. *Hai.* He was *Somebody* now! Everyone had heard of him. Was looking for him. *Iie*...was looking for the short-haired younger boy of the photograph in the newspapers. With his shaggy mop, and being so much older now, who would know him? *Hai*...he would lose himself in Usaka.

Ushered to his room, Jordan didn't bother to unpack. Listening to the maid run water into his tub, he sat upon the double bed to think. Yukiko would understand. He would explain everything and she wouldn't resist having his son go to the States...his son. He smiled at the familiarity with which he thought of him. Yukiko would forgive him, would let him make up for lost years. And if there was a husband—God, let him be reasonable; if only he didn't have to be considered. Well, if there was no man in her life, they couldn't resume the old relationship. That was long gone. Anyway, it hadn't been serious; they had done what everyone did in those days.

And they had a son.

Smiling, he reached for the telephone beside the bed to put a call through to Tokyo. Wanda would want to know he'd had a safe flight.

At daybreak, two *junsa* in a jeep drove past the empty steel drum, now lying upon its side. Ashes were strewn across the muddy ground, picked clean of nails and other salvageable metal.

"One day they'll try burning down the expressway, those cursed vagrants."

"They'd have done it by now had it been made of wood."

"You can see how they enjoyed themselves when the rains kept us indoors."

"I'd rather they have a place to congregate...we can keep an eye on them." There was shouting behind them, and they stopped the engine and turned to see. "What now?"

"It's the old wreck who lives in the shack beside the canal."

The derelict ran to them, sometimes favoring a leg so that he hopped several steps. He reached them and panted, clinging to the windshield frame to catch his breath. The *junsa* wrinkled their noses at his fumes. One said, "What are you excited about, *kojiki?* Are robbers looting your hut?"

"Where have you been? I've been waiting hours to see you!"

"Hai? What have you to do with us?"

"It's worth yen..."

Laughing, the policeman said to his companion, "Have you money to give him? He got my small change last time we were by."

"Oh, you may not pay so little for what I have to tell!"

They eyed the derelict. He generally avoided them unless desperate for a handout. He wore an expectant grin and was oddly elated. "Nothing along this canal is worth any money. Even the bodies you've netted for the morgue have been stripped of their valuables."

"Hai, that's true...true..." He dared not meet their

eyes longer, for he had never turned over a corpse without having given it his own autopsy beforehand.

"Are you reporting something that happened here in our absence?"

"Partly. But the main was done in Kyoto."

"Kyoto! We've nothing to do with another city, you idiot!"

The policeman keyed his ignition. "Let's go," he growled to his companion. The derelict grabbed at his sleeve and the officer was offended at the touch. "Get away from me, *kojiki!*"

"Call me beggar if you like, but I'm rich with knowledge you want."

"I'll want to break a baton over your skull next."

The other *junsa* soothed the man. "He didn't soil your uniform, so don't be so angry. It's only charity he's after."

"Then give him five yen or so or he'll be chasing after us."

"Here, you." The policeman passed a few small bills to the derelict, whose manner changed at once.

"Very well, I'll find other policemen to tell what I know of Jihei Segawa's murder and they will get the commendation." He swiveled about to trot back to his hovel. His words registered and both *junsa* shouted at him to return. He stopped, turned to them and waited. They ordered him to come to the jeep and he did so with feigned indifference.

"What's this about Segawa?"

"Ah...you recognize his name."

"Don't amuse yourself at our expense or you'll regret it."

"*Iie*...I won't regret anything. How would you like to be praised by your superiors?"

"What information have you regarding the actor's death?"

"How much will you give me?"

One policeman declared disgustedly, "The fool has nothing to tell us. What could he know of events in Kyoto?"

"I read what happened in the newspaper...I read about the *ainoko* they said was involved." As the jeep began to move, he blurted louder, "I've seen the murderer!"

The jeep stopped. The *junsa* glared at him. "You've been drunk, you say?"

"*Iie*...I've been sober and I've touched the boy with

these very hands." He displayed his filthy fingers, waggling them mischievously at the officers. The *junsa* exchanged a cautious glance and backed the jeep to be even with him. *"Hai*, you may not think so but I'm not lying to you: He was in my hut. Sick! I fed him and nursed him."

"How do you know he murdered Jihei Segawa? Did he brag of the deed to you?"

"Iie. He denied it."

"You accused him?"

"And be killed myself? *Iie*. I only hinted at it."

The policemen relaxed. One observed sarcastically, "You did not discuss the crime and he did not admit to one. So therefore he must undoubtedly be the fugitive everyone in the nation would like to seize. Be off with you, *kojiki*."

"The boy in my hut was an *ainoko*."

The engine of the jeep was switched off again. They were nervous about this information; it wasn't out of the realm of possibility and yet they were wary of the source. "There are many of them around. We see them frequently."

"Not like this one. He matches the photograph in the *Yomiuri Shimbun*."

"Where is he now?"

"Running. If you had been here sooner, you could have caught him."

"If you had tied him up, he wouldn't have run."

"I thought he was too sick to go anywhere."

The *junsa* conferred privately in whispers while the derelict waited. Finally they looked at him sternly. "Very well. We'll make out a report. It will go to the Chief Superintendent, so if you've lied you may count upon retribution."

"And if I haven't lied?"

"Then ask us for your fee."

They proceeded to interrogate him closely after that and wrote it all into their notebooks. He cooperated with less enthusiasm, not trusting the *junsa*. Once raised in rank because of him, they might not appear near the canals again. He should have wheedled his fee in advance.

Not much later that morning, Heinie Joe spoke to a man. "I don't have any money, but I'm hungry and I'd like something to eat."

He stood at the rear of one of many small restaurants which serve the working population of the shipyards. A truck, piled high with farm produce, had been parked in an alley to make a delivery. The driver was suspicious of him. Holding a heavy crate in his arms, tendons protruded like rails beneath his skin. In his business, pilfering was to be guarded against, most when a *garentai* like this one showed up.

"Are you allergic to work?"

"I'm hungry."

"Well then, if you would stoop to aid me with my morning route, I might let you have something."

The boy glanced at the truck. Mainly vegetables; it meant carrying many baskets and crates. "All right." If it got too much for him, he could quit...but the man would have to give him something anyway.

The driver snorted. "You had me fooled. At first I thought you were Matsushita himself, come slumming to see what he could do for me."

Heinie grinned. The multimillionaire named was famous for his welfare programs as well as for the elaborate and successful empire he ruled. No one was ever surprised to encounter the energetic fifty-year-old among his employees to see what he could do to improve their lot. Starting his work with determination, Heinie helped take produce from the truck to various littered alley doorways. He felt faint at times but was determined to be fed. Fortunately, the driver liked a midmorning break and he prepared a simple meal for both of them, which they ate sitting inside the cab of his vehicle.

"It's not easy to find work in Osaka if you haven't learned a skill, eh?"

"Hai.... It's not easy."

"You're new in this district."

"Iie. I once lived near Piss Alley with my mother."

"Where do you live now?"

Heinie Joe stuffed his mouth to keep from answering. He didn't want to be questioned. The man didn't press him.

"You don't have to gobble so. There's more if you want it."

"The work made me hungrier."

"Well, that's the way of the laborer," the driver agreed. "He's a prisoner of his stomach. Once he's taught it to eat, he must continue the lessons." A sleek limousine splashed through a puddle nearby. He indicated the grand folk and added, "Too bad we don't eat so well as the privileged ones, for then we could sell our turds and afford further delights for our intestines. Look at them. Must be nice to ride in a car like that."

"I did. A long time ago."

"Hai? How did that come about?"

"When I was young, some rich American lady took my mother and me to her house. You should have seen it. Big! Filled with lots of happy children, eating and singing."

"Ah, there was a party then?"

"Hai, but we didn't stay. My mother wanted to ride the car again so we went home."

"Well, she knew what you'd like best. You could play with children anytime."

"Hai...anytime..."

When they were tugging at crates again to remove them from the truck, the jeep with the *junsa* clattered down the path. The policemen greeted the driver cordially, knowing everyone on their beat. Heinie was scrutinized, the more so because of the story they'd heard from the derelict.

"Who's this? Not one of your regular helpers?"

"Hai, but he's very good if I keep prodding him." The driver put a crate into Heinie's arms and shoved him toward the kitchen they were servicing. The boy hurried inside and stalled, afraid to come out again. He listened to the conversation, ready to bolt through the establishment if need be.

"When did you hire him?"

Sensing their tension, the driver's infantry training came to the fore. Obstruct authority whenever possible. "Long time ago. Why do you ask?"

"Where's he from?"

"Osaka! You think I imported him?"

"You're certain he's from Osaka?"

"He and his mother. We were talking about her not ten minutes ago."

"So you know him, then?"

"We're friends."

"He works hard, you say? He's not weak, not sick?"

"You saw him carry that load without trouble, didn't you?" He tossed a large cucumber to each of them. "Lock

300

up your lady friends with those," he laughed. They kept the vegetables and drove on. Heinie stepped outside and watched till they were gone. The driver poked him, saying conspiratorially, "They always give my help a bad time. They think everybody's a hooligan."

They went back to work, and at length the truck was emptied well past noon. Heinie regarded the scraps left on the truckbed: Nothing fit to carry away for food. The man secured the tailgate and turned to him.

"You've done a good day's work. If you like, meet me when I return in the morning and we can do this again."

"I'll see; but don't count on me."

"Well, it was only a suggestion. I might not need you then, anyway. Not if my regulars turn up."

They bowed politely at each other, men who had shared the morning and were free of obligation. Feeling somewhat cheated, Heinie parted from the driver and headed for the waterfront, hungry. It wasn't fair to end the experience as he had begun. It was all to do again but he didn't want the *junsa* to see him a second time. The fogbound harbor stretched before him, so congested with ships and small craft he thought the bay had shrunk. It recalled the peaceful lagoon of his mother's village to him...shit. Who could go there?

The motor launch chugged industriously out of the crowded harbor of Osaka Bay. Lighters floated in massed rows awaiting their turn to be unloaded, having brought freight from ships anchored in the outer bay for lack of berths. The murky water was choppy, whipped by cold bursts of wind. On the exposed deck of the launch, Jordan stood muffled in a heavy woolen duffle coat. The sea took shape for him by degrees, grasping avidly at the limited light, revealing parts of the vast amount of ships at anchor bearing cargo for Kobe and Osaka, sister ports now welded into a continuous waterfront of docks and piers. As Awaji Shima unveiled itself partially of mist, Jordan tightened.

301

It had to be the same. Nothing was changed. The Inland Sea really was as it had been before. Throbbing diesel motors brought the *Bulman* to mind...as did the gateway the motor launch went through between Awaji and Akashi into Seto Naikai. The throat-cloying burned smoke of fuel snaked behind, curling back with stray tendrils to catch his breath. Smaller boats, looking bare without sails and tended by one or two men, were sailing resolutely through shifting currents, where they survived minuscule storms. They posed before picturesque inlets and islands, the same fog-shrouded extraordinary landfall he had seen long ago. The sun leaked through a hole in the gray sky momentarily to circle a piece of shore—it appeared newly painted, glistening with an overlay of frozen dew—and sent its perfume to seduce him with memory; he felt in his pockets for sticks of gum, for anything to offer the kids of the village. He needed Dave with him, he thought.

Jordan walked to the bow, eager to have spray touch him and to see the wake form. He leaned on the starboard rail and watched water part and foam into a widening wave before spreading into eddies behind the stern. A flying fish soared into the wind for an instant and then slid on—a dragonfly has that darting, hovering ability ashore—but was given twice the wings to liberate it into the upper airs. He waited for the fish to reappear and was mesmerized by the flow of the sea. Oil streaks became rarer...the water lifted and fell gently...patches of foam drew his gaze only to vanish, and yet he stared hard at where they had been. Fog made it more difficult to see the surface. With a start, he realized he was praying.

Christ, he hadn't done that since...when was the last time fear knotted him into belief? Within a fog deeper than this one? And he thought of fogs at other islands far south of here...it was near the end of the war when his ship was off picket duty and lying at anchor in Buckner Bay with the rest of the Okinawan invasion fleet. Battered hulks leaked slowly through their wounds, and the only protection from kamikaze attacks had to be created by the smokestacks of every ship there. They feverishly generated black fogs to cover themselves when the alarms sounded, fogs which thinned and opened treacherously. Ships foolish enough to fire blindly into the hidden sky had led the enemy down to themselves along the line of

302

tracers to their mutual regret ... portions of the dark vapor glowed orange whenever the atmosphere shook. So nearby! *Don't let us be next, Jesus ... don't ...*

And now he was praying again. He tried to see the boy's face, tried to imagine him, but the water drowned each image, clouding it and swirling into bubbles which never coagulated into features. *Jesus, let me find him. In the village. And if not there, let them tell me where to look for my son.*

When the long afternoon entered the darker cone of dusk, the motor launch was secured to a broad stone quay for the night. Being an established stop for many of the sea's voyagers, the community provided several choice inns for their comfort. Lanterns hung at doorways, remnants of another era which refused to succumb to modernity. Posts of cypress supported cedar doors, ironbound like fortress gates against seasonal typhoons. Mantled with fog and sea breath, evening descended. Jordan felt his hearing dull, his steps fade and he detected a soft *ching-ching* of a ghostly buoy tolling its warnings. He had taken a walk after the launch delivered him here, and he knew he should get back to his inn before it was impossible for him to see the path. A last look at the fading scene, scrimwashed with salt dew and forming haloes about a passing craft's running lights. How could they move so safely in this thickening brume?

Ching-ching ... ching-ching ... ching.

A voice floated loudly to him, followed by another, clear as though close to him on shore. He heard the rattle of anchor chain, a merry clanking after a loud splash from the dropped anchor. Turning sluggishly with the tide, pale moons rocked rhythmically in equal orbit. Red and green and diffused yellow. He gazed at them longingly ... they could have belonged to the squadron.

If he shared the inn with anyone, he could not tell. The building was strangely silent and its thin construction had joined forces with the encroaching fog to spirit him to the past. Mingled with fragrant woodsmoke, the odor of the tatami was dry and clean. This room, which was his dining room, bedroom and parlor, held him within its uncluttered space like a loosely packaged gift. He looked forward to his dinner, anticipating the indulgent service and solicitude which has spoiled so many men for carefully labeled generations.

Unlike the uniformed girls of city hotels, his maidservant wore her own ordinary clothing protected by a smock. She was soft-spoken and had the broad, flat face of a hamlet girl, unattractive as pie prepared for baking. Sitting upon his heels, Jordan wondered how many inn guests had taken her to bed. She didn't appeal to him sexually, no more than would a healthy animal moving around him. The lacquered bowls she set before him were on trays of assorted sizes, each calculated to please the eye as well as the taste. He dined under her unobtrusive watchfulness and she removed every dish as he emptied it, and he in turn observed her, searching for Yukiko... and not finding the delicate lark of memory. After the meal, he was to go into an alcove at the side of his room to admire a tiny rock and raked sand garden lit by iron lamps, and he would drink *ocha*, thin green powdered tea, until his *futon* and fluffy comforter were laid out upon the tatami floor. Enigmatic, the maid would leave him, giving no sign of her own desires, simply whispering, *"Oyasumi-nasai."*

Good night, she'd say to him... good night.

Preparing to sleep lightly, alert to anything which could disturb him, Heinie Joe made himself comfortable inside the unfinished hold of a tanker. Earlier, he had dodged unseen past watchmen of the shipyard and dashed up a short brow to the open decks of a squat hull. There were pieces of timber, scaffolding and tarpaulins for him to construct a snug nest; had he dared, he would have attempted a small fire, as the raw steel sides of the bulkheads could easily shield him from view, but having already stolen the paper-bagged food of one of the guards, he thought it best to remain in the cold dark. He ate everything except a tangerine, which he reserved for his breakfast. Bedding on planks above an ice-sheathed deck, he crawled beneath a stiff fathom of canvas which smelled of acetylene and burned metal cinders. Everything wore a dank, greasy coating. And he slept, cupping his private parts protectively with his palms, his eyelids sometimes twitching at muffled night sounds.

He was running awfully slowly, awful because his legs refused to function and the junsa behind was faceless and cutting at him with a wicked blade of frightening proportions. No matter which way he turned and twisted, the sword ate into his flesh, not stinging and hurting, yet drawing blood which oozed and congealed upon his tired body. Trying to hide behind a pillar of concrete, he saw the shining blade pass through it and the column tipped to dump a large section of freeway into the canal; cars and their screaming occupants feathered into the rancid sink of yellow muck; the angry people were shouting at him and blaming him for their doom, and he fled, gulping the foul air desperately, tasting the putrid exhalations of the derelict. Thinking to see him, Heinie looked back wildly but the faceless pursuer was now dressed in a bloody Marine uniform and uttering curious howling moans. The boy tripped over his own unraveling obi, went sprawling to the freezing ground, and he covered his head with both arms to ward off the fatal blow. How it stung! How the sword edge blunted itself against his skull!

"Tatte! Tatte! Get up, you wharf rat!"

A guard was beating Heinie with a billy club, striking at him without pause. He tried to fend him off with a section of wood which miraculously came to hand. Slamming at it, the guard knocked it away in a shower of splinters. Heinie Joe staggered painfully to his feet, hunched over and lurched frantically to the wooden brow. He thought himself trapped again in the molasses of his dream and forced his body to move faster. Halfway down the gangway, he was caught and beaten to his knees; the scalp at his forehead was split open. Blood rushed stickily to his eyes. If he couldn't get away, he knew the man would kill him.

"Tomaru . . . stop . . . why are you trying to kill me? What have I done? Stop, stop . . ."

The boy's anguished cries had no effect. The man struck harder at him and, in a surge of agony, Heinie scrambled down the rest of the brow. Cutting behind crisscrossed girders and cranes, he ran into the depths of the shipyard.

305

The watchman set up a hullabaloo to arouse his mates; racing footsteps and strong flashlight beams cut the gloom. Heinie Joe watched them from a cave of rust-pocked metal at the base of a dry dock. When the shouting faded, he took a long, shuddering breath. Then urgently he relieved his bladder against the rough concealing surface, welcoming the hot scent of his urine as something familiar and not to be feared. Its spattering shattered the silence and he would have stopped if he could; the cold returned and he was done. He listened. They were pounding down the other side of the skeletal vessel. A ray of light stabbed at the sky, smoking in the mist. Now! He had to get out now. Holding his wounded head, he slipped past machinery and slabs of steel. He had to find a safe place . . . and he'd have to clean himself up in order not to attract attention. There didn't seem to be blood on his clothing yet. Why did the man try to kill him?

After escaping from the shipyard, Heinie eased over the side of a retaining wall to reach a rocky strip of shore. Still too near the shipyard for comfort, he acted with speed. He washed in the salt water of the bay and winced as it bit the cut on his scalp. Pressing his hand to the place, he wondered how to stem the blood. A white rectangle danced in the shadows. Touching it, he found a length of toweling hanging from the wall and lost no time tearing the cloth into strips. He patted his wound and washed it again, then wrapped a strip firmly around his head like a *hachimaki*. Militant students wore it so as a badge in imitation of the kamikaze during the war. He felt stronger and braver with it on. He pulled himself to the top of the wall and tested his limbs. Soreness afflicted all of them. Travel would be difficult unless he could get a ride.

Without knowing his destination, Heinie Joe headed southwest. It was an instinctive impulse he had not analyzed or he would surely have changed direction. He was hurt, seeking the one human with compassion for him. The fevers were fingering his lungs again and he looked anxiously at the leaden sky. If it rained, he didn't think he could survive long enough to get to wherever he was running . . . to the safe place . . . where he could hide from

306

the *junsa*. Hide from everyone. They hated him. Had always hated him.

A blood stain seeped into the front of his *hachimaki*.
Like a red sun...

Reluctant to be done with working, the Chief Superintendent brought his latest reports home with him every evening. His wife told friends he worked from morning stars to evening stars, and she gave the information with ambiguity, for they had one day each week for themselves, provided he was not called to duty. This was to be one of those days of rest, but he had gotten up before dawn to throw a robe over his nakedness, and she heard him rustle through the papers from his briefcase beside the nightlight. She wondered if she was to lose her day with him. Sneezing once lightly to let him know she had awakened, she sat up, wrapping the comforter around herself. A kerosene stove beside the *futon* gave off heat.

"Shall I get up to order your breakfast?" she asked meekly.

He looked at her with surprise. "You're awake...I didn't want to disturb you."

"I wanted to rise early myself."

"Well then, have you something of importance to do today?"

"Hai, shujin..."

His hands dropped to his lap, the report forgotten. "What could that be?"

"To be with you."

They exchanged knowing smiles. He granted most of her wishes on the days they shared; she frequently asked him to remain beneath the comforter with her for a longer time, but now he didn't move toward her, and she regarded the briefcase petulantly. The girl within her took over at such moments to ruffle her staid married woman's bearing. She was a girl beneath the down-filled padding; a girl in

307

her husband's arms whenever he held her. And they did not speak of Hichiriki and they were young again each time.

"I'm afraid I must disappoint you today. There are preparations I must make."

Her training squelched her thoughts and she threw the coverlet aside to dress hurriedly. "Ah, then...what may I do to help you?"

"There's a while yet. I don't have to board my plane till the commuters' hour."

She paused to question him. "You're leaving Osaka?" she asked with concern. "For how long?"

"The day only. I've a foreigner to interview in Tokyo."

"Has it to do with Mr. Segawa?"

"Hai."

He took up his report to read again. His wife continued to dress. Then she came to him, kneeling as she secured her hair and craned her neck to see what he read. "What has a foreigner to do with the case?"

"Joe Shimada is an *ainoko,* you remember..."

"Ah..." She settled upon her heels. "You're seeing a man, then."

"Iie. A woman."

"Ah..." Her inflection varied; she was curious. Hidenori was amused.

"This came from the emigration office in Tokyo," he said, lifting the document to her. "It seems an American and his wife cabled from overseas in regard to my fugitive."

"They want the boy."

"They want the boy."

"Ah..."

"It is imperative I speak with the lady."

"Of course. Is not the man with her?"

"He's not. She checked in alone, though both came through Customs together. I venture to say he's looking for the boy."

"Ah..."

"It was fortunate the Americans gave the time and date of their arrival. We would not have known they were here."

"Ah..."

"Now that the boy has another interested pursuer, I must do something about the man if we are to take my suspect in charge as I planned."

308

"Is the man his father?"

"Yes. And there's no trusting his behavior under such circumstances. I must neutralize him somehow."

"Where do you think the boy is?"

He added the page in his hand to others in the briefcase. "The best indications suggest him to be in Osaka: There was a very encouraging report from a *junsa* patrol in the canal district near the shipyards. They claim there was a positive sighting of Shimada. And not long after, we received an account from night watchmen looking after the dry docks. One of them evicted a young vagrant from the bowels of an unfinished tanker. Naturally, he may not have encountered our quarry but some *garentai* spending his night out of the weather. However, the man said he wounded the intruder and that is another thing to make the boy stand out from among his peers." Hidenori pushed the briefcase aside and put his arms about his wife. "My department is scouring the warrens of Osaka in hopes of turning up an injured *ainoko*."

"Ah..." she said. He unfastened the collar at the back of her dress, then removed each of her garments with infinite care, taking time to admire the curve of her nape and spine as he unbound her hair. And when he carried her swiftly to the *futon* they had left, she said again, "Ah...*shujin*, ahhh..."

"How did you get injured?"

"Oh, that. It's paint! I wanted a *hinomaru* in front."

"No slogans?"

"They are to be decided." Heinie kept his face averted.

"You young people are so interesting." The portly man spoke easily, despite his unrest about the appearance of his passenger. It was obvious the boy had been rioting somewhere: The circular mark on his *hachimaki* was a bloodstain, no doubt of that! He was almost sorry to have plucked this student from the roadside as a means of relieving his boredom while he drove...frequently, hitchhiking schoolboys provided dinner stories to relate to his friends, who were always anxious to learn how the current revolution was going and what demonstrations would affect the course of business. The students were their own inadvertent pipeline to the establishment, reporting on the next national disruptions. *Hai,* an astute man could plan his monetary affairs accordingly. This boy hadn't been talkative, though. And there was a stink clinging to him. The man hoped it wouldn't contaminate his car. "Well, fight on," he said with assumed joviality. "You're still weak, you youngsters. It was different when I was your age. We had power then. We were within a bee sting of ruling all Asia. The Pacific was our pond, and our fleets were its carp."

Heinie watched the scenery unfold without interest. They had driven through Himeji, close enough to see the castle called the White Heron. His head throbbed. Well, it was behind them now. He had his glimpse of it and didn't care. Grateful to be riding, he knew he was expected to pay his fare. What was the man saying? Reply. Anything will do. "Oh...were you in the war?"

The man's mouth tightened. "Not exactly as a soldier. There had to be those of us to conduct the life at home. I spent many fierce days under the bombs." After a thoughtful interval, he declared, "Upon occasion, I suspect I would not be here had I been a soldier."

All gems glitter when polished, Heinie mused derisively, but said, *"Hai,* you don't look like the sort of man to surrender."

"Not that I condemn those who did," the man replied generously.

"It's not what I would have done, either."

"You?" He looked closer at the boy, then back to the road. *"You.* You look foreign to me. You are not of pure blood."

Heinie parried the sneer with the story he told to blunt the barbs. *"Ano-ne,* it's like this: You are quite right. But you musn't think I was a dropping of the Occupation. I'm much older than I seem...several years. My mother married one of the Doitsu-jin who flew his Messerschmitt fighter for us after the Luftwaffe was broken up. He flew it here and gave the Beikoku-jin many surprises they had not expected."

"A German? Flying with our own forces?"

That always impressed them. "*Hai!* He was one of our war aces! Everyone in our village honored him."

The man thought, it's not a bad tale; there are a few of the Doitsu living comfortable lives in concealment all over the world. "Where is your village?"

"Oh...very far. Near Iwakuni."

"Ah. Tell me, how is your brave father now?"

"Oh, he was lost. It happened over Okinawa. He was leading a wave of kamikaze. We had a fine funeral for him before he left."

The man's eyes flicked at the boy and he smiled. "Oh, you remember that, do you?"

Embroidering rapidly, Heinie stuttered, "That is to say...I was told of it. You know it was customary to have the funerals before any raid." He reddened with shame. It was the first time he'd offered that invention of a funeral but he told the story so many times it needed fresh material to make it seem real to himself. He hadn't said it with authority; that's why the man doubted him. "Everyone calls me the German Joe... all who know me well."

"Ah, is it so? That must make life very much easier for you, then. You know how the bastards of the Americans are disdained."

"Oh, yes...It's all very easy for me." He decided to get out of this man's car and catch another ride. Coughing uncontrollably, he sat closer to the door, thinking they were both poor liars.

When the boy asked to be let off, the portly man didn't try to dissuade him. He stopped the car and watched Heinie Joe walk to the bank of the road. The russet blotch on the *hachimaki* bothered the man considerably, as did the ridiculous fabrication about his background. Driving away, the man pieced together his suspicions, which had nagged him for some miles. He was certain the boy was in serious trouble. Wouldn't it be his duty to report this encounter? It could mean a minor delay, which he would minimize by making the report over the telephone. A personal visit to the police can be a drawn-out experience. Or perhaps he should let Fate take its own course and not do anything. He drove for five more miles before making up his mind. No, the boy was an *ainoko*. Not to be trusted. Not to be dismissed as an innocent hitchhiker...wasn't he evasive under questioning? *Iie,* an *ainoko* was not to be trusted, not after what had been in the newspapers these days. If they weren't robbing, they were murdering! He kept a lookout for the next place he could telephone.

Entering Kurashiki, he pulled up at the first lodging house he could find. The owner was distressed that he was not to be a guest but merely wished the use of the telephone. They fenced politely about it; the portly man had his way. After many involved transfers by the operator, he heard the clipped tones of someone in the office of the Osaka Police Bureau answering.

"May I help you?"

"My name is Michio Toba. I have a report to make."

"Proceed please."

"It happens that I was in Osaka to attend the marriage of my nephew and upon returning to my home in the South, I picked up a rider on the road, a boy of perhaps seventeen or more."

"Where are you at present?"

"I'm in...a poor establishment in Kurashiki." The owner of the lodging house darted a look of annoyance at him. Poor establishment, indeed! Wait till he asked to pay for the call.

"Why aren't you in contact with the *junsa* there, Mr. Toba?"

"I've no time to waste and you know what provincial policemen are like."

Silence. Then, "What about this boy?"

"It appeared to me that he had been injured."

"An accident?"

"I don't think so. It may have happened during a struggle with someone."

"Is he in serious condition? You should consult a hospital instead of us."

"You don't understand. The boy is in trouble, I believe. I suspect him of criminal activities."

"Did he threaten you?"

"No."

"Steal anything from you?"

"No."

"Mr. Toba, mere suspicion of wrongdoing isn't sufficient for you to call this bureau. Is that all?"

"I'm very alarmed about this boy. He is an *ainoko* and

312

his head is bandaged over a wound." The phone gasped emptily in his ear for a short time. He shook it impatiently. "Are you there?"

"An *ainoko*, you say? With a bandaged head? Is he still with you?"

"He insisted upon being let off a few miles back. I understood him to be going to Iwakuni or thereabouts."

"Could you identify this person from a photograph, Mr. Toba?"

There they go, always wanting to detain people with their procedures; it would be required to return to Osaka next. He replied firmly, "I doubt it. I was driving, you understand, and had to keep my eyes on the road, and his face was to the window on his side of the car while with me. You know how passengers do..."

"Can you think of anything to identify him further?"

"He's dirty...clothing too inadequate for winter. Hoarse voice, I think he has a cold. Ah! He calls himself the German Joe."

"So. I've noted that all down, Mr. Toba."

"I'm only reporting since I think these types are a danger to citizens."

"I understand."

"He's very suspicious-looking. I think he should be apprehended and questioned."

"Have no care, Mr. Toba. We will do what is necessary."

"Was I right to call you?"

"Yes, Mr. Toba. Is that all you can tell us?"

"Well, he's a fancy liar. I could readily see he didn't want to speak the truth about himself."

"Did he say where he lives?"

"I told you. Some village near Iwakuni."

"You seem to believe that, Mr. Toba."

"After all, he's heading in that direction."

"*Hai.* Where did he say he had been before you picked him up?"

"Oh...that. There was some mention of living in Osaka, but I don't know where in the city that could have been."

"Thank you, Mr. Toba."

"Wait, don't hang up! I had another thought."

"What was that, Mr. Toba?"

313

"Wasn't there an *ainoko* involved in the murder of Jihei Segawa in Kyoto?"

"Mr. Toba, you mustn't allow your imagination to run away with you."

"It was only a passing thought. I meant that all these types are a danger to citizens."

"You've stated that already, Mr. Toba, and I have it written down. Is that all?"

"You will convey my information to the Superintendent?" This said with an important look at the owner of the lodging house, who was unimpressed.

"When he returns from Tokyo. Is that all?"

The portly man was irritated that the owner of the place was busily adding figures in a column while referring to the sweep of the second hand on his wristwatch as it continued to tick off the duration of the phone call. *"Hai,* that's all. I've done my duty." He hung up and was presented with his bill. He studied the paper, then added the figures himself laboriously. He sighed. He shouldn't have stopped after all. Look at the expense the *ainoko* had put him to . . . which proved he should be removed from all contact with the citizenry.

The deceptively mild man walked soundlessly along a thick carpet in the corridor of the hotel. Hands clasped behind, he glanced at each door number in passing and halted before the one he sought. He knocked lightly and waited. After a moment, Wanda opened the door. She looked at him worriedly as he introduced himself.

"My office contacted you. I am Chief Superintendent Hidenori."

Her nervousness increased. Beyond being told to expect him, she hadn't been given an explanation. It had to do with Jordan, she was sure. "You're prompt. They said you'd be here shortly before noon."

"Forgive the intrusion. I won't be long."

"I don't mind," she lied politely. "Please come in." Step-

314

ping aside, she disliked the scent of his hair pomade. It seemed endemic to Japanese males. On her morning tour of department stores, she encountered the same odor everywhere. It added to the discomfort of being unable to communicate; English was spoken but she didn't think she was understood. Those funny smiles she'd seen now matched her own. He was strolling past her into the suite, which was starkly furnished in the Occidental style. A print of Degas ballet dancers hung above a sofa; two modern stuffed chairs, a coffee table and a writing desk hugged the edges of a square rug laid over wall-to-wall carpeting on the floor. "Would you like me to have lunch sent up for us?" she asked nervously.

"Thank you, no. This is an official visit, Mrs. Asche."

Upset, she shut the door, then followed a few steps after Hidenori as he went to the windows to admire a magnificent view. Past sliding glass, a panorama overlooking Tokyo from a considerable height spread before him under an unbroken gray sky.

"Like the terrapin, I find my feet stamping to go south," he observed enigmatically. When she didn't reply, he pointed out a flock of geese winging into the horizon. Turning, he asked with a disarming smile, "Have you seen the geese often from your windows?"

The effect was to perturb her further. "I'm seldom in my rooms. I'm here now because I had to wait for you."

"Pity. I mean about not seeing the geese. You are so close to them in this suite." He indicated the sofa. "Please be seated, Mrs. Asche." He waited for her to sit; his pleasantness kept her on guard. "I'm grateful you granted me this appointment."

"I could hardly refuse an order from the local police."

"It was a request, madame," he protested gently and added another correction. "This is not my prefect. I am normally to be found in my office at the Regional Police Bureau in Osaka." As she began to rise with alarm, he held out a placating hand. "Calm yourself, Mrs. Asche. Your husband is well, so I am informed."

She was nonplussed. "You seem to know about us, Superintendent."

"*Hai*...a trifle. Your arrival at the airport was noted."

"We weren't aware of being singled out."

"We are discreet, Mrs. Asche."

"What is this about?" She was both angry and apprehensive. Jordie should have been there to handle it. "Is there something wrong with our visa...or what?"

"Your papers are quite in order. Your landing cards state that your husband's business affiliation is Polychem. What is that?"

"He's part owner of a plant on Long Island...Long Island, New York," she added lamely to clarify it for him.

"What is the nature of his business?"

"Polychem creates new uses for plastics. Everything's being made of plastic now." His features remained blank but she could tell he found the idea repugnant. Impatient, she demanded, "Just why are you here, Superintendent?"

"Permit me to ask instead why you and Mr. Asche have come to Japan."

"My husband is here on a personal matter."

"Not a vacation, as claimed on your landing cards?"

"It's meant to be that, too."

"At the time your journey was booked, he also petitioned us for emigration procedures...concerning the son of Miss Yukiko Shimada."

"We're..." Including herself seemed false. She amended her statement. "Jordie is hoping to adopt the boy."

"Have you been corresponding with Joe Shimada?"

"No. Is that his name? He's very new...to both of us." Like it or not, she was involved and had to say so. She lit a cigarette irritatedly. He glanced out the windows again but the geese were no longer in sight. His next question seemed less innocent.

"Have you read the newspapers or watched our television since your arrival in Tokyo?"

"Neither would be comprehensible to me," she scoffed. "The set in there hasn't been turned on once." She nodded toward the next room, where she slept badly after tossing and turning to rid herself of visions of Jordie and his Japanese woman in each other's arms.

"Well, then...the hotel delivers English-language newspapers to foreign guests, is that not so?"

"Sorry, I don't bother with them."

His thoughtful pause was almost critical. She tapped ashes into a glass ashtray to show she didn't care. He asked, "I wonder if you are familiar with Jihei Segawa...the film actor?"

Baffled, she attempted to place the name. "He's...yes, he's the lovely man who got so many awards for a part he played in...I saw the picture...yes, *End of the Wheel*, wasn't it?"

"*Hai*, the very one. It's flattering you are aware of him."

She smiled as she relaxed a little, wondering why he was talking about a film star. "His movies are a tremendous success in the States," she offered, certain he knew but wishing to appear interested.

"As they are in the rest of the world, Mrs. Asche. Jihei Segawa was admired as the epitome of the samurai."

"I'm afraid I don't follow the gist of all this."

Hidenori was blunt. "Jihei Segawa is dead."

It was a rude change from his quaintness, and her tension returned. "Oh? I'm sorry to hear it." There was more coming and she prepared for it by grinding out her cigarette to be rid of its distraction. "Wasn't he a young man?"

"A young man," he agreed gravely. "Jihei Segawa was killed by a boy he was entertaining for the night." She stared at him aghast, suspecting the connection because there could be no other. "There is no confusion about his identity. His fingerprints were found throughout the house at the scene of the crime, and his friends knew he was expected to put in an appearance."

Unwilling to accept the dreadful conclusion, she asked without hope, "Why are you telling me this?"

He was impassive. Hidenori could have been speaking from a podium in answer to a student of criminal law. "Your husband is the boy's father."

The confirmation dismayed her. She wanted to deny it and couldn't, able only to breathe brokenly, "Oh, God..."

"I thought surely you had read of it in the newspapers...seen it on television...I apologize."

"My God, how terrible. We didn't know anything about the boy...nothing."

"A complete dossier exists. Would you care to see his photograph?"

As he reached to an inner pocket, she protested, "Please don't," but it was already being displayed to her. She covered her eyes. Hidenori regarded the glossy reproduction himself. Too small photographs printed side by side on a file card, with a history listed beneath. A felon's poses, so ordered by custom. The boy was handsome; nothing

317

marred the perfection of his face, and there was nothing marring his physical description. Not so much as a mole upon his perfect skin...intelligence in the eyes. The Superintendent thought it despicable that an *ainoko,* an impure blot upon the national honor, should be so well favored while his own firstborn was a tragic monstrosity. His jaw tensed; in Manchukuo, men had feared to see the sign, followed by rages. But he had control of those now. Only the malefactor need fear. "This is a copy of what we have at the Bureau," he said easily. "It is the usual head and profile. He was fourteen then, but it is a fair likeness, I think. We Asians age slowly."

"I said I didn't want to see it."

"Very well." He put the card away, then moved to a chair beside the sofa. "May I?" He sat without her consent and folded his arms across his chest. "The boy's mother has been on file as well, since the days of the Occupation when she was a licensed whore."

"I didn't know she was a whore," Wanda exclaimed, feeling a wave of revulsion immediately, as if she was herself unclean for having been touched by the same man. But sailors and whores...isn't that like fish and chips...salt and pepper? She said sadly, "I thought she was a respectable girl Jordie met when he was here. I thought she was..." She didn't say *like me.* The revelation made things worse. The more he talked about the boy, the worse it became.

"We have kept strict records of the *konketsuji,* the racially mixed children of GIs and Japanese girls, Mrs. Asche. It is an oddity that there are not many, considering the thousands of troops we entertained. I regret to admit the majority of our nationals are not tolerant of the children, who are without standing among us. They may not be listed in the family register. Predictably, it has been observed as these children mature, they were deserving of continued surveillance. They are thugs, panderers, addicts, thieves...and murderers."

Composing herself, she asked plaintively, "How am I to break this to Jordie?"

His reply was a warning. "You won't. My primary concern at this juncture is to apprehend your husband's son without interference."

"Do you know where the boy is now?"

He nodded. "We believe in Osaka. The *junsa* are conducting searches along the canals and waterfront districts."

Rising agitatedly, she paced to the windows. "My husband has already gone to the woman's village."

"*Hai*. He should arrive there today."

"Are we being watched, Superintendent?"

"Not aggressively, Mrs. Asche. But we have to know your movements since they relate to the boy."

"So...Jordie isn't going to find his son in the village."

"I haven't said that, Mrs. Asche."

"But you think he's in Osaka."

"He may be. Or may have left. There are over two and one half million souls in Osaka and as many places to go to ground. I understand these *ainoko*. I am of the opinior the boy will run rather than remain."

Sorrow overcame Wanda for Jordan and his hope...and another feeling lurked behind it, one she couldn't quite pin down.

"I asked for this interview to make a specific request of you, Mrs. Asche."

Dully, she replied, "What is it?"

"If I must go to the village to take the boy into custody, will you accompany me?"

"You think the boy is heading there?"

"*Hai*. I hope to have him sooner. However, the hounds must follow the brush of the fox or be caught yapping at a false trail."

"Surely, the village police are keeping watch for him?"

"They have been since the outset."

"Then why aren't they to arrest him for you?"

"They are residents of the island, Mrs. Asche." It meant nothing to her and he explained more fully. "It may be we shall have to remove the boy forcibly from his mother's house. I would not care to have her own neighbors take part in this incident officially. They've given her much injury since the birth of her child and she has many more years to suffer."

"I didn't imagine my husband would find her still living there...not after so many years."

"She was not a member of the community for some time. She returned to the village from the mainland when she lost her profession. Miss Shimada is not welcome there."

319

"She's not married."

"Hai. And lives alone."

"She's not married." Wanda wrestled with the distressing information. Yes, who would marry a whore? Who would love one? The Superintendent was *so Oriental* to refer to her *so* politely and be *so* concerned for her treatment. It was too complex—Japanese values were *so* twisted. "You said...you asked if I'd go to the village with you. But why? I'd rather stay in Tokyo to wait for my husband. Jordie promised to return right away if his son wasn't there."

"I won't disturb you in that case. But if the boy is there?"

She didn't want to meet the woman. That was the one reason she let Jordie have his way about going on alone. "Why must I be with you, Superintendent?"

"It's to be with your husband, Mrs. Asche. He'll need you. He'll need your sympathy. And I shall need your help to prevent him from behaving foolishly. You see, he can't carry out the plans you've both made. The boy can't possibly leave the country."

And the elusive feeling she couldn't grasp before clarified itself. She was free. She didn't have to go through with the adoption. She wouldn't have to live with it, after all. But Jordie...poor Jordie. How could anyone comfort him now? "I hope we don't have to go to the village," she said with ambivalent relief. "I sincerely hope it won't be necessary."

Moist overcast tarnished the sea and islands into a faded stereoscopic deception, shifting with the movement of the observer. Everything was glutinous yet impermanent; slightly fragrant with the decay of yesterday's catch and overlain with the charcoal smoke of an awakening community. Excrement's liquescent aroma snaked down from terraced hillsides where night soil carriers had done their work of fertilization. Jordan was glad when the launch coughed diesel fumes into the air and they got under way again. He had been presented with a small box when he left the inn, a gift of light dry cakes like pale golden chrysanthemums with jade green leaves. Thinking to save the lovely things for Yukiko, he retied the colorful cord carefully to duplicate the original intricate knot. The box bulged safely in a pocket of his duffle coat while he braced himself against the roll of the motor launch. As always, when subjected to a vessel's sensual stirring, he felt a surge of joyfulness, a sense of being home. Was it only because he had been a seaman, or was it deeper, a gladdening of the heart to be swayed by the original cradle once more?

Spray hissed into a flourish of air globes to feather into a flattening wake below which left a highway behind. It would endure, fragmenting unwillingly when currents and winds scuffed it over. Waves humped at the sides of the smooth lane, gathered strength as they fell apart to bounce other craft on their crests, and then hurled themselves upon myriad shores amid thunders of relief at having crashed to rest...as he had heard on that tender beach where he had played with the girl at being fisherfolk. Was that the island there?

A landfall revolved lethargically as the motor launch passed, displaying its clinging village, its tended steps of fields, its cloud-laced wooded coronet, and the tail of the wake crumpled whitely against sheer walls of rock, finding no cove other than a constructed recess below houses embracing one another beneath roofs of tile. It was so poor a community; plank stairs and catwalks were its streets. No...his island, their island, was better endowed. If the weather improved, he would ask to picnic again and take his son along. The launch picked up speed entering a decent anchorage, past an assembled catalogue of floating tradesmen, past a breakwater forming an artificial lagoon, toward fishing craft drawn up in rows upon a man-made beach of algaed cement, below a comfort of dwellings laddering into cultivation which ended in pines and mist. Jordan threw back the hood of his coat and stared. It was Yukiko's village. As it had been.

As it had always been.

Suitcase in hand, he stood nervously on the stone wharf. The motor launch muttered into the distance, heading for its next stop. A squad of boys chased tangled kites wobbling down upon the line of fishing boats. One boy remained behind to gaze at Jordan. Without expression or movement, child and man regarded each other. As though the clouds had been upended, it began to rain. The boy ducked his head and ran up the ramp to the village, followed closely by his friends. Jordan pulled his hood over his head and trudged after them. The rain strafed the ground, flooding rapidly down the cement incline; the village hid within the streaming curtain. His shoes and socks felt like slick dough and he didn't bother to walk around puddles but tramped through them after the boy.

He couldn't find the place which had fallen into the sea during that long-ago typhoon and realized they would have rebuilt there. It was necessary to climb to the path which led to Yukiko's house by another route. The village seemed deserted; no one could be expected out in this downpour. If people saw him from their homes, he was not aware of it, though there was a semblance of the dread he knew once, not here. The rain beat harder upon him and he marched doggedly upward. How little had changed! Paintwork had the same peeled spots, and the same gates stood awry from their posts; a heavy burnt carbon tang was held fast by the wet and he crinkled his nose at odors less appetizing; and over everything was the refreshing chill wash of the rain...

When he arrived at the house, he hesitated before stepping under its protective eaves. A finger of smoke beckoned above the roof. The shutters were locked against the weather, and all was still as a mountain shrine but for the steady thrum of drops upon stained-clay tiles. Stepping beneath the overhang, Jordan sat on the stoop. He removed his wet shoes and socks to store against the dry wall with his overnight bag, and got to his feet. What a practical custom, after all. Nerves jangling, he knocked softly at the *fusuma* and called out, "Hello?" Water splashed in barrels beside the house, advancing balletically to the rim in variations which swooned over the edge without stop. He tried again. "Hello. Is anyone home?" Then, thinking he could not be heard above the drumming rain, he slid the door aside and entered.

The room, illuminated only by sallow light from papered windows and the glow of the fire pit, was quite dark. Swathed in a padded blanket, a figure sat in an accustomed place as if no time had passed since Jordan had last seen it. Her head was down, chin fallen to her sleeping breast. He didn't want to frighten the old lady; he coughed loudly a couple of times and scraped his bare heels over the mildewed tatami. The woman's head raised and she spat into the ashes at her feet.

"Ooba-san? Ooba-san...it's me. It's Jordan Asche. I'm here to..."

She looked at him with a sudden thrust of her head, like an asp striking out blindly. He wasn't to finish his sentence. Heat swept over him...she was not Ooba-san. "Oh, Christ," he said, sinking helplessly to his knees. He sat back upon his legs and looked pityingly into Yukiko's aging face. "It's me," he offered softly. "It's me, Yukiko... Jordan...Jordan Asche...remember?"

It was forever before she answered. And then she rasped, "I never remember...because I never forget."

Devastated, he reached into the pocket of his duffle coat and struggled to extract the box of *higashi,* the little dry cakes from the inn. When he extended it to Yukiko, she didn't move to take it and he placed it upon her lap.

"Is this something you bought for me...or is it inn trash as is given to every departing guest?"

He was speechless, unhappy she'd found a flaw in him so soon. She pushed the box from her lap to the coals, where it smoldered before flaming. They watched the box burn, its cord breaking and spiraling into umbilical life, turning back and falling to ashes, and finally the wood split apart to show the chrysanthemums. The imitation flowers burned rapidly, a more living gold than they had been until they were rubescent jewels among the twisted black strips of what had been joined strips of cedar.

"I'm sorry, Yukiko," he mumbled inadequately, and repeated it because he meant more. "I'm terribly sorry."

She glanced at him and back to the fire.

"You'll want to know how it is I'm here," he began. The heat was unbearable; he was sweating. "Dave Bell—my old buddy, Dave Bell—we hadn't kept in touch over the years and he was in New York." He smiled wryly. "They say everyone you ever knew will eventually show up there, so I suppose it's true." Was she listening? "Dave told me...he told me you had a son."

Not looking at him, she retorted gruffly, "I also told you."

"I got your card...a long while ago."

"A long while. How long was it before my message reached you?"

He strained to recall the card and its postmark but could not and calculated roughly. "It must have been a month after you sent it."

She smiled at him then; it was not nice. "Ah. And you were anxious to acknowledge it."

Jordan's throat sanded. "I couldn't read the Japanese, Yukiko. Only the address made sense to me."

"But you knew the *hagaki* was from me."

"Why didn't you write in English?" he demanded defensively. "You could have...or Dave would have done it for you."

"I could not paint the words in your language beautifully." She hesitated, then asked coldly, "Could no one read it to you? Many of my people live in your country."

"There was no one...and I didn't think the message was important."

"You didn't think it important."

"I was getting married at the time...preparing to go on my honeymoon." He thought she didn't know what that was. "It's the interval a man spends with the woman he has newly wed."

Yukiko was thoughtful. "So," she said reflectively, "the dance of lions." He didn't understand and winced as she observed with quiet malice, "How interesting for you to become father and husband within the same period."

"Yukiko...I swear I wouldn't have gone through with it if I had known what was written on your card."

"You think not?" When he didn't reply, she hugged her

324

body with her arms, hands buried inside the sleeves of the heavy jacket she wore under the blanket. After an indecisive moment, she asked, "What did you do all these years with the woman you took to wife? Have you been busy rearing fair-haired, blue-eyed children?"

"My wife...we didn't have any children." A strand of tatami was loose beside his knee. He toyed with it; it broke and came away in his fingertips.

"*So desuka?* Was the woman barren?"

He searched her face. She was asking a woman's question and he didn't mind answering, though it had been his greatest source of pain. "Yes...that was it."

Yukiko nodded to herself. "She cannot conceive and you have finally learned you have a son."

"Yes."

"Did you know the woman could not bear children before you married her?"

"Neither of us knew. We learned much later...and we resigned ourselves to it."

Breath hissed inward between her teeth before she taunted him, saying, "You missed a great joy. And she. You must know that children are indispensable to a woman. When they are born, they give reason for lust, and forgive her the pleasure she took for her body by paining it at the time of delivery...and when dire days befall the woman, the child can aid her in her work if he is old enough."

"Have you married?" She flicked a scornful glance at him and he winced again. It was so easy to offend here.

"I am less eligible than the fairest women of Nagasaki and Hiroshima," she explained simply. "At least they may find someone rash enough to risk the condition of their wombs...but mine is considered far more defiled."

Jordan picked at the ragged strands of the tatami. She had said a monstrous thing in an ordinary tone of voice. He said helplessly, "Then you've been alone since...and you've raised the boy yourself."

"*Hai.* Myself."

"Had I known, I would have sent money."

Her scoffing amusement was unexpected. "Your countrymen provided me with sufficient yen," she chuckled. "*Hai,* the Occupation had its advantages."

The straw in his fingers had multiplied into many

pieces now. He flipped them into the coals, where they bent back and forth as they heated, then flared into torches and turned dark.

"My family was not alone in wishing me to give up my child of mixed blood," she mused aloud. "The people of this village held a *hanashiai* and gave an ultimatum to my father, which he passed on to me. I went to Osaka, taking your son with me. There were Christian ladies in Osaka who imprison children like him in their establishments, lavishing strict care and affection upon them as the Ainu upon the bear cub they raise and slaughter after a few years of worship. The Christian ladies and the Ainu speak of love and prayer, but their saints end upon two logs. Would I leave him there? *Iie*, and not with our own Japanese welfare organizations, who have their kennels, too. And I would not give him to some *hakujin* woman without the womb for the task. *Iie*, I would not let them have him. At first, I thought my message would bring you. Then I hoped for an answer only. Over the years, I even foolishly asked for you among uniformed men . . . and the sailors . . . how I asked in vain! It seemed to me that surely among so many, I would hear of you."

He was unable to meet her questing eyes.

"There was no shame in Osaka . . . and in those days, the life I had was not against the law. What better profession for a discarded woman? Ooba-san knew. She had the gift of knowing what was to come—they say it is compensation for aging. Old Ooba-san knew everything. When the laws were changed and the Occupation had long been discontinued, there were still your countrymen to be seen everywhere. As they are even now. They expect to find women like me. But today . . . a son must lead the men to his mother's bed in stealth."

Appalled at the matter-of-fact delivery of her story, he stammered, "I can't . . . I can't believe your father was so cruel . . . or that your family would allow him to send you away to a life like that."

"How easily you judge!" she admonished angrily. "In these islands, no man survives without his neighbors. And if they refuse to help him, his family suffers, too. The punishment most feared on Seto Naikai is *mura hachibo*, which is decreed for extreme offense . . . the total denial of aid. My father and his relations would be shunned because

I bore your child." Her mouth twitched at the next grievous thought. "My father could have taken your son's life but sent us from home instead." A single spark at her feet flew up and died in the rising, disappearing in midair.

"The boy...you brought him back with you?" His disjointed croaking was all he could muster.

"*Hai*. I brought him. To my father's house. But the child got no farther than the threshold. Being spoiled, city-bred and seeing the backs of those scorning him, he knew he had no place in this village. Being unacceptable to flesh of my flesh, he left me."

"Then he's gone? He's not here?"

She straightened to look at him directly. "Did you bring cigarettes for the old one?"

She confused him; he wanted to talk about his son. "Cigarettes? No...no...I didn't think to bring anything for your grandmother. I haven't any with me."

Yukiko was disappointed. Scratching at an itch, she slumped again and grumbled, "I would have accepted the cigarettes of Ooba-san. She has no use for them. She was buried when I lived in Osaka."

"I'm sorry. And what of..."

"No one. The parents I disgraced, I now mourn. My sister is no more my sister and her door is closed to me. There is no one now."

"But the boy. What of the boy? Where is he?"

She rocked gently, nodding over her knees like a frail leaf. "The winds know. He visits sometimes when the villagers cannot see him. At night only...and seldom. But they know when he is here."

"You must have some idea where he can be found."

She shrugged. "None. It could be anywhere. The boy is his own man."

Jordan was sapped of energy. This wasn't what he'd expected, wasn't as it should be. Yukiko shifted to crawl from her place at the fire pit. He eyed her dully.

"You shall stay here for now," she advised him with firm practicality. "We are too humble a community to have an inn. It has been a while since I served you last..." She laughed without humor, knowing he had no desire for her. "Bring in your belongings and put your coat aside. I shall prepare a meal. The launch will make its rounds and by tomorrow morning, you may leave me."

Rain shook the roof violently. A few leaks dripped into soggy pools on the tatami. Humming as though a girl, Yukiko busied herself with kitchenware. Jordan removed his coat dejectedly and listened to the woman and the storm.

Heinie Joe's fevers were back in force. He'd never be dry again! As the truck bounced away into the heavy rain, he muttered imprecations against the driver for making him ride on the open bed of it. There had been room inside the cab but it was dry there and the driver refused to let him foul it with his sodden clothes. The wind straddled him, buffeted his ears. He could see nothing of the surrounding countryside. This was miles before Iwakuni and he had to find the beach. Shaking under the scourge of wet chills, he slogged along in the mud toward the sea. The weather was in his favor; he intended to steal a boat, if he found one. There was scant chance of anyone working on the beach, less likely he'd be seen prowling there. He ran like a wraith past a shuttered hamlet whose windows and doors deflected the chattering strings of the liquid loom. Was it illness singing in his head?

Brown sands absorbed huge droplets with a flat sound; the surface of the sea beyond twitched with small white explosions which patterned without repeating themselves. As he reached some beached boats, he was dismayed to find them too big to handle by himself. He groaned, thinking he should have tried to stow away on the daily motor launch from Osaka, but that was impractical: There was nowhere to hide on those craft. The rain drove him underneath one of the boats and he tried to worm into a dry corner against a hull. No good. Water ran down the side of the planking and blew along the keel at him. He would have to find better cover.

Thinking there'd be something useful in the fishing gear, he crawled over the side of the boat, slipping under canvas lashed down to keep the interior dry. It would have been wonderful to stay until the rain stopped but the fishermen would be back to launch the boat and he mustn't be found there. What's that? He felt a thickly folded pad. It was of bright yellow canvas and upon opening it, he discovered a deflated survival raft, one of the war surplus items diverted to peacetime needs. Searching more, he located compressed air capsules, which could fill the raft; two paddles lashed together completed its equipment. Gleeful, he eased the plunder from the boat and dropped to the sand to take it down to the water. There, ankle deep in a simmering surf, he charged the raft with air. In a few moments, he was adrift and paddling with short, chopping strokes into the sea. A current seized him; it would help speed him to his destination. If the storm continued, he'd make his landing without notice. It wouldn't be dark for a while and he couldn't feel safe till then.

The voyage was hazardous. Heinie Joe's weakness resigned him to let the power of the current keep him on course. Waves broke over the raft and he sat in several inches of freezing water. His attempts to paddle kept his circulation going, though most of the warmth he felt came from his fevers. When he was opposite the lights of the village on the island, the current threatened to carry him past; he had to thrash at the water furiously to break the raft from its grip to float into the safety of the lagoon. It was less difficult there. Rain-tanned swells pushed him toward shore, lurching forward in a long motion and pulling backward in a short one, making each yard gained in sliding stages. He retched, seasickness adding to his woes. Several panicky moments occurred as a riptide veered him from shore. Again, he had to dig his paddle into the sea to ride along with it obliquely until he was out of its grasp. Then the raft seemed to lie still and he knew he was not being pulled seaward but heading to shore. He slid lower on his spine, discerning glimmers of lamps in the opaque screen before him. The community would be confined indoors and shouldn't see him arrive, but there was the risk of someone having business out in the rain: He'd have to take the same care he always did not to be seen.

Now waist deep in the sluggard float, he was insensible to cold and wet. He plunged the small wooden blade mindlessly into the water . . . down and pull . . . down and pull . . . it was as if he made no progress whatever. He grounded stroked down and pulled, stroked down and pulled, stroked and stroked and stroked...and saw there was no farther to go and fell from the raft into the shallows. The paddle floated from him, soon joined by the swamped raft. Half submerged, it was sucked out into the lagoon till the riptide bore it deeper into the channel of the sea, where it started a longer journey. Heinie Joe forced himself up to his hands and knees. The surf rushed under his chest, supporting him and pushing him to land, helping him to creep onto the cement ramp of the village.

It was dark here, as dark as he could have wished; a premature nightfall due to the rain. Any sensible policeman was under a sheltering roof and could not be on watch for him. If he got to his mother's house, there would be safety there...*iie*, would there be? This wasn't where he should be, but there was no place else...nowhere for him to go...nowhere...and he staggered to his feet and climbed painfully and cautiously toward the lights, a long stumble forward with a steadying half step back, still seadazed and controlled by its action upon him. His second paddle, forgotten and unused, bobbed against the ramp, where it was beached and twitched under the raindrops like a live thing.

It was that which alerted the village *junsa* patrolling the wharf and shore. He crouched over it, peered into the rain and heard the boy fall between two boat hulls. He went toward the sound warily, stopped as the boy pulled himself upright again; both listened to the night, sensing the other. But Heinie was willing to believe himself undetected and continued his stealthy entry. The *junsa* followed at a discreet distance.

The enmity remained. Despite Yukiko's gladness to see a man partake of food from her hand once more, she could not forgive Jordan. Serving him, she thought how different this could have been for them. She would have told how it was when the child came; how she had risen, sweating, to her knees to see the caterwauling beast, slipping in her arms like an eel trying to escape the sudden enormity he had entered, butting her with his head and crying out in rage. *Oh, Joe dan-ash, how beautiful he was, our son! I was so proud to see his stem, a protuberance making a rosebud knot between his strong thighs. I have his umbilical yet, wrapped in silk and safely stored . . . but his afterbirth could not be buried inside the threshold of my family home nor near the village itself, for none of this community would wish him to return to it once gone. Hai, he brought unhappiness to others . . . but none to me. Not then. Only now, when I do not know where he is.*

"When was he here last?"

She answered, "Last year. In the fall. He moves like a transient bird, south with the cold, north with the warm. But he doesn't stay with me more than a day or two."

"What does he look like?" Jordan waited expectantly. His question had blurted past his hunger to ask it.

She considered her answer. How does one describe her sole treasure, the object of her yearning and adoration? "He is not unlike any other boy becoming a man. Somewhat taller than most. Had he your coloring, he might resemble you."

"Have you his picture?"

"No. But it isn't needed."

There was accusation present, directed at both the man and his son. Feeling oppressed by her decaying house, Jordan tried to eat what she had given him. The food was unpalatable, being laced with generous portions of an ill-favored seaweed, *wakame,* which soaked in thin ribbons in his broth. He put the bowl down. Rain hammered over their heads insanely.

"You've come for the boy," she said flatly.

He nodded slowly.

"He's not mine to give up any longer."

Jordan hastened to explain, "I would never take him without your consent. You must know that."

"Do I? What man can be kept from his own flesh? It's not me you must deal with, at any rate."

"I suppose not. He'll want to make his own decision."

"If you find him . . ."

They listened to the rain.

"Where shall I look, Yukiko?"

331

"I raised him in Osaka."

"Will I find him there?"

"When I last saw him, he said he was living in Kyoto."

"Where in Kyoto?"

"That I cannot say. You'll have to determine it for yourself."

"Is it that you won't tell me or that you don't know?"

"I don't know where he lives."

"Do you believe he's in Kyoto now?"

"Perhaps. It's as good a city as any to turn upside down for him. But you won't find him in the respectable districts."

A heavy downpour walked across the rooftop, springing yet another leak in the far corner of the room.

"Do you know what they call your son and those like him? *Ainoko*...the love child. And having conferred so sweet a name, the people of my nation promptly gave them hatred. It has made an impression upon those children. It is possible you shall not wish to have him, after all."

Jordan examined her to ascertain her thoughts; she wasn't being vindictive. He asked uneasily, "Has he turned out badly?"

Returning his gaze levelly, she allowed him to answer for himself.

"Well, that can be changed," he argued. "Once he's away from his old life..."

"*Nan no hana desuka.* What is the name of the flower? If you change its location, shall it transform itself into a tree?"

"If he's been soured by your people's prejudice, he'll forget it in my country."

"So. There is none for him in your country."

"No." Her smile angered him and he admitted feebly, "All right, goddamnit, there's a hell of a lot but I can help him fend it off."

"What will they call him in Beikoku?" she goaded, expecting no answer. "Do they have endearing titles for his like? I would be pleased to hear what his title will be in your America." Though he hid his face from her, he was listening and she continued relentlessly to flay him with her words. "I learned many epithets from your countrymen. at my trade. Shall it be one of them? Men were entertained to teach me indecent words and phrases before we whores

332

engaged a student tutor to grant us knowledge of others. Nevertheless, I studied my lessons from both sources well and separated the good from the evil. You had put me upon the right path when you began my instruction—my daydreams led me to think I was preparing myself to live among your people—but after accepting your absence as permanent, the study of your language became merely something I did to make myself more attractive to my customers. A man likes to discuss ambitions and calamities with the woman he buys. He suspects the body she lends him is divorced from affection, so she must pretend a little nonexistent homeyness. Thus, you see, it was good and profitable for me to speak Ei-go with as much skill as yourself."

The rain fell on and on and on to tap a din underscoring the desolate mood they shared. Taking the bowl from his side, she emptied its contents into the iron pot above the coals. She didn't bother to say the slightest amount of food was not to be wasted. When she sat by him again, he could smell her: no more the crushed-pine scent of her maiden days, but acid and stale, smoke-cured and clad indifferently in yesterday's clothing. She was a stranger to him.

"Hey, Oka-san, you running an inn? Maybe you have room for me."

Heinie grinned shakily at the startled couple. He slid the *fusuma* wider and leaned against it, then fell on his face, breaking the fall with his arms. Yukiko and Jordan scrambled to his side. Jordan stared at him. He knew. A son, returning home, does not knock to enter. The weather blew in at them and he ran to close the door. Yukiko began peeling the boy's wet clothing from his shivering body and as she struggled with the sopping material, Jordan hurried to help her.

"There are towels in the *tansu*," she said rapidly, indicating a chest of drawers with her head.

He crossed the room to open a drawer. From an assortment of linens, he took a scrap of knubby cloth; returning to her, he snatched up a quilt which lay heaped into a corner. It required both persons to remove Heinie Joe's trousers, each resenting the thinness of the figure revealed. Yukiko rubbed his skin dry, bitter over his illness. Tucking him into the quilt, they carried him closer to the fire pit. His eyes were shut; his flesh had a green cast, with every vein starkly visible beneath the skin. A pink trickle of blood oozed below the *hachimaki*.

"He's hurt," Yukiko exclaimed with alarm and unwrapped the filthy bandage. She made a woeful noise over the cut on his forehead, which was not bleeding excessively but white from saturation by seawater and rain. Jordan examined the wound anxiously.

"He should have a doctor."

"There are none on the island. We are our own practitioners. When there is serious ailment, the launch takes the patient to the mainland. This is an injury I can mend. For the rest, I'll warm him and feed him. We shall see how he is by morning."

She scurried off to obtain clean strips of cotton cloth and a bottle of sake, which she spilled into a pan to heat over the coals. There was nothing for Jordan to do; he felt useless, impatient to do something for his son. His hands moved involuntarily to touch the boy. He wanted badly to hold him against himself.

Looking at him, he saw little to recognize. The boy did not appear to be tall; if anything, he seemed little more than a child. The tilted folds of his eyelids were as pronounced as that of the woman...hair an uncombed ebony mane...and yet Yukiko said there was a resemblance. He couldn't see any. But that was because he had forgotten the face of his own boyhood. For her, they were identical, merging blue and brown and black and blond into the same golden creatures of her thoughts. Jordan smoothed the boy's hair and held his head as Yukiko fed him sips of hot wine. Reviving slightly, Heinie opened his eyes to look at them. A quizzical wonder manifested in his scrutiny of Jordan.

"I know you...shit, yeah...I do..."

Jordan frowned. The boy had gleaned gutter English from GI friends and foreigners encountered since childhood. What could he expect to hear? "I don't think so," Jordan denied gently. "We've never met."

"But I know you.. I've seen you."

"I don't think so," Jordan repeated. He had no recollection of the incident in front of the hotel in Osaka.

Heinie Joe fought to stay awake. "Well, shit...what are you doing here?"

Jordan was about to reply but the boy lost consciousness. Yukiko put her pan aside at once and cautioned, "Let him sleep. I must do something about his injury and it is best he doesn't know of it." She ran to her cabinets and returned with a small basket. She took a needle from it and a spool of fine silk thread.

"You're not going to sew the wound?" he asked, horrified.

"I must. I've sewn worse in Osaka when troops brawled with each other on our street. This is a minor cut so you needn't fear for him."

She sterilized the needle by turning it over red embers and washing it in the hot wine. While Jordan held their son's head still, she sewed tidy stitches, binding the lips of the wound together. There was blood again but she dabbed it with her scrap of cloth. The boy felt pain within his faint and attempted to pull away but Jordan wouldn't permit it...and then, finished, Yukiko used her strips of cloth to fashion a new bandage around the boy's head. A small red sun bloomed on the cloth at his forehead. She took her sewing basket and the pan away and started to get a pillow for the boy but Jordan stopped her.

"Don't bother with that," he pleaded. "I'll hold him like this for a while."

Acquiescing, she rested upon her heels and watched the man and the boy with sidelong contemplation. In the fire pit, coals rustled as they broke from heated cores into ashen satellites. Jordan could not take his eyes from his son's sleeping face.

"Yukiko," he whispered hoarsely, "what did he look like when he was a child?"

"As you see him. But not so thin. A man sleeps showing his earliest countenance...the dream robs him of his conscious mask..."

The boy looked dreadfully young for his age. Jordan

attributed that to his Oriental ancestry, another Asian trait he found baffling. "What does he know about me?"

"There was a time I used to tell him about his father...but after being jeered at by other children and cursed by adults, he didn't ask to know further."

"When did that happen...when his questions stopped?"

"Ah. It was long after we left this village for Osaka. When he was past six years of age."

Jordan bit his lip. There were father substitutes entering the boy's life then...a succession of them...each for the time it took. Despair welled up in him and he said sadly, "I wish he had continued to think of me."

"Do you truly? What a cruel man you are. He was happier to shed his father's phantom."

Pained, Jordan tried to shift the blame. "I deplore what your people have done to you as a result...what your own family forced you to do..."

"My family had honor," she interrupted. "Until we met. I do not condemn them, for the fault was mine and I freely admit it." And she laughed softly, thinking, *Ask of the honeybee...*

"I share your blame," he said.

"So much that you had no inclination to learn what was written upon the *hagaki* I sent with such hope and gladness."

He recalled the thin postcard with a depiction of the Daibutsu on the face of it—a souvenir card, not an urgent thing to receive. "I've explained why I didn't!" he retorted.

"Hai. A man betrays himself not by answering questions but in explaining himself to everyone." After spitting into the coals, she studied how he sat cross-legged with the boy's bandaged head cushioned on his lap. One of Jordan's hands stroked the damp hair while the fingers of the other curled about the boy's cheek. The meter of the rain was that of a waterfall in their past and she felt the stickiness of her body under her clothing. There was a moistness between her thighs. She got up, really aware of herself for the first time since his arrival.

"With such an abundance of fresh water available, I should take advantage of it."

Jordan watched as she prepared a bath. Bringing small tubs of rainwater from the barrels outside the house, she heated a quantity. When it was hot, she carried it to an alcove, disrobed, and using a discolored chunk of crude soap, she lathered her body. He saw her as a middle-aged woman fleshed with unfirm padding and so unconcerned with his audience that he understood how often she must have done this before other men. Dipping into the water with a clay bowl, she rinsed suds from herself and they ran through the floorboards to the ground below. She dried herself with the same material she used on her son; already dampened, it left her clean skin glistening with moisture. As she dressed again in the sour clothing, he wondered if she had nothing else to wear. He fished out his wallet without disturbing the sleeping boy and removed the money from it.

"Look. Is it possible to get anything you want?"

"Anything is possible with money."

"I meant ... in spite of the rain ..." She was determined to keep him off balance, he thought.

She smiled at him crookedly. "When have you seen a merchant close a shop door with a customer in sight?"

In a hideous way, they seemed to be discussing something else entirely. "I thought that since the boy and I are here ... there must certainly be things you need."

"I have always been in need." She wound her scarf about her head to cover her hair, still long but without its luster, and she said, "Do you want to bathe? There is water in good measure."

"No. I'll just stay as I am." Heinie Joe stirred under his hands, pressing his face against him; he had ceased trembling and had begun to sleep peacefully. Jordan held out his money. "Here. Take this."

She took the money from him without seeing how much it was, the practiced gesture she learned in Osaka. In her day, she could know the amount by touch. Donning a transparent plastic raincoat, she plucked an oiled paper umbrella from the side of the doorway. "I won't be long," she advised him. "No one gossips with me." Not expecting a reply, she let herself out.

Jordan stared down at the boy. He stroked his hair ...

Her *geta* were mud-spattered at once, but tall enough to keep her feet out of the muck. Facing the umbrella to the wind, she forged through the slanting rain. It was a temptation to run so she might accomplish her task quickly and sit once again in the presence of her men. Anger and resentment had been banished during that frugal bath, but it was hard to give up the habit of so many years; the man had aged, of course; they both had aged. And gotten plumper with the wealth of their years. Her heart sank somewhat. She knew she had not fared so well as he. He still bore the fair, young look, the same blueness of eye which had filled her with excitement...she would have to speak with less vitriol when she returned to her house. They might pretend they were truly a family and share a few hours of a life denied her and the boy. Their son. He was unpredictable. It was going to be a peculiar evening, no doubt.

Arriving at the entrance of a shop, she furled her umbrella and stood it to drain outside the door. She clattered across a foyer paved with irregular squares of cement, broken concrete which had been salvaged for the purpose. Counters bearing groceries lined the walls beyond and there was a long table in the center of the shop for fish and meat and other sea produce. A man was there to wait upon her: Masao Masuda, the soldier she and Jordan had seen when the government first brought men home, the same man her friend Natsu had married. Of the handful of village returnees, only he remained; the rest gathered up their shame and went elsewhere, for it was easier to bear the condemnation of strangers.

Masuda watched her silently. She wasn't given a greeting; no one was seen to speak to her whenever she left her house. Yukiko chose a chicken carcass and picked among the better vegetables. And remarkably, she smiled at him. He looked over his shoulder to the room at the rear of the shop. Natsu had her back to them.

338

"You're not unhappy?" he murmured softly.

She laughed with surprise. "I have no reason to be! I have guests in my house." She selected some mushrooms and poked into layers of carrots and asparagus.

"*Hai*...I know. It is said a man is there."

"*Hai*. And my son. *Hai*."

"*Hai*. And your son..."

She wasn't fazed. The spies and busybodies kept the community informed of everything. Why did he look so solemn? "Be pleased for me...as I was for you."

He knew what was meant. After being ostracized socially on the island, he was amazed to be approached by the go-between for the daughter of the shopkeeper. Natsu had witnessed his return and would have no other. Her mother convinced the villagers that Masuda lacked the opportunity to forfeit his life for the Emperor and was an acceptable candidate for the projected marriage. This woman, once the close friend of the bride, had been at the forefront of those to offer him congratulations...but her friendship was lost after she was branded *fushidara na onna*, a slut, for bearing an *ainoko*. All but lost. There were nights when he crept to her *futon* and they copulated furtively and silently then, and he pressed a sum into her hand and stole back to his suspicious wife. It pleased him to think he was being charitable, but he had not visited her since learning the news of the murder of Jihei Segawa. The Shimada house was now being watched by the village *junsa;* everyone knew it. The world itself had its eyes on the village; the name of Joe Shimada and that of the village of his birth had been in the newspapers, on radio and television; the *yoryokusha* were in a sweat to have him apprehended and no longer connected with the community. It was very intriguing. Yukiko wasn't behaving like a woman with trouble.

"I'll take these," she said, indicating her selections. He packed them into a large shopping bag, wrapping the fowl and the vegetables separately. He then added a few tangerines. The gift was observed by the virago in the room at the rear.

"Those *mikan* are overripe," he lied in a whisper. "No one will buy them now. It would be a favor to me if you add them to your meal."

339

"But I have money! I can pay for them. I was given many yen for a feast."

He bowed stiffly. "I didn't mean to offend you."

Seeing his discomposure, she sought to rectify her error. *'Tie.* I am supremely grateful. We shall enjoy your kindness. I only meant that I was able to buy whatever I wish this time."

The air cleared between them. She counted out her money and paid him. As she took the bag in hand, he asked in an agony of embarrassment for doing it, "Who is the man?"

"Why...the boy's father. Who did you think he was?"

"Ah...the American sailor."

"You remember him?"

"I recall everything about that day. I saw him like a tower above the folk on the ramp. I wanted to hate him as I passed...you were so young and beautiful...and he..." He stopped to check his wife's activities. She did not seem to be listening but was occupied with household tasks. "I had never been so close to one of the Beikoku-jin...not even when we were herded aboard the steamships. So...he's back. At such a time." She said nothing, and again he was perturbed with her lack of concern. "Tell me: What is there about him to have misled a Japanese girl?"

"Nothing," she said with a smile. She reflected, picturing Joe-dan-ash sitting on the mat with his son's head upon his lap. "Nothing. He's quite ordinary. He's a very ordinary man, indeed."

They bowed to each other and she left the shop, pausing to take up her umbrella and open it. The rain was merely a sprinkle ruffling puddles at her feet. She felt Masuda's eyes upon her. How should she have answered him? There was no way to explain how a girl gives herself in love once, never to do it so completely again. Nor how that man is forever engraved upon her heart in an exalted place which even he, himself, cannot topple by anything he might do later; that first mystic consummation can never be repeated or duplicated. How many times had she conjured up Joe-dan-ash in her mind while in the arms of another? And then wept...and the man atop her was flattered to think she shed her tears for him. As recently as with this soldier turned shopkeeper, whose visits to her house had been regular as the menstrual tides of his wife. She heard Natsu's high-pitched voice shriek at him within the shop.

"What was all that discussion with the whore?"

"We were agreeing upon a price."

"And which of you was to pay it?"

The taunt was followed by an angry tirade. Yukiko ran from the waspish sounds. Natsu, whose name was summer, resenting autumn's fan. They should still have been sharing confidences and sympathies...but none would do that with her now. She was isolated. When Joe-dan-ash left, she was alone till the child replaced him. The shopping bag thumped heavily at her knee. She slowed to rest a moment and to look at the lagoon below, where flurries of rain whirlpooled on the sea. Azure patches of sky showed temptingly through ragged holes in the clouds, and several sunbeams of the sinking sun straddled an island in the channel. Did Joe-dan-ash think of that island as she did? She smiled at it and resumed her walk. Her unaccustomed cheerfulness prevented her from noticing that she was being watched from every dwelling surreptitiously...and that no one had come outdoors. Like a respectable housewife taking home her purchases, she returned to Jordan and the boy.

"I'm going to be gone for a few days, Hichiriki," Hidenori remarked casually. His son gave no sign of hearing but stared steadfastly at a small screen on the platform of the *tokonoma*. Flickering black-and-white images flashed the sudden starts and stops of a samurai duel. Another Segawa film. A villain fled into a forest and dissolved into a soft-spoken pleasant girl reciting the merits of a new motorcycle. Hichiriki wriggled on his elbows impatiently; he wanted to see what was in the forest. His father pushed a lacquerware bowl to him, offering the candy it contained. Hichiriki accepted a chocolate square, dipping his head to take it from the bowl with his lips. "Not like that," Hidenori reprimanded; the child-man could be infuriating

341

with his animal habits. He gave the bowl to the old nurse-maid angrily. She concealed it behind her back; whatever offended the master of the house was best unseen. Hidenori dissipated his annoyance by directing it at the salesgirl on the screen. "Stockings," he criticized as she perched beguilingly on the shining machine and crossed her legs. He resisted the change in women of his country. Prosperity and technology were very well in their place, but the young people of Japan were too enamored of Western notions. Stockings. To see tourists anywhere was to see everyone dressed alike. Japanese tourists; foreign tourists. Melding. Becoming faceless. Marrying. *Hai,* nationals marrying foreigners. But legitamacy did not alter the bloodlines of the child. And he felt again the rage he had against himself at the birth of Hichiriki, whose lineage was impeccable. What he would have given to show both his sons to the world! Every man stokes the furnace of his anticipation for his firstborn son. Alas, to be unable to accept the felicitations of peers with fatherly pride... and not to exhibit a son. There was a dreadful compensation. There remained an infant to love within the man. No matter how Hichiriki behaved, it was with the innocence of an undeveloped mind. He could be loved openly here, beyond public view — here, in the humane confinement of his suite.

Hidenori thought he'd better do something about phoning Tokyo again. He'd been trying to get Mrs. Asche since receipt of a communiqué from the island village. She must come to Osaka at once. The film resumed on the television screen and Hichiriki pointed excitedly at it. *"Hai,* I see," Hidenori said. "There is a deer running and hiding." He thought, there is a boy running and hiding, too... as he knew he would. The net was drawing tighter after the signal from the traveler in Kurashiki. What a simpleton the fugitive was to give his name! That, with the description Mr. Toba supplied of the boy's appearance, confirmed his identity beyond doubt, and now it was verified that Joe Shimada had forsaken the unrestricted mainland for the false security of his mother's house. The *ainoko* had been slow to do the obvious, but it was inevitable so long as he had freedom to travel. If his head wound was bad, he'd be getting care and rest. What a simpleton to feel safe there.

Hidenori tarried till his son was totally absorbed in the

television drama and then eased from his side. He stood and bowed curtly to the nursemaid, who lowered her head over her knees to the floor. "Don't forget to unplug the set and remove it when the film is over," he instructed her. Her head knocked once upon the mat. Hidenori exited quietly from the room. He followed the hall to the rear of his house; the servants had their own television set going, tuned to a variety show. Someone was playing an electric organ while another person sang. Television. No one lived the right way anymore. Once the evening meal was done, the new family shrine received worship. In most households, the cyclopean box held sway constantly, to be turned off when the last pulsating picture became a blank radiation without sound, illuminating hunched spectators whose shoulders were thrust forward into the blue glow with fatigue. They regard the screen with surprised indignation, as if to find fault with it for having lost the program. And then they dutifully twist the knob, which will be switched on again before many hours have passed to bring the next day's fare. Hidenori wondered why anyone insisted upon deluging themselves with babel in a city filled with noise. It was such a luxury, recordings were being sold to listen to with earphones—the speed of silence at 33 1/3; television sets were advancing into the whole of the land; it was a race to see which would be pushed into the sea first, the growing mass of population or their mushrooming electronic toys.

He arrived at the closet of the banished telephone. Consulting his notebook, he dialed the operator. It was a matter of seconds before he was connected with Mrs. Asche's hotel in Tokyo.

"This is Chief Superintendent Hidenori again..."

"He's still sleeping."

"That's good." Leaving her umbrella outside, Yukiko slid the *fusuma* shut, set down her shopping bag and removed her raincoat. "The rain is ending...there is sunlight over the water."

Jordan was as she had left him, the boy sleeping soundly with his father's hands resting lightly upon his head. Yukiko busied herself with the food, starting to clean and cut it for their meal. Everything was done with an economy of movement; a feeling of domesticity prevailed in the room. When she sat at the edge of the fire pit to cut vegetables into a bowl, she caught Jordan's eyes with a long look. Both smiled sadly.

"He doesn't seem to be bleeding now," Jordan said.

"I've patched him before...he always recovers."

"In the States, we've read of violent demonstrations in Japan. Is he involved with those?"

"I doubt it. But I don't know anything of what takes place on the mainland...or anywhere, for that matter. No one tells me anything."

"Don't you have a television...no radio, either?"

"Now you sound like the boy! I don't want them. I've no need for what they have to say. This is my universe." And her gesture included himself and the boy as well as the room. It inhibited them from speaking.

They wanted to talk about the past years but neither wanted to mention her life in Osaka again nor the woman Jordan married. It was the hearing of it they avoided, not the telling, for what is not heard can be remote and not yet real. They could retain a fiction about themselves. At least they tried. Unsuccessfully.

Jordan started to say, "Do you recall..." and broke off the sentence to begin anew. "There was a child at your sister's house...next to the theater...when I saw you. An old man was teaching him to dance, singing with him. I

344

often found myself thinking of them. What became of the little boy?"

"*Hai*. My sister's son. It was her husband's father who instructed him in the arts of the theater. He is grown now, part of the actor's company, as all the men of the family were. They are traveling now, performing on other islands in Seto Naikai."

"What of the old theater here? Has it been closed?"

"Temporarily. The company will return soon; this is their home, after all. If you were to stay till they are in residence, you could see them perform...and see the child grown up and a man."

"I'd like that but I haven't the time to spare. There's too much to do to get my boy to the States."

It was impossible to converse easily. Everything inevitably led to their sleeping son. He was at once their link and their barrier. The tenuous spell of euphoria evaporated. Yukiko cut precisely at her vegetables. Jordan felt the rise and fall of Heinie Joe's regular breathing.

"You don't want him to go, do you." He'd made a statement of the question.

"Does it truly matter to you what I want? And as to his going, he has already left me. He did that as a child...as I told you. I wished to preserve him and keep him with me, but I lost him...and fear the losing more than most mothers would. You cannot expose a child to depravity and expect him to remain untainted. What was I skilled in? Having learned from you that my body gave pleasure, I used it to provide for your son." She bent over the coals toward him, the reflection casting a red cruel glint into her eyes. "You may not have approved of the home your child and I had in Osaka but it served us well. Much being destroyed in the city, we lived in the shell of a bus. Its broken windows were papered over for privacy...and we had none. Your son conducted riders to me and I collected the fares. Can you imagine what it was like for a frightened girl to give herself to strangers deliberately, not because she wished but of necessity?" Her voice quivered with past injury. "And it was not then a disgraceful choice I made. I sometimes have thought I was condemned less for being promiscuous than for having your son. It was only after his conception that I was rejected...and it was for his father that he was despised." She looked lovingly

345

at the boy for a moment, then said bitterly, "He thought the life we led was normal. And after I was accustomed to having him interrupt my work with his childish intrusions, I permitted him to take up the same game all his friends played. The competition of the infant pimps. And among them he was outcast as anywhere else. Think of it: I have never heard him mention one word of a confidant—a comrade, a girl, a woman—to whom he entrusted his thoughts. He doesn't with me. Who has he spent his hours with? I cannot believe he is always alone. I haven't questioned his doings. It was safer not to know."

They became aware that the rain was over. A concert of inconsistent water cymbals clanged brokenly on the tatami where each leak ended. The papered windows were coppered by the setting sun, now unclouded and painting the countryside and sea from the bottom of the horizon before it sank for the night. And the interior of the room gradually darkened and grew smaller with the fading light.

"There, you see? There is no avoidance of our past. But I shall not ask after the woman of your own house. I have dreamt of a face of chalk and I will not have a body put to it." She may have sensed he was on the verge of telling her Wanda was waiting in Tokyo. Taking up her bowl and knife, she concentrated on her work and continued, doggedly, "But you asked what my wish was in this matter. It is that of any mother for her son. I should like to have him with me always, and I would rather he followed good fortune. It is possible he can make a name for himself if given the chance. Then it matters little who his parents are, and the ashes of my ancestors will cease to stir in the clay. The villagers might even deign to wash from their faces the dirt I kicked there." She pared a radish into a thin unbroken wide sheet. "If my son should choose to go with his father, then he is not altogether lost to me." And she smiled contentedly at the thought. "The beloved are never too far apart to be near...as I have kept you since younger days, so may I keep him as I age. However, Joe-dan-ash...you shall have to ask the boy."

Not since his arrival had she called him by name, and the familiar way she used it now wrenched at Jordan's heart. Something simple occurred to him. "The boy...what did you name the boy?"

346

Her smile broadened. "I once heard that the Beikoku-jin keep the ghost of the father alive in the son...it was before the war when I was very small and a missionary tried to influence the village. And so I named him Joe."

Jordan suppressed a wry laugh. "You named him Joe. I should have guessed."

"Surely it is the best of names in your country?" she asked anxiously. "I knew so many with the name..." Her sentence trailed to a stop. She didn't want to talk about the Joes, the legions of Joes.

"It's a fine name," Jordan reassured her. "Known all over the world..."

Finally at ease, they grinned at each other. The shadows in the room spread and became night. Lighting an oil lamp, Yukiko prepared the meal and served it without awakening the boy. When they had fed, she brought out two *futons* and heavy coverlets, and after undressing without shyness, they lay down side by side. She blew out the lamp. In the faint light of the embers, he could discern the outline of her body. He felt regret for her and nothing more. Averting his head, he studied the face of his son and gradually joined him in sleep.

For Yukiko, sleep came slowly...yet it came. But not before she deplored the sight of Jordan's scars. They were not there before, nor in the vision she'd kept of him throughout the years. A woman sees her lover's form with forgiveness for its faults; whatever new brand appears she regards as a blemish upon herself. Yukiko yearned to smooth the brutal cicatrices from his flesh to restore him to perfection, to make him as he was. Shutting her eyes with remorse, she thought of herself—as she was; what she had become. There would be no change for her...and none for him. The waters of the stream they had shared was run and they would rise from their rest never to meet again.

Heinie Joe held his breath while listening to that of the others in the room. It had been a nightmare when he first awoke, very like the days of his childhood when he heard snuffling sounds in the dark...and upon crawling to his mother's side would be thrown roughly away to console himself. They weren't awake. It was only the regular sighing of two sleepers, but it was a frightening recollection for him. His racing pulse calmed and he noticed the dim outlines of windows and a vague apparitional indication in the fire pit. He tried to remember his arrival—touched his head to feel the new bandage—*hai,* someone had been with her, a man he thought he knew. No. It was the American tourist he'd seen in Osaka. How'd the son-of-a-bitch find his way here? Some old customer must have directed him to his mother's house. But who would want to sleep with her, with the pick of Dotonbori available to him? Or perhaps he was the old customer. That would be funny...and they could have traveled together. It hurt his head to think so hard.

He was hungry. The fevers weren't bathing him in sweat now and he disliked the cool dampness he felt under the musty quilt. He wondered where his clothes were...shit, he was forever looking for his clothes. Then the reality of his situation reasserted itself and he watched the sleepers. If she had to entertain this man, she was useless to him and he'd have to leave. He should leave, anyway. What was he doing on the island? He had to clear off, that was certain. Throwing aside the quilt, he crawled to the fire pit. How cold the room was! The iron pot should have something to eat in it. He dipped a bowl into its tepid contents and was treated to morsels of chicken. He smiled at the obscure lumps on the *futons;* the man must have given her money for food. It would have been nice to stir up the coals for heat. He drew his knees to his chest to keep warm and sat closer to the ashes. The chicken was good.

In the dream, Jordan had his arms around both of them and was saying, "This is your new mother." The woman under his arm cuddled near and smiled as she looked at the boy.

"But he isn't a baby, Jordie. You promised me a baby."

"No, I didn't! Don't you remember, Wanda? It's impossible for you to have a baby."

Her face clouded and underwent a change. Her eyes grew slanted and her hair disordered. The boy leaned to her across Jordan's chest to say, "I know you ... I know you ... I know ..."

"Sure you do, Joe. She's your new mother. I knew you would like her."

"Yeah ... we lived in a bus in Osaka. I know her." The boy grinned at him, and Jordan squeezed his thin figure into a cedar box with white cranes painted above green pine trees on the lid. He carried his son into snow outside the brownstone. Dry fluff crunched under his heels, leaving a flat wake behind. They passed through brick ruins, festooned with streamers of dry kelp. Jordan smelled the sea and saw the Triborough Bridge leading emptily to a destroyed city.

"Shall we pick some kelp?" he asked, and turned the box over to let his son float to the ground. The boy shrank as he fell and when he was waist high, he ran to the ruins and grew even smaller so that he was a little boy leaping high into the air to get at the kelp. Grabbing a handful which broke into brittle cakes, he stuffed the pieces into his mouth and chewed and chewed and chewed and chewed ...

"That's it, you dumbbell! That's the way to do it!" Yukiko snuggled closer to Jordan and he held her with both arms. "You see? He's just as you wanted him to be."

"I didn't want him at all. You're the one wanting him. You want to take him away from me, don't you?"

He was confused. Hadn't his wife said she wanted a little boy? "We can change his name if that's what's bothering you."

She was Yukiko in Wanda's clothes and a young girl again. "What would you change his name to? Would that make him better?"

"Don't you like him?"

"Do you?"

349

He was perplexed. He looked at the little boy beside the ruins and saw him urinating into the snow and sending up a minute column of steam. "I don't know," Jordan confessed plaintively. "I don't know anything about him."

Squirming in his arms, she turned her back to him. They were lying flat upon the snow and he held her as hard as he could. It seemed to make them warmer. He could hear the boy moving around under the kelp and wondered what he was searching for...

It was the man's clothing he found. Automatically, he went through every pocket and was chagrined to find Jordan's wallet empty of yen. She'd been there ahead of him, he thought. Dropping the wallet to the mat, he searched the room until he found his things hanging from a rafter. Not dry; not too wet to wear. He swore softly. She could have hung them nearer the fire pit. The house was a veritable sieve; nothing was really dry in the room. Putting on his shirt and pants was an ordeal; both were like discarded eelskins retaining the frigid air of the rafters overhead. Hair rose from his puckered skin in protest. On tiptoes, he went past the huddled sleepers and slid the *fusuma* ajar enough to get through.

It was so still outside, he thought he heard the stars snap with each twinkle. The air was crisp, swept clear by strong breezes from the sea; there was not a light to be seen but for running lamps passing by on a channel in the harbor. A buoy clanged faintly, calling him. He saw his shoes on the veranda and tried to put them on. They were soaked. Holding them, he stepped to the mud of the path. It was slick beneath his bare feet and wormed icily through his toes at each step. The man assigned to watch the house missed seeing him go.

At the edge of the ramp, Heinie paused. Pushing any of the boats would make noise on that surface; he had to choose one he could handle easily. He walked slowly along the row, measuring and judging. Halfway down the line, he came upon a one-man dory, the perfect boat for him. He gave it a tentative shove and it slid easily, rasping the cement with a thick keel. Heinie pushed faster, propelling it to the sea. The bow hit water and lifted. He was straining to raise the stern in order to push the boat farther when someone clapped heavy arms around him. Heinie fought

350

wildly, kicking and punching in panic. His assailant tripped and was on one knee, shouting, as Heinie made a dash for the village. More shouts were raised, this time from some of the houses. People were calling to each other near the ramp. He dodged into an alley, cut from there to another path. The noise grew fainter as he went higher. Where was he to hide? Where?

Vaulting over a fence, he landed in a courtyard with potted plants defending a low, large building. Banners and posters from a departed production decorated its entrance. It looked gap-toothed with squares of damp cloth...and the door was unlocked. His mother had told him of this place: the theater belonging to her sister's family. It smelled of dust and actors' paints and of cedar and pine planking. The one scent missing was that of the audience animal and its countless delicacies, a creature essence found only where the circus of escape is celebrated. Heinie Joe moved cautiously in the dark, inching deeper into the auditorium and black imaginings. Reaching the polished stage, he could see nothing but felt the smooth, level surface with his hands. He lifted himself to it and crawled blindly across. Suddenly the floor gave way beneath him. The trap had sprung and he dropped into a darker place, as though through the crust of the charcoal burner's mound...and his scream of terror was muffled by a something which enveloped him and wrapped him within itself as he fought. He saw the black woman, her eyes gleaming hellfires as she closed around him, and when fear drained his strength entirely and he thought he would perish, there was nothing; the heat was of his struggle, and there was no fire and no burning and no smoke and no choking charcoal fumes. Just the dust. He was inside the *seridashi*. Alive. And the black woman was a heavy cloth with threads patterning it in whorls. Only cloth. Embroidered brocade for stage plays.

The twin-motored cabin plane taxied to a corner of the civil airfield; its propellers spun faster, then stopped. A limousine rolled smoothly beside it and parked. Quiet prevailed except for the gusting wind, which blew unimpeded across the flat expanse of tarmac and runway lights. A driver got out of the car, shrank into his business suit at the cold and waited. When Wanda stepped from the plane, he ran to her and saluted by bowing and touching the brim of his fedora, which he then whipped off, and he bowed again.

"Ohayo, ohayo!" he chirped enthusiastically as he admired her long sable coat. She brushed past him to head for the car. He was in a dilemma, first legging toward her and then the plane, unable to decide whether to help her into her seat or to take the suitcase handed out from the plane by a uniformed *junsa*. He opted for the luggage, grabbed it and carried it to the side of the limousine, where he peered through the window and again bowed at her, low, to conceal his collection of wealth: gold-rimmed glasses, a gold bridge artfully constructed to contain his horse teeth, and nuggets stabbing his tie, strangling his wrists and finger as well. He was obviously a success as an official chauffeur for the Police Bureau ... and perhaps a failure as one of their detectives. She wanted none of his hospitality.

He stowed her suitcase into the trunk of the limousine and eagerly returned to his seat behind its steering wheel; hot air poured from the heater under the dash, warming him before reaching his passenger, seated numbly behind him. Against her hope, Hidenori had asked Wanda to join him and his staff on their mission to the Inland Sea. She had been required to leave her comfortable hotel suite to be flown to Osaka within moments of his call, escorted every second by sleek young men with military bearing. They were more like highly trained soldiers than police officers, she thought, and she felt like their prisoner. They conjured up nonsense from old movies: atrocities, beheadings, rapes, pyramids of short men planting meatball flags. It was oilly. The young policemen were ultrapolite to her. It made her more fearful.

She was driven through empty stygian streets for some time before they reached the waterfront area. It appeared doubly threatening because of the trash and shuttered warehouses. The pier helped; she welcomed its string of weak light bulbs lighting the distance to the launch. The car rumbled over loosened slabs of heavy planking, sometimes rattling wide iron sheets nailed over deteriorating sections. Fishermen eyed her glumly as she went past. They sat patiently in their established niches, knowing today would be like yesterday, and brooded over their handlines with resentment for the car's loud motor and the vibration it transmitted from pier to sea.

Stopping the car cautiously a dozen steps from the end of the pier, the driver leaped from his seat to get at Wanda's door. He hid his treasure trove again, hissing so lengthily that she longed for a stick. While he got her suitcase, she looked at *junsa* taking it easy among stacks of crates destined for villages and communities along the scheduled run. Men were unloading the cargo from the big launch, stowing it in the center of the pier. People with baggage under their arms appeared from the shadows to move toward the gangway and were stopped by several of the policemen to be advised in low, earnest voices. Hidenori left the group to greet her.

"Thank you, Mrs. Asche."

She wrapped her fur tighter against the chill. The dilapidated motor launch was unappealing. "Is that our transportation?" she complained fretfully.

They gave way for the chauffeur to take her suitcase to the deck of the boat. Hidenori said, "I hope you will manage to sleep during our voyage."

"Is it far?"

"Ordinarily, this launch would call at many ports and be delayed long hours with handling cargo. One would have been obliged to stop at an inn before continuing."

"I'd like that."

He was apologetic. "I intend to reach our destination as soon as possible. We shall make no stops and proceed at high speed all the way."

She glanced at the waiting civilians. "What about them?"

"They are being informed to take the next scheduled launch and will not board with us."

"Just what triggered this burst of activity, Superintendent?"

"Ah... forgive me for not having enlightened you. We were, of course, hoping to arrest young Shimada in Osaka but did not, and expect to do so after we reach the village."

"You're confident you'll find him there?"

"I wouldn't have inconvenienced you otherwise."

"What's to prevent him from slipping away from you again?"

"He can't possibly leave the island now. The boats of the community are under guard and a watch is being kept on the house of his mother."

"He's with her."

"And with your husband."

Wanda ground her teeth. The cold made her shiver. The cold, surely. She hated being there. She commented nastily, "I wish I'd had more warning."

"I didn't want you to do anything foolish."

"What did you think I'd do, Superintendent?"

"You might have attempted to communicate with Mr. Asche had you more time."

And spoil Jordie's reunion, she thought, and said glumly, "I understood there were no telephones... no means of contacting each other from there."

"Every island community has shortwave radio facilities, Mrs. Asche." She smelled of whiskey, he thought. And of the mothball mustiness of her fur coat. Black, lined with red satin, and folded around like wings to keep her warm. But she was cold as ice with him. He disliked her attitude; she wasn't being coerced into taking part in this incident; it was for her husband's benefit. She should be thanking him.

"Are you always so dedicated when nabbing your juvenile suspects?"

Thanking him instead of mocking him. But he replied with unruffled courtesy, "It's particularly important that this boy be brought to trial, Mrs. Asche. I assure you, he will not be treated as an ordinary criminal."

"Is his trial to be some sort of show?"

"We can't avoid one. Think of what the boy has done to Japan."

She scoffed at him. "A *cause célèbre* over the murder of a homosexual?"

"Jihei Segawa's amatory preferences were his own private affair. If not actually sanctioned by us, they are not condemned, either." His polite smile altered and was gone. "The loss of any artist is irretrievable, Mrs. Asche," he said somberly. "We thought of Mr. Segawa as a national treasure. His talent was a gift from heaven and we shall not see his like again."

He turned from her to inspect the preparations. Done with the cargo, workers had stopped to smoke cigarettes and talk. The *junsa* behaved like groggy family pets impatient to seek pillows; they watched Hidenori for a sign to board the emptied launch. He glanced at the sky. Because there was no moon, the stars were brilliant. Each day makes certain demands; he knew this morning would have a scarlet beginning. He snapped an order at his men and they scrambled into the launch. Then he inclined a slight bow at Wanda and suggested, "If you step aboard now, I believe we may get under way."

He followed her down the short gangway onto the launch. Raw diesel flared their nostrils and a gentle heave weighed them as they walked across the deck to the wheelhouse, where the captain gave them a sloppy salute. The jovial blue-jawed man wore a Taiwan plastic slicker, shredded with use; his legs waddled beneath it inside mismatched gum boots cut open in front to make room for his toes. Hair stubbled from his shaven head in serrated tufts attesting to self-barbering. He was aware something of significance was in the wind for these gentlemen and the foreign woman to disrupt his cargo deliveries. Full Speed! He had always wanted to see what his craft could do unloaded and with the engines pushed to their limits. The honor of transporting the Bureau Chief Superintendent of Kansai Province was in itself a dish to relish. Emboldened by his good fortune, he attempted to engage the great man in conversation.

"It is seldom a sparrow may mix in the dance of cranes, Chief Superintendent!"

Hidenori was abrupt with him. "This lady will have her breakfast in here, Captain."

"I have it ready for her." He produced an oily rag with a flourish and wiped the seat of a stool welded to the deck beside the wheel and gestured at it, leering at Wanda like a bandit. *"Koshi kakeru,"* he invited. She sat down gingerly, remembering with a guilty twinge the cleanliness of another place and another person wiping dust from an immaculate chair.

Hidenori nodded amiably at her. "He'll bring your tray when we are at sea...and later there is a bunk prepared where you may nap."

"I don't think I'll want to, Superintendent."

"As you wish." He barked at the captain, "Get under way."

"Hai, at once!"

They cast off, lighting their course with red and green lanterns at the sides of the launch. The bay was crowded; barges were bound together near the piers like captive whales. Nothing else moved in the harbor but the motor launch, humming and coughing itself awake. Drowsy merchant sailors standing port watches yawned to see the early departure and flicked cigarette stubs into the water in meteoric farewells which snuffed out under its pinking surface. The bay was a bowl of tinted colors emerging slowly from the lifting night to reveal the pine-hooded islets, for once not shrouded with fog. Only the persistent morning mists stretched shredded strands one to another in coves. The widening wake of the motor launch raised swells undulating to the plump cargo ships, tilting them off center to look down at the disturbance with their masts and hoists before settling firmly back upon Plimsoll marks with contempt. And for a while, a mauve hue dominated everything but failed to hold off the inflexible advance of an unseen sun...

Jordan stirred, opened his eyes and stared at the woman in his arms. The drop in temperature had brought them together in the night for warmth. She slept soundly, shut away from yesterday and today and the thing neither knew was to come. Examining her closely, he saw the unguarded face with all its wear exposed...a woman-mask in that balm which falls graciously upon the living in recurrent swoons to accustom them to eventual oblivion. Do we age in the waking or always? And if always, then the practice is wickedly disarming. When a boy, Jordan bemoaned the loss of hours given over to sleep; he did it still, though yearning for the peace brought him...provided he did not dream. Dream? Was Yukiko dreaming? She breathed evenly and her closed lids twitched. What was she seeing? Hadn't he dreamed of his son? He turned to look at him.

Jordan sat up, almost calling out with dismay. The bowl at the fire pit was mute evidence that the boy had eaten. His rumpled quilt lay untenanted upon the floor. The walls of the room reflected dim light from the windows; shadows were climbing imperceptibly to the rafters to wait for night again. Reaching to where it had been dropped, Jordan picked up his wallet. He opened it sadly, saw the empty compartment and wished he had left something for the boy to take. Well, Joe couldn't go far without money. Joe. Joe...he wasn't sure he thought of him as Joe yet. So far, it was always "the boy" or with chary conviction, "my son." Turning his wrist to the meager light, he tried discerning the time on his watch. There was ample time to get to the wharf. The launch wasn't due for hours. The boy... Joe...couldn't leave the village any sooner. He'd see him there. Christ. The kid didn't even know who he was.

"So. He's gone again."

Jordan didn't move. He replied optimistically, "I'll catch him before he can leave. On the wharf."

Yukiko wanted to console him. She had awakened at his movements and watched silently as he discovered the

357

absence of their son. "He would have stolen whatever he found in your wallet."

"I know that. But he doesn't know I'm his father."

"He would have taken it anyway."

Annoyed, he turned to her. She was smiling at him, an understanding twist of mouth which said much of her acceptance of what the boy had become. But what lurked within her eyes was different; there was unhappiness and fear and mockery and frustrated longing. And Jordan saw regret, the accusatory expression of a woman rising from her bed after a loveless night, untouched and undesired by the man at her side. The flicker of mockery was for herself; she would have been fornicating again in the presence of her child, just as she had with her thousand Joes of yesteryear. And there was also her realization that she was not the girl Joe-dan-ash had loved but only an aging, retired whore. Jordan could not guess her thoughts. He drew his scattered clothing to himself and began to dress.

Rising, Yukiko took up the familiar duties of her day. She went naked to the coals and blew them to life while stoking the fire with fresh tinder and charcoal...*hai,* she could have been an inn servant tending to the man's needs. She spat into the fire pit and Jordan thought he heard her chuckle.

"I'd like some coffee," he said, and felt foolish. He was treating her as though a paying guest.

"*Hai.* I'll have it shortly. It is made with a powder. Is that all right?"

"Sure." They were mad for instant coffee in the Orient. He'd had the same on the plane, and at the inn, and now here. She put on her clothing and prepared the coffee for Jordan. He drank it with quick sips when she gave it to him in a thin cup which scalded his fingers. Yukiko put the *futons* away, lingering over the boy's quilt as she folded it, and then she sat across from Jordan with her own cup. The room was warmer. And no longer dark.

That's how they were when Superintendent Hidenori knocked politely. Unprepared, Yukiko crossed the room to slide the *fusuma* open. The sky flared outside, searing aquamarine and bright blue with fading red streaks. Against the light, the man and the American woman were hard to distinguish, and Yukiko squinted at them with puzzled concern. The Superintendent had done this many times... and he did it well.

"I am Chief Superintendent Hidenori of the Regional Police Bureau... and this is Mrs. Asche. I believe her husband is your guest."

Behind her, Jordan was taken by surprise. He rushed to the door with amused disbelief. "I thought you were in Tokyo..." Wanda shrugged at him. He looked at Hidenori and noted there were no smiles. Jordan gaped uncomprehendingly at both visitors, then at the *junsa* on the street.

Yukiko studied the foreign woman with terror; she brought misfortune with her, of that she was sure. Hidenori addressed her again. *"Anohito wa kaetta kimashita."*

Darting her eyes at him helplessly, she clasped her hands and admitted, *"Hai,* he came back. But he has gone again."

The superintendent cleared his throat. "It would be best to speak inside your house."

Yukiko reddened. *"Gomen nasai,* excuse me! Please to enter!" Bowing deeply to hide her dismay, she backed from the door. She did not wish to see the *junsa* waiting on the street.

Hidenori, shoeless, entered with Wanda. Her heels made round holes in the tatami, which sprang smooth again after each step. Unease ruled the quartet. Without being obvious, Hidenori surveyed every detail of the room. Jordan said apologetically to Yukiko, "I was going to tell you: My wife has been waiting for me in Tokyo."

Frightened, she backed from him and the others. "Is it by force you wish to take my child from me?"

359

Appalled at her assumption, he tried to go to her but she backed more. "No...that's not..." He looked angrily at his wife. "For Christ's sake, what are you doing here? I told you to wait for me."

Wanda's throat was dry; she wished she had a drink. The flask was in her pocket but she couldn't use it openly here. "I was invited," she answered shakily.

Then he couldn't restrain his excitement and exclaimed, "I saw my boy! I've got to chase down to the wharf to keep him from leaving. The launch wasn't supposed to be here for hours."

"He's not going anywhere, Jordie," Wanda interrupted harshly. "Not without company." Unable to continue, she said, "Superintendent?"

Jordan had a sudden foreboding. They were too serious. He appealed to the man with his wife. "Okay...what's he done?" He plunged on without waiting for the explanation. "The boy's done something stupid, yes? Stolen something. Look...let me fix it." When Hidenori didn't respond, he shifted to being confidential. "Look...I want to adopt the boy. He's my son. We're going to take him back to the States with us. You'll never have to worry about him again."

"I'm not concerned with theft."

Jordan blinked at the man, then looked to Yukiko. She advanced a step, saying hesitantly, "He has not stolen?"

Hidenori was astonished. "You know nothing of what your son has done?" He thought it impossible, but it was so. He pitied her.

"So...he has not stolen..." Her voice cracked on the last word. She needed Jordan's support badly...and would not seek it. She noticed a draft of cold air streaming through the house and went to close the door. It was a thing for her to do, a busyness to let her mind sidestep what the Superintendent was saying. Or not yet saying. He was going to confirm her growing apprehension. He would tell her that her son had done a frightful deed. This official and the foreign lady would put out the sun...her son...the shining fabric she had woven out of distress and her loneliness. She shut the door slowly, sliding it with deliberateness against the inquisitive world outside, against those who told her nothing, carrying out the task with as much delay as she could muster for fear of hearing it now.

"Where has the boy gone?"

Yukiko did not lift her head. "We believe he went down to wait for the launch."

Hidenori grunted. "He was near the wharf but not for that. We've come too early and he would not have guessed at our arrival."

"*Hai*, you've come early," she said flatly. Yukiko hurried past to hunch down into her accustomed seat at the fire pit.

Jordan stared from one person to the next. His face was drawn; the fuse of his temper shortened. "What the hell is this?" he demanded impatiently.

Hidenori cast a short look at Wanda before answering. "Your son is wanted for murder, Mr. Asche."

Stunned, Jordan challenged him derisively. "Just like that? Is that all? Is that how you tell me?"

"My regrets, Mr. Asche. You asked...and I replied."

"Jesus..." Jordan choked, "it's a game with you, isn't it?"

"I consider my work a lifelong profession...or obsession, if you like. Keeping order requires little finesse."

Jordan blustered vehemently, "This is a young kid we're dealing with. He's not a man yet!"

"Quite so. If you think of it, murder and violence are the acts of children. They begin with games against each other and by warring with their elders...and the combatants invariably become one as the young are absorbed into the ruling class, that very same army which reproduces its own enemy again. Only the Law and its officials remain truly parental." Hidenori sat beside Yukiko upon the tatami and inhaled the aroma of her hot coffee appreciatively. She still had some heating in a small pot over the coals.

Jordan couldn't believe this dispassionate behavior. He complained to Wanda impatiently. "Wanda, he doesn't understand."

"There's nothing we can do, Jordie."

"No, you have to make this guy understand. I want my son." He clutched at her arm. "I've got to have him."

She removed his hand forcibly, pulling the fingers away one at a time. She didn't like being physically hurt, and his grip would leave a bruise in spite of the thick fur of

361

her sleeve. "Don't be a fool," she snapped. "The Superintendent has a job to do. It's his duty, Jordie."

"It's my son!" Jordan cried out indignantly.

Her mouth twisted. "Yes, your son. And he's about to become famous."

He echoed, "Famous?"

She sounded remote as she continued. "He killed a celebrity, Jordan. But you shouldn't have me tell you. Ask the Superintendent about it."

Her strangeness alarmed him. "You haven't any intention of helping me," he accused, caustic with realization.

"What can I do?"

"You're happy as hell about this, aren't you?"

"Not in the least. I wish we had never made this disastrous trip!"

They were shouting now, without regard for the onlookers. "Goddamnit, you agreed to let me find the boy!" The Japanese averted their faces from the Americans and listened uncomfortably to the argument as it raged.

"Under duress, Jordie. I had no alternative. You forced me to make this effort for you."

Jordan choked up, feeling betrayed. Punishing words burst from him. "No matter what you promised, I sensed that you would never really want him. You and your fucking noble effort," he raged. "Well, I don't give a shit. He's for me, anyway. Not for you. For me! Just because you couldn't have a child doesn't mean I'm to be deprived of mine!"

She retorted defiantly, "I'm here, Jordie. I was determined to do everything, suffer anything to keep you. When we met, you hadn't known me half an hour before saying you wanted me to be the mother of your children. I wasn't a virgin but I remember blushing. I was already in love with you and it was all I could do to keep from leaping into the nearest bed so we could begin making your babies. Well, it's not ending happily ever after, Jordie. We got the shitty end of the stick, you and I. I know what this boy meant to you...and how I felt about him. You can't have this baby either. He's set up too many obstacles, far more than I thought to overcome." It made no impression on her husband. He was regarding her stonily. "I can't help you with this, Jordie."

362

"I wish we'd never met," he said unreasonably. "You've given me nothing and you're still giving me nothing."

His injustice infuriated her. She lost her head, wanted to hurt him in retaliation. "I'm not taking that, Jordan," she stormed at him heatedly. "Every expert and quack I saw said we lose and you agreed it wasn't my fault...but that didn't stop me from feeling guilty. I've tried to drink it away, Jordie...but it didn't do it. You were so busy feeling sorry for yourself, you've forgotten about me. I've had to try to overcome my misery without your love and understanding...and now you want my sympathy. Well, I used it up, Jordie. I used it up on myself because I didn't have someone to ask for any...someone I'd known forever as you did." He whirled from her, shaking his head. He didn't want to listen, but she taunted him pitilessly. "No, I don't want the son you have here, the son of your whore. Do you want the rest of the details? Shall I tell you what else your son is?"

He recoiled from her cruel attack; weak-kneed, he willed himself to stand. The boy's ingenuous face had been under his hands for most of the night; he had taken him into a blissful future of partnership and continuation. They'd be father and son together, men together. "No," he said bitterly. "No...I don't want to know. Not from you." He rasped at Hidenori, "You tell me. You do it. That's your job, right? Do your fucking job."

"Well, then. Your son killed the actor Jihei Segawa."

"Go on."

"It happened at Mr. Segawa's house...in his bedchamber. They were known to be...intimate friends."

"Don't pussyfoot with me. You're telling me my son killed some lousy pervert. What makes you so goddamned sure the man didn't deserve it?"

"That may or may not be true. However, the boy is not a lotus flowering in the mire of our society, Mr. Asche. He has led a dissolute childhood and grown up in criminal ways. His fate was sealed at the moment of his birth."

"How can you say that? The man was a homosexual...a sick man with a healthy boy."

"Is it healthy to carve someone into bloody meat with multiple strokes of a sword?"

"You bastards should know."

Jordan stumbled from him to sit on a chest below the

window overlooking the lagoon. Wanda was exhausted. She saw no other seat and went to sit beside him. He kept his head bowed over his clenched hands, ignoring her ... then muffling his hurt, he pivoted to throw open the papered window. Sunlight blinded him.

Yukiko was old Ooba-san again, snugged fast to her ashes. There was no reading her face. Spitting into the coals, she felt the heat and wondered if her son was warm. The growls about her had turned garbled and indistinct and it was an effort for her to concentrate upon what was being said ... yet, if she was to know what was to become of her son, she had to maintain contact. The trouble was thinking of every place of hiding he might choose ... and she was fearful that the very thoughts would transmit themselves to the man sitting next to her, the inoffensive-looking gentleman with the power of life and death in Kansai Province. Mindful of her duties, she meekly poured him a cup of coffee from the pot on the fire and he kept his gaze fastened to her over his cup ... and there was no menace there. It wasn't necessary. If anything, she detected sorrow. That was remarkable to her. She swallowed hard and spat again because it helped to keep tears from forming.

Superintendent Hidenori set down his cup. "You have relatives living in the village."

After he was born, she used to take him over the water to the love island and they would spend the day. It took them from the sight of the villagers and they could be tranquil for a while, unchallenged by scorn. The boy made mounds of sand, tunnels, deep pits for unwary fiddler crabs and sand hoppers ... or they went high into the mountain, he riding on her shoulder and arm like a coddled prince. He was too young to retain the memory but he had seen the place where he was conceived.

"An elder sister ..."

"Do you think the boy is with her?"

364

"I know he is not. She has not spoken to me since we were young girls. She despises the boy."

She had placed the child on the ground near the pond. It would have been good for them to share it as she had with his father but the water was too cold and she would not risk the child. The sun warmed them. The boy would have loved that glen had he grown to know it.

"And can you tell me if there is anywhere in the village or its surroundings some hiding place he might have used when he was a child here?"

"He was only a baby here. We left before he learned to walk."

"Then he does not know the village?"

"Not at all." Her gaze remained centered upon the ashes. "I am all the village he has ever known. He could hide only in my arms."

How often she had yearned for the child of the arms, the helpless babe that clings with loving ferocity. She had told Joe-dan-ash the boy left her after they returned to the village... but it wasn't entirely true. The child leaves the parent with the first unheld footstep, when it discovers that breathtaking freedom of walking without the tether of the hand. The small male becomes a man upon raising himself from a fall with triumphant laughter, pushing to his feet and surveying the world slyly as he continues his tremendous adventure; he has left the land of the beast, the creepers upon four legs; he is bound no longer by earth and can regard the stars with speculation.

"I see." The smile the Superintendent formed with his thin lips was mirthless. Tracking the quarry was simplified by the boy's circumstances. It would not be in the home of a neighbor that he would be found. Standing, he went to the door and opened it. The local village *junsa* stood sleepily on the roadbed with the dapper men who had descended upon the community from the hold of the launch. All turned attentively as the Superintendent spoke. "He is not here. You will make an inspection of the village and its environs. It isn't necessary to search the households since the boy is an *ainoko.*" He dipped his head in acknowledgment of their salutes and pulled the *fusuma* shut.

Yukiko was staring at him, probing for his thoughts with a curious, spellbound calm. He had seen a pigeon

365

once, held prisoner by a large orange cat. The cat had straddled the wings with both front paws from behind so that the pigeon squatted beneath his jaws and could look over its back at the cat. The cat stripped feathers from the bird's body and tail, using its smiling fanged mouth with precise delicacy, and paused sometimes, eyelids half closed with ecstasy to look into the eyes of its victim—whose little eye, rounded into an appalled exclamation, mirrored the benign furred countenance; and yet the pigeon seemed detached from its own destruction. Hidenori recalled how human the skin of the bird was beneath the feathers, rapidly being exposed and dimpled like that of someone badly chilled. As the woman was now. He could almost hear the fluttering pulsation of her heart.

"They will look for him but have received prior orders not to attempt to take him. I shall do that myself when he is found."

Staring, staring. Fearing. She saw how implacable he was, and she crossed her arms over her body, over the first house of the child, over the dry, choking sobs that were spawning inside like screams beneath water.

"*Hai* ... you will do that when he is found."

Hidenori understood her meaning. He hoped it would not come to violence, that the boy would be reasonable and would give himself up readily. Moving forward, he stood beside Jordan. Wanda edged away, not wishing to be intrusive.

"Mr. Asche.... I wonder if you will assist us."

Tilting his head slowly, Jordan regarded him with open hostility. "Why should I?"

"To help your son..."

A savage snarl ripped from Jordan's mouth. "To help my...! What do you want me to do, lead him out for you? Tell him I'm turning him over to you for his own good?" Resentment ravaged him. "Christ, I want to get him away from you. If you let me out of here, I'll damned well try to find him before you do."

"You are perfectly at liberty to do as you wish, Mr. Asche. In fact, I would be pleased if you would seek the boy and find him first. He would be less apprehensive of his father than of a police official."

Jordan lurched to his feet and crossed the room to the door. Feeling stifled, he threw the *fusuma* aside with a rough thrust of his hand. *Look at that. That's sunlight out there. The street looks scrubbed. The houses of the village have a sparkle. It isn't fair,...the fucking day doesn't give a damn about my son.* Numbly, he declared, "The boy doesn't know I'm his father." In the silence following, Hidenori and Wanda exchanged a startled glance. As Jordan walked out onto the veranda, he mumbled, "I didn't get a chance to tell him..." And he sat down out there, in the knifing crisp air with a hint of warmth far out of reach.

Wanda shifted disconcertedly as Hidenori approached to sit beside her. He must regret having brought her, she thought. Though suspecting he wanted to talk, she stood abruptly, fishing in the deep pockets of her coat for a package of cigarettes. She found it pressed to the flask. A book of matches from the hotel was in her other pocket. If only she were in Tokyo! She lit a cigarette, then held the spent match fastidiously to take to the fire pit to dispose of it. As it dropped to the ashes at Yukiko's feet, the woman looked up sharply at her. Wanda returned the gaze steadily, concentrating to control the involuntary trembling of her fingers as she raised her cigarette to her mouth. How could Jordan have slept with anyone so ugly? On impulse, she offered the cigarette package. "Smoke?" Yukiko took one and accepted the matches. She noted the crest of the expensive hotel on the cover of the matchbook before tearing a match free to light her cigarette. "Have you been there?"asked Wanda, and caught herself, knowing it had been stupid to say. The woman could never have been there.

"*Arigato,*" Yukiko replied and returned the matches. She resumed staring into the fire pit while she smoked the tobacco. Past its tang, the lady beside her smelled of many perfumes.

Wanda felt Hidenori's interest boring into her back. It wasn't possible to ignore and she sought to convince him she was unconcerned. The obvious out was to engage the Japanese woman in some inconsequential conversation. Wanda didn't want to go so far as to sit beside her on the unsavory tatami, so she spoke while standing. "I was wondering..." Yukiko raised her face to her. "The Superintendent has told me of the sad life you've led. How do you manage now?"

Yukiko compressed her lips, then decided to answer.

"If it had been me, I would not have asked your question."
Her glance flicked toward Hidenori for an instant. "I am
not engaged in my old profession," she declared, thinking
of the village men who also denied it to their wives.

"Surely you have means of support?"

Hidenori listened with a fixed expression. Yukiko knew
he waited for her answer, too. The foreign lady was a nettle
she could not shake.

"Who looks after you?"

"Who, indeed?" With reluctant compliance, Yukiko got
to her feet to go to a nearby cupboard. "I have an agreement
with a merchant of Mihara. Because I was taught *kimi-
komi*, the art of dressing dolls, he sends me scraps of silk
and brocade." From the cupboard, she produced a small
unfinished figurine. Although the painted head was clown-
ish without its wig, the body was already clad in a kimono
and obi. Yukiko reached into the cupboard for another
doll, this one unclothed and stiffly postured—a frozen
white succubus with a livid, passionate face. Yukiko
glanced from it to the other woman with recognition of the
resemblance and said, "I am sent also the dolls and cloth
and spools of thread on a regular basis and work with
them when I please." She raised the figurine for Wanda
to see. "You may think this a toy...but this is a woman.
She permits a man to touch and enter her secret places,
thinking his desire is to pleasure himself. But she is wrong
if she thinks that only. He seeks to return to his beginnings. He does not reflect upon the awkwardness of the
coupling for he seeks to reproduce himself...for through
his child he lives again." Yukiko held Wanda's eyes im-
placably with her own. "The woman may not know she is
to open the door to forever for him. She tries to bind him
with nests and cages to make herself secure. She may do
the best she can...which is to bring forth his son. And if
she cannot...what is there to hold the man's love? I have
not been a wife, but I would have called your husband
shujin had he been mine. Do you know the word? It is one
of two we have here, each a function of loving and giving.
Shujin is 'my lord and master'—what every wife dutifully
calls her husband. And the other word is *shinju*—an in-
version of letters, barely noticeable—but now meaning a
double suicide. The ultimate gift exchanged by people
deeply in love. But you need not fear...Joe-dan-ash did

368

not love me so much. Which is why I am here. Is it why you are here?" Expecting no reply, Yukiko returned both dolls to the cupboard. "A woman must give all and beyond that when she has nothing else to give." She underlined the remark with a slight accusatory pause, then shut the cabinet door and padded back to the fire pit.

Wanda felt cold. Exposed. The rebuke was too pointed. She puffed her cigarette with irritation. When the Superintendent spoke to them, the women turned as one. Hidenori's features were complacent as he indicated the doorway.

"Mr. Asche has decided to help us."

The veranda outside was empty.

There are those who will say unused theaters who emptiness . . . and they would be in error. The space is filled with phantoms, inhabitants of fables who have become too real to be swept away. Sighs and abrupt sounds announce spirit performances, and the applause is created by the rustle of mice in the pit. There is never any emptiness. If one concentrates and looks very hard, the masked figures will become visible . . . from the rotting stones of Greece to the scented runways of Seto Naikai. And if the pine trees are not similar, the outer surroundings seem to be . . . and if not that, then know that the inner temple is unchanging. Those who dance before mankind give up mortality to take on the trappings of gods; they speak thunders; they bestow the balm of escape. But do not go into their dens, behind the draperies, past the painted doors, under the stages. Not when they are not there. For then the silks and velvets hang like shrouds, the swords and lances lie in disarray and the phantoms are envious clouds of smothering dust moving fitfully. You see, they want to live again . . . they never wanted to die.

And should you come alone into their presence, and should you fall asleep, it may be you will not wake again.

Or it may be that when you waken, the play is about your-
self...and it is the final scene...and it is a tragedy.

Heinie Joe was rolled into a ball, one arm flung over
his face and covered with a length of old embroidered silk
someone had stored beneath the stage. It would have been
good to sleep, he thought, if only to pass the time, but he
could not. There were movements beyond the corners of
his eyes which turned his head but he saw nothing that
might have made them, and so he hid his face in the crook
of his arm while beneath the cloth his other hand comforted his crotch; a man resumes childhood easily when
he is alone and prodded by fear. A board stretched somewhere in the theater, pressing noisily upon another to force
itself room. The temperature was rising slightly and the
theater had to accommodate itself to a dew-encrusted roof
beginning to steam vapors under the sunlight. There were
whispers in the rafters. For the boy under the stage,
swathed in faded jade and gold, it was terrifying.

Like a lodestone, the theater pulled Jordan along
cramped streets to its courtyard. He stopped before the
weathered façade, once more seeing garish posters and
gaudy cotton banners and slick photographs. Dust layered
edges where wind and rain had not scrubbed, and the
entrance had the faceless aspect of something closed and
unused. Past the guardian potted plants, the house of Yukiko's sister shed rainwater and basked in the wintry
morning light with shadows peeling from its walls. There
were only women's clogs beside the door, spaced out of
habit, leaving room for those of the family's men, who were
on tour. Two young hens trod resolutely in the mud, raking
their feet industriously and pecking into the furrows with
questing beaks. A cock, scrawny from the chase, jittered
luxurious tail feathers and stalked each bower in turn only
to flee with alarm when the hens denied him. He glared
from a short distance, first with one lascivious eye and
then the other. He expanded his chest and made believe
he'd had them both. He crowed magnificently but it was
a sham which gave itself away by the rueful attempt he
made to approach again. The arrival of the man disturbed
him. A leg poised in midair each time, the cock stepped
warily and haltingly and finally sped around the side of
the cottage to consider how best to mount the hens.

Jordan put his hand to the gate on the wooden fence

and it creaked open, a small nattering not unlike that of a wailing cricket. Entering on the toes of his own shadow as it preceded him, he had no doubt but that this was where he would find his son; there was nowhere else the boy could have gone. He really didn't want to flush him out for Hidenori and had gone seeking the boy with the despairing thought that there was yet something he could do. Of course, it was cruelly ludicrous: There was no eluding the tightening net of the police, and it was impossible to leave the village except by sea. The Superintendent had only to wait for the boy's surrender.

This time, Heinie definitely heard a man-made sound. He recognized the stealthy opening of the main door and then hesitant footsteps which made a short entry and now scuffed quietly in place. Tense, he listened for the next movement. Whoever it was chose to stand there...doing what? He would have risked a look but was afraid any activity he initiated would be detected. It was better to wait...and it would be wise to arm himself. There were plenty of things here —props for plays, yet lethal, for they were not toys and had been fashioned by skilled armorers. He took up a quiver of arrows and a short bow, a slender weapon which curved back upon itself like the horn of a gazelle. He let the aging cloth slip from him and stood with an ear pressed to the flooring of the stage above his head, listening.

The man sighed heavily once. His weight shifted. Then he called softly, "Joe?"

The boy listened.

The phantoms paused, looked haughtily at the scene and then assumed positions in the sectioned auditorium to watch the drama unfold. Jordan advanced another step, gazing restlessly around the theater. Behind him, sunlight stabbed from the open doorway into the dimness to push a third of the distance to the stage before the lintel pinned its edge to the clay floor. From the past, an old fear leaped into being. There were bogeys in the darkness surrounding him and he had to discern them before they reached him— they were closing in, drawing near with incredible speed and awesome purpose; diving, diving into the beating silence. Heartbeats of silence. As at the edge of sleep the twin of death. I'm afraid, thought Jordan, but he's afraid, too. We are both fearful...as I was then and am again.

And there is no smiling, sallow man to welcome me and explain what takes place here this time.

"Joe? Joe?"

More silence.

"Joe?" A scampering in the eaves. "Hey... are you here?"

Intense listening.

"Don't be afraid..."

Silence.

"You hear, Joe?"

Silence.

"Hey, Joe... you hear me? Come out where I can see you..."

A word sibilated out in a long, thin whisper which ended in a hard, plosive exhalation. A street word... but a word. His face relaxed and he almost smiled; the leopard in his gut ceased to sharpen its claws. Sinking to his haunches, he stared at the stage. The expletive hummed in the air. They had established communication.

Listening. Listening.

"Look... about what's happened. I know how a thing can get out of hand. A kid gets propositioned by some queer and doesn't know how to handle it. We can get you out of this. The man forced his advances on you and you defended yourself. That's how it was, wasn't it? You can't be charged with murder..."

What is he saying? thought the boy. That's not what happened to me... not in Kyoto... and not in Osaka... and not anywhere.

"Please... you've grown up thinking you didn't have anyone on your side..."

How did he know?

"But you've got me now..."

The sun was withdrawing subtly, unwilling to stay.

"Please trust me..."

Cash on delivery and no credit. Unless I like you and I don't know if I do.

"We could have talked last night but I wanted you to sleep..."

Talk, talk, talk. Why is this man so persistent?

"And you left before anyone was awake so we didn't get the chance to find out about each other..."

My mother said when a man talked much it was because

372

he was shy or because he needed more than he paid for with his yen. What is this man's need that he wants to talk?

"You were sick last night. Are you better? I'm worried about you...please answer...you've got to trust your own father. That's who I am, Joe. Your mother calls me Joe-dan-ash..."

So. This is Joe-dan-ash. And he wants to help. Where the hell were you all these years, Joe-dan-ash? Where, when I was young? Do you know what a little boy likes to do best? He likes to hold the hand of the giant who is his father and tries to match his stride. I have held the hands of many men, matched many strides to lead them to my mother. And now I am no longer a little boy. You can't hold my hand now. You mean nothing to me, Joe-dan-ash. Go away, go away.

"When I was told about this...I thought everything was finished. But it can't be. We can't lose now...both of us. I'll get the best attorneys there are to defend you..."

Go away, Joe-dan-ash.

"And when it's all over and everything is all right again, I'll take you with me...to the States..."

To the States. The magical journey. The dream of my mother. Mine. When this is over? Oh, Joe-dan-ash, what a lot of...

"That's why I came here. To find you. To tell you...and to take you home with me..."

Home?

"Do you understand, Joe?"

What is "home"? Where is the dwelling of my father? Do you know where I have lived, Joe-dan-ash? My home was anywhere I slept. And others have asked to take me...and some I asked. Does anybody hate you, Joe-dan-ash? Does anybody use you like a package they can throw away in the morning?

"Joe...are you listening?"

Listening. Listening.

"Joe...Joe, you're important to me. You're...you're the only...son...the son I've ever had...could have..."

Something wrong. He's stopped talking.

"Oh, Joe...I don't want to...to...lose..."

Joe-dan-ash is crying. Oh, shit, Joe-dan-ash, go away. You are going to make me weep and that is not the way of the warrior. Why does Joe-dan-ash cry? And why should I care if he does? I have no need for another man's tears.

It was damned hard to suppress his emotion. Jordan didn't want to weaken before the boy; hell, how could the boy expect help from him if he went to pieces so easily? For a few moments, he cupped his head between his palms and steeled his stomach muscles against the spasms unmanning him. He watched the retreat of the sun through his fingers...shadows were gliding to him on the floor, reaching back for territory they had lost. Jesus, crying; crying for a boy he scarcely knew. "Okay," he said, "I'm going to leave the building and I'll look around as though I hadn't found you. I'll see if they won't follow me to some other place..."

And Heinie Joe broke his silence. "So. You are not alone." Sneering, he continued, "Where will you lead them? You know the path to my mother's mat. Is that where you're going to take them, Joe?"

Jordan winced. The boy addressed him as they do white men in the Orient: as a nameless name. Not Joe-dan-ash. Simply as *Joe...you*. He replied, "No, I won't go to her house."

"Why not? You find she's too old now? Maybe the *junsa* won't think so. Maybe they will pleasure themselves as you did last night."

Twisting, turning; so many dark tunnels to follow. "There was nothing between us last night."

"Not even sweat? I saw you in each other's arms." His words were rude with disbelief.

"I didn't come to Japan for her. I came for you."

"Ah. Is that the explanation? Are you a lover of men?"

"No!" Another blind alley. How could he reach the boy? "I am willing to love you as my son."

"The only love I know comes blanketed in yen."

"We're not talking about the same thing."

"Then what have you to do with me?"

"I'm your father. Isn't that enough?"

More than enough and too much...it didn't need saying.

"Give me a chance, Joe."

"Piss on your chance."

"Don't talk like that."

"How do you want me to talk? 'Hey, Joe-dan-ash! You

374

want fuck, you want suck? Hey, Joe-dan-ash, I get you anything you want!' Is that okay talk for you?"

"Stop it! You know damned well it isn't!"

"First words I learned of my father's language. Very good for taking care of my mother...taking care of myself, too. Because there was no fucking Joe-dan-ash to take care of us. We waited a long time to hear from you."

He said *my father*. He was getting closer. Closer. "She told me. God help me, I'm sorry I'm so late..."

"But she must be happy now. You will be regular Oto-san, and she's going to be Oka-san, and the three of us will go live in your house in America."

"That's not what I planned. It's just you I'm taking to the States."

The boy laughed darkly. "What did she do, sell me to you? How long will you keep me, Joe? How many months, weeks, nights before I get replaced? I know what it is to go from one to another so it's nothing to me. But I want to know: How long do you think you will keep me, Joe?"

Ignoring the boy's angry gibes, Jordan answered softly, "As long as I live...if you can forgive me."

Silence.

And within it the wyvern grew once more. Upon two legs; dragon-jawed; aiming. Hearing no sound, Jordan stood and started toward the stage.

"Ugoku to utsu!"

He stopped, his weight thrown forward upon his foot. "What? I don't understand."

"If you move closer, I will shoot."

"Joe...please," Jordan pleaded.

"Bakayaro!" Heinie Joe raged. "Because of you, who am I? What am I?" A suspicion dawned and he asked with cunning, "How is it you show up right now?"

"Get down out of there and we'll talk."

"You could be anyone...sent to fool me."

"You're wrong, Joe."

"Prove it."

"Your mother can vouch for my identity."

Silence. Thinking.

"Why should I believe her?"

"Can't you trust her, either?"

"I don't trust anyone."

Aiming.

"The only way you'll learn the truth is to go back to the house with me."

Aiming. Thinking.

"You want me to go out there? To the *junsa?*"

"I'll be with you."

Aiming.

"No. I know you now," the boy panted. "I know what you are doing here. The *junsa* are using you to trap me for them."

Diving.

"Please, Joe ... please ..." And Jordan stepped from the maze.

Superintendent Hidenori and Yukiko and Wanda in her long black sable coat ... and the brilliant white winter sun blinding the old house ... and the door still open and the room turned polar ... and the feeling being not so cold as that within the heart ...

After Jordan had been gone for a time, Wanda lit another cigarette. She offered one to the patient man and tossed one more to the woman at the fire pit. The fragrance of tobacco and that of the ashes in the hearth blended with grave rot sneaking moistly from the worn tatami.

"The sun is rising," said Wanda to disrupt the silence.

Yukiko and the superintendent eyed each other warily over an interplay of medusa coils of cigarette smoke, blue and gray and weaving into nothingness. Yukiko shook her head. *"Hi ga kakureku,"* she announced in cryptic answer, "The sun hides itself." Hidenori blinked at her and did not speak. She looked away to stare at the veranda, at the spot where Jordan had been.

Listening. Listening.

Marching with regular tread, crunching mud and gravel beneath heavy boots, the local policeman came to report to the Chief Superintendent of the Kinki Regional Police Bureau of Kansai Province, who was himself here in the village to see justice done. The rural *junsa* was a ramrod automaton who knew how to behave in the exalted presence. Halting outside the house, he faced the veranda and bowed to his knees. He would have saluted in the military manner with a stiff hand to the bill of his cap but the doorway was too dark behind the glare of sunlight to see where His Excellency could be. Standing erect, he delivered his report in a staccato shout that penetrated the neighborhood.

"The Beikoku-jin was seen to enter the theater! It is certain the boy is there! The men of the chief superintendent are in position to prevent an escape!"

A voice thanked him laconically out of the darkness and asked him to stand by at the theater. Again the deep respectful bow and the *junsa* trotted importantly to his post. A tile popped on the rooftop, cracking as it absorbed the heat of the sun. Nothing moved in the house.

A flighted arrow is a blur and a strong chanting whisper that becomes a death symbol only after it has struck. Jordan was startled when the feathered shaft stung him. He looked with amazement at the neatly made end protruding from his chest and saw each fine grain of black and white feathers, cut and fitted to a rounded slim rod shining with maroon lacquer and bands of silver. He felt as though hit by someone's playful fist. Reaching for the arrow to pull at it instinctively, he gasped at the pain he induced. Dumbbell, he thought. It's barbed; not a target arrow. Now the damned thing hurt like a son-of-a-bitch.

"What are you trying to do, kill me, you crazy bastard?" The words roared out on impulse and he tried to recall them remorsefully as he uttered the last word. "Oh, Jesus, Joe. I don't mean that..."

There was a readjustment of trembling motes; the sun had reached the exit and was departing in measured grandeur. Over the stage, the indistinct gloom showed a black maw where the trapdoor had been removed in the center of the prim setting. It held Jordan's eyes, though he could not see into the *seridashi,* where a taut thong tracked him.

"Joe...don't be scared. I didn't come to harm you..."

Damn, that hurt. He decided he'd be better off to sit down. Each movement, even the talking, made the pain worse.

"Listen...you can't gain anything by holing up here. No matter how long you try to hold out, they can get you."

Sinking with difficulty, he made it to the floor and then cried out when he sat back off his legs because the maneuver jarred the imbedded arrow.

"Joe...all they need do is wait. You'll have to give up eventually. Don't make them come in after you."

The second arrow missed his head by a millimeter. Ducking wildly, he rolled to one side and clutched the ground, suffering the searing disturbance of his wound. Outside, a city *junsa* dashed past to take a fleeting look at Jordan. A dart chased the man, sounding like cloth tearing quietly overhead. Goddamnit, don't push the boy! Give him a chance to think it out. He hasn't learned yet that there is never any refuge, any escape. We are all doomed, all of us...to this life, this death, this seldom happy, unhappy day after day after night after night which ends always with the loosening of bowels into the next man's path. Hey...Dave...wish you were here. You don't owe me anything anymore: You told me she had a son. And he's here. And I'm here...

Several of the *junsa* ran to the veranda. They shouted at the house to say the boy was armed and had shot the foreigner. Yukiko covered her face with her hands and began a moaning ululation. Hidenori prevented her from rising. He pressed her back to the tatami, saying gently, "Please wait a little. It is best if you remain in your house." He addressed Wanda, who had not moved from her seat. "Mrs. Asche, this is when I need you."

She answered coldly, "What do you mean?"

"Your husband..." He was going to tell her Jordan was injured but decided not to, for it could possibly make her unmanageable. "He will complicate the arrest, I fear. We can avoid that if you intervene."

She shrugged. "Jordie will do whatever he pleases, Superintendent. He's beyond reasoning so far as the boy is concerned."

"You refuse to aid us?"

"I don't give a shit, Superintendent." Offended by the crudity, the man stiffened but she didn't care. "Jordie and I are through. You saw the end of our marriage. Whatever happens out there, Jordie will go his way and I'll go mine. So go get your fugitive, Superintendent. I'll meet you down at the launch."

"You are wrong about your husband, Mrs. Asche."

"No. He thinks I've deserted him... and I've made him hate me."

"His words were spoken out of the disintegration of his dream."

"I was willing... I was willing to try this adoption... and the boy made that impossible himself. I can't help it if Jordie's son proved more of a disappointment than myself."

"A woman's failure sorrows a man," he reproved her. "That of his son can destroy him... or make him violent. You can prevent that."

"I don't know how to be kind anymore. Is that a sign of having any love left for Jordie?"

"That's for you to decide, Mrs. Asche."

He gave her a dignified salute, then went to the veranda and slipped into his shoes before stepping down to the path, where he shifted to a jogging run. When he arrived at the courtyard, he stopped to examine the spent arrow, which had been retrieved by a villager. Roused by others observing the activity around the theater, the people of the community thronged to the place. Hidenori ordered them to stand clear, and the folk massed silently at both ends of the street. They stared at the ominous building. Its banners were lifting in a breeze which sounded in their ears hollowly. The alert *junsa* watched the entrance of the theater intently; Hidenori debated his next move. From every household in the village, men, women and children arrived in numbers.

Waiting.

The dirt was against Jordan's cheek and in his nostrils, smelling faintly of dried tangerine skins and peanut shells. Reminiscent of circus tents, trained animals and clowns. With black and white and red makeup. Bright red. Like the red welling up around the arrow in his chest. The pain pulsed now, keeping time with his heart and picking out another tempo with the labored rise and fall of his rib cage. Someone was walking to the theater entrance; he could hear footsteps displacing pebbles in the courtyard. As he was about to call a warning, the footsteps came to a stop.

"Mr. Asche..."

So you're here. Not raising his head, Jordan answered, "I'm all right. Don't come in."

"The officer tells me you've been shot."

"It's not bad...we can take care of it later."

Listening.

The Superintendent remained in place.

Listening...

Jordan coughed suddenly; tidal waves of agony wracked him. The clay floor in front of his mouth was flecked with deep vermilion and sudsy pink bubbles. Not bad, he had told the Superintendent...and now it was worse. He felt panic and quelled it at once. What did it matter? The measured voice of the man outside did more than announce his presence...it meant he had taken charge. He would bring order. He would remove the boy from the sanctuary of the haunted theater and walk before him to the stone wharf. His aides would flank the prisoner, comforted by the clink of chains upon his wrists, and they would escort him aboard the motor launch. And the boy would be taken to the prison, to the court, to that dispassionate final house of steel cells and rigid security. And the boy would count the vanishing days, hours, minutes, seconds, until he was done with counting, done with waiting...done with living.

Shall I be able to bear that? Jordan wondered. I will

not have him; he will not be me, and his children will not be an extension of ourselves into eternity, and we shall become less than nothing...which at least has a name. There will only be the bitter sadness with Wanda again, and the thinking and the accosting of each other in dreams...and the remembrance of his sleeping face in my hands and his breath against my fingertips. I will not have you, Joe...

Oh, Joe...oh, Joe...how it hurts to die...and how it hurts not to die...how it hurts not to die...

Wanda hesitated at the doorway. She would have gone to the launch but was held by the still figure of the Japanese woman. Yukiko had more purpose to remaining than to obey the Superintendent...but what was it? Outside, the village was portentously quiet; everyone had vanished from the road before the house. No. There was someone looking at her. A boy...almost a man. Was he anything like Jordan's son? His calm gaze gave nothing away of his impression of her...no smile...no frown...nothing. Just the unemotional inspection. Uncomfortable, Wanda stepped back into the room. Yukiko was knotted into herself, rigidly still and impervious to the thin smoke rising out of the fire pit to veil her. What was the woman thinking? Wanda shivered, drew her coat together. Where did Yukiko get her strength?

It couldn't be due to subservience. To give beyond having nothing to give takes enormous strength. She and the Superintendent wanted Wanda to overcome her bitterness toward her husband...the woman for her love of Jordan and his son...and the man to make his job less complicated. But what of herself? If there was nothing for her to gain, why shouldn't she walk away from their oblique lectures? What would be left for herself and Jordan when this was over? His loss of his son was insurmountable...and how could she survive the loss of her husband? But she didn't want to lose Jordie. Just as the woman at the fire pit had known it and was waiting for her to know it. In his need, here in this dire place, Wanda was giving Jordie nothing, thinking she had nothing to give. Was that Yukiko's meaning?

Head lowered, Yukiko left her seat at the fire pit swiftly, brushed past Wanda and ran over the veranda and down the path. She hadn't put on her *geta* but had gone in bare feet. Like a peasant. Like a woman with a destination. Yukiko gathered speed as she got farther, her long black hair lashing her onward with writhing strands. Mud flew from beneath her drumming heels to leave a spoor of craters behind until she was out of sight. Within seconds, nothing moved on the road but the water welling in each mark along the length of her journey.

Yukiko uttered a keening that was heard like the opening mouths of clay images which emit no sound and are yet horribly loud in the soul. The people parted for her as she appeared, seeing a woman grieve and honoring its exposure; they were mostly the old ones who were here so they were part of the tragedy, part of the punishment, part of the suffering. There were those who remembered the man...and the birth of his son...and the ridicule and expulsion of the girl and her *ainoko*...and they saw her pass, bent with tears, now running upon laggard feet, afraid to arrive but with the necessity to be there.

Superintendent Hidenori caught her as she entered the courtyard and pulled her to one side out of range of the lethal doorway. Thinking to free herself, she struggled with him but he would not loosen his grip. Seeking help, he appealed to a woman nearby, asking her to take charge of Yukiko. The woman declined. She was Yukiko's sister, concerned that the theater be not damaged by these events. He tried another woman and was refused; Natsu had also turned her back years ago. Hidenori growled at the man beside her and the ex-soldier jumped forward to take Yukiko into his arms. Masao Masuda held her tenderly, firmly, cringing from his wife's glare but obeying the instruction of authority. Yukiko fought the restriction and whimpered that she did not want her son to be hurt. "He's only armed with a bow," Hidenori reassured her. "We're not going to shoot him." She glanced fearfully at all the *junsa* surrounding the theater and demanded to know why

382

they held pistols in their hands. "That's usual," he soothed. "They have to follow procedure."

"He's not responsible for what he's done," she pleaded hysterically, "and not for what ho is he can never be as you are. He's not responsible...not responsible..."

And he thought of Hichiriki, the prisoner he kept at home, who was also not responsible for what he was...a prisoner, sentenced to live out his life...as this woman's son would not. She didn't believe him when he said he understood. Seabirds soared from overhead, diving to scrutinize the inquisitive crowd and the cautious policemen poised at vantage points around the theater. Yet another arrival occurred: Hidenori saw Wanda push to the front of the onlookers. He went to her quickly.

"I love him," she confessed simply. "I love my husband. Let me go to Jordie now and I'll help you with the boy."

"I can't permit you to enter the building, Mrs. Asche."

"Why? Isn't this what you wanted me for?"

"Your husband has been injured."

Wanda threw a panicked look to the theater and he blocked her path. "Damn you!" she cried angrily. "You and your men knew Jordie was only trying to protect his son."

"It was his son who hurt him."

She groaned, believing it her fault for not having been with Jordan.

"We've not been able to verify the seriousness of his injury."

"How was he hurt?"

"His son found weapons in there...items used for performances. He's become agitated and has been firing arrows at anyone he sees. Your husband called out to me that it is not a bad wound. We'll know better when he's outside."

"When will that be?"

Hidenori wasn't encouraging. "We don't know his situation, Mrs. Asche. I shall do what I can to end this peaceably."

Wanda breathed, "Please, Superintendent...don't let both of us be too late."

He ordered two policemen to prevent her following him and left to sidle close to the doorway of the building. The spectators were tense with anticipation, cringing as though from the next arrow. Hidenori spoke into the dimness.

"Mr. Asche?"

On the floor of the theater, Jordan lay inert. He was breathing shallowly and blood had turned the earth to mud beneath his body. After a moment, the Superintendent called to him again.

"Mr. Asche?"

The gulls floated above the theater.

"Heinie Joe...this is Chief Superintendent Hidenori speaking. I want you to put down your weapon and come out. Do you hear me?"

The boy was listening to the irregular gasps of his father. He could not see the man's face nor distinguish more than a dark smudge on the ground against the light from the open doorway, but he felt the intense blue stare directed at the stage. There was pain wrinkling the corners and the man would not look away...the man claiming to be his father. Joe-dan-ash.

"Come out!"

Heinie sent another bolt sighing into the courtyard. The arrow slammed into the wood fence and quivered with a flat nasal whine. Hearing its deadly whisper above him, Jordan started to say something to his son only to find he could not speak or move. His hands fluttered feebly on the ground where he was sprawled, fingers clawing the dust. He had the impression he had lain there for hours, imprisoned by a sneaking paralysis which had taken him unawares. Otherwise, he felt everything—the uncomfortable pebbles goring into his flesh, and beneath one hip, a sharp stone—and the unending consuming pain swelling and receding between his efforts to find air to fill his lungs. And the charnel smell of the hot wetness mingling redly with his urine. How messy it is, he thought. They'll have a hell of a time cleaning me up. His head jerked slightly with distaste. It was like floating in a cesspool of his own making.

Oh, God, I can't help him now...I can't do anything to help him. They are getting impatient out there and they'll come after him with the guns. God, let me say something that will keep them from hurting him...

His mouth worked with great strain and he tried very hard, harder than he had done anything in his life...and all he achieved was to force some negative tics of his head which were so limited the dust was scarcely disturbed. The

384

only sound he made was a desperate intake of quickening breaths. Why didn't they do something sensible out there? Where was Wanda? She must surely be out there with the Superintendent. She and Yukiko...his thought was unfinished as he heard a noise through his agony.

There was hectic scuffling beyond the entrance and he heard someone cry out. He could not turn his head to see; when he felt her touch his face, it was not his wife. Yukiko had burst into the theater to kneel beside him.

"*Sumi-masen*, Joe-dan-ash...*Sumi-masen*..."

After comforting him, she regarded the stage. Her hair had fallen over her shoulders and in the weak light she was transformed into a young girl again. Jordan yearned to speak to her. Nothing issued from his throat; only the gasping, only the tongue working between his teeth in a dreadful, useless way. Help him, Yukiko, help him.

Leaving Jordan, Yukiko shuffled to the stage across the length of the expectant shadows. Heinie watched her with the bow ready in his hands, arrow half drawn. She stopped before the stage, stumbling humbly, like a petitioner.

"I think you've slain him. Put down your weapon and do as the Chief Superintendent asks."

The boy stared at her steadfastly. "Is it really him?"

A flicker of annoyance passed her brow, for she thought her son was proud to have attracted the attention of the authority who kept order in Kansai Province, and then she understood he meant the man on the ground behind her.

"It is truly him, isn't it?"

She could not read Heinie's eyes. And she replied, "*Hai.* It is he."

"I knew it. I told him I thought he was from the *junsa*. But I knew him. And then I shot him."

"Because he was from the *junsa*?"

"No, Oka-san. Because he fathered me."

The boy rose out of the *seridashi* to the stage and stood above her, growing tall like a player in a drama, and his mother gazed at him, seeing every aspect of her son, absorbing the sight of him as a rapt audience might. A rustle sounded at the entrance to the theater. She looked to see the Superintendent with drawn pistol in hand, not held threateningly but hanging loosely and pointed to the ground. He did not enter. Yukiko turned back to the boy and said again, "Put down the weapon."

The bow fell from his fingers, shedding the arrow noisily onto the polished boards of the stage. Walking to its edge, he leaped lightly to the ground, then passed his mother and went to the stricken man. Looking down at Jordan's waxen face, the boy kicked his prone figure in the crotch.

"Stop it!" shrieked Yukiko, running at him, and Heinie threw her to the earth, where she lay horrified as he kicked his father again—lazily, as he would a broken mannequin. Hidenori raised his pistol.

Then the boy squatted at the man's side and touched his moist skin; it was oddly greasy under his fingertips. The blue, clearest of blue eyes glowed at him from the suffering face. Joe-dan-ash looked at him fiercely, as though he would speak through them, as though he could will all he wanted to say to pour out of his soul and be transmitted through that savage regard. A tear formed and made a runnel down the boy's cheek. Father and son were bound by what they saw in each other's eyes. Suddenly the man shuddered, shrugging off the world, and his frame became rigid. There was an odor of feces and his breathing stopped. A profound struggle took place, soundlessly racking his body. Then Joe-dan-ash relaxed, his eyes took on a look of wonder and his mouth had the semblance of a smile. It was finished. The boy began to cry aloud, openly and unashamedly, and he bent to his father tenderly to kiss his lips. Joe-dan-ash was gone, never to return. Never.

Never.

Outside, Wanda tried to break past the restraint of the *junsa*. "Jordie! Jordie! Jordie!" she screamed. The policemen stood like a wall before her. She fought them, beating futilely with clawing fingers. Then she saw Hidenori holster his pistol at the entrance of the theater and he turned toward her. "Superintendent," she begged frantically, "is my husband all right? You have to do something for Jordie! He should be taken to a hospital!" Hidenori walked to her and motioned the men to let her pass. She ran to him, begging, "Can't you have a helicopter lift him out of here?"

"The motor launch is all we need, Mrs. Asche."

"God...then he's not hurt badly?" she asked on the verge of relief.

Hidenori buttoned down the flap of his holster smartly. The villagers were a patient herd waiting to be released from their spell. But the foreign lady waited, too.

"He's dead, Mrs. Ascho."

And the rest occurred as Jordan had known it would. They escorted the boy to the wharf, one hand chained to the other, with the Superintendent leading and the *junsa* flanking the prisoner on either side. Behind them, Yukiko had to double her steps to keep pace. The people of the village stood upon different levels of the paths and watched mutely as some of the men brought up the rear with a litter bearing a covered body, the man Joe-dan-ash, concealed with the fading embroidered cloth of pale jade and gold from beneath the stage. Despite the sun, it was cold enough to see the exhalations of the marchers as they breathed. One last participant followed slowly. Wanda set one foot carefully before the other as she walked alone upon the road. Yet she wasn't without company. During that dreadful march from the theater, guilts and recriminations walked with her to bring the recognition that there was to be no forgiveness. Not from Jordie.

Never from herself.

And down she went after the cortege, through the village and past the cement ramp with its fishing boats lined high and dry from the edge of the sea, and onto the stone wharf, which stretched into the wayward currents.

And the boy was led aboard the waiting launch, the litter carried to rest upon the deck, and the *junsa* arranged themselves along the railings. Hidenori glanced to the wharf but Yukiko hung back and did not move to go aboard. He drew out a notebook and began to inscribe a meticulous report. Wanda walked the long measure of the wharf to the gangway, high heels tapping loudly upon the stones and her fur coat whipping open unheeded as she approached. She stopped when she reached Yukiko and looked at the launch. Heinie Joe sat crouched beside the corpse, head bent to stare at the salt-bleached deck. He seemed hypnotized by numerous fish scales which had adhered to the planks like opal shavings. His captors smoked with unconcern, dropping ashes into the water where darting bream mouthed the sinking dust. The men were phlegmatic Buddhas dispersing vaporous lianas of smoke, forbidding as jungle ruins. They unnerved her. She had ceased thinking of them as foreign and had herself become alien. Her solitude was intensified by their disdainful quarantine. Yukiko was granite; and on the launch, Hidenori stood with head thrust over his notebook, penning exuberant combinations of dashes and slashes. Everything was incomprehensible. There was no shriving anywhere.

Chilled, she gripped her coat tightly at the collar and crossed the gangway unsteadily to enter the launch. Her flask was empty, thrown away. No one reached to aid her as she stepped aboard. She stopped again to look at the boy. He had lain his head against his father's body; his face was innocent, the visage of a dreamer without care. Because she had lost everything and he was all that was left of it, she sank to the deck beside him. Opening her coat wide, she pulled him from Jordan to nestle between her breasts. "I hate you," she mourned, "I hate you." And she folded the coat over him to keep him warm and rocked to and fro...to and fro...to the rhythm of an old nursery tune she would never sing.

The crew cast off their lines, leaped aboard to haul in the gangway. As they coiled each rope into neat round carpets upon the deck, the vessel backed from the battered stones. Engines thundering, it cleared them, arced slowly and set course for Osaka. Those departing could not endure the sight of the grieving woman remaining on the wharf; they averted their eyes and busied themselves or stared out to sea. Dead, dying...soon to die...Yukiko watched them diminish, saw the flutter of brocade covering Joedan-ash, saw the huddled pair beside him. A squadron of gulls careened in shifting patterns as they sped to hover over the stern of the launch before diving over and over again through fumes rising above the wake.

Diving...diving...
Diving...

Diving and uttering melancholy cries which echoed in the channel, only to be borne away by a sharp cold wind . . a wind which stripped the enchanted mist from the entire length of Seto Naikai . . .

From

"The Bestselling Novelist in America."
Washington Post

Rosemary Rogers' new, daring novel is set in the 1840's and sweeps from sultry Ceylon to Paris, Naples, Rome, London and the English countryside. It is the passionate story of the love-hate relationship between spirited young heiress Alexa Howard and sensuous, arrogant Nicholas Dameron.